Shadow Walker

Allyson James

BERKLEY SENSATION, NEW YORK

THE BERKLEY PUBLISHING GROUP
Published by the Penguin Group
Penguin Group (USA) Inc.
375 Hudson Street, New York, New York 10014, USA
Penguin Group (Canada), 90 Eglinton Avenue East, Suite 700, Toronto, Ontario M4P 2Y3, Canada
(a division of Pearson Penguin Canada Inc.)
Penguin Books Ltd., 80 Strand, London WC2R 0RL, England
Penguin Group Ireland, 25 St. Stephen's Green, Dublin 2, Ireland (a division of Penguin Books Ltd.)
Penguin Group (Australia), 250 Camberwell Road, Camberwell, Victoria 3124, Australia
(a division of Pearson Australia Group Pty. Ltd.)
Penguin Books India Pvt. Ltd., 11 Community Centre, Panchsheel Park, New Delhi—110 017, India
Penguin Group (NZ), 67 Apollo Drive, Rosedale, Auckland 0632, New Zealand
(a division of Pearson New Zealand Ltd.)
Penguin Books (South Africa) (Pty.) Ltd., 24 Sturdee Avenue, Rosebank, Johannesburg 2196,
South Africa

Penguin Books Ltd., Registered Offices: 80 Strand, London WC2R 0RL, England

This is a work of fiction. Names, characters, places, and incidents either are the product of the author's
imagination or are used fictitiously, and any resemblance to actual persons, living or dead, business
establishments, events, or locales is entirely coincidental. The publisher does not have any control over
and does not assume any responsibility for author or third-party websites or their content.

SHADOW WALKER

A Berkley Sensation Book / published by arrangement with the author

PRINTING HISTORY
Berkley Sensation mass-market edition / June 2011

Copyright © 2011 by Jennifer Ashley.
Excerpt from *Primal Bonds* by Jennifer Ashley copyright © by Jennifer Ashley.
Cover art by Tony Mauro.
Cover design by George Long.
Interior text design by Kristin del Rosario.

ISBN: 978-0-425-24182-0

BERKLEY® SENSATION
Berkley Sensation Books are published by The Berkley Publishing Group,
a division of Penguin Group (USA) Inc.,
375 Hudson Street, New York, New York 10014.
BERKLEY® SENSATION and the "B" design are trademarks of Penguin Group (USA) Inc.

PRINTED IN THE UNITED STATES OF AMERICA

10 9 8 7 6 5 4 3 2 1

"Addictively compelling . . . I can't wait to read more about [Janet and Mick]."
—*All Things Urban Fantasy*

"If you're looking for a book that packs romance, adventure, passion, and magic, then pick up *Stormwalker* and ride the lightning."
—*Dark Wyrm Reads*

"WOW!! That was my primary reaction after turning the last page in this paranormal gem by Allyson James. *Stormwalker* grabbed me from the first page and took me on one wild and crazy roller-coaster ride."
—*The Romance Dish*

"Allyson James weaves a wonderful story full of intrigue, mystery, suspense, and romance while at the same time tempting the reader with what might be next for Janet and Mick."
—*Romance Novel News*

Mortal Seductions

"This story will hook you from the first word to the last one . . . A very tempting read."
—*Night Owl Reviews*

"A very modern story with lots of homages to ancient cultures and lots of hot, powerful men. Amazing characters kept me involved from beginning to end. Ms. James brings the heat, adventure, and juicy surprises that readers are demanding. The sex is smokin' hot . . . Both sensual and amusing."
—*Just Erotic Romance Reviews* (5 stars)

Mortal Temptations

"The balance of intrigue, romance, and unbridled sexual fantasies makes James's story of gods, demigods, and mortals a sizzling page-turner. This book is the start of a series featuring these delicious characters."
—*Romantic Times*

"Hot! Hot! Hot! It doesn't get much hotter than this one . . . If you enjoy stories full of action, both in the bedroom and out, this is one story you will want to read." —*The Romance Studio*

The Dragon Master

"Superb . . . A masterful tale."　　　　　*—Alternative Worlds*

"If you're looking for a book that's full of passion, characters who'll capture your heart, and some truly great storytelling, look no further: *The Dragon Master* is here. Get your copy today!"　　　　　*—Romance Reviews Today*

"For a fantastic romantic fantasy suspense with a delightful ethnic twist I recommend *The Dragon Master*."
　　　　　—ParaNormal Romance

The Black Dragon

"One of my favorite authors. A unique and magical urban paranormal with dragons, witches, and demons. Will keep you enthralled until the very last word!"
　　　　　—Cheyenne McCray, *New York Times* bestselling author

"A fabulously delicious read."　　　　　*—Darque Reviews*

"Begins with a bang and the action never lets up, not for one single, solitary, wonderful moment . . . The story is unusual, wonderfully original, and filled with intriguing characters."
　　　　　—Romance Reader at Heart

Dragon Heat

"[A] delightful romantic fantasy . . . A fun tale of life between a mortal and her dragon."　　　　　*—The Best Reviews*

"This story has a wonderful fairy-tale feel about it. Allyson James does an outstanding job of creating and bringing these mystical creatures to life with characteristics and emotions that you can't help but fall deeply in love with." *—TwoLips Reviews*

Titles by Allyson James

DRAGON HEAT
THE BLACK DRAGON
THE DRAGON MASTER

MORTAL TEMPTATIONS
MORTAL SEDUCTIONS

STORMWALKER
FIREWALKER
SHADOW WALKER

Anthologies

PRIVATE PLACES
(with Robin Schone, Claudia Dane, and Shiloh Walker)

HOT FOR THE HOLIDAYS
(with Lora Leigh, Angela Knight, and Anya Bast)

WEDDING FAVORS
(with Nikita Black and Sheri Whitefeather)

HEXED
(with Ilona Andrews, Yasmine Galenorn, and Jeanne C. Stein)

Acknowledgments

Many thanks go to the readers who have enthusiastically followed Janet, Mick, and Coyote and their adventures. I very much appreciate your support. I'd also like to thank my editor, Kate Seaver, for loving Janet as much as I do.

And, as always, I need to thank my husband, who, in spite of not being a dragon shape-shifter with fire magic and dragon tatts, still manages to be awesome.

Read more about the Stormwalker series on its series page: http://www.allysonjames.com/stormwalker.html.

One

Nothing quite makes your night like falling two hundred feet into a sinkhole.

My motorcycle spun as the solid pavement of the highway opened up under me, and then I was falling down, down, down into the bowels of the earth. An avalanche of rocks, dirt, trees, and the speeding sheriff's SUV followed me into the abyss.

My bike and I separated, and it smashed against the side of the hole and broke into many pieces. I tried to stop my fall, to grab on to roots that protruded from the breaking wall, but I fell so fast, my hands could close on nothing. The SUV ground its way down with the boulders, metal groaning, glass flying to mix with the shower of dirt and gravel.

I'd been wearing padded leather against the January cold, which protected me somewhat, but all my padding wouldn't help me if Nash Jones's SUV fell on top of me. I tried to reach into myself and draw on my magic, but I'm foremost a Stormwalker, which means I can channel the power of a storm, but I need a storm to be present to work the magic. The night, though raw with cold, was stubbornly clear.

I also had Beneath magic in me from the world below this one, but I had to be in a steady frame of mind to temper it with my Stormwalker magic. If I didn't, I'd blow up the sinkhole and me and Nash with it.

Falling a couple hundred feet down a sheer drop with an SUV did nothing to put me into a calm frame of mind. I could only flail and claw, gasping for breath as dirt leaked under my helmet and threatened to suffocate me.

I don't know why I didn't die. Maybe the gods and the universe had other plans for me. I tumbled over and over, and at last came to rest on an upthrust boulder, while mud, roots, grass, and gravel poured on around me. A bone in my arm snapped, the pain sharp and numbing.

The sinkhole proved to be a wide one, and the SUV landed about five feet from me, wedged on its side between two colossal boulders. I sprawled like a bug on top of the mud-coated boulder, amazed that my heart still beat.

The landslide ceased but sent up a choking cloud of dust that cut off all air and light. The SUV went silent except for the creaks and hisses of engine parts.

I pulled off my helmet with my good hand—which sounds easy. What I really did was fruitlessly claw at it, crying with fear, until it at last unstuck from my head.

I thanked every god and goddess who might care that I'd bothered with the helmet. Sometimes I rode bareheaded, which was perfectly legal in this state, but I'd been traveling back from Chinle, and I didn't like to ride on the interstate without my helmet, especially at night. If I hadn't bothered with it, my brains would now have been wet smears on the rocks around me.

It was pitch-black down here, the moonlight blotted out by the dust. Coughing, I crawled to the SUV, drawing breath through my teeth when I touched the hot metal of the engine. The vehicle was wedged in tight, the passenger door facing upward. I climbed onto the door, my hurt arm clenched against my side, my legs clumsy. The window glass had broken away, leaving a gap in the darkness.

"Jones," I croaked. It didn't even sound like a word, just a guttural noise.

Nothing moved. Everything inside was dark, the sheriff's radio and computer interface dead. The SUV was nothing but a silent hunk of metal, plastic, and fiberglass. I groped for Nash, half falling into the slanted cab.

Sheriff Nash Jones had been chasing me out on that lonely highway, because when I'd taken the turnoff to Flat Mesa, I'd driven right through his speed trap. I hadn't been paying attention, thinking about the nice day I'd spent at Canyon de Chelly snapping photos, after an equally nice visit to my father in Many Farms. I'd flown past the clump of cedars on the deserted road, and Nash had burst out from behind them, lights flaring, to pursue me like a hungry lion.

Damn you, Jones, don't you have anything better to do with your nights than parking behind a tree with a radar gun? You seriously need to get laid.

I touched a warm body, Nash Jones in an unmoving huddle against the far door. I tugged off my glove and found his face, his neck, but I couldn't feel a pulse. I put my fingers under his nose and exhaled in relief when I felt a tiny breath touch my skin. He was alive.

Now what?

No radio, no cell phone, because I'd left mine behind at my hotel, and Nash's, once I dug it from his belt, didn't work. The piece of magic mirror, which had been ground into the mirror on my motorcycle, must have been smashed along with every bit of my bike. The mirror was why I hadn't been carrying my cell phone—magic mirrors were more reliable.

The full magic mirror, which hung over the bar in my hotel, would know that its slice had fallen into the sinkhole, that is if the damned thing was awake. It liked to nod off at the worst of times. I hoped it was screaming at the top of its obnoxious voice that something was wrong, alerting Mick, my dragon-shifter boyfriend, and Cassandra, my Wiccan hotel manager. Only the magical could hear the mirror, and I wanted them to hear it now.

Without being able to see past the dense cloud of dust, I had no way of knowing how far down we were. Or whether we'd continue to fall if the rocks shifted. Had we hit bottom, or had the rubble built a shelf that would stabilize awhile before again breaking apart?

I'd read somewhere that sinkholes were formed when groundwater finished eating away at the roof of gigantic caverns far below the surface. Once the layer is gone, then up to a thousand or so feet of rock above it collapses straight down, dragging everything on the surface with it and leaving a sheer-faced sink for everyone to ponder. The upland deserts are riddled with the things. They're very interesting when you read about them in a book, not so much when one forms right underneath your feet.

Was this SUV rigged to send out a distress signal if it crashed? Nash's deputies would notice that they'd lost radio contact with him—wouldn't they? I had no idea where police technology stood these days, or whether Hopi County had enough money to keep up with the rest of the world. All I knew was that every communication device in the SUV was dead and silent. Nash himself still wasn't moving.

"Come on, Mick," I whispered. "Cassandra. Someone."

The truck shifted and my heart raced, my adrenaline off the scale. I felt my Beneath magic wanting to strike out in response, to get me the hell out of there. The magic was as tense as a coiled rattlesnake and just as deadly.

I closed my eyes to try to still my mind, but my heart was still pounding so hard it made me sick. The Beneath magic responded, bright and white and strong enough to destroy the world. I didn't want to destroy the world: I wanted to get out of this damned hole.

I jumped when I saw light flicker through my closed lids. I popped my eyes open, hope flaring. Was it the moonlight filtering through dust, or the flashlights of rescue workers?

Neither. The glow didn't come from the surface, but from the rocks around me. As I watched, thin lines of light began moving across the boulders. The lines looked like petroglyphs, pictures left from the ancient people of this land, but these glowed with phosphorescent-like light.

The lines thickened, multiplied, still glowing faintly, and then under my watching gaze, they sprouted skeletal hands. I went utterly still. Bony fingers started flowing across rocks, making no sound, groping, searching.

I gripped the seat of Nash's truck and swallowed bile. I'd never seen anything like them before. Were they the gods of Beneath trying to get out through a vortex down here? Or was this some new horror?

I touched my Beneath magic again, my only weapon. Using it might either rip a hole in reality or make my brain implode, but I knew with ever-increasing certainty that I didn't want those skeletal fingers touching me.

The hands multiplied as they poured across the surface of the boulders, sliding through them like fish through water. The sickly light increased until it lit up the inside of the cab, illuminating the blood black on Nash's head and face. His skin was pasty, his lips bloodless. He'd die if I didn't get him out of here.

Mentally, I closed my fist around a ball of Beneath magic and drew it to the surface. Oh, it hurt. It hurt like holy hell, as though someone had thrust a lit firework into my chest. I held on to the magic as hard as I could, knowing that if I lost control of it, I could kill me, Nash, and every living creature within five miles. But at least I could try to send up a signal, like a magical flare.

I opened my imaginary fingers, releasing a bit of light. The skeletal hands stopped, fingers moving slightly, each hand pulsing in exact time with the other. Like a heartbeat, I realized. *My* heartbeat.

In panic, I let out more of my magic, and the moment I did that, the hands oriented sharply on me.

The scream that came out of my mouth was more of a croak. I closed my mind over the Beneath magic, frantically shutting it down. As soon as my magic retreated below the surface, the hands stopped, stilling, waiting.

Shit, shit, shit. If the Beneath magic excited them, and I had no storm, then I was essentially screwed. All I could do

was sit here with the dying sheriff and watch the hands fill
the sinkhole to the right and left, above us and beneath.
They started moving again, enclosing the SUV in a bubble
of light, and I was so scared I wanted to puke.

A face appeared in the middle of the unnatural glow, an
animal face, long-nosed and pointed-eared. It looked more
like a glyph of an animal rather than a real one, but I grasped
at the hope.

"Coyote? Damn it, help us!"

The animal faded, but the bony fingers didn't. They were
touching the SUV now, sliding through the metal and fiberglass, and the whole truck began to groan.

I grabbed Nash and lifted him the best I could, cradling
him against my chest. I feared to move him, but I feared
those hands even more. Nash himself was some kind of
magic void—which meant that his body somehow negated
all magic thrown his way, even the most powerful stuff.
Whether he could negate these evil hands, I didn't know, but
I had to take what I could get. They were all around us now,
crawling across the hood toward the broken windows.

I couldn't sit here and do nothing. The hands had homed
in on my Beneath magic, but maybe, if I was fast enough, I
could take them out before they could touch me.

I reached down into myself for the ball of white magic
again. Coyote had told me he didn't want me to use my
Beneath magic unless I tempered it with my storm magic,
but Coyote wasn't here, was he? And it wasn't my fault
there was no raging storm overhead. I was stuck in a sinkhole with weird petroglyphs coming for me, and I wanted to
go *home*.

I had to let go of Nash—I knew from experience that he
could negate my magic, even the strongest of it. I laid him
gently against the far door and braced myself on the dash to
push up through the broken passenger window.

I screamed as I threw the snake of Beneath magic at the
hands on the truck. Screams echoed through the sinkhole—
my screams—absorbed by the hands and thrown back at
me. The hood of the SUV melted, hoses breaking and fluid
erupting. And the hands kept coming.

I had drawn back for another strike when red light and sudden heat burst high above me. Hot orange light poured down the hole like a thousand bonfires strung together, burning the dust into little yellow sparks.

The skeletal hands froze, and as I held my breath, clenching the Beneath magic, they retreated. In the distance, I heard the bellow of a gigantic beast and then felt a downdraft as a huge dragon flapped his wings.

I started to laugh, tears streaming down my face. "Mick," I tried to shout, but all I could manage was a clogged whisper.

"Mick," I whispered again. "Down here."

Two

Mick couldn't reach us. A gigantic dragon weighing who knew how many tons would never get into that sinkhole without killing us. Even the wind from his wings started a small dirt avalanche. With another dragon shriek, he flew away.

But he'd found us. He'd sent a light spell down to me, one fiery and warm and everything that was the goodness of Mick.

The next thing I heard was sirens, the joyful sound of emergency vehicles. Many of them, which meant the sheriff's department plus the town police were responding, maybe even some state DPS. A helicopter chopped air, and magnified voices spoke to one another, unintelligible to me.

I crawled painfully to the top of the SUV and into the glare of their searchlights, waving my good arm and hoping they saw me. The voice of Paco Lopez, Nash's senior deputy, answered me, and I wanted to fly up there and kiss him.

Eventually a paramedic got lowered, carefully, down to

me. He checked me over, his flashlight painful, and moved to Nash, talking to those above through a static-filled hand-held. I was left alone for the moment on top of the boulders, and damn it, I couldn't stop crying. As much as I told my-self that tears in my eyes wouldn't help me right now, the sobs kept coming.

A harness came down, and the paramedic helped me into it. They were taking me up first, which made me even more worried about Nash. When the paramedic gave a thumbs-up, the rope tautened, and the helicopter started to haul me up. At least the tears stopped as I concentrated on holding on.

As I rose from my rocky grave, Mick's light spell dis-persed, and the skeletal hands reappeared with a vengeance. They poured from the rocks straight for me, and at the last minute, I felt spidery fingers close around my ankle. My leg froze to the bone, and I kicked and kicked in panic. Then the harness dragged me inexorably upward, and the fingers were forced to retreat.

When I made it over the lip of the gaping hole, other hands reached for me, these human and whole and warm. Deputy Lopez; Chief McGuire and Lieutenant Salas from Magellan; a paramedics woman who'd patched me up on another adventure; and Mick, in human form. Dressed in a T-shirt and jeans despite the cold, Mick came at me, shaking off the paramedic trying to hold him back. I charged past her and flung my arms around Mick's neck.

Male warmth had never felt this good. Mick kissed my hair and my face, raw kisses, his hands hard on my back. My handsome, sexy man had come for me. I was so happy to see his square, hard face, his black hair, and his blue, blue eyes.

His healing magic flooded me too. Mick possessed the clean fire-magic of dragonkind—he never had to steady himself or meditate or fight himself to use it. He simply decided to let the magic come. Now it flowed into me, heal-ing my hurts.

Mick tilted my head back until I looked into his eyes, which were turning to dragon black and laced with fire. "Janet." His voice was rough. "Gods, I thought I'd lost you."

I couldn't speak, because I thought I'd lost me too. I held on to the solid heat of Mick, shaking reaction setting in.

"Nash," I croaked. "Is he all right?"

The paramedics woman was at my shoulder. She gently dragged me away from my lover, and Mick let her take me. He *let* her; if Mick hadn't wanted me to lie on the stretcher with the oxygen mask on my face, there was no way she'd have gotten me there.

"Nash," I repeated through the plastic mask. "Is he dead? Just tell me."

The paramedic snapped a blood pressure cuff around my arm. "He's alive," she said curtly. "They're bringing him up."

Many people had gathered around the lip of the hole, the helicopter hovering. As the paramedic spoke, a knot of DPS and paramedics pulled up a stretcher. Nash was so strapped in I couldn't see him as they rushed him to the helicopter.

Lopez leaned over my other side, the usually easygoing young man looking a bit green. "They're airlifting him to Flag. He's bad, Janet. Real bad. What the hell happened?"

"Sinkhole. Wasn't there one minute. Next minute . . ."

I clutched the stretcher, reliving the terrifying confusion of falling, falling. Mick took my hands and held them hard. More healing magic flowed through me, relaxing my mind from the remembered horror.

I grew warm and drowsy. And horny. I wanted to go home, wanted a warm shower, soft sheets, and Mick in bed with me.

Lopez continued, "Someone should have seen the pavement going bad. Someone should have cordoned it off. Why didn't anyone see it? Why didn't they know?"

"Take it easy," I said, my voice still painfully scratchy. "Sinkholes happen. It's geology."

The guy was miserable. "It's my fault."

"You made the earth collapse? Nice trick. Only the gods can do that."

Gods. Oh gods, what a thought. That hole *happened* to open up the moment I rode over it? And then those hands down there? What supernatural entity had it in for me this time?

"No, I mean it should have been me," Lopez said. "I was

supposed to be manning the speed trap tonight. I asked Jones for the night off, and he agreed to switch shifts with me."

I reached for Lopez's hand, reflecting on the irony that I, the survivor, had to comfort one of my rescuers. "No, blame Nash. I was only going about eight over the speed limit. *You* would have let it go. And hey, at least it was me, not some tourist's RV full of kiddies."

The speech grated out of me, the effort wasted, because Lopez still didn't look happy. He'd carry the guilt for a while, poor guy.

The paramedics loaded me up and took me to the clinic in Flat Mesa. They let Mick ride with me, and he held my hand the whole time. I started to drift into exhausted sleep, but as soon as I closed my eyes, I saw those skeletal fingers reaching for me. I jumped awake, gasping, motion-sick in the swaying vehicle. My leg still burned with cold where the hands had touched it.

The doctor in the clinic's ER was surprised I hadn't sustained more injury, but Mick's healing spells outdid medical technology any day. The doctor puzzled over the frostbite on my ankle, and Mick sent me a grave look. I'd given him a garbled account of the hands while we rode in the ambulance, and I didn't like it that Mick didn't seem to know what they were.

The doctor wanted me to stay overnight for observation, and Mick overrode my objections and went to check me in himself.

"How's Nash?" I asked the doctor. The doctor hadn't been at the scene, but he would have heard all about it by now, officially or unofficially.

"He's going into the ICU in Flag. That's all I've heard. Alive, at least. They're trying to stabilize him."

Damn Nash anyway. I still wasn't sure whether we were friends or enemies—it depended on the situation—but one thing I knew about Nash: he always came through when I needed him. I prayed he was all right.

"Someone should tell Maya," I said. Maya Medina, the beautiful Hispanic woman who was my on-call electrician, was madly in love with Jones.

"His mother will be there," the doctor said.

I blinked. Nash Jones had a mother? He was so cold that sometimes I believed he must have hatched out of rocks in the desert. But no, Nash had a brother, so it followed they must have had a mother.

"His parents live in Flag," the doctor explained. "I called them."

That relieved me a little. I wondered if the parents knew Maya, and whether they'd contact her.

Mick returned, and the doctor, finished with me, left us alone. Once in my small, private room—which Mick had arranged—I was out of the bed. "Shower."

I had to jerk the IV needles out of my hand, but that tiny pain was nothing compared to the bone-jarring ache in my leg.

Mick followed me into the bathroom and closed and locked the door behind him. He stripped off, the pale fluorescent light brushing the dragon tatts that encircled his arms and the stylized flame that rode across his lower back. Mick was six-feet-six of honed muscle, his black hair touching his shoulders, his eyes blue as summer skies. I'd tried to kill him the night I'd met him, after a bar fight. He'd laughed at me as he'd sucked down my storm power, enjoying it, and I'd fallen madly in love with him.

"Let me see that ankle," he said.

I demurely put my right foot on the toilet seat. The bathroom didn't have a tub or shower stall, only a showerhead high on one tiled wall with a drain beneath it. Mick knelt and put his hands around my ankle. The skin was blackened, like a deep bruise, in the exact shape of the fingers that had touched me.

"You don't know what they were?" he asked.

"They were dead things," I said, and shivered. I'd been raised to abhor death and dead bodies—bodies were simply the shell of a person, and the shell could rise as a ghost. Even all the science I'd been taught in school, plus the couple of years at college, hadn't erased my deep-seated dread of death.

"I would have said they were auras," Mick said. "Of the

ancient dead, many accumulated in that spot. But auras don't do this." He drew his finger across the frostbitten skin.

Under his healing touch the blood vessels started to knit, bringing some of the feeling back to my ankle. And with it, pain. Excruciating pain. I grew nostalgic for my IV drip.

But I wanted to be clean. I stripped off my hospital gown and turned on the water, needing to wash myself of the dirt and sweat and blood from the sinkhole.

I'd been holding it together well enough, but now reaction hit me. I'd cried as I'd waited for the harness, then my tears had dried because I'd had to do things and talk to people. I'd thought I was over it. Nope. As soon as the water cascaded from the showerhead, I crumpled into a heap on the tiled floor, sobbing, cursing at myself for being so weak.

But Mick was there. He lifted me from my huddle and stood me back against the wall, fitting his large, hard body over mine. He kissed my face, his lips taking away my tears. I felt his erection solid against my belly, but he didn't try to make love to me. Not now. His touch was healing, comforting, tender.

He held me until my crying stopped, then he lathered me up with soft soap from the wall dispenser. I let him wash my entire body, loving the feel of his fingers on my thighs, my cleft, my breasts, my legs. My ankle burned as it healed, but that was better than it being numb and frozen.

Mick rinsed me, and then he held me against his slick body, his own reaction emerging. "I thought I'd lost you," he whispered brokenly. "I thought my girl was gone. I thought I'd be all alone again."

I heard the tug of grief in his voice, saw in his eyes the sadness of an ancient being, who was lonely more often than not. "I'm all right," I told him. "I made it. I'm tough."

So tough that tears leaked from my eyes again. He kissed them away.

"Shh, baby, it's over," he said. "I'll take care of you now. I won't let them get you."

"It's not that." I wiped my eyes, sorrow filling every space in me. "It's my bike. She's at the bottom of a sinkhole in about a million pieces."

* * *

They let me out of the hospital right before lunch the next day. My hurts were almost gone, thanks to Mick's healing spells. Some of the healing spells involved Mick and me twined together in the bed, him making love to me so hard that I was surprised the hospital bed made it intact.

I called Lopez first thing, to see if he had any more news about Nash. Still in the ICU, Lopez said. He told me he'd called Maya and broken the news, and she'd rushed up to Flagstaff. Good.

I was greeted at my hotel with sympathy and concern. Cassandra brewed a cup of tea for me and made me drink every drop. There was magic in that potion, because afterward, my already healing body came alive, and the lingering pain in my ankle vanished altogether.

After Mick made sure I was all right and in good hands, he left again, saying he wanted to go to the accident site and see what could be salvaged of my bike. I didn't want to think about my motorcycle smashed up in the hole, and I was grateful to him for sparing me that. I knew I'd have to go back to the sinkhole eventually, because if there was a new evil in town—or an old one awakened—I needed to learn everything I could about it.

But I was content to let Mick reconnoiter while I recovered. I planned to sit in my office sipping Cassandra's magic teas and wait for Lopez to report about Nash, but after only an hour of solitary bliss, Cassandra knocked and entered, looking harried.

"I'm sorry, Janet. I tried to put him off when he came earlier this morning, but he's back now."

I looked at her blankly. "Who? I told Lopez everything I can remember."

"It's not about the accident." As usual Cassandra had every blond hair in place in a French braid, her linen suit unwrinkled. "It's worse. He's a hotel inspector."

I sat up in alarm. The very word "inspector" made my stomach churn. I'd restored the Crossroads Hotel from a derelict old building that I'd basically had to gut and redo from the inside out. I'd filed every form, passed every inspection, paid every fee, and kept meticulous records. I knew that. If this was a snap inspection, it must be only a formality, but if so, why did Cassandra look so worried?

As Cassandra went out to fetch the man, I tried to stay calm, but my mind whirled with questions. Those weren't butterflies inside my stomach; they were angry bees.

Cassandra was nothing but calm as she entered again with a tall man behind her. "Janet, this is Mr. Wingate. County safety inspector."

"Ted," the man said in a jovial baritone.

I stood up as Ted held out a tanned hand and shook mine with firm pressure. He was about forty or so, hard-muscled as though he worked out, with brown hair and light brown eyes. He wasn't so much good-looking as striking, with a white-toothed smile and a deep tan that made his skin golden all over.

"I don't think I recognize you," I said, looking him up and down. I'd only lived in Magellan nine months or so, but already I'd met everyone who lived in the area.

"I'm new," Ted said. "The wife and I moved to Flat Mesa a few weeks ago. I work for the county now."

I strove to remain polite. "Welcome to our little corner of the desert. What can we do for you?"

"I heard you had an accident last night." Ted gave me a once-over as though he'd add the fact that I'd wrecked my bike to his report.

"Out on the highway, yes. I was lucky. The sheriff, not so lucky. We're still waiting for news of him."

"That's too bad." Ted set his soft leather briefcase on my desk and extracted a clipboard. "Now let's get down to business. I have a few questions for you about your little hotel."

I bristled at "little hotel," but I tried to remain calm. "All the reports are filed at the county records office," I said. I looked to Cassandra for confirmation, and she nodded.

"They are." Ted kept up his jovial smile as he started flipping pages on the clipboard. "But there are a couple of discrepancies you need to clear up."

Discrepancies? What the hell was he talking about?

"Discrepancies of what nature?" Cassandra asked smoothly.

I knew that Cassandra would know what was on every word of every sheet of every record for the Crossroads Hotel. She was that kind of manager. She'd worked in luxury hotels in Los Angeles and knew every aspect of the business, many that I didn't. I couldn't pay her one-tenth of what she'd made in California, but she seemed content to live in this backwater and run my hotel with breathtaking efficiency.

Ted flipped pages. Watching him, I decided that his clean khaki work trousers and white polo shirt were obnoxious. The last inspector had been as threadbare and grimy as the workers whose work he'd checked, and he'd been easygoing, the kind of guy you said hi to in the diner. But he'd retired to end his days fishing on Lake Powell, and now, apparently, we had Ted.

"I've a whole list of things." Ted smoothed his hair with nails that had been manicured. "Your piping is out of date, electric boxes are old, you've got smoke damage on the walls of the saloon—not to mention a broken mirror that should be taken down before the glass falls out. Speaking of that, the alcohol permit doesn't look right. Your parking lot—if it can be called that—is a mess, you don't have enough outdoor trash receptacles, your roof is too easily accessed and doesn't have a guardrail. Windows too small for the fire code, and you have inadequate fire escapes. If you had a fire on the first floor, it would draw through that gallery like smoke up a chimney."

Cassandra and I stared at him. He cleared his throat to go on, but I interrupted. "This is a historic building. Some of those things, like the windows, are waived to keep the property as close to its origins as possible." Small windows in a hot climate made sense, and this building was solid brick and adobe, not a fire hazard.

"You'll have to take that up with the preservation branch," Ted said. "I'm safety, and I'm here to tell you little gals that this hotel is unsafe."

Cassandra fixed him with a cold gaze. I could have told

Ted that the "little gals" remark was a big mistake. I half expected the ultra-feminist Cassandra to turn him into a toad.

"I'm sure we can come to some sort of agreement," she said.

"You wouldn't be trying to bribe me now, would you, sweetheart?" Ted asked her.

I winced, waiting for Ted to turn green and start croaking. "Of course not," Cassandra said. "Most of those things you mention have been fixed since the last inspection, or we've acquired a waiver for them. It's all in the records."

Ted waved the clipboard. "These are the only records I've got, honey. And they say you're in so much violation, I could close you down right now. So what are you going to do about it?"

Three

I ground my teeth, resisting the temptation to toss him out the nearest window, but Cassandra gave him a cool look and held out her hand. "May I?"

I'd have ripped the clipboard from Ted and smacked him over the head with it, but Cassandra took it calmly and started flipping through the papers. Her sangfroid wavered as she continued to read. "This makes no sense. These records have to be old, or tampered with."

"Nope," Ted said. "My checklist, which you'll find on top, I made while conducting an inspection this morning. They match the records. Did you know that you have two gallons of fresh blood in your walk-in refrigerator? Sitting in gallon milk jugs. What the hell are those for?"

I knew what the blood was for—Ansel, my resident Nightwalker—but I couldn't very well tell Ted that. Ansel had been staying here for a few weeks, and he was perfectly civil, and even nice, as long as he got his daily dose of cow blood. My cook, Elena, who thought I was crazy—and I thought she was too, so it was mutual—agreed to keep the blood stocked for him.

"My cook trained to be a gourmet chef," I extemporized. "She uses it in specialty dishes. Ask her."

"I tried. She threatened me with a knife. I couldn't understand a damn thing she was saying. She Hispanic?"

"Apache."

"Whatever she is, she's dangerous. I fired her."

"What?" I sprang from my seat, all injuries forgotten. "You can't fire my employees!"

"You had no authority," Cassandra said.

"Yes, I do, gals. You're lucky I didn't call the police."

I had the benefit of knowing that calling the police on Elena wouldn't do any good. Assistant Chief Salas would have showed up and calmed her down, because Elena, for some reason, liked Emilio Salas. Elena liked him, and she liked Mick, and that was it. Everyone else in Magellan, including me and Cassandra, she didn't consider worth her time.

I sensed Mick come into the office before I saw him. Usually he left me to conduct hotel business on my own, but he must have returned from the crash site in time to hear my shout of outrage.

Mick made the room smaller, not only because he was tall and a big man but because Mick dominated any room he walked into. Lesser men faded to nothing in the face of my biker lover with his black hair, blue eyes, leather, and tattoos.

Most people, upon seeing Mick approach like an animal stalking a kill, would swallow and take a nervous step backward. Ted Wingate gave him a little smile that was almost a sneer.

"I see," he said to me. "Having your bodyguard threaten me won't help you keep your hotel open."

Mick's eyes were changing to black with little sparks of red swimming inside them, the dragon in him ready to come out and play. "Whatever business you have here is one thing," he said. "How you conduct it is another. Tell Janet what she needs to know and go."

Ted consulted his clipboard. "You are Mick Burns? You aren't listed on the title deed or the payroll."

"I don't work here." Mick folded his arms. "I live here."

"You don't seem to have a lot of documentation anywhere, Mr. Burns."

"I like to keep a low profile."

Ted's eyes almost gleamed. "No one's profile is that low. Nice tatts." He cast a glance at the dragons, bared by Mick's short-sleeved shirt. "My wife is always after me to get tattooed, but I don't care to."

Tattoos might mess up his pretty tan, I guessed. I had tried several times myself to get inked to match Mick, but the etchings always faded by the next morning. My magic, maybe, healing my skin whether I liked it or not. I never scarred, either.

"Tattoos are not for everyone," Mick said in a mild voice.

Mick's calm told me how angry he was. If Cassandra had fond thoughts of turning Ted into a toad, Mick would be waiting to flame him to a cinder. Between them, we'd have roasted Ted–frog's legs.

"Why don't you leave your list with me?" I suggested. "We'll look it over and make the necessary repairs. How's that?"

"That's exactly what you'll do." Ted took back the clipboard, ripped off the top sheet, and handed the paper to Cassandra. "You don't, you get shut down by the county sanitation and safety department. You have one week to come up to code."

"One *week*? How am I supposed to have all this done in a week?"

"Well, now, that's not my problem, little gal," Ted said. "It's my job to make sure it gets done. Here's my card." He handed Cassandra a small rectangle and walked past us, tapping his clipboard to his thigh as he went. "Have a nice day."

I slammed my office door behind him and started to swear. I swore long and hard in English and in Navajo and every other language in which I knew bad words. Mick and Cassandra watched me in silence until I collapsed to my desk chair and buried my head in my hands.

Mick, bless him, came up behind me and gently kneaded my shoulders. Cassandra, still the cool professional, flicked a pristine nail down the checklist Ted had left.

"We can appeal most of this," she said. "It's ridiculous. The wiring is up to code, and so is the plumbing. That was all checked. And many of these things are open to interpretation."

"But we'll have to fix some of it," I said. "Like the parking lot." It was a dirt lot, full of potholes, and I shared it with the Crossroads Bar. Barry, who owned the bar, didn't seem in a hurry to grade his half, and his side was where most of the trash collected. Sure, I'd love to have my half of the lot leveled and graveled, but that took money.

I'd used the money I'd made from years of selling my art photographs to buy this place. I was making enough to pay bills and the salaries of my small staff, of which Cassandra was my only full-time employee, but I had nothing left for extras. I could have footed a few repairs, sure, but not a complete overhaul.

"Don't worry about the cost, Janet," Mick said. "I'll help you."

Mick always did seem to have money—cash money, no plastic for my dragon shape-shifter. I never asked him where he got it, and I wondered whether he, like dragons of legend, had a cave somewhere piled with gold. He'd told me he had a territory on some island out in the Pacific, but never much more than that.

"I don't want to take your money," I said to him. "We agreed."

Me not accepting money from Mick and running this hotel on my own was my way of taking control of my life. Abandoned by my hell-goddess mother, I'd been raised by my grandmother and my father, my grandmother never letting me forget that I was different and dangerous. I had never fit in anywhere and believed I never would. Becoming a photographer and buying this hotel was my way of establishing my independence.

Cassandra broke my thoughts. "You may not have a choice, Janet. How badly do you want to stay open?"

"Bad enough." I looked up at Mick. "We'll talk about it."

"I'll start going through this and make notes for you," Cassandra said. "Don't worry. We'll make that inspector eat this list." She walked out, high heels clicking on the tile floor.

"In a weird way, I think she'll enjoy this," I said.

"Cassandra likes a challenge," Mick rumbled.

"What about you? Do you like a challenge?"

Mick smiled at me in a way that made my heart feel light. "I do, baby."

I hoped Mick would follow up on the wickedness in his smile, but he merely kissed the top of my head and picked up his jacket. He took a camera from his pocket and set it on the desk in front of me.

I stared at the camera in astonishment. "It survived?" The camera had been in one of my saddlebags.

"DPS was lifting out the remains of your bike when I got there, and they let me take this."

I didn't like the word "remains." The camera, an expensive digital model, looked whole and unblemished, but when I clicked the on switch, it did nothing. I pulled a cord from a drawer and hooked the camera up to the laptop on my desk. Drawing power from the computer, the camera came on and obediently uploaded what was on the memory card.

"What about the magic mirror?" I asked while the computer worked. "The one on my bike, I mean."

"I didn't see it, but your motorcycle was in a lot of pieces." Mick gave me a look of sympathy as I winced, then he gestured at the computer screen. "You got some nice shots."

I'd spent the day before the accident taking many photos in Canyon de Chelly. I'd planned to enlarge and frame the best of them for my friend Jamison Kee for his upcoming birthday. Jamison was a sculptor—a somewhat famous one—who'd helped me get my start as a pro photographer. I didn't do anywhere as well selling my photos as he did his gorgeous sculptures, but I'd always been grateful to him. Jamison had grown up in Chinle, right next to the canyon, but now he lived here in Magellan with his wife. I wanted to give him something to remind him of his home.

The pictures had turned out well, if I did say so myself, but then, it was difficult to take a bad shot of the canyon. Canyon de Chelly is full of colors, shadows, and sudden flashes of light, breathtaking spires and vistas of sheer beauty. I smiled as I clicked through the photos, happy that my work had survived.

I stopped. "Hold on."

"What?" Mick leaned over me, smelling of dust and dragon warmth.

I enlarged the photo on my screen: Spider Rock, a lone spire that stuck up from the canyon floor. Storytellers said that Spider Woman, the goddess who taught weaving to the Diné, lived there. She liked to throw people who displeased her from her aerie to the canyon floor, where they were found as a pile of bones. Not a woman to mess with.

I zoomed in and moved around until I found the spot that had bugged me. "There. What's that?"

At the base of the rock was a mark that looked like a petroglyph, tiny compared to the rest of the photo. But the chill in my bones told me it wasn't a glyph. The line of light ended in a sprawl of lines that resembled a skeletal hand.

"It's the same as the things that came for us in the sink-hole," I said.

Mick's breath was pleasantly hot on my neck. "You sure?"

"Very sure."

He reached around me and tapped and clicked to zoom in even closer. The photo lost resolution, the lines growing fuzzy.

"You told me they moved *through* the rock," Mick said. "Like fish beneath the water's surface. They didn't crawl across the rock?"

"No, that's what was so creepy. They even moved through the metal of Nash's SUV. Silently. No skittering or scratching. I'm not sure how the last one grabbed me, but I bet my leg brushed one of the boulders as the rescue team pulled me up."

Mick's brows quirked as he studied the photo. "In-teresting."

"Not interesting. Scary as hell." Lines on rocks might not

seem threatening to a big, bad, fire-breathing dragon, but *he* hadn't been trapped in the hole with them.

"I mean it's interesting that you snapped a picture of one, and later they're with you in the sinkhole. Plus your camera was miraculously spared. Too many coincidences for my comfort."

"Don't tell me that I captured an image and carried it with me, and then it and its friends attacked me. That's too far-fetched." I stopped when Mick didn't answer. "Isn't it?"

"Probably. But you might have awakened something."

"From Beneath?"

Mick rubbed the lines of his dragon tattoos. "Doesn't seem right for Beneath. Too . . . dead. Beneath was so alive."

So alive it had nearly killed us. But when evil things from Beneath emerged in this world, they changed. Skinwalkers looked almost beautiful Beneath but were putrid and foul here. They were equally deadly in both places.

Mick studied the picture again. "When they came toward you in the hole, were they aiming for you or Nash?"

"I don't know. I was too busy being terrified to notice. I don't think they were *aiming* at all. Just coming for us."

"Nonsentient, then."

I gave him a blank look. "What?"

"I mean, they didn't have minds, couldn't think or perceive. The hands came at you blindly."

"I don't know about that. They seemed pretty damned determined for something moving blindly."

"You said your Beneath magic seemed to draw them, but the fire I sent down scared them off?"

I nodded. "When your fire started to fade, they came at me again."

Mick continued to study the photo, his look too inquisitive for my comfort. Mick was a dragon with a dragon's curiosity, plus he had a dragon's total lack of fear. He liked to solve puzzles no matter how dangerous they were.

"Don't you dare go down into that hole looking for them," I said.

He flashed me a look of innocence that was purely contrived. "Aren't you interested?"

"No."

That was a lie, and Mick knew it. I wanted to know about these things, because I needed to learn how to fight them. That didn't mean I wanted a bunch of skeletal hands that could freeze flesh from my bones surrounding my boyfriend and smothering him with their cold touch.

"Did you get any more pictures of them?" Mick asked.

We looked at each photo—and I'd taken many—but as much as I magnified and searched, we didn't see any more of the hands.

When we finished, Mick rose and stretched. "Up for a ride?"

I was still stiff and sore from the wreck, a little nervous about sinkholes opening up under me again, and more than a little worried about this hotel inspector. Then again, maybe a ride was what I needed. I could hang on to Mick and put Ted and skeletal hands and certain death out of my mind.

"Where to?" I asked.

"Flagstaff. I want to talk to Nash."

"He's still out. Lopez said he'd call me as soon as anything changed."

Mick stood up and closed the laptop. "Then we'll be there when he wakes up."

I felt a little guilty leaving Cassandra with the long list of Ted's demands, but she told me she thought I should go check on Nash. I was right about Cassandra enjoying the challenge. She waved us away and went back to tapping her computer with grim determination.

The hour ride to Flagstaff flew by as I wrapped my arms around Mick's strong body and gave in to the road. The high desert gets cold in January, so we both wore thick leather and gloves, but the Stormwalker in me felt the power in the icy weather. The sky was clear for now, but the wind was hard, and I felt myself reaching out to draw it in.

I'd lived in Flagstaff for a couple of years while I worked on my degree in fine art. I warmed to see the familiar tall pines flowing through the city, the mountains soaring behind it, the black volcanic rock everywhere. I also remembered the discomfort I'd had living side by side with so many other people. In all this beauty, why live in a box that shuts it out?

Mick dodged his way through traffic up to the hospital that now housed Nash. The nurses at the front desk said we could go to the floor where Nash was, but not inside his room.

Nash lay in a bed on the other side of glass doors, his skin as pasty white as it had been in the SUV. Tubes snaked into his arms, and machines behind him flashed gently.

Mick kissed my cheek, said he was off to the bathroom, and asked if I wanted any coffee. He was ready to wait it out.

As Mick walked away, I looked back at Nash, a man I struggled to understand. Nash was an Iraq War vet. He'd been inside a building in Baghdad when a bomb went off, and the building had buried him and his men. Nash had been the only one who'd made it out.

That event had scarred him both mentally and physically, though he never spoke about it. He suffered from PTSD, though his method of dealing with that was ignoring it, working out like a maniac, and being as much of a pain in the ass as possible.

"He'll be all right," someone said next to me.

I turned to find a middle-aged woman with the same lean sharpness as Nash and the same cool gray eyes. "I keep telling myself that," she said. "He's strong, my boy. He'll pull through."

"Mrs. Jones?" I'd been surprised to learn that Nash's parents lived here, so close to Magellan. They never came down to visit him, and Nash never, ever talked about them.

"Ava. Are you a friend?"

"Janet Begay. I was in the accident with him."

She looked me over, reassessing me. "Thank you for helping him."

"I didn't do much. Nothing I could do."

Ava turned to watch Nash again. "He'll pull through. We raised him to be strong, to let nothing stop him. He's weathered worse. He'll come out of it."

I knew she said these things to keep her hopes up, but the short phrases explained a lot about Nash. He was strong to the point of insanity—Nash never took a break. This was the first time I'd ever seen him stop and lie down.

I heard footsteps approaching and glanced down the hall. When I looked back, Ava had gone.

The person approaching wasn't Mick, but Maya Medina. Maya loved Nash desperately, and from the way she scowled at me as she approached, I knew she was trying to figure out how to blame me for the accident.

"I didn't cause the sinkhole," I said without greeting her.

"Are you sure about that?" Maya was beautiful, with creamy dark skin, black hair, and thick-lashed brown eyes. Plus she had five inches on me that I envied. She'd resented me when I first came to Magellan, but now she was the closest thing I had to a best girlfriend. "Weird things happen around you, Janet."

I couldn't argue. I shared Mick's suspicion of coincidence, and the fact that the skeletal hands had been at Spider Rock and then again in the sinkhole bothered me a lot.

"I'm glad to see his folks here," I said, to change the subject. "I was just talking to his mom."

Thick silence greeted my words. I turned to see Maya staring at me with a peculiar expression.

"What?" I asked.

"Janet, you couldn't have been talking to his mom. Nash's parents are both dead. They died ten years ago."

Four

I dragged Maya down to the cafeteria and told her to explain what the hell she was talking about.

She angrily stirred a latte. "They died in a wreck out in California. Ten years ago—a little longer than that. Nash doesn't like to talk about it."

"The doctor in Flat Mesa told me he called them," I said. Mick slid into the seat next to me and set a cup of black coffee in front of me. Its heady aroma made my mouth water.

"The doctor in Flat Mesa used to live next door to them," Maya said. "He knows they're dead."

"Then who did he call? Why did he tell me he contacted them?"

"Janet." Mick's rumbling voice was gentle. "I didn't hear the doctor say anything about Nash's parents."

"You'd gone to check me in when I had that conversation. All right, I admit that I was full of painkillers and not very coherent at the time, but I'm not on painkillers now. I met her. A woman called Ava."

"That was her name," Maya said.

"The doctor didn't mention their names to me, and I've never heard anything about them before now. So how would I know that?" Score one for me for not being completely crazy. Maybe.

"It could have been a woman pretending to be his mother," Mick said. "Knowing that you wouldn't know who she really was."

"Why would someone pretend to be Nash's mother?" Maya asked.

I looked at them both in sudden horror. "Because only relatives are allowed in his room."

Mick and I were up before I'd finished the sentence. The three of us ran out of the cafeteria, taking the stairs instead of waiting for the slow elevators. We dashed down the eerily deserted hall outside of intensive care to Nash's room.

Nash slept on behind the window, unchanged, the machines still pulsing their rhythm. The woman I'd met stood over his bed, reaching toward him with a long, thin hand. The machines beeped faster as her fingers neared his chest.

Mick flung open the door. Maya stared at Mick, bewildered, and I realized that she didn't see the woman in the room. But Mick did. He rushed inside, flames dancing in his hands.

"Hey," he shouted at the woman. "Touch him and die."

I was pretty sure there were flammable gasses in that room. I was also pretty sure I didn't want that woman touching Nash, not with that bony hand.

I reached for my Beneath magic and found it ready and waiting. As soon as I had a bright ball of it in my hand, the woman jerked from Nash to fix a furious gaze on me. Her eyes had changed from human light gray to black voids. She opened her mouth in a soundless shriek and lunged at me.

Mick got in her way, hands on fire. He pushed those fiery hands into her chest, and she screamed, a high-pitched sound that threatened to blow out my eardrums. I stepped behind the woman and shot her with the Beneath magic.

That turned out to be a mistake. She sucked up my magic without harm, her eyes glowed a sudden silver, and she swatted Mick across the room. Mick crashed into Nash's machines and went down with them. Something hissed into the room. Definitely a flammable gas.

On the bed, Nash gasped, and I heard the pounding feet of orderlies and nurses.

Mick untangled himself from the machines, his eyes black with fury. I had the presence of mind to find the valve that shut off the oxygen tank before Mick blasted the woman with flames, but the tanks were still sitting there, waiting to explode.

Mick's fire surrounded the woman, and she screamed again, just as the orderlies and nurses poured into the room. I could tell that they couldn't see the woman either—they only saw a big man with fire steaming from his fingers flaming the middle of the room. Two nurses shoved Maya and me out of the way to rescue Nash, and the orderlies went for Mick.

Under Mick's fire, the woman burned. She screamed as her face peeled back from a bone-white skull, she clawed at it with her skeletal hands, and then she disappeared.

An oxygen tank strapped under the foot of Nash's bed burst, and the residual fire dove for it, embracing it like a long-lost lover. I wrapped Beneath magic around the tank and tried to smother the explosion.

Incredible pain filled me as my magic struggled with forces of nature. I wrapped that fireball down, squeezing the life out of it, while it tried to burn the life out of me. I existed and I didn't; I heard a tear and a flutter of wings as a hole ripped in the fabric of reality. Great. I was about to destroy the universe trying to put out a fire.

And then my magic won. A flare of energy yanked at me, and the explosion reversed, then died.

I let out my breath, feeling curiously light. The last thing I remembered was Mick's worried, midnight eyes as he dove for me, and the floor rushing up to crash into my face.

I woke up on Mick's lap with his arms around me. I liked it there, a safe and peaceful place. My head rested on his shoulder where I could inhale the good scents of Mick and leather.

When I found the energy to open my eyes, my sense of peace fled. We were in a waiting room at the hospital, surrounded by a ring of security guards and police officers.

"Hey, I *stopped* the explosion," I croaked.

"You all right, baby?" Mick asked, leaning over me.

"Fine." I felt like someone had torn out my insides and sewn them back in but, other than that, fine. Physically, I hadn't been hurt, but magically, it was a different story. "Is Nash all right?"

"He woke up." Mick smiled with his usual warmth. "He's pissed off at you."

"He must be all right then."

Maya wasn't there, and I clamped my lips closed over questions about her. If she'd had the sense to disassociate herself from us, good for her. She might be with Nash, holding his hand and refusing to leave his side.

One of the city police officers informed us that he was arresting us for attempted assault, attempted arson, and vandalism. We'd be looking at attempted murder too, he said, if they decided we'd been trying to burn Nash alive in his hospital room.

"Thank you," a familiar voice cut in. "I'll take it from here."

I was startled into standing up, then regretted the swift move and fell dizzily back to Mick's lap.

A tall, broad-shouldered Native American of indeterminate tribe pushed his way through the ring of security and cops. He was dressed in a black suit with a string tie and cowboy boots, and had his hair in a neat braid. His face was hard and without its usual grin.

"FBI," he said, flashing an ID that looked authentic. "These two are in my custody."

The head uniform cop frowned at him. "I didn't find any outstanding warrants for them."

"They use aliases," Coyote said. "The girl sometimes calls herself Lucky Lucy. Works the Indian casinos all over the state and in New Mexico, cons innocent men into giving her their winnings every night. I've been after her for a long time."

Oh, for the gods' sake. I closed my eyes so no one would see me rolling them. Mick said nothing.

"What about the arson?" one of the nurses said. "They had that room on fire, nearly killed the patient."

"We'll add it to the list. But they need to come with me. I have a wagon waiting."

Mick and I went quietly. The nice FBI agent said that he saw no need for handcuffs, but I had no doubt Coyote that would have pulled them out of thin air if he'd wanted to.

Coyote really did have an SUV waiting, black, with smoked-glass windows and metal grills on the inside. I had to wonder where he'd stolen it from.

Mick and I were ushered into the backseat, and Coyote had the security guards lift Mick's big Harley into the back. The local police weren't happy, but I got the feeling they were just as glad to not have to deal with us.

Coyote swung through town at top speed and shot onto the freeway heading east. He swerved around a couple of eighteen-wheelers in as much of a hurry to leave Flag as he was, his speedometer climbing.

"What the hell was that?" I demanded as soon as I found words.

Coyote grinned at me through the grill separating back-seat from front. "Me saving your asses. Neat trick, huh?"

"You couldn't have magicked us out or made everyone forget we existed?"

"Way more fun this way. I always wanted to pretend to be an FBI agent."

Mick put his arms around me. "Thank you," he said.

"Not a problem." Coyote gunned the engine and swung around more trucks. We hit ninety and kept accelerating.

"Who was that woman?" I asked, to take my mind off the vehicles flashing by much too swiftly.

"Don't know," Coyote said. "But she sure wanted Nash. She was full of magic, though, so why would she risk Nash sucking it all out of her?"

I wondered the same thing. The freeway dropped down

out of the mountains, and Coyote drove faster. The SUV reached one hundred as we whipped around an RV and nearly rear-ended a flatbed.

"Pull over!" I screamed.

"What for?"

"Just do it."

Coyote shrugged, swung across both lanes of speeding traffic, and roared the SUV down an off-ramp. He overshot the road at the bottom and rolled straight into the desert, skidding to a stop in a cloud of dust.

"Out," I said. I kicked the back door open and hopped down, my legs like rubber, and wrenched open the driver's side.

Coyote chuckled as he scooted over and let me scramble into the driver's seat. But he was a god—if he wrecked the SUV, he'd survive. Mick could turn into a dragon and heal himself. Me, I'd end up in the hospital again, if I made it. I'd survived one accident this week—I didn't want to go through another.

Once we were on the freeway again, me driving at a careful pace, we continued to speculate on the woman but drew no conclusions.

"I saw you in the wall," I said, hands firmly on the wheel. Clouds were building up over the San Francisco peaks behind us, and I felt the icy tingle of an approaching snowstorm. "I thought I saw a glyph of you, anyway. Did you see the hands? Did you have anything to do with them?"

"Nope. I saw you all banged up, and I contacted Mick through your mirror. I didn't see anything else, babe. My eyes were only for you."

"Figures," I muttered.

The snowstorm hung back in the higher elevations, so the late afternoon was still sunny in Magellan by the time we pulled into the parking lot of the Crossroads Hotel. Coyote and Mick off-loaded his bike, and Coyote drove off in a burst of gravel, hopefully to return the SUV from wherever he'd acquired it.

Instead of coming inside with me, Mick said he wanted to go back to the sinkhole and continue investigating. I wasn't easy about him being out there, but those hand things had feared his fire magic, and he'd probably be safer from them than I'd been.

Mick kissed me and held me hard, told me to keep resting, and said that he'd continue the healing process with me when he returned. I knew what he meant by that, and I warmed with anticipation.

Cassandra was still looking over Ted's list when I went in, her optimism that we could defeat the inspection beginning to fade. The sun was already sinking, but I wanted to solve one problem before I shut down for the night. I called Assistant Chief Salas of the Magellan police and asked him if he would drive me to Whiteriver.

Most people in Magellan liked Emilio Salas, and so did I. He was good at his job but not arrogant about it, and he knew everyone in town, being related to half of it. He was hung up on Maya, but by now even he knew that a relationship with her wasn't likely. Maya loved Nash, and that was that.

Salas drove me up in his squad car. The sun disappeared behind us as we drove south and east, the twilight clear and cold, stars pricking out in abundance.

Whiteriver lay in the heart of Apache country, the town south of the Mogollon Rim, following the contours of the White River. Salas drove me to my cook's daughter's house, where Elena lived whenever she didn't spend the night in Magellan. Elena herself answered the door.

Elena Williams, even if she was temperamental—and yes, sometimes dangerous—cooked the best food I'd ever tasted. She'd worked in top restaurants in Manhattan and Los Angeles and could have gotten a job anywhere she wanted, but she'd come to my hotel because it was an hour's drive from her daughter and grandchildren. Elena wasn't the most reliable of employees, some days choosing not to show up at all, but she mostly put up with the weirdness that went on in my hotel and cooked like a dream. I would beg to keep her.

Salas flashed Elena his most charming white-toothed smile. "Hey, *chica*," he said. "Janet scared the bad man away.

Come back down and make me some of those frijoles and squash. Please? They taste like heaven."

Usually, Elena softened under Salas's winning smile, but tonight, she ignored him and pointed a stiff finger at me.

"You, Stormwalker, bring evil," she said, her voice tight with anger. "A Shadow Walker seeks you. I see the shadows, fluttering in the night." She stepped back. "I stay here, so they don't get me too."

Before I could draw breath to ask Elena what she was talking about, she slammed the door in our bewildered faces.

Salas could do nothing but drive me over the mountains and back to Magellan again, cook-less.

Five

Mick didn't return from his sinkhole exploration until three in the morning. I lay in bed awake, worrying about him and other things. I was minus a cook, plus I'd seen how Cassandra had shaken her head over Ted's list before she'd left for the night. I contemplated the ceiling above my bed, while a shard of magic mirror lay on my nightstand humming. Badly.

All in all, things had not been good for me since my visit to the Dinetah. It had been beautiful up there during my week-long vacation in Many Farms and Chinle. Cold blue skies. Peace. Beauty. My father and I had driven the land in silence, both of us soaking up the splendor as we'd always done.

My aunts and cousins had been too busy with their kids' school sports to criticize me much, which had been a bonus. I'd accompanied them to a basketball game and a gymkhana, sitting with my aunts and father in the bleachers to cheer on the next generation. A good visit all around. My grandmother had wanted me to stay longer and hadn't hidden her annoyance when I said I needed to go. I wondered if she'd put a spell on me to make my life hell because I hadn't obeyed her.

At three I heard Mick come in the back door and down the hall. I breathed a sigh of relief. The magic mirror cut off its hum in mid–"I'm Gonna Wash That Man Right Outa My Hair" and went strangely silent.

Mick walked in, not looking at me, dropped his leather jacket on a chair, and sat on the edge of the bed to unzip his boots.

"Hey," I said.

He didn't respond except to pull off his boots and drop them one by one to the floor. *Thud. Thud.*

I rose on my elbow. "Everything all right?"

Mick still didn't look at me. "Fine. Why are you awake?"

"I was worried about you poking around in that hole. Plus worried that one of the deputies would find you out there naked if you decided to go dragon." I laughed, expecting him to flash his smile at me, but he didn't.

"They never saw me," he said.

"Did you find anything?"

"You mean in the sinkhole? Nothing. Just rocks."

"You went all the way down inside?"

No answer. Mick had left ten hours ago, a damn long time not to find anything but rocks. I touched the small of his back, where the flame tattoo lay under his shirt. Sudden heat seared through the fabric, and I jerked away.

"Mick, are you all right?"

He snarled. "Damn it, I said I was *fine*."

I stared in shock. One thing Mick had never done, since the night I met him, was snap at me. He didn't always agree with my decisions, and we could argue, even rage at each other, but he never, ever bit my head off for no reason. Something must have happened out there that he didn't want to tell me about.

"Mick." I touched his back again, and he sprang to his feet.

I sat up. "Sorry. Did I hurt you?"

Mick swung on me, and when I saw his eyes, I fell back

into the pillows. Mick's eyes were usually human blue or filled with black. Tonight he looked at me with white gray irises, his pupils nothing but tiny pinpricks.

"Mick, what is wrong with you?"

"Nothing." His voice was harsh and wrong. "Stop berating me, Janet." He turned away, taking that awful gaze with him. "I'm hungry. I'm going to raid the kitchen."

His aura was flickering, white and gray weaving together. That was wrong. Mick should be solid black with streaks of fiery red.

Shadows.

"I'll come with you," I said, starting to get out of bed.

"No!" Mick glared at me with those white eyes, and I froze.

He stood silently over me, and I sat back down on the bed. If I had to fight Mick, I'd have to use my Beneath magic, which meant I'd either kill him quickly or lose. I didn't want to do either.

As Mick watched me, the white receded from his eyes. When his irises became dark blue again, he rubbed his hand through his hair. "Sorry, baby," he said almost in his normal voice. "I just need to eat something. You go to sleep."

Mick turned his back on me and walked out. I was out of bed as soon as he closed the door, and as I suspected, he went nowhere near the kitchen. I heard Mick's bike start up behind the hotel, and I yanked open the blind in time to see him ride past my window and roar off. His red taillight flashed as he slowed to turn onto the highway, then the sound of his motorcycle faded down the road.

"Oh, girlfriend," the mirror breathed from my nightstand. "Our Micky did *not* look good."

I snatched up the shard. "What's wrong with him?"

"I don't know. But he's touched evil. Or evil has touched him."

"What kind of evil?" There were so many different kinds.

"I don't know, sugarplum. I wish I did."

"Keep an eye on him," I said.

"If I can."

I dropped the mirror shard into the drawer and closed it and then got back into bed. But I didn't sleep and didn't turn off the light. I leaned against the headboard with my knees drawn to my chest, sitting in the circle of lamplight until gray dawn touched the sky.

Mick didn't return, and I went through my morning routine with worry lodged in my throat. Deputy Lopez called me around nine to tell me that Nash Jones had recovered enough to insist on leaving the hospital. I could imagine Nash yanking the tubes out of his arms and storming out of the ICU, demanding his clothes on the way.

"At least he let Maya drive him home," Lopez said. "She's there with him now, feeding him chicken soup." He snorted with laughter. The idea of big, bad Sheriff Jones being spoon-fed by Maya was funny.

I thanked Lopez for letting me know and hung up, relieved that Nash seemed to be all right. As I said, the man was tough. I hoped he'd be smart enough to lie low and recover, but with Nash, who knew?

I had other problems to face today besides figuring out what was wrong with my boyfriend. I had no cook, and though a local bakery delivered bread and muffins for breakfast, by lunch I'd have nothing.

"The saloon's closed for meals," I said to Cassandra and Fremont Hansen, my plumber, who'd come in response to Cassandra's summons. "Drinks only."

"Aw, no," Fremont said, his plain face distressed. "I was hoping Elena would be fixing those squash blossom things. I love those."

"She's gone for now," I said. "Maybe permanently." I remembered how Elena's dark eyes had gone flat when she'd said there were shadows around me. She'd sounded pretty certain.

"Damn," Fremont said, with feeling.

"Help me fix the hotel, and maybe we can persuade her to come back."

Fremont pushed back his cap and scratched his forehead. "But there's nothing wrong with the hotel. The plumbing's fine. I stake my rep on it."

Cassandra handed him a copy of Ted's checklist. "According to the new county safety inspector, we have to do all this by next week."

Fremont's eyes widened as he took in the long list. "You've got to be kidding me. This is that Ted Wingate, right?"

I wasn't surprised that Fremont knew the man's name. Fremont knew everything there was to know about everyone in Magellan and Flat Mesa.

"That's him," I said.

"He's from Seattle. What the hell does he know about buildings in the desert?"

"Enough to shut us down," Cassandra said.

"I told you, there's nothing wrong with my plumbing." Fremont looked around the lobby. "Have you told Maya yet? She's gonna go ballistic."

She would. Maya had worked for months to replace the ancient electrical system of the once-derelict hotel. She'd done a beautiful job according to our last inspector, who'd let us open. Why the hell had he retired to fish, leaving us with a jerk like Ted?

I heaved a sigh and snatched a copy of the list from Cassandra. "I'll go tell Maya right now," I said.

I asked to borrow Fremont's truck, because I had no other transportation now that my motorcycle was gone. I tried not to think about the broken wreck of my Sportster, because I'd be lost in grief if I did. I loved my bike, which had carried me all over the country for the last six years. At times she'd been my only friend.

I drove to Nash Jones's house in Flat Mesa, remembering where it lay from the last time I'd come out here. That time, I had been in a panic, and it had been cool September. This time, I drove sedately, and January cold forced me to run the heat in the truck. Fremont's truck was less than a year old and the heater was in great shape. I was toasty warm by the time I parked in front of Nash's long, low house.

Nash's roof was peaked to help winter snow slide off, and his gutters managed to be free of debris from the cotton-wood trees along his property. A couple of cedars dotted the strip of land that separated him from his back-door neighbor, but the yard held no sign of fallen leaves or branches. I swear Nash vacuumed his yard. Maya's truck was out front, as was Nash's black F-250, obsessively restored from its last adventure.

I knocked on the door, but my knocking couldn't compete with the shouting inside. Maya's voice rose, Nash's started to drown hers out, then Maya's screech cut through that.

"You are one stupid, stubborn son of a bitch!" she yelled.

I turned the knob, found the door unlocked, and pushed it open. "Quiet down now, kids," I said.

Nash didn't have much in his living room but a weight machine and a rack of free weights, and he used his break-fast bar for his dining room. A folding table now reposed near the window, two folding chairs drawn up to it, Maya's work presumably. Maya and Nash looked up at me from this table, which held the remains of a meal.

"Tell him he can't go back to work today," Maya said with vehemence. "The stupid idiot had a concussion, and he's supposed to rest for a week."

Nash glared at me as only Nash Jones could glare. His eyes were clear light gray, his hair black and cut short. A square white bandage covered the base of his scalp.

"What do you want, Begay?" he growled.

"I came to see whether you were all right. And to find Maya."

"You escaped FBI custody?" Maya asked, her eyes gleaming.

I grinned at her. "He was lenient."

Nash, who'd been out during the attack on his hospital room, came alert. "FBI custody? What the hell have you done now?"

"Calm down." I hopped up on the stool at the breakfast bar. "Didn't Maya tell you what happened?"

Nash transferred the glare to Maya. "No."

Maya flushed, but she didn't stop me as I told him, in

detail, about what I'd seen in the sinkhole, the woman in the hospital room and how Mick had killed her, finishing with Coyote's ploy that got Mick and me out of Flagstaff.

"She pretended to be my *mother*?" Nash asked, enraged, when I'd finished. "Who was she?"

"We don't know. She died fast under Mick's fire."

"You should have kept her alive for questioning."

"We didn't have a choice," I said, exasperated. "It was the only way Mick could stop her."

"What are your conclusions? Or Mick's?"

I rubbed my head. "I think she was connected to what I saw in the sinkhole. Her reaction to my magic was the same—it made her stronger, not weaker. I thought the hands in the hole were coming for me, but maybe they were coming for you. The women in the hospital didn't seem interested in attacking me, or Mick."

Maya's brown eyes widened. "Someone's after Nash?"

"Looks that way," I said.

"Why?" she demanded.

"That's a good question," Nash said. "There's no reason anyone should be hunting me, especially not someone magical."

"I can think of dozens of people who'd want you dead," I said. "Every person you've ever gotten sent to prison, for example. And magically, you're special. Unique. You have the ability to soak up magic, nullify it, not be hurt by it."

"Exactly what I mean." Nash dismissed the drug dealers, thieves, and assaulters with a flick of his fingers. "If, according to you, a magical attack won't work on me, why would someone try it?"

"Maybe they weren't trying to kill you, but capture you. To figure out how you work and how they can make your non-magic work for them."

"That's a lot of suppositions," Nash said.

"It's all I have right now. You need to be careful. I can ward your house if you want, or better still, Mick or Cassandra can do it. They're skilled, and their magic is earth-based. My brand obviously makes whoever it is stronger." Which really bugged me.

"None of this means I need to stay home," Nash said stubbornly.

"Nash," Maya began. Her voice was waiting to return to the screech, I could feel it.

"I'll sit behind my desk and write reports," Nash snapped. "I'm not stupid enough to chase criminals through the desert when I know I'll pass out after ten strides. I have deputies. I'll use them."

I pitied the deputies. If Nash couldn't run around himself, he'd make sure his deputies covered every inch he couldn't and report every detail to him.

"I also came to talk about this," I said, pulling Ted's list out of my pocket. "You wouldn't have had anything to do with hiring the new county inspector, would you?"

"Wingate?" Nash looked surprised. "No. Why?"

Maya grabbed the list and read it with widening eyes. "What the hell? Is he crazy? I've done all this. There's nothing wrong with *my* wiring."

"Ted Wingate is a huge pain in the ass," Nash said with conviction.

I was surprised. I thought he'd be the kind of guy that Nash liked—obsessive, annoying, and arrogant. "I take it you've met him?"

Nash nodded. "One of the first things he did was come to my office and tell me I didn't know how to run my jail."

Damn, I was sorry I'd missed *that*. "What happened? He looked healthy when he talked to me, so you obviously didn't break his neck."

"We came to an understanding."

That must have been an interesting clash of wills. Nash had been Special Forces in the army, and he liked to run things his own way. His sense of his own rightness was unshakable.

"Why is a jerk like him working for our county, anyway?" I asked. "Can't you arrest him for something?"

"Not until he commits a crime." By the tone of Nash's voice, he'd thought about it and wished he could.

"People aren't exactly signing up to work out here in the back of beyond," Maya said. "Counties with bigger populations pay better. So why is he here?"

"Maybe he likes the quiet life," I said.

Maya snorted. "No one likes things this quiet. Maybe no one else would hire him."

That was more likely. Hopi County was small, sparsely populated, and far from cities. Most people didn't even know we existed, except that Magellan had the reputation for being steeped in woo-woo magic. The biggest industry in the county was magical tourism—though I knew that the tourists saw the façade, the fake magic. They wouldn't be able to handle the real magic.

"He's nuts if he wants this all done in a week," Maya said. "I'll need to order more supplies. Besides, he's a liar if he says there's anything wrong with my wiring."

I believed her, just as I'd believed Fremont. "Could you take a look, though? To prove it's fine? Then I can get a lawyer and rub Ted's face in it."

"Be careful of Wingate, Janet," Nash said. "I got him to back down, but he's a troublemaker, the kind who will use the letter of the law to get at people. If he comes after you, it won't be pretty."

I knew that. Strange, I usually only feared people with powerful magics, but plain old Ted had me sweating.

Nash ended the discussion by standing. "You can take me to work, Janet. I agree I shouldn't drive until the dizziness goes away, but Maya won't take me anywhere."

"Damn you." Maya jumped up with him.

Nash walked away from her down the long hall toward the bedrooms in the back of the house. Maya started to follow, then stopped, looking unhappy, when Nash shut his bedroom door in her face.

"Take me out to the highway," Nash said as we pulled away from his house. "The one to Holbrook. I want to look at the scene." He'd dressed in his sheriff's uniform, every crease knife-sharp, his boots shining. He wore a heavy uniform coat against the January cold and his usual black sunglasses against the glare.

"Why?"

"For my report. I want to see it."

"Big hole, lots of debris. Mick went out there last night—he said he found nothing." And Mick had returned home acting strangely, and I hadn't seen him since. I didn't bother mentioning that.

"Mick had no business being out there. The area's cordoned off. A danger zone."

"Like police tape is going to stop Mick. He's a fire-breathing dragon, remember?"

"Yes." Nash's lips firmed. "Now I want to see what *I* can find. Turn here."

I took the backstreet he pointed to and, after dipping through a wash, emerged on an intersection with the highway. I guessed that Nash had probably asked Maya to drive him out here and Maya had refused. Maya Medina was the only person in Hopi County who could stand up to Nash Jones and get away with it.

About three miles down the highway we reached a barricade. Lopez had closed the road here, but I drove around the barrier through the dirt at Nash's instruction and proceeded to the site.

Six

I hadn't gotten a good look at the hole I'd fallen into, and now that I was standing on its edge, I was glad I hadn't. The fact that Nash and I had survived at all was a frigging miracle.

A hole about forty feet wide gaped across the highway and into the desert beyond it. Asphalt buckled at the hole's edges, twenty feet separating the two ends of the road. Boulders, red earth, roots, grass, and the remains of a cedar filled a ledge just inside the hole. Then that too broke off and plunged down into darkness. The sides of the hole were sheer and straight, as though cut by a razor.

"Sheriff!" Deputy Lopez made his way around the huge hole from the other side in his usual brisk stride. He regarded Nash anxiously. "You all right, sir?"

"Fine," Nash said.

"We're holding the fort, sir. You can stay home and rest if you want."

"I'm going crazy doing nothing at home. I'm heading to the office to catch up on paperwork."

I hoped Maya never heard that Nash considered staying home with her doing nothing. "You were home, what, half a day?" I asked him.

"I'll rest again tonight. Any sign that someone caused this deliberately?" he asked Lopez.

"Completely natural, sir," Lopez said. "We had a geology professor out here this morning. Underground caves collapse, the roof over them comes down. The pavement was probably weak and ready to give, and then you two happened to drive over it. You were damn lucky to get out alive."

I sat down near the edge of the hole. Sitting, I didn't get as disoriented, and I could look into the hole without feeling queasy. "Deputy, do you have a flashlight? You wouldn't have any binoculars too, would you?"

"Don't get too close," Lopez said. "The geologist said more could collapse."

Every instinct I had made me want to scramble back at that news, but I made myself stay put. "This won't take long."

Nash was interested in what I was interested in. He ordered Lopez to provide what I required, and Lopez gave him a salute.

"Good to see you're feeling better, sir."

Lopez didn't have binoculars, but Nash found a pair in Fremont's truck. I lay on my stomach on the edge, digging the toes of my boots into the hard earth.

I turned on the flashlight and stabbed the beam into the darkness. At first, I saw nothing but boulders, large and small, slabs of sandstone, weeds, tree branches, and the flash of metal that had been a piece of my motorcycle or Nash's SUV.

I felt warmth on my right side as Nash stretched out beside me, his bandage white against his black hair. He peered down with me, saying nothing.

I moved the beam back and forth, lower and lower, and froze. "What is that?"

Nash gripped the lip of the hole. "Looks like glyphs."

Not, as I feared, the skeletal hands. I saw a tight grouping of them: spirals, stars with coronas, a crescent moon.

Lopez looked over our shoulders, as curious as we were. "Were those on one of the boulders that fell in?"

"Nope." I moved the flashlight over the pictures chipped into the sandstone, light red against darker brown. "These are on the cliff wall."

"That doesn't make any sense," Lopez said. "How can someone make glyphs on a buried wall?"

"If it wasn't buried at the time." I played the flashlight over the area, turning up more and more glyphs. I hadn't seen these when I'd been down there, but then, it had been pitch-dark, plus I'd been distracted by the scary skeletal hands. "There might have been dry caves way down there once, maybe with the entrance now sealed."

"Interesting theory." Nash pried the flashlight from my hands and trained it over the glyphs. "I don't see anything that looks like skeletons."

"Skeletons?" Lopez asked in alarm.

"Something I thought I saw," I said.

I didn't see the skeletal hands now either. The glyphs were similar to what were in nearby Chevelon Canyon and up at Homol'ovi: observations of the night sky and natural events, plus drawings of men, animals, and strange beings New Agers claimed were aliens. No thin lines that ended in spidery hands.

But I sensed something down there, something that made my skin tingle and my blood chill. It wasn't so much a presence as a cold air seeping up through the rocks. Seeking.

I grabbed the flashlight from Nash. "Time to go."

"What's the hurry?"

"Lopez said the edge was unstable, and I don't feel like falling back down there."

Nash gave me his annoyed look, but he got to his feet with me and moved from the edge. "You know, neither of us should be alive after a fall like that."

"I know."

"So, what happened?"

"Why would I know?"

"Because you usually do," he said.

I handed the flashlight back to Lopez. "Not this time. I have no idea why we didn't break our necks or splatter all over the rocks."

Nash stared at the hole, rubbing the bandage on the back of his head. "I want to know."

Lopez shrugged. "God had other plans for you, maybe."

Nash, the Unbeliever, frowned at him. "I want to know *what* plans. Janet." He hesitated.

I raised my brows. "You want me to look into it? Is that what you're trying to say?"

"This is your specialty, isn't it? Poking your nose into things that don't make sense?"

"Yes, but usually you tell me to stay the hell away and mind my own business."

"But something's going on I should know about," Nash said. "I want to know why glyphs came to life and tried to grab you, and why someone pretended to be my mother and tried to kill me. I don't have time for woo-woo crap; you do. I have real criminals to catch."

"You can be so flattering, Nash." I was aware of Lopez, standing next to us, listening hard. "Sure, I'll do it. I'll even give you a discount."

Nash's eyes narrowed. "I thought you didn't charge for your investigations. You're not licensed."

"I was joking. Why should I need a license to look into woo-woo crap, as you put it?"

Nash shoved his sunglasses back on. "Just do it. Now drive me to my office. I have work to do."

The man didn't have a gracious bone in his body.

I dropped Nash off at the county jail and sheriff's department and didn't ask how he'd get home. I suspected that Maya would be back here at dark, prodding him out and into her truck.

I returned to Magellan, still worried about Mick and hoping that he'd returned. If I'd found the petroglyphs without looking very hard, Mick must have seen *something* in the sinkhole. I wanted to know why Mick's eyes had gone white, why he'd snarled at me, and why his tattoo had burned my fingers. Whether or not the skeletal hands were responsible for all that, we needed to fix him.

I gave Fremont back his keys when I reached the hotel and went into the kitchen in search of food. Mick was there, making himself a sandwich.

"Hey, baby," he said when I stopped in surprise. He lifted the bread knife well out of the way, came to me, and kissed the top of my head. "Want pastrami? Or turkey? If your guests are okay with sandwiches, I can be head chef."

He went back to slathering mustard onto bread, his muscles working. His eyes were blue and warm, his aura black and fiery as it should be.

"Mick," I said cautiously. "Are you all right?"

"Sure." He smiled his bad-boy Mick smile. "Why wouldn't I be?"

"What did you find out at the sinkhole last night?"

"Not much. Dark and quiet." He chuckled. "Nash's guard was asleep."

"What did you see down there? Any glyphs?"

"No."

"You were pissed off about something."

He gave me a puzzled look. "When?" He sliced the turkey sandwich in half, put it on a plate, and handed it to me.

I didn't take it. "When you came back last night."

Mick set the plate back on the counter. "I didn't come back here last night. I looked into the hole, didn't see anything but rocks and dirt, and I left. I got back this morning in time to see you drive off in Fremont's truck. Fremont told me you went to find Maya. Did you talk to her?"

I stared at him, openmouthed, until he put down the knife and gave me a look of concern.

"Mick, you came back in the middle of the night, got mad at me, and took off again."

"I didn't, Janet. I was out all night. I went into Flat Mesa and had a beer. I didn't want to wake you."

"Bars close at two."

"And then it was nice and dark and quiet, and I decided to get dragon. I don't have much chance to do that. It felt good to stretch my wings."

All of which made perfect sense. Of course Mick would enjoy himself flying around while the rest of the world slept. Except . . .

"Mick, I didn't dream you coming back here. The mirror heard and saw you. It said shadows had touched you."

"Magic mirrors exaggerate. Especially that one."

I put my hand on his. "Let's eat in the saloon. It's closed, and we can be alone."

"You want the mirror to read me?" Mick flashed me a grin. "Fine." He scooped another sandwich onto a plate, snatched a beer from the refrigerator, and followed me out.

The mirror was strangely silent as Mick and I took a table near the bar. I looked up at the mirror where it hung broken in its unbroken frame. Pieces were missing from one corner, where Mick and I had pulled off bits to put in other parts of the hotel or carry with us. Magic mirrors were a hell of a lot more reliable than cell phones, and this one had saved our butts more than once.

If I didn't repair it, Ted might demand I haul the mirror out of the saloon and throw it away—at least, he could try. I'd protect the mirror with all I had—it was damn powerful and I owed it. Magic mirror repair was a bitch anyway. Only specialized witches could do it, and then you had to worry about the witch claiming a share of the mirror's loyalty.

"Well?" I asked it impatiently.

Glass tinkled as the mirror shivered. "He's cold. Shadow touched."

Mick's skin had been plenty warm when I'd taken his hand in the kitchen, not to mention the heat of the flame tattoo on his back last night. "What do you mean?"

Mick went on eating, unconcerned. "A shadow found him," the mirror said. "It's freezing me."

Mick looked up, his eyes black with sudden rage. Fire flared on this fingers. "Get warm, then."

"Mick, don't you dare—" I lunged at him.

Too late. The fire left Mick's hand and engulfed the mirror in flame. It screamed, a loud, long, fingernails-across-glass scream. The fire burned merrily for a few seconds; then, the instant before the flames threatened to crawl onto the walls, Mick closed his hand, and the fire vanished.

I plopped back down in my chair and stared at Mick. "What the hell did you do that for?"

Mick shrugged and picked up his sandwich. "That thing has always bugged me."

"Mick, what is the matter with you?"

"Nothing. I'm trying to eat my lunch in peace, that's all. Give it a rest."

I stood up, fists on the table, and tried to peer into his eyes. "Did something come out of that hole? Did it possess you, maybe?"

Mick looked up at me, his blue eyes as clear as ever. "Do I look possessed to you?"

Not really, but something was going on. Cassandra must have thought the same, because she came rushing in.

"What the hell was that? What's wrong with the mirror?"

"Oh, honey," the mirror cried. "It was terrible. Our Micky, he *flamed* me!"

Cassandra drew a breath to ask why, but I cut her off. "Can you check and see whether Mick is possessed?" The possessed don't always realize they are.

Mick gave me a long-suffering look, but he let Cassandra take his face in her hands and study him, looking deep into his eyes. Mick returned her gaze without flinching.

Cassandra finally drew away, shaking her head. "He's himself. His aura hasn't changed either."

It had last night. But today Mick's aura was back to normal: black with crackles of fire. The fire crackled even more as he shoved aside his plate and stood up.

"I came here looking for lunch, not an interrogation. Next time, I'll try the diner."

He opened the outside door and walked out into the sunshine without looking back. We watched as he mounted his bike and drove away in a cloud of dust.

Cassandra watched him speculatively. "I can't read his

thoughts, Janet, but something's up with him. It might be magical or it might be mundane, but something's upset him."

"Shadows," the mirror groaned. "I'm telling you."

"What does that mean, exactly?" I asked in annoyance.

"Search me, honey. I'm just a mirror. I reflect impressions; I don't interpret. Now, if you want to get into his pants and see why he has ants in them, I don't mind watching."

"I can see that the fire didn't damage you too much."

"That kind of fire can't destroy me, sweetie. I'm hard to get rid of."

Tell me about it.

"If you need a spell . . ." Cassandra began.

"No," I said quickly. A good truth spell might get something out of him, but Mick wouldn't thank me for it. Which rankled a little. Mick was in the habit of minding *my* business whether I liked it or not. Everything I knew about *him*, I'd had to pull out a tiny piece at a time.

"Have a sandwich." I pushed my plate to Cassandra. "Or give it to Fremont. I need to go talk to a petroglyph expert."

I meant Jamison Kee, my oldest friend, who knew everything there was to know about ancient glyphs and the stories that went with them. But as I walked into the lobby, Maya came hurtling out of the door to the basement, followed closely by Fremont.

Maya waved a bundle of wires in my face. "Janet, what the hell is this?"

"Wires," I said. "Why are you pulling wiring out of my walls?"

Fremont was pale and breathing hard from running up the stairs. "This is bad, Janet."

I didn't get a chance to ask why. Maya went off in Spanish, then said in English, "Some son of a bitch has been down there, ruining all my wiring. There's some kind of nasty disintegration, and everything is worse than it was before you started renovating. Like I never fixed it at all."

Seven

I stood in the basement with Maya and Fremont and looked at the destruction of nine months' worth of work. The electricity still functioned upstairs, but Maya showed me stripped and corroded wires, strangely rigged splices, and entire junctions dead.

"I didn't do this," Maya wailed. "Someone sabotaged me." She started up in Spanish again, calling the unknown person a string of filthy names.

Fremont was quieter but just as angry. He removed a panel to show me pipes coated with rust and green corrosion. He also pointed out mold rotting the studs and beams that held up the hotel.

"We gotta replace everything," Fremont said. "All the plumbing plus the infrastructure, or the whole building is going to come down."

Maya was right—this was new. Last May, I'd followed the former inspector all over the hotel while he'd gone through his meticulous checklist. Everything had been in pristine condition. There was no way we could have had such deterioration in nine months.

"Did we have leaks? Faulty joints—something?"

Fremont looked indignant. "Not with my plumbing. I used all new piping and the most effective sealant. Plus a little of this." He wriggled his fingers.

Fremont fancied himself a mage, and he did have a tiny bit of magic in him, but not enough to have done this much damage even if his spells had backfired.

"And I'd never have done anything like *that*." Maya pointed to a knot of wire that looked as though it could burst into flame any moment. "That's plain shoddy workmanship."

"Are you two saying someone came down here and re-wired and replumbed my hotel?" I asked. "Incompetently? While no one noticed?"

Maya's dark eyes smoldered. "We're saying *we* didn't do this. We're saying we're better than this, but if you don't believe us . . ."

I held up my hand. "No, no. I believe you."

This was Magellan, a town that had been built close to vortexes, which were swirling sinks of magic. Who knew what kind of mystical energy flowed through the ground, not to mention the water? A strange kind of spell could have reversed everything they'd done.

"It makes me look incompetent," Maya said. "A stupid woman trying to do a man's job."

I studied the mess behind the panel, knowing that the entire basement probably looked like this. "I know you didn't do this, Maya, don't worry. But it doesn't matter. Whoever did this—I need you to fix it and fix it fast."

"A week, you said," Maya answered. "This is a month's worth of work and more."

Fremont agreed. "I need to get more supplies, and then I'll have to rip out everything. You'll have to tell your guests they won't have any water or electrics for days."

Damn it. "That means I'll have to close. Perfect."

No guests meant no income. I had insurance, but I didn't think it covered magical weirdness ruining the infrastructure.

"I can pay you double," I said. I couldn't pay them much at all, but I was desperate.

"Doesn't matter," Fremont said. "More money won't make time stand still so we can get it done."

"Hire more people to help you, as many as it takes," I said recklessly. "I'll buy the supplies and pay up when it's all done." My mind whirled—I'd have to sell more photographs, maybe go down to the bank and try to get a loan. There were programs for Indians and women-owned businesses—who knew what I might be able to get?

And maybe, just maybe, I could talk to Ted and get him to extend me another week. I'd promise to have it all done perfectly, if only he would give me a little more time. Maybe I should have Mick talk to him with me. The sight of Mick's muscles might persuade him.

Except Mick had torn out of here in a rage. I had no idea where I could find him, or even whether he wanted to be found.

"Start," I said to Maya and Fremont. "Do whatever you can. Please."

Maya gave me a skeptical look, but she began touching insulated wires and tracing things with a professional eye.

Fremont settled his cap. "Got a good-for-nothing nephew who needs to learn a trade. I'll bring him on for free."

I wasn't sure I wanted a disgruntled young man working on my plumbing, but I might not have much choice. Maya and Fremont turned away to get on with their assessment, and I left them to it.

Outside, the big crow that liked to keep an eye on me perched in the juniper near the edge of my parking lot. She cocked her head and gave me an admonishing look, but I didn't have time for her right now.

I asked Cassandra for a loan of her car, not wanting to impede Fremont's getting on with the repairs. My plan to talk to Jamison about the mysterious glyphs and skeletal hands would have to wait. First I needed to tackle Ted. I didn't enjoy the thought of begging and pleading with him, but again, I didn't have much choice.

Black clouds were forming to the north, rolling down from the mountains and highlands to the plateau on which Magellan lay. The growing wind had an icy bite, which meant there would be snow before dark. Swirls of wind danced in my fingers as I drove the twenty miles to Flat Mesa.

By the time I reached Ted Wingate's office, I was giddy with the storm, wanting it to come down so I could play. I held it together and entered the small county building that wasn't far from the sheriff's office.

The receptionist looked up from her computer and told me listlessly that Mr. Wingate was busy, and I'd have to wait. I hadn't sat long in the uncomfortable plastic chair, though, when Ted himself walked down the hall to greet me.

He smiled a broad smile, his teeth very straight and white in his tanned face. He should be out playing golf on some high-priced golf course, not carrying a clipboard through the linoleum-tiled halls of a county office.

"Ms. Begay," he said, sounding happy to see me. "How are you? Let's talk in my office."

Ted's office was sparse and lacked personality. The desk and chairs were gunmetal gray, and the only things on the walls were official certificates of training and licenses Ted had received. The white metal window blind was raised a precise one-quarter of the way, an angle that shut out the enormous and beautiful sky in favor of a slice of parking lot.

Ted's smile held as I put in my plea for more time.

"Not possible," he said. "I'm on a deadline too, Ms. Begay."

"What deadline? I had to pass inspection to open, but even then the county didn't give me a deadline. I just couldn't open until I passed."

Ted leaned against the edge of his desk. His light brown eyes set off his tan, as did his white polo shirt.

"Well, you see, little gal, that hotel is sitting on prime real estate. If the county seizes the property, we can sell it for a pretty penny. Hopi County can always use money. Now, I wouldn't want to see this happen to you." He set the clipboard on the desk with a decisive click. "I want to help you keep your cozy hotel, I really do. But the county says that if it's not up to code by end of next week, I have to shut it down."

"I have a team working on it." My mouth hurt as I said it.

Ted's smile widened. "I'm sure you do, sweetie. I'm sure you do. I'm not your enemy, you know. I've always liked Indians, and I want to see them catch a break after so many years of oppression. What can I do to help you out?"

If he were so sympathetic, why did his sympathy grate on my nerves? People existed who really did want to help Native Americans, some of them not very effectual, some clueless and doing more harm than good, but many were well-meaning and even kind. Ted, however, was in the condescending, what-will-make-me-look-good class.

"Give me another month," I said. "That would help."

"Now, that I *can't* do. Although . . ." Ted stepped around me and shut the door, giving me a furtive wink in the process. "Maybe we can talk. My job gives me some pull." He brushed by me again to close the blinds all the way. He smelled of fresh soap and toothpaste, not bad smells, but for some reason I didn't like them.

"My electrician showed me where the wiring has been sabotaged," I said, folding my arms. "I don't know who did that, and I don't know how, but I know she didn't do it."

I'd have suspected Ted himself, but the extent of the damage was vast and would have taken a long time. Someone would have noticed Ted repeatedly trotting down to my basement. No, something else was going on.

"I can't give you more time," Ted said. "Honestly I can't. But maybe, you know, when I come back to inspect next week, I can cut you some slack."

Again with the winking. Did he know how annoying that was?

Winter wind struck the building with a crash, rattling the window panes and howling around the eaves. Wind danced in my fingers, and I closed my fists to contain it.

"Sounds like a nice storm brewing," Ted said. "So, how about it, little gal? Want me to help you out?"

I wasn't stupid enough to believe that he'd help me out of the goodness of his heart. "In exchange for what?"

Another wink. "You know, we could be friends, Janet. *Good* friends."

The tips of my fingers began to crackle. "A free drink in my saloon?" I asked, letting the sarcasm drip. "Or a room for any friends and relatives who want to visit?"

Ted chuckled. "Your hotel isn't exactly four-star accommodations, and my family are too citified to come to a godforsaken place like Magellan. I was thinking something a little more . . . personal." He stopped an inch in front of me, smarmy smile and all.

I'd known damn well what he was getting at. "You've got to be kidding me."

"Come on, little gal. You're a cute thing, and my wife, she's always busy. So busy, you wouldn't believe it. If you keep me satisfied, I'll make sure your hotel will pass its inspection."

He closed his hands over my wrists. I tried to yank away, but he held me fast. His face was coming down to mine, his mouth open. He had to be crazy. All I had to do was mention this incident to Mick, and Ted would be toast.

I fought, but Ted slammed me against him, arms around my back. His breath was minty fresh, but I didn't want it mingling with mine.

"Let go of me." I tried to shout, but Ted slapped a hand over my mouth.

"No you don't, little gal. You make my cock happy, or I shut you down. Your choice."

The arm at my back was iron hard, Ted's hand over my mouth biting into my face. He knew how to pin me—his body held me in place as he thrust his hand up the back of my shirt.

No one can say I didn't give him a chance. I really, really gave him every opportunity to let me go.

Ted's hand still covered my mouth, but I didn't need to speak. I reached for the snowstorm, smiling as wind and ice surged through my body.

My blood burned with cold, my skin goose-bumped, and I exhaled frost. Ted's eyes widened as my frozen breath coated his hand; they widened more when I reached up and touched his face.

Ice.

Ted yelled and shoved me away. He stared in blank astonishment as the walls of his office iced over, and snow started falling inside.

I gathered ice in my hands, whirling it around and around my cupped palms while Ted watched in horror. Faster and faster the ice shards flew, and then I released them.

Ted screamed and threw up his arms. The icicles hit him, cutting his face, and the window shattered behind him. Wind exploded through the office, whirling up a cyclone of papers, glass, snow, and ice.

I ducked past Ted and ran out. Ted screamed and cursed behind me, his face dripping blood. The receptionist sprang up in alarm, and I shouted at her as I ran past.

"The storm broke the window. It's a mess in there, and Ted's hurt. Get some help!"

The receptionist dashed to Ted's office, and I ran out and leapt into Cassandra's car. Wind and snow slapped it, but I spun out of the parking lot and sped out to the open highway to Magellan.

Straight into a whiteout.

I slowed as the wash of snow met the windshield, the wind pushing and buffeting Cassandra's tiny car.

I laughed out loud. The storm was still whirling within me, me part of it. I lapped up the elements and danced in them. I was the goddess of ice and wind and I loved it.

My golden brown skin was turning pale, my lips blue, but I felt no cold. I beheld my strange face in the mirror, my eyes burning with fire in the middle of the cold.

I slowed the car to a crawl but didn't stop. I knew mine was the only vehicle on the road—I'd noted that before the world had gone white. No one else was stupid enough to be driving out here.

But I could sense the road beneath me, its cold texture different from the soft pockets of desert to either side. I was doing fine, singing in Navajo at the top of my voice, enjoying the freedom and the wildness of pure Stormwalker power.

The shadow of a human being reared up in front of my window. Gasping, I jerked the car to the right, but I felt a dull thud as the driver's side fender hit whoever it was.

I'd been going maybe ten miles an hour, but even that could knock a person down and do serious damage, especially if they'd been blundering around on the ice. I got the car stopped and opened the door, shoving hard against wind and swirling snow.

I scrambled to the body on the road. It was a woman, lying facedown, wind whipping the hood of her parka and her long black hair.

I was afraid to touch her with my snow queen thing going on, but I had no choice. I grabbed the woman under the arms and dragged her to the relative safety of the car.

She was light, and I tucked her into the passenger's seat without problem. Her parka hood flopped over her face, and she never looked up. The car was still running as I slipped back inside and slammed the door, shutting us into silence and warmth.

"You all right?" I didn't want to touch her again in case my crazy ice-fingers hurt her, but she didn't respond. "I'll take you to my hotel, and we can call for help from there."

No answer. My heart racing in panic, I put the car in gear and moved it slowly forward. The tires spun a little on the side of the road, but with a boost from my storm power, I got back on the highway. I cranked up the heater to counteract the cold my own body radiated and drove on.

Beside me, the woman stirred. She pushed back the hood of the parka, and I found myself looking into the face of a young Native American woman I'd met once before. She'd introduced herself last fall by the empty railroad bed behind my hotel, and when she had, my world changed. She was Apache, and her name was Gabrielle Massey.

"Hey, big sis," she said, flashing a smile. "How've you been?"

I hit the brakes, and the car spun in a tight circle. Gabrielle smiled at me, right before the car exploded.

Eight

The car didn't blow up in a big ball of flame. The doors and roof ripped away, the windows burst, and glass and snow poured in, wind whipping the shards into a frenzy.

Gabrielle disappeared, but I saw her on her feet a little way from the car, her arms outstretched. The storm wasn't touching her. She'd enclosed herself inside a bubble of stillness, against which the snow beat.

Gabrielle was a child of Beneath. My mother the hell-goddess had created her, even though the hell-goddess had looked me in the eye last year and told me that I was an only child. That was my mother for you.

Most people would rejoice at finding a long-lost sister, but *my* long-lost sister was evil incarnate. The last time I'd seen Gabrielle, it had been a clear, sunny day in September. We'd talked, no battling, but I'd realized then that her Beneath magic was as strong as mine, maybe stronger. Since then I'd been working on tempering my Beneath magic with my Stormwalker magic, drawing on the strengths of both without letting either control me. It wasn't easy. I was too new to using the Beneath magic, while Gabrielle had been training in it her entire life.

I wondered why Gabrielle had chosen to attack me during a storm, because now she faced a Stormwalker in her element. The storm tried to beat and ravage me, but I reached into it and made it my own.

The blizzard became a part of me, my body growing colder to blend with it. Ice spewed from my fingers, and I spread my hands and laughed. I was part of the storm, dancing in the wind, my touch turning the world to ice. It was orgasmic, this power, making me crazy with desire at the same time I was crazed with the need to destroy.

Gabrielle stood calmly behind her bubble of magic, watching me. "So that's what you do."

"I'm a Stormwalker," I said. "This is a storm. Put it together."

"It's earth magic." The words came with a sneer.

"Earth magic is strong. It's old, grounded in the bones of the world."

"Beneath magic is older," she said.

"But earth magic rules here."

Gabrielle's smile widened, and her bubble expanded. "Don't challenge me, big sis. I dream of taking you down, but this isn't the time. Not yet."

"Why not?" I smiled too and blasted her with ice.

Her bubble wavered and, with it, her smugness. "You don't want to mess with me, Janet."

I could kill her. I knew it. The storm magic was winding around my Beneath magic, honing me into a precise, efficient weapon.

I'd promised everyone who cared about me that I wouldn't use the Beneath magic to go on a rampage. I'd made the promise to a Koshare, a Hopi spirit who watched over this land, and to Coyote, who watched over those he wanted to watch over. Both had made it clear that they'd kill me without remorse if I turned into anything like my mother.

But they couldn't fault me for destroying Gabrielle before *she* went on a destructive rampage, could they? And besides, I could do this using Stormwalker magic only.

Gabrielle's bubble splintered into glittering pieces, but not because of me. Her Beneath power rose like a sword, and she sliced it at me.

The blizzard whipped away her strike before it could touch me, and I answered with another barrage of ice. The ice struck Gabrielle like bullets, tearing at her face before she deflected it.

"Fine," she panted. "If you want to do this now . . ."

"I want you gone now. This is my town, my people. Leave them alone."

"Your *people*. Oh, the arrogance of you. Mother tried to warn me."

Her power stabbed at me. We fought, Stormwalker to Beneath magic wielder, half goddess to half goddess. We were going to destroy each other.

We'd also destroy the world. Ice and snow tore up the ground, chunks of frozen earth heaving upward in seismic eruption. Black clouds swirled around us, a tornado in the making. If the storm got loose from me, it would flatten the two small towns sitting out here under endless sky.

I was freezing. My body had become the storm, my hair coated in snow, ice forming on my lashes. I was cold inside and out, which meant that all compassion, all warm feeling—any love I'd ever cultivated—was gone. I was ice: hard, uncaring destruction.

Gabrielle's power hit me, and I fell. I landed hard on snow-covered rock and heard a couple of bones snap, but I didn't feel a thing. I was on my feet again, the pain nonexistent. I slapped Gabrielle with wind. She fought back, the two of us smashing, grappling, falling, climbing to our feet to smash again.

She was testing me, and I her. We hadn't been ready to fight, but neither of us could stop now.

A shadow blotted out the snow, a huge black object that swooped through the storm. Red-hot fire streamed in front of it, melting the snow and ice down to bare earth.

The dragon's fire sent Gabrielle tumbling. She rolled over and over, coming to rest on the snow-covered road. I laughed, my triumph ringing out, and then the dragon turned on me.

"Mick—no!"

Fire blossomed in an arc around me. The ice melted, my body returning to normal temperature with a bang. Pain roared through me, and I screamed.

Mick lifted me in a clawed talon, and his wings blew snow in all directions as he launched into the sky. The storm reached for me, and I reached for it, but Mick's fire kept it from touching us.

The blizzard receded as Mick flew south with me, leaving Cassandra's wrecked car in the middle of the road, and Gabrielle nowhere in sight.

I groaned as Mick peeled my clothes from my body. The blizzard raged outside, but I lay on my bed inside my warm hotel, teeth gritted against the pain of cracked bones. Mick tried to be gentle, but I was broken and battered, my storm power still pounding me.

"Gabrielle?" I croaked.

Mick's eyes were black all the way through, his dragon tattoos red and writhing. "She's gone."

He was naked, his body so warm it hurt. Mick dropped the last of my clothing on the floor and lay down on top of me. I was shivering hard, but Mick's soft kisses heated my blood.

Fire danced in his eyes as my storm power sought him. The first time I'd met Mick, he'd dared me to blast him with lightning. He'd stood back and laughed as electricity crawled all over him, and then he'd swallowed it down and smiled at me.

What he did now wasn't quite the same but had similar effect. He absorbed the ice and cold I still radiated, inhaled it as he nuzzled my cheek and licked my skin. Mick's body shuddered with the cold, but dragon fire blazed along the lines of his tattoos. He drew the lingering storm magic out of me, until my body felt like it was roasting.

Caught in the frenzy, I wrapped my legs around him and pulled him down to me. My mouth sought his, my body welcomed him.

Mick went slow, mindful of my hurts. As he made love to me—deep, satisfying love—my cracked bones grew warm and whole, the heat of the healing nearly searing the sheets. I laughed, imagining my bed a smoldering cinder when we were done.

Mick smiled at me, his strange moods gone. This was *my* Mick, the man who'd watched over me for years, even when I hadn't been aware of it. I loved him for that, with everything I had.

He touched and kissed me, and once I felt stronger I touched him back. I knew what he liked, and I smiled as I licked him, tasted him, stroked him, teased him. Growling, Mick let me play, and then he showed me how much he appreciated the pleasuring.

The blizzard unwound into straight, heavy snowfall while Mick made me wild. At one point, I was facedown on the bed, my arms spread out across the mattress while he loved me until I was mindless with it. Nothing existed but him and me, and this feeling. Nothing.

Much later, we slept, curled together, my healing complete. But when I awoke to gray morning and freezing cold, I was alone.

I'd kicked off the covers in my sleep, and I now lay exposed to an ice-cold room. I grabbed the blankets and jerked them over my naked body. "What the hell happened to the heat?"

"Don't know, girlfriend," the magic mirror said from my bedside table. It wasn't in the drawer, where it was supposed to be; it sat happily on top. "But it sure was hot in here for a while. That was *good*. Dragon-boy has stamina, not to mention a gorgeous butt."

"Shut up." My injuries from the fight had healed, and the storm was gone, but I felt groggy and annoyed, not to mention cold.

I turned on the lamp, which glowed with light. The electricity was on, at least.

I got up and started to run a shower, then I gave up and turned off the water when nothing but cold poured from the pipes. I dressed with shaking fingers, pulled on my coat, and went out to the lobby.

Cassandra was there, the only one. She had a fire going in the fireplace, and she was dressed in the same clothes she'd worn yesterday, though covered with a white fake fur coat.

I went to the fireplace and held out my hands to the blaze. "Cassandra," I said. "About your car . . ."

"It's insured," Cassandra replied in her brisk voice. "I knew when it wrecked, because my wards on it alerted me. I called Mick, and he went to find you. The car can be replaced, and I'm happy to see you back in one piece."

"More or less," I said. "I'm sorry you had to spend the night here."

She shrugged, her sleek hair showing no sign of her having slept on it. "Even if I'd had a car, I couldn't have made it home in that weather. Fremont and Maya were stuck here too. Heat's out, and so is the hot water, but we have plenty of wood."

All the rooms, including mine, had been fitted with wood-burning stoves or fireplaces in addition to the central heating. Guests liked the extra fire, and desert winter nights could be severely cold.

"At least we have electricity," I said.

"We didn't even have that, but we have Maya. She got it back on, and she and Fremont are working on the heat. The only guest last night was Ansel, and he doesn't mind the cold. Good thing—he was the one who brought in all the wood. He wouldn't let me go out to get it."

Ansel would be asleep now, hiding from what little daylight there was. "I never thought I'd say this, but thank the gods for Nightwalkers."

"At least for Ansel," Cassandra agreed.

"If it wouldn't drive him to a killing frenzy, I'd open a vein for him myself," I said. "It sounds like the storm's pretty much done, though. When it gets lighter, maybe Fremont and Maya can get home. You too. I can handle things today."

Cassandra gave me a hesitant look. "Do you know what time it is?"

"No." I hadn't bothered to glance at a clock.

"Noon," she said. "You slept a long time."

Noon? I did a mental readjustment. "Why is it so dark? Is there another storm coming?" I didn't feel one, so I knew as soon as I asked that this wasn't the case.

For answer, Cassandra crossed the lobby and threw open the shutters. The lobby windows were supposed to look across the parking lot toward the open desert on the other side of the Crossroads, with part of the Crossroads Bar in view.

I saw only blank white. A bank of snow reached all the way to the top of the windows, cutting out the light.

It's handy to have a boyfriend who can wield fire. Mick came down from the roof, where he'd been surveying our surroundings, and melted a path from the front door, across the parking lot, and to the road. We decided to let the snow remain piled everywhere else, because it insulated the hotel and kept it warmer now that we had no central heating.

I climbed up to the roof, which shared a floor with the building's third story. I huddled in my coat and looked down at the bank of snow that rose to the second-floor windows.

Cassandra stood beside me. With her hands in the pockets of her white coat, she looked like a supermodel showing off winter fashions.

"I heard that half the Navajo Nation is cut off, same with the Hopi," she said. "Roads to remote areas are impassable."

"I believe it." The highway between Flat Mesa and Magellan, a major road, was blanketed with several feet of snow. Except for where Mick had cleared it, the snow lay unbroken for miles.

I'd already called my father. He'd assured me that in Many Farms they were cold but fine. They had a pile of snow, but their heat worked, at least, and they had a well-stocked stove in the family hogan.

Maya and Fremont were in the basement trying to coax the heater back online. We had food, I'd checked, and Ansel's gallon jugs of blood were still there. Ted hadn't thrown them away, and I silently blessed Elena for chasing him out before he could.

I told Cassandra what had happened at Ted's office, and Cassandra's brows shot up. "He tried to force you? And he's still alive?"

"I hit him hard. He won't be touching me again."

Cassandra's eyes blazed with outrage. "Men like him can't be allowed to get away with sexual harassment, Janet. You should report him."

I contemplated holding Ted upside down over the sinkhole Nash and I had fallen into until he retracted his demands. Screaming. Much more satisfying than suing him. I sighed. "He's not worth the hassle. Let me make sure my hotel is safe, and then I'll ask Mick to have a talk with him."

"You can take him to court about the inspection. Have the county supervisor make him prove his case."

"I would," I said, "but have you seen the garbage behind my walls? I don't know how it happened, but everything's a complete mess. All Ted would have to do is get an independent inspector in here to confirm his report, and we'd be done for. We have to fix it."

"I can help—come up with some spells."

"I'd appreciate that. I have to wonder whether Gabrielle is destroying my hotel just to prove she can. But I have wards that would go off like crazy if she comes within ten feet of the place. I'd know."

"The damage might simply be due to water and dry rot," Cassandra said. "It happens."

"That quickly?" The deterioration was strange, and there had to be an explanation besides the weather and the arid climate. This hotel had been abandoned three times in its life, the owners simply walking away. I wondered if the deterioration was the reason why. But if something magical had caused the damage, we'd have known, wouldn't we?

Between Mick, me, and Cassandra, we had so many magical warnings in place that we'd be able to detect a gnat that had been magicked to death.

Mick came out onto the roof with us, leather coat pulled closed against the cold, his breath steaming. He gazed about at the whiteness, then put his arms around me from behind. "Looks like we're not going anywhere for a while."

Cassandra smiled at us as she headed for the door. "Wonder what you'll find to do."

She left us alone. I closed my eyes as Mick kissed my hair. All signs of his anger and his white eyes were gone—I could only conclude that he'd taken care of whatever had happened to him.

"Any sign of Gabrielle?" I asked.

"Didn't see any when I went to move Cassandra's car. I thought maybe my flame had gotten her, but I don't think so."

"She hadn't come to kill me." When I reviewed our fight in my head, I realized that Gabrielle had been holding back. Scary thought. "This is the biggest storm we've had all winter. She came to see what I could do when I was in the height of my storm powers."

"For what?" Mick tightened his embrace. "I don't like the thought that she's planning to move against you. If I lost you, Janet, I don't know what I'd do."

This beautiful man with the dragon tattoos and the fiery eyes loved me. I never could believe it. He'd even made me his dragon mate, which meant that other dragons weren't allowed to have me or kill me. Most of them wanted to kill me.

"I'd like to know what she wants," I said. "But don't worry, I won't let her win. If my mother sent Gabrielle to best me, I won't let *her* win either."

We stood in silence, contemplating the snow and the crisp blue sky, now free of clouds. The mountains to the west were stark and clear in the brilliant air.

With Mick behind me, I didn't need a heater. Maybe I could get him to create a wall of flame or something inside—one that wouldn't burn the place to the ground.

Mick spoke before I could bring it up. "There's something I've been meaning to ask you," he said.

"What's that?" I felt safe with him. Nothing could touch me up here, high above the snow, with my dragon lover holding on to me. I thought of other ways Mick could keep me warm—the two of us in bed under the covers, his naked body cuddled up to mine. I would make sure the magic mirror was shut in the drawer this time.

Mick nuzzled my ear. "Among the Diné," he said, "how does a man approach a woman to ask her to marry him?"

Nine

I broke away and swung around, my breath fogging in the cold. "What?"

Mick watched me quietly, arms folded, eyes dark blue. "I'm interested in human customs and marriage rituals. Tell me about yours."

"Why?" I asked in a strangled voice.

"I'm curious. I've never asked you about these things before, and as much as I live among humans, I don't understand the intricate details of their customs."

Why on earth did he have to know about them right now? We had Gabrielle and skeletal hands to worry about, not to mention Ted and my hotel problems. "I'm sure a storyteller like Jamison can tell you better than I can about Diné customs."

"But I want *you* to tell me."

He studied me, dragonlike, with his head tilted, his eyes taking on a black gleam. Whenever I let myself be lulled into thinking that Mick was human, he'd look at me with that intense stare, reminding me that he was a couple centuries older than I was, not to mention a giant reptile.

"Traditionally?" I asked.

He shrugged. "If you want."

I drew a breath. "Traditionally, among the Diné, when a girl reaches marriageable age, her father goes out looking for a good match. He approaches the father and uncles of young men of other clans who are ready to marry. Fathers and uncles negotiate. There's a lot of talk, a lot of bargaining, before the couple in question even meet. But that's traditional. When my cousin April married, she simply accepted her boyfriend's proposal. Knowing April, I'm pretty sure the whole marriage thing was her idea. Her husband looks perpetually confused about how he came to be part of my family."

Mick listened, smiling a little. "What if the eligible bachelor is alone in the world? No family?"

"That's rare. Most Diné, even orphans, have some family—aunts, uncles, grandparents, cousins. Family is more than parents and children." I had so much family I couldn't turn around without tripping over them. That was my father's doing. I was his illegitimate daughter, mother unknown to all but him, but my usually quiet and subdued father had refused to give me up. The family had accepted me—grudgingly, but they'd done it.

"Among dragons, it's more common to be alone," Mick said. "We need so much territory, and when humans overran the world, there wasn't a lot of room left for us. We've been dying out for centuries."

Mick didn't talk much about his dragon background, only occasionally feeding me bits of information. He'd once told me about a lady dragon he'd planned to take as mate, long ago. She'd been stolen from him by another dragon, and she'd later died. He'd been alone since.

The dragon council, a triumvirate who enforced dragon law, had assigned Mick to watch over me. The original assignment had been to kill me, but Mick had turned things his own way. He was still watching over me.

"Dying out?" I repeated.

"Slowly. Nothing to worry about. Dragons live a long time."

"Maybe, but do Stormwalkers?"

Mick's smile vanished, and I saw a deep and ageless pain in his eyes. "I don't know. That's why I want to enjoy every minute I can with you."

I knew what he meant. He would watch me age and die before he changed much himself. He knew he'd lose me, and he was already preparing himself for it.

"You should find a lady dragon," I said, trying to make my voice light. "Someone who can be with you for another couple of centuries, someone who can live inside a volcano with you."

Mick laced his fingers through mine. "A lady dragon hasn't snared me. You have." He leaned to me, his eyes darkening. "*Mate* isn't just a word to me, Janet. It never has been. I want you as my mate in all ways, in bed and out of it. I want to give you all I have, all that I am."

A breath of freezing air swept over the snow and made me shiver. "Maybe we should talk about this later."

"When? There's always something crazy happening around you, around us. I have to talk about this when I can catch you alone for five minutes."

That was true enough. "Mick . . ."

Mick closed on me again, hands cupping my shoulders. "What are you afraid of?" he asked. "Me?"

I wasn't sure. Obligation to be the perfect wife, which I was convinced I never could be? Fear of producing children with the touch of evil I inherited from my mother?

"Everything," I said. "I'm afraid of everything."

"I know. I want to make sure you're never afraid again."

Gods, he'd break my heart. The fact that Mick wanted to be with me and me alone stunned the hell out of me. But all my life I'd been watched, restricted, controlled. Things had happened to me in the last year that I hadn't quite come to terms with, one of them being having Mick back in my life.

"I love you," I said, choosing my words carefully. "I love being with you, believe me. And I love knowing you have my back. I love that you claimed me as your dragon mate to protect me from the other dragons. We're partners, lovers, best friends." I closed my hands on his hard ones. "Right now, that's enough for me."

Mick's eyes turned blue again, the human eyes that had persuaded me to give him my virginity years ago. He reached out and traced my lips. "But it's not enough for me," he said.

He released me and walked away, his boots grating on the sanded roof. Mick went back inside, and I was left alone in the white, icy world with tears that froze on my cheeks.

No big surprise that by the time I went back downstairs, Mick had gone. Snowed-over roads wouldn't stop a dragon—he'd probably flown back to his Pacific island to bask on the beach while we froze our butts off here.

At least Maya had gotten the heat working. Cassandra and I cheered when a blast of hot air came out of the vents, but we kept our coats on until the place warmed up. Fremont and I scrounged through the pantry and freezer and put together brunch. Maya could cook like a dream, but she'd already done enough work coaxing the heat pump back on, so I was happy to make cornmeal pancakes and let her rest.

We toasted Maya with orange juice and fell to eating. I was hungry after my battle with Gabrielle and my wild night with Mick. I tried not to think about Mick and the way he'd walked away from me, because that way led to hurt and confusion.

"I called Nash," Maya said. "He got stuck at the sheriff's department overnight."

"Nash's dream come true," I said. "Not being able to leave work must be heaven for him."

"I'm still pissed off at you for driving him in yesterday," Maya said. "He needs to rest."

I pointed a pancake-filled fork at her. "You should thank me for saving your relationship. If you'd forced him to stay home much longer, he'd have thrown you out. You know it."

"I know." Maya ate glumly. "He doesn't like being taken care of."

"Bullshit. He likes it, but he needs to think it's his choice."

Maya thought about that, and she started to smile. "So if I told him I'm done with babying him, he might find a way to keep me around?"

"Maybe."

Fremont chuckled. "Jones has to be crazy. If a woman wanted to move into *my* house and spoon-feed me, I wouldn't say no. I bet if you wore sexy lingerie while you fed him, he'd change his mind real quick. And if you want to model it for me first, I won't stop you."

Maya made a face at him, but I could see she didn't think Fremont's suggestion of putting on skimpy lingerie to nurse Nash was a bad one.

By two, the snowplow from Magellan had made its way to the Crossroads, which lay two miles north of the town, then headed up to meet the plows from the county. Magellan had only one plow, which was driven by one of Fremont's many cousins. The cousin stopped at the hotel and warmed himself with a cup of coffee before driving on, releasing us from our snowy prison.

Maya and Fremont could get home now, but that would leave Cassandra and me stranded without vehicles. Cassandra said she didn't mind staying at the hotel while we worked on it, and I let Fremont give me a ride into town so I could run errands and stop by Cassandra's apartment to grab her some clothes.

Cassandra lived with a Changer, a shape-shifter who could turn into a wolf. Pamela had dark hair and Native American features, was tall, as most Changers were, and had dark eyes except when they turned gray like a wolf's. Those wolf eyes peered at me in suspicion when she opened the door a crack, then flicked back to brown when she saw who I was.

I was never sure where I stood with Pamela, but she tolerated me because Cassandra liked me. When we'd first met—if you could call it that—Pamela had tried to choke the life out of me.

"If Cassandra's staying at the hotel, so am I," Pamela told me bluntly. "I'll pack a bag for her."

"I don't have a cook or a maid up there right now. I might have to close until I get things straightened out."

"I can make my own bed, and cook in a pinch. By the way, Janet, I saw your boyfriend talking to a woman yesterday afternoon."

I gave her a blank look. "And?"

"A woman I'd never seen before. She was blond and beautiful, wispy, in the 'I'm a helpless female and I need a big, strong man' kind of way. I saw them behind the library, and she was doing a lot of talking."

Something tightened in my chest. Mick hadn't bothered to mention this woman to me, but maybe he'd been too busy blowing my mind talking about marriage.

I'd never met a fragile blonde in Magellan or Flat Mesa. Most women in Magellan were hardworking and knew how to cater to tourists. There wasn't much for a helpless female type to do here. The fact that it was a blonde chilled me a bit. My mother liked to possess blond women, and my heart beat a little faster. But my goddess mother was still sealed into the vortex, contained. Mick and I checked all the time, and so did Coyote. It couldn't be her. I prayed it wasn't her.

I mulled this over as I walked the couple of blocks to my next stop, the house where my friend Jamison Kee lived with his wife and stepdaughter. Jamison's wife, Naomi, ran the town's plant nursery, which was closed today, due to the weather. I found Naomi at home with Jamison and her daughter, Julie, in the house behind the nursery.

Jamison was a Navajo from Chinle and had met me one summer day in Canyon de Chelly when he'd come out to enjoy a storm. He'd found teenage me huddled, wet, and alone, crying because I couldn't control the lightning that tried to take me over. Jamison was the first person to teach me how to start mastering my powers. Jamison was also a shape-shifter, a Changer who could become a puma. As a storyteller, he knew all kinds of history of the Diné plus that of the ancient Pueblo peoples that had populated this area. If anyone knew about petroglyphs and what they meant, it was Jamison Kee.

Naomi's eyes danced as she hugged me. I didn't much like hugging, but I made an exception for Naomi. Jamison, the tall Indian who'd grown up declaring that he wished all white people would vanish from the face of the earth, had fallen madly in love with Naomi and her blue green eyes. They were insanely happy together.

I'd drawn some of the petroglyphs I'd seen in the hole, and Jamison smoothed out the drawing on the kitchen counter. Naomi perched on a stool at the breakfast bar, and Julie, Naomi's eleven-year-old daughter, ducked in under Jamison's arm to look. Julie had been born with total hearing loss, though she could now speak and was a master at sign language.

Jamison's hands were strong, a sculptor's hands. He traced the glyphs with his roughened fingertips, dark brows drawn in a frown.

"This one is a comet," he said, touching one that looked like a starburst. "This one a bright star. Did you draw them in sequence?"

"I tried. There were so many, kind of blobbed together."

"I'd love to be able to see them all."

Jamison took on a thoughtful look, and Naomi frowned. "Jamison, no."

Jamison looked at Naomi in innocent surprise. "What?"

"No, you are not climbing down into that hole to see for yourself."

Jamison continued with his "would I be planning that?" expression, and I broke in. "Listen to your wife. There's something evil down there. I survived because of Mick's light spell, and Nash survived because he's a magical black hole. I'm pretty sure magic pulled us down there."

"I thought it was just a sinkhole," Naomi said.

"So everyone has been telling me. But why should that hole collapse at the exact moment Nash and I happened by? We were going fast—in another second or two, we'd have been clear of it. Something wanted us down there, and if Mick hadn't come along, that something would have had us. You're tough, Jamison, but you're not that tough. Besides, even if you climb down there as a mountain lion, you likely wouldn't be able to get back out."

"I planned to use climbing gear," Jamison said indignantly.

"Nash's boys won't let you near the place anyway. It's unstable and dangerous."

"And you're not going," Naomi repeated, scowling at him.

Jamison held up his hands. "All right, ladies, all right. I give up. It's just that I could read these better if I saw them in context."

"When I can get out there again, I'll take my camera and get some good photos," I said. "In the meantime, can you tell me anything about them?"

Jamison studied the drawings again. "These glyphs are observations of the night sky, made over time." He touched the page. "Here are constellations, the moon in different phases. Changes. Significant changes."

"These were already down in the hole, not on pieces that fell from the surface. They must have been inside the caverns themselves."

Naomi looked interested. "If that's true, then there must have been a separate entrance at some point. I wonder how extensive the caves are."

"Now who's talking about dangerous exploration?" Jamison asked.

"It fascinates me," Naomi said, not looking contrite. "All this under the ground, and we don't even know it."

"There has to be more to this than what you're telling me, Janet," Jamison said. "These glyphs are fairly common, if used in an unusual way here, but you didn't come to me because of drawings of a comet. What else worried you down there? A vortex?"

I shook my head. "I'd have sensed that, and the hole is too far north of our vortexes." Vortexes came in clusters— there were some in Magellan, some in Sedona, some in the foothills of the Sierras between Las Vegas and Death Valley. What humans called Area 51 was swamped with vortex energy.

"What then?"

I glanced at Julie, who followed the conversation with interest. I knew that if I tried to ban her from the room, she'd find a way to figure out what we were talking about anyway. Julie was a smart, and determined, kid.

I sighed and told the tale of the skeletal hands, including how one had shown up in a photo I'd taken near Spider Rock. Jamison listened, his expression grave. When I finished, he grabbed a pencil and started drawing on my paper with an artist's precision.

"Did it look like this?"

Under his fingers, the hands I'd seen took shape. My blood chilled as he swiftly drew the thin lines that ended in bony digits. Then he drew another, and another.

"Yes. Stop it."

Jamison lifted his pencil halfway through the fourth hand he drew and dropped it. "Sorry. You're right, these are dangerous."

"What are they? What can they do?"

He looked troubled. "The ancient word for them is something like *karmii*. It's no longer a word in Diné or in any Pueblo language, but that's as close as I can figure. The glyphs don't stand for anything. They're like harbingers. They point the way to evil. From what I've read, when the *karmii* find evil, they multiply, gathering in hordes to try to smother said evil."

I remembered how the hands had burgeoned on the walls as I'd brought up my Beneath magic, remembered the eerie glow surrounding them and lighting up the truck.

"They were homing in on Nash and me. I know my Beneath magic can be considered evil, but *I'm* not evil. Neither is Nash. Irritating as hell, yes, but that's not the same thing."

Jamison studied what he'd drawn, gaze riveted to it as though he couldn't look away. "The *karmii*, they're mindless. Primal, created by shamans using ancient spells that never faded. The *karmii* were to protect the shaman from evil spirits while he performed his rituals. If they are triggered, they multiply and smother the threat. Maybe they sensed your Beneath magic and wanted to get rid of it. Nash was just in the way."

I thought of the woman at the hospital who'd pretended to be Nash's mother and tried very hard to kill him. She certainly hadn't been made of drawings of hands, but I couldn't help but believe the two incidents went together.

"They didn't like Mick," I said. "Didn't like the dragon fire at all."

"Firewalkers have clean earth magic. Not evil."

"So dragons can be destructive shits, but not evil?"

Jamison grinned at me. "Exactly."

I folded the paper in half, shutting out the drawings. Jamison said he couldn't tell me much more, so I thanked him and said I'd go. He'd given me a lot to think about.

Naomi and Julie tried to get me to stay for dinner, but I knew I'd better return to the hotel. I hugged Naomi again, and then Julie, and departed.

Fremont picked me up in front of the nursery and drove me back to the hotel. Pamela's pickup sat in the snowy lot when we arrived, but Mick's bike wasn't there. The Crossroads Bar was optimistically open, and sure enough, about a dozen motorcycles were parked in the snow in front of it.

Fremont followed me in through the hotel saloon, probably hoping I'd reward him with a beer, but as soon as I walked inside, I smelled the heady odor of cooking from the kitchen. Mouthwatering, familiar cooking. Someone was making stew and fry bread.

"Oh, honey," the mirror in the saloon moaned as I made for the kitchen door. "I couldn't stop her. She's way too powerful for little ole me."

I ignored the mirror and hurried into the kitchen.

A small Diné woman stood in front of my stove, stirring stew in a pot. She had iron gray hair, long skirts, and a pinched expression on her wrinkled face. I stopped in dismay.

"Grandmother," I said.

"About time you got home," she said. "Don't you stop for meals anymore, Janet?"

Ten

"Grandmother, what are you doing here?"

Ruby Begay glanced up at me with her black eyes and went back to stirring. "I heard you needed a cook. So here I am. Cooking."

"But how did you get here?" My grandmother could turn into a crow. I had visions of her flying across the snowy landscape, a speck of black in the sky—carrying a bundle of clothes in her beak? The vision fled.

"Your cousin Thomas dropped me off on his way to Flagstaff," she said. "Do you know there's a hole in the highway from Holbrook? We had to go all the way around through Winslow. Took a long time."

She spoke Navajo, so I replied in the same language. "Yes, I'm well acquainted with the hole in the road."

Grandmother turned the fry bread over, then slid it onto a plate, and my mouth continued to water. No one made fry bread as good as my grandmother's.

"I thought you'd have something to do with that," she said.

I didn't bother arguing that I hadn't opened up the sinkhole on purpose. Arguing with my grandmother was always futile.

"I can have as many as twenty guests here at a time, you know," I told her.

"I don't see that you have any guests at all. Just a witch and a Changer who ought to be ashamed of themselves. And I can cook for twenty people. Didn't I raise four children on my own? Don't I feed all my grandchildren and great-grandchildren when they bother to come see me?"

Yes, but she'd trained us to shut up and eat what we were given and be grateful, which guests didn't always do. We *had* been grateful, though. Grandmother was one hell of a cook.

"Guests don't always want the same things," I tried.

"That's your fault. Have a set meal, and if they don't like it, they can go someplace else."

Again, I gave up the argument. I did need someone to make basic meals, and once the roads opened and guests returned I'd try to get her to go back home.

"I don't like witches," Grandmother said.

"Cassandra's Wicca, not *chindi*." Witches were hated in my world; they were seen as people who used dark, evil magic for personal gain.

Grandmother didn't look convinced, and I knew Cassandra's relationship with Pamela annoyed her as well. While Grandmother believed that women were far superior to men, she did not believe that women should shut men out of their lives entirely. Women were meant to carry on the family line, to have children who would inherit their mother's lands and goods. The family would stop if a woman didn't marry and have children.

I suddenly wondered what she'd think about *me* having children.

Grandmother ladled out a heaping bowl of stew, slung the piece of fry bread over it, and handed it to me. Argument won. I got a spoon, sat down at the kitchen table, and devoured the meal.

Mick hadn't returned. That meant I couldn't ask him about his blond woman, nor could I borrow his motorcycle for my next errand.

I borrowed Fremont's truck again instead. It was sturdy and heavy and had a four-wheel drive; the afternoon sky was clear and hard blue, and I had confidence I could return it unscathed. Fremont, happily working in my basement, tossed me the keys and waved me off.

Because the road to the sinkhole from my end of town hadn't yet been cleared of snow, I had to drive all the way through Flat Mesa to the freeway, then along the 40 to Holbrook and the turnoff I'd taken a few nights ago. That road had been plowed, so that county deputies and DPS officers could come and go to the hole as needed.

The orange and white wooden barricades had been replaced with waist-high black ones forming a solid and snowy wall. No one was guarding the place, so they must have decided the barriers were warning enough to keep people out. I hung my big camera around my neck and climbed over them, heading for the sinkhole.

Not wanting to slide in, I'd brought a harness and rope, which I attached to a solid boulder that was three times my size. Secured, I crawled to the lip of the hole, focused the lantern flashlight down on the petroglyphs, and started snapping pictures for Jamison.

My camera had a zoom feature that let me fill the screen with the glyphs. I finished and backed away from the hole, only to collide with the legs of a young woman standing over me.

I was on my feet in a flash, unclipping myself, and stepping well away from the hole. I reached for my Beneath magic, but Gabrielle held up her hands.

"I'm not here to fight you. Truce?"

"What do you want?"

"Janet, you are so very suspicious. Maybe I just want to talk."

"You know where I live," I said. "Everyone does. Why don't you come talk to me there?"

Gabrielle laughed. "In that heavily warded hotel? You've put alarms up just for me. I'm flattered. Besides, you have so many friends there."

"Are you afraid of them? If you are so interested in a truce, why only come to me when we're both in the middle of nowhere?"

"So I'll have a chance. Of course I'm afraid of them, big sis. You've got so many earth-magic friends—a witch, a couple of Changers, a dragon, and a magic mirror—how can I compete? Not to mention you're best friends with Coyote."

"I wouldn't say that."

She smiled the cute smile that wrinkled her nose. Gabrielle was actually a very pretty young woman, with soft Native American features, a compact but curvy body, and glossy black hair. "He's not really friends with anyone, is he? Coyote doesn't trust you, and he doesn't trust me, equally, because you and I are cut from the same cloth."

"No," I said. "We're not."

"Oh, please. Your father is Navajo, your biological mother unknown. I was born to an Apache man and raised by his wife, a nice woman. They're gone now. But we both know who our true mother was."

She mentioned the death of her parents without a flicker, but I thought I saw something in her eyes, some sadness. I hoped so, and I hoped, for their sake, that they'd never known what their daughter was.

Gabrielle went on. "I know what you went through, growing up. People sensing you're not quite right, treating you differently, not really accepting you. Not fitting in with your own people and not fitting in anywhere else. No place in the world for us."

I slid my camera back into its case. If this came to a fight, I didn't want the precious camera to get broken. Mick had given it to me as a birthday present. "I've made a place."

"Yes, your little hotel. Your *friends*, who'd turn on you in a heartbeat. Come to think of it, they have turned on you once or twice already, every single one of them. Haven't they? Except the mirror, but that's enslaved to you. It doesn't have a choice."

I didn't like that what she said was very close to the truth. "Did you come out here to make a point? If not, I have things to do."

Gabrielle stepped close to me. I tensed, but I didn't sense her power at the ready. "My point is that you're a fool. You were offered the world, the universe, and you turned it down. For what? A dump of a hotel in the middle of nowhere and so-called friends who don't trust you."

How the hell she knew all of this—that my mother had offered to make me a goddess if only I'd stay Beneath with her—I didn't know. It unnerved me, but I kept my voice even. "I made my choice. And I'd make it again."

Gabrielle sighed. "Janet, my poor sister, life is hard. Don't you get that? We're different from everyone else, and people don't like different. We're American Indians in a world in which Indians no longer have any power."

"Life is hard," I agreed. "But I like my life. I'd like it better if you'd go away and leave my friends alone."

"I haven't done anything to your friends."

"Not yet."

"I hate that you don't trust me." She almost pouted. "You really should trust me, you know."

I was tired of the conversation. "The world is a large place, Gabrielle. I'll take Hopi County and the Navajo Nation, and you can find someplace else. We don't ever need to see each other again."

"What are you afraid of? I came to interest you in a partnership. Together, my sister, we can kick some serious ass."

"I don't want to kick serious ass. I want friends and family who aren't afraid of me. A strange concept for you, I know, but that's my world."

I turned around and walked away from her, going back over the barriers. I didn't have to justify my choices to Gabrielle, the daughter of our bitch-queen-from-hell mother. If

Gabrielle wanted to follow in our mother's footsteps, fine. That was *her* choice. I'd try to stop her, of course, before she did too much damage, but I didn't like Gabrielle pretending that she and I shared this special bond.

I felt a sudden burst of power from her and ducked, but the only thing that happened was that Fremont's tires hissed and went flat.

"That's childish," I said.

She climbed over the barriers after me. "I'm not finished talking to you. You're adept enough to change a few tires, aren't you?"

Yes, but not what I wanted to do on a cold, snowy afternoon, when the truck had only one spare. "What do you want, Gabrielle? Spell it out. Do you really want us to be friends and partners, or are you here to size up the competition?"

Gabrielle snorted. "Like you could ever be competition for me."

"Don't push me, sweetie."

"There's no storm, Stormwalker. You have Beneath magic, sure, but your storm powers keep it dampened. Without a storm, I could kick your butt from here to the Pacific, and you couldn't stop me."

That was perfectly possible. Gabrielle was powerful like an out-of-control tornado—I knew that from fighting her—but she was a little too confident.

"I'm not worried," I lied.

She laughed at me, long and hard, as though I missed something she thought hilarious.

"I was giving you a chance today," she said. "A chance for us to be friends. But you're too hard to reach, too damn stubborn. I won't hold back when we meet again, all right?"

"If you touch anyone close to me, you'll regret that you were ever born."

"Threats. I love it."

"I'm not kidding. I've seen what you can do. Coming after me is one thing, but you leave my people alone."

"See?" Gabrielle laughed. "The 'my people' thing again. You *are* arrogant, Janet."

"I take care of them. They think they take care of me, but it's the other way around. So if you touch them—*I* don't hold back."

"Oh, this is delicious."

Gabrielle called me arrogant, but the conceited surety in her eyes was too strong, too certain. I knew then that she'd not stop at anything to humiliate me. That's how she would see it—humiliation—but I was concerned with more basic things. Survival. Protection. I would protect Mick and my grandmother and my friends to my last breath.

Whatever we'd have said to each other, and whatever we'd have done next, was cut short by flashing blue lights in a brand-new county sheriff's SUV. Nash Jones pulled to a stop next to Fremont's truck and climbed out. He wore a parka against the winter cold, sunglasses against the glare, and a bandage still stark and white on his black hair. I could see his right fingers twitching, not for his gun but with eagerness to write a citation.

"What are you girls doing out here?" he asked.

I pointed to Fremont's tires. "They went flat."

"You know this place is blocked off for a reason."

Gabrielle was smiling at him, the kind of smile a woman reserves for a man whose pants she wants to get into. The smile was sultry, a woman certain of her charms. Nash, true to form, completely ignored her.

"I'm fascinated by places where I nearly died," I said.

Nash gave me an expressionless look from behind his sunglasses. "If you visited them all, you'd never have time for anything else. Get in. I'll call a wrecker for Fremont's truck."

"Why don't you change the tires, Sheriff Jones?" Gabrielle asked.

Nash looked at me, not Gabrielle. "Janet, who is she?"

"Gabrielle Massey," I answered. "She's Apache."

"Like Geronimo," Gabrielle said, and giggled.

Nash opened the back door of his SUV. "Ladies."

I climbed in. Gabrielle smirked at Nash as she climbed in beside me, and she actually wriggled her butt at him. Gods help us.

Nash was quiet as he drove us back, which told me he still hadn't recovered all the way. Nash loved to interrogate. Gabrielle, on the other hand, sat forward in her seat, fingers on the grill that separated the backseat from the front.

"Nice ride, Sheriff," Gabrielle said. "I think I'd like it better in the front seat."

Nash flashed me a look in the rearview mirror. "*Who* is she?" he repeated.

I knew he didn't mean her name. "Oh, just someone I met in a wash."

"Don't be coy," Gabrielle said. "Janet's too shy to tell you. We're sisters."

"You don't have a sister," Nash said to me. "I've read all your records."

"Half sister," I corrected. "Sort of. It's complicated."

Nash continued to stare until a curve in the plowed road forced his eyes back to it. Gabrielle continued to simper at Nash, and Nash kept on ignoring her.

I suggested Gabrielle be dropped off at the small bus terminal in Flat Mesa that ran a once-a-day shuttle to Winslow, though I had no idea where Gabrielle was living. "So she can leave the county," I said in a hard voice.

"I'm not a taxi service," Nash snapped.

"Drop me off too, then," I said. "I'll call someone."

Gabrielle grinned at me. I felt magic spark in her, and I came alert, but all she did was open the door of the moving SUV. Nash had locked it, but the door now swung wide, and freezing air swept inside.

"What the—" Nash hit the brakes, but by the time he got the SUV stopped, Gabrielle was gone. Vanished into the wind and the vast plain of snow.

I dragged the door closed again. "I told you," I said to Nash. "It's complicated."

Nash dropped me off at the hotel, but he declined to come in, racing away almost as soon as my feet touched the ground. The lobby was warm, and Cassandra told me that Maya and Fremont were still working in the basement.

The two of them weren't speaking at all, which, Cassandra told me in a strained voice, made a nice change from their arguing.

I'd have to tell Fremont about his truck, for which Nash had radioed in a tow, but I decided I'd wait until Fremont was in a better temper.

Pamela had moved into one of the empty rooms, Cassandra with her. At least they were happy.

"Janet!"

The voice came from the kitchen, the word shouted as only my grandmother could. She used names like weapons.

I felt seven years old again as I entered the kitchen. "Yes, Grandmother?"

"How many of you do I need to feed tonight? Is that Hispanic girl and the magician-plumber going to stay? Where's Mick? And did you know you have jugs of animal blood in your refrigerator?"

"Those are for Ansel." I braced myself. "He's a Nightwalker."

Grandmother slammed down her spoon. "A *Nightwalker*? So this is an all-service hotel, is it?"

"He's a nice Nightwalker," I tried. "He's sworn off human blood. He collects stamps and watches old movies." I sighed when her glare didn't soften. "Let him have the blood. He's really trying, and he's handy to have around."

"Handy. A Nightwalker." She didn't exactly say *humph*, but I heard the sound hovering. Grandmother went back to chopping vegetables, her silence screaming disapproval.

I ducked into the saloon and drew myself a beer. My bartender had taught me how to draw from the taps, so I could fill a mug with frosty brew and give it just enough of a head for foamy satisfaction. I took a slow sip, knowing that if I drank it too fast, I'd end up passed out in a short space of time. I'd learned long ago what a lightweight I was. I didn't touch alcohol often.

Maya came in, covered with dust and grease and looking out of temper, so I drew her a beer too. She took it gratefully and looked less sour after she drank and wiped her mouth.

"I need to tell you something." We sat at a table together,

and she gave me a grave look from her dark eyes. "I know I'd want you to tell me if it were Nash. I saw Mick with a woman. Yesterday."

"A blond woman?"

"Yes."

I nodded. "Pamela told me." As long as she wasn't my mother in another woman's body, fine, I told myself.

Maya took off her work hat and tossed it to the chair next to her. Her black curls were matted with sweat. "Don't be blind, Janet. I wouldn't have mentioned it if he'd been talking to her at the diner or something. Mick is friendly. But this was Mick taking a woman behind the library and looking damn worried about anyone seeing him. And then talking to her intensely. *Very* intensely. I think you know what I mean."

I folded my hands under my chin. Even Mick flirting with another woman wouldn't bother me as much as my mother trying to hurt him. There were degrees of badness here. "Was he having sex with her?" I asked. "Out there behind the public library? You think he'd be more discreet."

"I'm not stupid, Janet, and you shouldn't be either. They talked like they knew each other very well, but I have no clue who the woman was."

Yes, this was bothering me. Mick didn't always tell me everything he did or about everyone he talked to, but if this woman was important, he would have.

"Thank you for the information." I picked up my beer and took a bigger swallow, feeling my nose tingle.

"I know I've just pissed you off. But like I said, I'd want you to tell me if it were Nash. No matter what."

I shrugged. "You're right. But I'll take it from here, all right?"

Maya's stare skewered me. My grandmother bellowed from the kitchen that supper was ready, and the discussion had to end.

A discussion like that, however, doesn't simply vanish from your brain. I was already in bed under several layers of blankets that night when Mick slipped in, kissed me on the forehead, and told me to get dressed and follow him.

Eleven

It spoke a lot about my trust in him that I grabbed my clothes and jacket, slid into them, and followed him out the back door.

Yesterday's storm was long gone, and the night sky was clear and cold. Stars stretched from horizon to horizon, a white smudge of more distant stars visible under the nearer carpet of brightness. My breath formed a crisp cloud as I tilted my head back and looked up as far as I could.

"Beautiful," I said.

Strong arms came around me from behind, and I felt his lips in my hair. "I brought you out to show you this."

A gift of sight. I leaned against Mick's warm, hard body and stared at the rope of the galaxy stretching before me. The snow hid the desert in a seamless white blanket, rippling a little when it hit ridges to the south and east. All was silent, the hotel asleep, the bar closed, only a few lights glowing in the town south of us.

Mick put something into my hand. A box. A small velvet box with a hinged lid.

"I asked around about human mating customs," he said in my ear. "I don't know if this is the traditional Diné way, but I was told it was essential."

I opened the box with shaking fingers. Inside lay a silver ring encircled with turquoise interlaced with onyx. The ring was finely crafted, beautiful.

"I was told diamonds are most common," Mick whispered, his breath warming my skin. "But I knew you'd want turquoise."

The ring was gorgeous, exactly the kind of piece I'd wear, with craftsmanship that spoke of talent.

Mick tugged the ring from the box, lifted my left hand, and slid the ring onto the fourth finger. The silver band was cool, and I felt warmth from the turquoise. "I know you're not certain," he said. "But will you wear this for me while you think about it? If you decide no, you can give it back to me."

I turned in his arms, my eyes moist. Mick so rarely asked me to do anything just for him. I didn't know what to say, so I asked the first question that popped into my mind.

"Is this what you were talking to the blond woman about?"

Confusion filled his blue eyes. "Blond woman? You mean Cassandra?"

"No, the one you talked to behind the library. The blond woman everyone in town is so eager to tell me about."

"I haven't been anywhere near the library, and I haven't spoken to anyone lately you don't already know. Are they sure it was me?"

"Sure enough. You're kind of distinctive. It wasn't my mother, was it?"

Mick drew back. "Gods, no. If I ever thought I was talking to your mother, I'd alert the forces, and I wouldn't have had time to get the ring."

I chewed my lower lip. "I'm a reasonable person, or at least I try to be. If she was someone you knew when we were apart, after I left you, I mean, I wouldn't blame you. I walked out on *you*."

Mick smiled suddenly, blindingly. "Are you asking me if there's someone else? I like questions I can answer easily. No." He came to me, putting me inside his warmth. "After I met you all those years ago in that roadhouse, there was no one else for me, Janet Begay. Only you."

"We lived apart for five years."

"Doesn't matter. I found you, and that was it."

My heart warmed. Meeting Mick had been it for me too. I'd told myself that I'd avoided other men when Mick and I were apart because I was afraid I'd hurt them. My magic was powerful stuff, and Mick was the only one I knew who could take it. But I realized now that I simply hadn't wanted to make memories with anyone else but Mick.

"No mysterious blonde, then?"

"No woman of any hair color. No dragon, no Changer, no human. I'm in love with you and you alone." Mick shot me a sinful smile, and my heart tripped. "My crazy, beautiful Stormwalker."

His kiss was dark and hot. I felt the silver ring heavy on my finger, Mick's hands warming my back, his solid body against mine. He lifted me, hands under my buttocks, and kept on kissing me, despite the cold, despite the sharp wind coming out of the frozen desert.

We made it back into my room, stroking, touching, kissing. I had the feeling there would be no safety words tonight.

The shard of mirror on my nightstand sucked in a breath and let out a long, terrified wail. "Shadows," it sobbed. "Shadows everywhere. They're all over him. Make them go away!"

Mick snatched up the shard of mirror, yanked open the window, and hurled the mirror hard out into the snow. I watched, mouth open, as the glint of mirror skated across the drifts, still screaming. It came to a stop at the feet of a big coyote, who stepped on it.

Mick calmly closed the window, shutting out the cold. His eyes were still as blue as ever, his aura unchanged. He growled a long, animal snarl, and landed on top of me on the bed.

"Mick. *Gods.*"

Mick didn't answer. He was filling me, pressing me, his fists bunched on either side of my head. His sweat dripped to my face, and his eyes were so intensely blue I could drown in them.

My bed rocked, Mick's thrusts fast, faster. I held on to him, too breathless to make a sound.

Mick squeezed his eyes shut. His damp hair swung as he threw his head back and let out a heartfelt groan. He opened his eyes, and the strange gray flashed through them, gone before I had time to decide whether I'd seen it.

Mick grabbed my hand and kissed the ring, his teeth scraping my finger.

We both came at the same time, moaning and panting. Mick collapsed on top of me, his hands and mouth all over me.

"More," he whispered. "I need more of you. Janet, I can't get enough."

I didn't mind. I rolled over with him until he was flat on his back, me on top. I straddled him, Mick holding my hips. I made love to him as hard as he'd done to me, and I didn't see the gray white flash again.

Somewhere before dawn, Mick woke with a noise of pain. I popped my eyes open to find him sitting on the edge of the bed with his hands pressed to his head.

"What is it?" I sat up beside him, unable to sense anything that could be hurting him, physically or magically. The wards were quiet, as was the mirror in the saloon, everything peaceful.

Mick dug his hands into his temples, as though trying to grind out one hell of a headache. His body gleamed with sweat, and the dragon tattoos on his arms were shivering.

Shivering. I'd seen them move before, sometimes circling his arms in impatience, the dragon in him wanting the change. I'd never seen the tattoos shiver like scared puppies.

I touched a tatt, and Mick scrambled to his feet and stared down at me, eyes wide.

"Are you all right?" I asked. I knew damn well he wasn't. "What's happening to you?"

"Make it stop." Mick dug at his temples again. "Make it stop. Please, Janet."

"I'm not doing anything to you."

I slid out of bed and reached for him, but he jerked away. I dropped my hands to my sides but caught and held his gaze, trying to read him. If someone were possessing him I needed to know who, and how to stop it. The problem was, I didn't feel anything through my wards—nothing was in my hotel that shouldn't be in my hotel. No spell, no intruder, nothing.

Mick's aura changed. As I watched, it went from familiar fiery hot to gray and white and cold. Shadows began to swirl around him like thin clouds. His eyes burned that strange gray white, and his lips curled to a snarl.

I had to help him. I gathered the Beneath magic in me, mentally twining it with the Stormwalker magic I could feel but couldn't use without a storm. As was my practice, I squeezed a small white ball of magic into my hand.

"Let Mick go," I said in a stern voice. "Whoever you are, whatever demon I'm talking to, don't even think about possessing my boyfriend."

"It isn't possession," Mick growled.

Those scary gray eyes focused on me right before Mick lifted his hand and shot an arc of fire at me.

Instinctively I brought up my ball of Beneath magic to deflect it, but the Beneath magic suddenly wanted to fill the room, to grab Mick and squeeze him in half, to eliminate the threat. To eliminate Mick.

I squished out the magic and dove to the floor, landing facedown as the fire punched a hole in my plaster wall.

"Janet."

Mick sounded horrified. I looked up, my hands and

knees burning from skidding on the tile floor. Mick stood at the bedroom door, stark naked, the whites of his eyes fading to sane blue.

I expected him to come and help me up, to tell me how sorry he was, that he didn't know what had happened. But he just stood there. The dragons were now running up and down his arms like live creatures, and I saw in the mirror above my dresser that the flame tattoo on his back was bright red.

"Mick, what the hell?" I climbed to my feet and went for him, but he backed away, hands out.

"Janet, when you see me again, don't try to help me, don't try to fight me. Just run."

"Don't you dare go anywhere. We need to pull this thing out of you. Stay here. I'll get Cassandra."

"It's not possession." Mick's voice rose in fury. "You promise me you'll run the other way. That you won't let me come near you. *Promise me*."

"I can't. I'm waking Cassandra, and we're binding this thing."

"Let him go, Janet."

It was my grandmother's voice. She stood in the hall, beyond Mick, small and stubborn, swaddled to her throat in a thick robe. She didn't seem in any way perturbed by Mick's nudity, but I could see her eyes sparkle in disapproval at mine. I snatched up the quilt.

"Grandmother, get out of here," I said. "Go back to bed."

Grandmother sniffed. "I know a thing or two about Fire-walkers. He's not possessed, he's enslaved. If you don't let him go, he'll destroy everything around him in order to get to his master." Her lips pinched. "In this case, mistress."

My mouth fell open and stayed there. Enslaved? I remembered something Cassandra had said to me, offhand, a few months ago. *Dragons can be useful to witches, if the witch is powerful enough.* What the hell did that mean? Was this blond chick Mick had been seen talking to the witch? And who the hell was she?

The blue departed from Mick's eyes, and they became white and hard again. Right before the blue flicked out for good, he whispered, "Remember that I love you, Janet."

Mick shoved my grandmother aside, strode down the hall and out of the hotel, still naked, and ran across the white snow. Grandmother and I watched as he stretched out his arms and morphed to a dragon that took off over the ice-shrouded land. Mick's footprints faded, leaving behind unbroken snow and no sign that he'd ever been there.

Twelve

Cassandra fed me coffee in the saloon the next morning, but even her delicious brew couldn't cut through my anxiety. "Explain it to me again," I said.

I'd been grilling her since she'd come downstairs, repeating my questions as though she'd give me the answer I wanted to hear if only I asked her often enough. Cassandra, the good woman, was exceedingly patient. Grandmother, not so much. She scowled at me after a while and trudged to the kitchen to bang pots.

Pamela had risen at the same time as Cassandra and now sat across the table from me, sharing in the coffee and listening to the interrogation. Pamela was strong, as most Changers were, her muscular shoulders emphasized by her pale sleeveless shirt. She kept her black hair pulled into a braid, and she sucked down coffee faster than Cassandra could pour it.

"A witch has to be damn powerful to enslave a dragon," Cassandra said. "I'm strong, and even I couldn't do it. I've studied the theory, but that's as far as I'll ever go. Even if I could control a dragon, I wouldn't. I don't believe in using slaves to do my dirty work."

"Good for you," Pamela said, giving her an affectionate look. "So what would a witch use a dragon for? If someone is powerful enough to control a dragon like Mick, wouldn't her magic be kick-ass enough already?"

"Yes, but dragons have amazing magic," Cassandra answered. "Very different from witch magic. Dragons are born able to do things that witches can only dream of—perform spells simply by thinking about them, shape-shift, even cross dimensions and maybe time, theories say. Plus dragons are good muscle to have around. But the problem with enslaving a dragon is that the dragon has to be totally controlled. One tiny slip, and the dragon turns on the witch and solves his dilemma by taking out the witch."

I balled my fists on the table. "This is *Mick* we're talking about. He's powerful even for a dragon, some kind of dragon lord. Who the hell would be strong enough to hold him? Gabrielle?"

Cassandra frowned and tapped her mug with well-manicured fingers. "I doubt it. Dragon enslavement takes control and strict discipline, and from what you tell me about Gabrielle, I don't think her control is very good. She's more like a loose cannon. This witch would have to be trained, focused, learned, and powerful. Much more powerful than I am." Her voice held a trace of envy.

"The blond woman he was talking to?"

"Possibly," Cassandra said. "You'd never seen her before?" she asked Pamela.

Pamela shrugged. "Nope. But I didn't get an 'I'm a hugely powerful witch' vibe from her at all. More like 'I'm lost, help me.'"

"A hugely powerful witch can become any kind of person she wants," Cassandra said. "Mick is a protector. If he saw a woman in trouble, he'd help her, and then . . ." She reached out one hand and snapped it closed.

I shivered. "Fine. It's the blond woman. Or the blond woman is an innocent tourist he doesn't remember. I don't care. I want to find her, find out, and help Mick. How do we get Mick free?"

Pamela lifted her coffee mug. "Kill the witch?"

"Sounds good to me," I said. My Beneath magic stretched and tingled, wanting to find the woman and kill her *now*.

"It's tricky," Cassandra said. "We have to be careful."

Pamela started to sip her coffee but put the mug down instead. "Tricky, yeah. She's now a witch protected by a dragon."

"An enslaved dragon," I said. "Wouldn't Mick welcome a chance to end that?"

Cassandra gave me a look of sympathy. "Understand, Janet. Mick will be *completely* enslaved. Which means if she orders him to kill us, he will. If Mick hadn't already been totally enslaved when he flew off last night, he'd have killed the witch himself and be sitting here telling us about it."

"So what do we do?" I growled. "Sit around and wait for her to be tired of him?"

At the glance Cassandra sent Pamela, I shot forward across the table, sending my coffee cup spinning. "What? What aren't you telling me?"

Cassandra spoke gently. "When a witch commands a dragon and uses his magic, she drains him. He can't stop it, and the more powerful the witch, the faster the drain. In the end, the dragon dies."

I jumped to my feet, white magic crackling in my hands. "Then we find the bitch and take her down."

"I agree," Cassandra surprised me by saying. "Someone like that has to be stopped. But we have to be careful, as I said. If she dies while the spell is in full force, it might kill Mick too. Plus Mick will be compelled to protect her. We need to respect just how difficult fighting Mick would be."

Damned difficult. Mick was a dragon, huge and magical, and he could shoot fire, not to mention that in dragon form he possessed gigantic, jagged teeth.

I thought about what he'd said to me: *When you see me again, don't try to help me, don't try to fight me. Just run.* Mick had known.

"What can we do, then?" I asked. "If we can't get behind

him to get to the witch, how can we get him free? What kind of spell does the witch use? Can we break that?"

"The witch uses the dragon's true name to bind him." Cassandra looked hopefully at me, but I had to shake my head.

"I know you don't mean the Latin-sounding name the dragons call him. Mick told me his true name would sound like musical notes, but he never told me what it was."

The true name, Mick had said, was sung to a dragon in the shell by his mother. True dragon names were similar to Native American spirit names, given to a child by his or her father and told only to the gods.

"How would this witch find out his name?" I asked. "If Mick wouldn't even tell me?"

"I wish I knew." Again, Cassandra betrayed a trace of envy. "I know dragon names leave vibrations on places that they frequent, like dragon lairs. If the witch was able to find Mick's lair, she might be able to piece it together, but dragon lairs are well hidden. Do you know where Mick's is?"

"No, but I know who does." I itched to get my hands on him—Colby, a snarky dragon who'd come to help Mick last fall. Colby did things for his own reasons, but I had to admit he'd stood by Mick's side against the mighty dragon council when Mick was in trouble. I also knew that Colby at one time had confronted Mick on his own territory—a big no-no according to dragons. And, come to think of it, I knew someone else, even more powerful than Colby or any witch alive, who possibly knew.

"Coyote," I said. "I think Coyote's been there."

Cassandra gave me a skeptical look. "Sometimes finding Coyote can be just as difficult as discovering a dragon's name."

I couldn't argue. I thought I'd spied Coyote outside last night when Mick had thrown the shard of mirror out the window. I'd ask it. Other than that, I hadn't seen Coyote since he'd dropped us off after getting us out of Flagstaff.

"Colby too," I said. "At least he answers his cell phone."

"It's worth a try," Cassandra said. "But be careful what you tell the dragons. The one thing dragons dread is enslavement. The dragon council might convince themselves that the only way to help Mick is to kill him. And if there's a witch out there who knows how to discover dragon names, they might kill her before we can get Mick free."

"Terrific." I dropped my fists to the table. I didn't like the way Cassandra looked at me—pity mixed with knowledge that the odds of getting Mick free were slim to none.

I couldn't let myself believe that. I was a damn powerful Stormwalker and I had the power of Beneath inside me, and some witch had just stolen my boyfriend. There would be no power on earth that would stop me getting him back. If Mick died because of that witch, I'd make sure every breath she took became absolute hell. And then I'd kill her. Slowly.

I stood up again, determined. "We do this. Cassandra, research like crazy about how to get him free. Pamela, see what you can find out about this blond woman, and I'll hunt up Coyote."

Pamela and Cassandra exchanged another glance, as couples do when they share an opinion without saying a word. But they both nodded and rose to put the plan into action.

They left me alone with cooling coffee and a magic mirror, its voice subdued. "We'll get our Micky back, girlfriend," it said. "We'll save him. We have to."

The mirror told me it didn't remember a thing after Mick threw the shard out into the snow. It had been so panicked, the mirror said, it had blacked out its vision through that shard. So it hadn't seen the coyote and couldn't tell me if it had been the god Coyote. Lots of help that was.

I went out the back door of the kitchen into the bright snow to try to get Coyote on his cell. The weather was changing already, the morning warming. Local birds had already ventured out to eat the corn I'd strewn at my back door, and the corn my grandmother had also tossed outside the kitchen door.

Getting Coyote to use his cell phone wasn't easy. He didn't answer this time either, and he didn't have voice mail.

I sighed and clicked off the phone. I stood a long time

watching the black birds pick through the snow for the corn, debating whether to call Colby. Colby hated the dragon council, so the odds that he'd rush and tell them the tale of Mick's enslavement were slim. Still, I didn't need him deciding he needed to kill Mick or the witch, but then I didn't think Colby was strong enough to take on Mick and win. It was a risk, but if he could help, I had to try.

"Hey, little Stormwalker," Colby sang when he picked up. "Please tell me you kicked out Mick and want to trade up."

I studied the turquoise-and-onyx band on my finger as I gathered my thoughts. Mick had given the ring to me as an engagement ring. Had he bought it before or after he'd been enslaved? And had the entire idea to ask me to marry him been the witch's? The thought made me ill.

"Colby." I stopped.

He must have heard something in my voice, because his amusement died. "What's wrong, honey? What happened?"

I told him. I tried to be cautious, but the entire tale poured from my lips. When I finished, I was wiping tears from my face. Colby was absolutely silent.

"You still there?" I asked.

"*Shit.*" Yep, still there. "Who did this?"

"We don't know yet."

"Well, you need to find out. Anyone who can enslave Micky is going to be one powerful witch. And anyone who can enslave Micky can enslave *me*. Every dragon could be screwed, because— Hey—"

His outraged cry faded into the background, and a dark but cold voice took Colby's place. "Janet Begay, you need to discover who has done this quickly. When you have, report to me."

Oh, crap. It was Drake, a dragon who was head flunky to Bancroft, one of the three members of the dragon council. So much for not letting the dragon council in on the secret.

"Nice to talk to you too, Drake," I said in a hard voice.

"We will be waiting for your call."

"Wait, I still need to talk to Colby—" *Click.*

A callback went to Colby's voice mail, so I assumed Drake had confiscated the phone.

What Colby was doing with Drake I had no idea. Colby was like the juvenile delinquent to Drake's dragon law enforcement. I couldn't imagine Colby not doing as he damn well pleased, though, so I left a message for him to call and hung up.

Damn it. I went back into the kitchen, where at least it was warm.

Grandmother was chopping vegetables. It was her answer to all problems, cooking. Either that or cleaning, but whenever I was at home, she usually made me do the cleaning.

"How did you know what had happened to Mick?" I asked.

She went on slicing carrots without looking at me. "I told you. I know about Firewalkers."

"Can you tell who has him?"

Grandmother shrugged as she put the carrots into a pot and started rinsing the beans she'd soaked. "The woman everyone saw with him with is a good prospect. A Shadow Walker, as I heard it."

"What's a Shadow Walker?"

Grandmother looked impatient, as though I should have been born with an encyclopedic knowledge of magic. "A witch who wears her magic like shadows. Strong and nasty. The blond woman is a likely candidate, but I'd like a serious talk with your sister."

Her lip curled when she said the word *sister*. Grandmother was all about family—which I'm sure is why she hadn't tossed me to the coyotes when my father first brought me home. Grandmother had known there was something wrong with me, and watched and mistrusted me all my life. However, she'd protected me as well, and she was still protecting me, because I was a Begay. I was family.

But though Grandmother was all about family, she wasn't about to let Gabrielle in. Neither Grandmother nor I had known about Gabrielle until last September, when Gabrielle had come to me and announced herself. Because Gabrielle wasn't technically blood related, and not even Diné, Grandmother had felt no need to find her and draw her into our clan.

"Cassandra says it's probably not Gabrielle," I said.

"If there's mischief, then Gabrielle is somehow involved."

"You used to say that about me."

Grandmother gave me a severe eye. "And I was right. Don't defend her. She's not like you."

Grandmother, in her crow form, had been with me when Gabrielle had revealed her existence to us. Grandmother's first impression of her had been of pure evil, and nothing had changed her mind since. I had to admit, Gabrielle hadn't done much to change my opinion either.

"I'll find the witch," I said. "And Coyote. He can help us."

"Never put your fate in the hands of a trickster."

"I don't plan to. But I need his help."

Grandmother added the beans to her pot. "Best go find him then."

I left her to her cooking. Grandmother wasn't sentimental. When something was wrong, she declared that it should be fixed first, cried about later. I had to admire her philosophy.

I went back to my office. I tried Colby again but added no message this time. I could only hope that the dragon council would have as hard a time locating the witch and Mick as I did.

I had an advantage, though, and his name was Nash Jones. Nash liked to keep tabs on anyone who came and went in his county, and the woman had been seen in Magellan by several people. If she'd been acting the part of a passing tourist, it would be tougher, but Nash would have found out *something*. Emilio Salas kept the same kind of eye on Magellan, if in a quieter way. I scrolled through numbers on my cell phone, happy I'd finished putting them into my new one. I was hard on cell phones, the last one dying because it somehow wound up in a potted plant that got watered.

Before I could push the button to dial Emilio, I heard a yell and swearing in Spanish from the basement. Dropping phone to desk I sprinted out and down the basement stairs.

Maya and Fremont had returned early to work on repairs, going downstairs before I'd even gone up to wake Cassandra. They didn't know yet what had happened to Mick, because I was hoping Cassandra would have a quick fix and it wouldn't be necessary to tell them.

"What?" I asked testily as I hit the bottom step.

"This!" Maya pointed to wires that looked as corroded as the ones she'd showed me yesterday. "I replaced those. Yesterday afternoon." She flipped the dead wires and more copper crumbled from them. "Let me put it in an English phrase you'll understand: It's all fucked-up again."

"Same thing here," Fremont said. He sounded sad rather than angry. "Brand-new PVC, the kind that's flexible, and it's as disintegrated as the copper."

The three of us studied the ruin of my pipes and wiring, our combined frustration and defeat keeping us quiet.

"It's a spell," I said, my voice hollow. "It has to be."

Fremont poked a green encrusted pipe with a wrench. "Like Penelope."

Maya glared at him. "What? Who the hell is Penelope?"

"In the *Odyssey*," Fremont said. "She promised she'd chose a new husband from the men who hung around her house—they wanted her to declare Odysseus dead and marry one of them so they could get their hands on Odysseus's estate. But they agreed to let her hold off deciding who she'd marry until she finished weaving her tapestry. So every night she unwove what she'd done that day to buy herself more time."

"Oh, thanks, Fremont." Maya scowled. "Very helpful."

"Only none of us are doing this on purpose," I said.

Fremont adjusted his hat. "But Janet, there's a problem with it being a spell. You and Mick have magic wards all over the hotel. Wards are like a net," he said to Maya. "Or a barrier against malevolent magic. Nothing magical can get in, and if someone is strong enough to penetrate the wards, Janet and Mick are alerted, like a magical burglar alarm. Only you haven't said you were alerted."

"No." I touched the brick wall, feeling the magic, Mick's and mine, running through it. Strong, tensile, unbroken. The fiery bite of Mick's magic made me want to cry. But the taint that came when I touched the wiring was there. Faint, but destructive, like a colony of termites.

Termites. I was pretty sure we'd find those too.

"Mick let the spell in," I said, realizing.

Even Maya gaped at that, and Fremont looked at me in confusion. "Why would he? Mick lives here too."

I explained to them about Mick's enslavement. I deluded myself that I kept an even tone and relayed the information with calm detachment, but I must have sounded as dejected as I felt. Maya, who disliked hugging almost as much as my grandmother, came to me and enfolded me in her strong arms.

I didn't want her to do that, because I didn't want to cry. I would be useless if I broke down. But Maya's warmth comforted me, and I allowed myself to rest against her for just a moment.

I felt Fremont's shy pat on my back. "But Janet, Cassandra and Pamela don't have to scour the town looking for the mysterious blond woman. I know who she is."

I pushed away from Maya. Of course. Fremont, the biggest gossip in Magellan, knew everything there was to know about everyone.

"Who, then?"

"If I'm right, she's Vonda Wingate. Ted Wingate's wife."

Thirteen

Ted Wingate.

My Beneath magic woke with rage. A streak of white-hot power shot from my hand, and Maya and Fremont jumped as bricks behind them exploded.

I grabbed Fremont's wrench from him and tossed it into his open toolbox. "Enough. Don't work on this another second. I'm going to make Ted tell me everything he knows, and I'm going to enjoy it."

"Janet," Fremont said quickly. "All I know is that I saw Wingate's wife talking to Mick behind the library."

If that was supposed to calm me down, it didn't. "I'm going to find the Wingates and see if they have Mick, and I'm getting Mick back. If Ted had any part in this, I swear to the gods I'm roasting him whole."

"But . . ." Fremont looked fearful, but even fear couldn't keep Fremont quiet. "Why would Ted Wingate have his wife put a spell on your hotel? To give her something to do?"

"To make me close and move out." I shoved more tools

into Fremont's toolbox and slammed it shut. "Mick and I are the strongest mages around; maybe Ted's helping his wife move into my territory."

"Why?" Maya asked. "It's *Magellan*." She spoke with the incredulity of someone who has lived in a spectacular place all her life and doesn't understand what other people see in it.

"Because of the vortexes," I nearly shouted. "You know, the swirls of mystical energy that tourists flock to see? A powerful witch could do so much with vortexes. She might even try to open them, which would seriously suck, trust me."

If Vonda Wingate opened the right vortex, my mother would come out to play. Mother dearest would kill Vonda immediately, of course, which might kill Mick in turn if Cassandra was right. After that we'd have a bigger problem. My mother.

Maya, of all people, was the calmest of us. "You're saying that Mrs. Wingate captured Mick so she could do witchy magic on some pipes and wiring, so you'd give up and move out? That's far-fetched, Janet. If Ted's wife wanted you out, why wouldn't she just have Mick burn down the hotel?"

"I don't know." It was a good question, and it frustrated me that I didn't know the answer. A witch who could enslave a dragon could do much more to me than mess with my plumbing. "The best way to find out whether Vonda Wingate has Mick is to ask her. If getting to her involves strangling Ted, so much the better."

I started up the stairs. I'd read the phrase "towering anger" and never understood what it meant, but I did now. I felt tall, burning, strong, unstoppable.

"Talk to her, Maya," Fremont said behind me.

"When she's being crazy Indian on the warpath? No, thanks."

"We have to stop her."

I looked down the stairs. "Why don't you come with me, Fremont, if you want to keep me calm? After all, I don't have any transportation."

"Okay, but I'm driving." Fremont came for the stairs. "I just changed those flats you put on my truck last night, *and* you blew up Cassandra's car. You're hard on vehicles, Janet."

Maya, at the last minute, caught up with us and jumped into the cab of Fremont's truck beside me. I think she was more worried about me than her cynical comments let on.

Fremont drove to Flat Mesa far too slowly for my liking. The road had been plowed, but the current thaw filled it with dirty slush and standing water. Fremont navigated carefully, and the twenty miles seemed to take forever. The sky was clear and blue, but the snow had been so thick that it still blanketed the desert, blinding whiteness stretching to the horizon.

Once we reached Flat Mesa, Fremont drove to the residential area. I looked around at the old bungalows mixed with modern houses, some yards pristine, others filled with junked cars, old tires, and snowed-over swing sets. "How do you know where they live?" I asked him.

"They moved into my cousin's best friend's house," Fremont said. "She sold up and moved to Albuquerque."

Fremont's knowledge of the comings and goings in the two towns would make an FBI agent green with envy. He turned down a slushy street, past kids throwing snowballs and dogs chasing up and down. Fremont finally halted in front of an ordinary suburban house half-hidden by a squat cedar that took up most of the front yard.

I felt the wards on the house as soon as I hopped out of the truck. I could see the white blue aura of them, rippling and sizzling, wanting to keep me out. My heart almost broke when I recognized a touch of Mick's fire in them.

I didn't need to charge in through the wards and start fighting to find out what was going on. I simply walked to the front door and rang the doorbell.

Ted answered it. I was surprised he wasn't at his office on a weekday, with the roads now clear, but I was too angry to care. Ted's tan was as pristine as ever, his hair as well styled, his handsome face as irritating. He didn't look pleased to see me, but he gave me a smug look, knowing I couldn't hurt him while he stood safely behind his wife's wards.

"Well, now, little gal, changed your mind about my offer, have you?"

"Where is he?" I demanded.

"Where is who?"

I tried to look past Ted, but it was gloomy in his house, and it smelled a bit. "Why don't you let me in, and I'll tell you?"

"I'd be a fool to do that. We can talk fine with you out there."

I reached for him, not with magic but with my out-stretched fingers. Some wards won't let magic through, but a human body can penetrate them with no problem.

Fire snapped around my hand, and I jerked back. Ted smirked. "Talk or go. It's getting cold. I want to shut the door."

I yanked one of Ted's checklists out of my jacket pocket, tore it into shreds, and threw it at him. The wards let the harmless papers through to flutter to the floor at his feet.

"Fuck you and your inspection. If you want war with me, you've got it, but you leave my hotel and Mick out of it."

"I didn't come here to make war, little gal."

"You've got it anyway. Tell me why your wife wants me out of the hotel."

Ted tried to give me an innocent look, but he wasn't good at innocent looks. "My wife's got nothing to do with it. I'm just doing my job."

"Bullshit. There's a spell on the hotel to keep me from bringing it up to code so you and the county can shut me down. You tell me why."

Ted shrugged, smiling. I had the sudden feeling that he wasn't stonewalling me; he really didn't know why. He wasn't the one with the power here. He'd been assigned a role and was playing along.

"Janet," another voice rumbled behind me. "I told you what to do if you saw me again."

I turned. Mick stood in the front yard next to the cedar, in shade cast by the bright sunshine. He wore his leather jacket, hiding his tattoos, but I sensed them beneath the coat, writhing and shivering as they'd done last night. His eyes were dark, dragon eyes, in his hard face, and they watched me with no friendliness.

"Mick."

He regarded me with a coldness I'd never seen in him. Correction, a coldness I'd never seen him direct at *me*. I'd watched him take down plenty of enemies while wearing that expression—calculating, intense, deadly.

"Grandmother and Cassandra explained the enslavement to me," I said hurriedly. "I can break it, but only if you give me your true name. I'm strong enough to get you free, but I need the name to do it."

Mick's expression didn't change. "Give my true dragon name to *you*? How stupid do you think I am?"

The words cut, but I held it together. "I could kill the witch who holds you, but if I do that, you might die too. Your name is the only way."

Mick's lip curled. "You have no idea how to use that power locked inside you, Stormwalker. What would happen if I gave you my true name? You'd blunder around and shatter the name, and me, trying to figure out what to do with it. I'm not idiotic enough to give the gift of my name to someone like you. You'd kill me with your incompetence."

More cutting. I swallowed. "It's the best I can do. If the dragon council finds out you've been enslaved, they'll come for you, and they won't care who dies. You, the witch, Ted, the kids playing down the street. I kind of want to prevent that."

Mick's black eyes flickered in annoyance. There was nothing of the blue in them, nothing of the Mick who'd smiled at me so devilishly in that restaurant in Las Vegas, before he'd taken me back to his hotel room to make deep love to me.

"Do you remember what I told you when I left?" he asked. "I said that when you saw me again, you should run? You'd better start running, Janet Begay."

I folded my arms. "If you think I will roll over and give

you to a witch, especially one with the bad taste to marry someone like Ted, you don't know me."

"No." Mick smiled. "You don't know *me*."

I sensed his surge of magic the split second before a fireball shot from his hand. I dove desperately behind the cedar, landing flat on my face in the mud, and the tree took the brunt of the blast. The cedar burst into flames, its dry branches sucking in fire, a sharp, sweet smoke rising from it. I heard Maya shriek and Fremont shout. Ted swore and slammed the front door.

As I climbed to my feet, Mick stood calmly on the other side of the burning cedar, his eyes still deadly cold despite the red tinge in them. The tree hemmed me in between the house and a corner of the six-foot block fence that separated Ted's yard from his neighbor's. Mick blocked my escape to the street.

Mick started for me. No sympathy, no love showed on his face that the fire illuminated. His expression was blank, determined, his eyes going gray white again, and I had no doubt about what he was determined to do.

Mick opened his hand and let fly fire. I was up the six-foot wall, toes desperately scrambling, fingers scraped raw as I climbed the fence like a rat. I made it to the top as the fireball struck below me, the cement blocks popping as dragon flame melted them.

I jammed my feet under me and sprinted along the top of the wall, praying to keep my balance. I reached the back of Ted's yard and leapt to the ground on the neighbor's side. The neighbor hadn't fenced the rest of that property, but a stand of cottonwood trees lined a narrow creek behind it, water trickling between frozen banks. I ducked into the trees' shadow, my feet breaking through the ice, freezing water pouring into my boots.

I stopped, panting, realizing that I heard no one chasing me. Not Mick, not my friends. Mick had let me go, but who the hell knew what he was doing to Maya and Fremont?

Tears froze on my cheeks as I burst from the trees and sprinted through another yard back to the road. As soon as I stepped onto the asphalt, Fremont's truck roared toward me, tires screeching as he pulled up. Maya flung open the door, and I leapt in beside her, my feet so numb I could barely feel them.

Fremont accelerated before I'd managed to close the door, and the momentum snapped the door shut.

"He just stood there," Fremont yelled as he tore out of the neighborhood. "Mick watched you run, but he didn't try to follow. He didn't seem interested in us at all."

"Not that we'd know," Maya said, throwing Fremont a dark look. "Fremont took off the minute Mick started throwing fire around."

"I decided we should get the hell out of there," Fremont said.

"Good call." I folded my arms across my chest, my hands bleeding and smarting.

"What now?" Fremont asked. "Still want to interrogate Ted?"

I'd never get to Ted with Mick protecting him. I hadn't even learned whether the witch was in the house at all, but the visit had at least confirmed Vonda Wingate as the witch who'd enslaved Mick. Mick's magic had been mixed in the wards guarding the Wingate's house, and Ted had looked so damned smug.

I bunched my hurt hands. "Back to the hotel," I said. "I need to change the wards."

I held myself together while Cassandra lit the sage smudges. Then she and I traced runes over every door and window and on every beam, wafting sage smoke into every corner of the hotel. My grandmother watched this witch magic with a scowl on her face, but she didn't interfere.

It hurt me to work the wards, because not only was I erasing traces of Mick, Mick was the one who'd showed me how to do wards in the first place. He'd taught me so much, not only about magic, but about myself, and now I was clearing the walls and rooms of all traces of him.

Cassandra and I finished, meeting in the lobby. She chanted a final spell, and we left the sweet-smelling sage burning in a bowl on the reception counter. I excused myself to clean up and made for my bathroom in the back.

The hot water still worked, thanks to Maya. I filled the tub, poured in scented bath salts, stripped off my clothes, and sank into the water's warm embrace.

My unbandaged hands stung, and my bruises complained. I paid no attention. I drew my legs up to my chest, rested my head on my knees, and cried.

I cried hard, sobs racking my body. My chest kept on heaving even when I had no tears left, my throat raw, my face wet.

At Ted's house, Mick had looked at me not with hatred but with cold indifference. He'd viewed me as an enemy to be stopped, nothing more.

I could have fought him. I could have gathered my Beneath magic, hurled it at him, hurt him, shut him down. But none of that would have brought him back to me. All the strength of my magic wouldn't have broken the spell and made Mick look at me again with love in his eyes.

Unbidden came the warmth of his voice when he'd said, *I'm in love with you, and you alone. My crazy, beautiful Stormwalker.*

My tears returned full force.

Someone walked into the bathroom. I raised my wet face to see my grandmother seat herself on the closed lid of the toilet, the folds of her long skirt falling modestly about her feet. I curled into myself, not wanting her to see me like this but not having the strength to tell her to go away.

She spoke in Navajo. "Janet, you need to do something about this."

I wiped my eyes with the heel of my hand. "I did do something. I erased Mick's wards and covered them with mine and Cassandra's. He can't come back here to hurt anyone. I shut him out. Do you have any idea how hard that was for me?"

"I have some idea, because you're in the bathtub crying like an infant."

I sniffled. "I thought that when I saw him again, something inside him would reach out to me and want me to get him free. But there was nothing. She took it all away. Everything Mick felt, everything that's between us, is gone. He would have killed me and not cared. I know it's not his fault—the witch has him—but that look in his eyes made me want to die. You can't possibly understand how much that hurt."

"No, because I was born an old woman and have never fallen in love."

I leaned my head against the cool tile wall. "That's not what I meant."

"I know what you meant. The young always believe they are the first to experience grief, or love, or loss. But let me tell you a story. It's about a young Navajo girl named Ruby who foolishly fell in love with a white man who came to the reservation fifty years and more ago."

I blinked. "You did? What about Grandfather Begay?"

"This was before I married. I was eighteen. The man worked with a mission, and he was kind to me. He wasn't all that handsome now that I recall, but he was young and he was different, which made him exciting to me. I fell hard for him, and he was happy to take advantage. When the time came for him to return to the Midwest, I had all kinds of dreams in my head—he'd propose to me and take me home with him to meet his friends and family. He'd adore me, and we'd be so happy. But in those days the chasm between white and nonwhite was vast, and this well-off young man had no intention of marrying an Indian girl or even admitting he'd been involved with me. The last day I saw him, he stood up in front of the congregation and said a sad good-bye, but it was general good-bye, nothing to do with me. When I tried to speak with him after the service, he looked right through me, as though I didn't exist. And I didn't exist to him. I was just a naïve Diné girl, ignorant of the ways of the world."

I listened with my mouth open. I'd never heard this story, not from Grandmother, not from my father, not from anyone. "What did you do?"

"Cried. I cried pretty hard. Wallowed in it. Then told myself to stop living in a romantic daydream and get on with my real life."

"And that's what you're telling me to do?"

"Partly. I shared that story with you to tell you I know how it feels to be rejected, even if it happened in primeval times. Wrapping yourself inside another person can hurt. I learned that again when I lost your grandfather, although what I shared with him was a true love, not girlish infatuation. Now, you need to ask yourself this: Do you want to lose Mick?"

I rubbed my face. "Of course I don't."

"Then finish your grieving and get back to work. Mick can't help you, so you need to help yourself. I like your Firewalker, as good-for-nothing as Firewalkers are, and you need to get him free."

I couldn't help but smile even as I wiped away more tears. "Yes, Grandmother."

"We need to start by finding Gabrielle. Where has she got to?"

"I have no idea." I tried to think. "She grew up on Fort Apache with a family called Massey. That's all I know."

"It's a place to start." Grandmother rose creakily from the toilet.

"But Gabrielle doesn't have Mick. Vonda Wingate does."

Grandmother gave me an impatient look. "Janet, there's a child of your goddess mother running loose, and there's mischief about. The coincidence makes me suspicious. You focus on the witch, and I'll try to find Gabrielle."

"No!" I hauled myself up, water everywhere, and grabbed a towel as Grandmother moved swiftly out of the bathroom. I yanked the towel around me and hurried after her. "Stay away from Gabrielle. She's dangerous."

Grandmother had her hand on the doorknob. "So am I. And so are my friends."

"*Grandmother.*"

She ignored me and left the room. I couldn't run after her in my bath towel, so I quickly rubbed myself dry, fuming. I'd get her out of here even if I had to ask Fremont to help me truss her up and haul her back to Many Farms in his pickup.

"Hurry up, Janet." Grandmother's voice floated back to me through the closed door. "There are more Firewalkers out front, trying to get in."

Fourteen

I reflected, as I tugged on my clothes and ran out to the lobby, that Grandmother's story had effectively stopped my crying jag. Her tale had surprised and touched me, but it had also pulled me out of my self-pity.

Grandmother had slammed her way into the kitchen by the time I emerged, but someone was indeed pounding on the locked front door.

"It's Colby," Cassandra said.

"Why haven't you let him in? I need to talk to him."

"He's not alone."

I felt the second dragon then, one more powerful and far colder than Colby. I recognized his aura with some dismay.

Colby thumped again. "Let me in, Janet. It was a long drive, and I need to pee. And a beer."

I opened the door. Colby hadn't changed a bit; still massive and dark haired, still inked all over, yakuza style, except for hands and face. Behind him stood a man with sleek dark hair and dark skin, the ends of his dragon tatts rising above his collar to touch his cheekbones. Drake was tall, hand-some, and brusque, and he didn't like me. He worked for a member of the dragon council—I called him a flunky, but he probably called himself an executive assistant. Drake was the dragon version of Nash Jones, all law and order all the time, only Drake was quieter about it.

I let them in. Drake's nostrils widened as he took in Cassandra, scenting a witch, and a powerful one at that. The derisive curl to his lip let us know what he thought of her, and of Pamela the Changer standing protectively behind her.

Colby charged past me to the saloon, and I turned to Drake. "Did Colby say *drive*? No flying, either as dragons or in a helicopter?"

"Flying either way attracts too much attention." Drake gestured to Cassandra. "She is not the witch who enslaved Micalerianicum?" Drake only used the Latin names for dragons, sneering at the shortened versions humans needed. Drake's name was really Draconilingius, but damned if I could pronounce that.

"She wouldn't be standing here if she were," I said. "We know who the witch is."

"Then why has she not been killed?" That was Drake—strike to the heart of the matter, worry about who gets hurt later.

"Because I haven't been able to get to her. Mick is pro-tecting her, and killing her might kill Mick."

Colby back came out of the saloon, looking less tense. "Hey, Pamela." He winked at her. "Switched teams yet?"

Pamela gave him a derisive look. "Even if I had, you'd still be my last choice, dragon."

"Aw, too bad. But a dragon's gotta try. All right, Janet. How are we going to get the bitch?"

Colby struck to the heart of the matter too. Dragons were like that. Mick liked to talk and play, but always in the back of his mind he was working the quickest solution to a prob-lem. He was probably doing that even as we stood here.

"I need to find out Mick's true name," I said. "Cassandra says that clues to it might be in his lair. Is lair the right word?"

Colby's expression changed to one I'd never seen before.

All humor, anger, and impetuousness left him, and he looked at me with an ageless gravity that showed me what an old and powerful being he really was.

"True names are serious shit, Janet. No dragon is stupid enough to leave it lying around."

"It's impossible for any of us to know another dragon's true name," Drake said.

"Vonda knows it." I tugged at the cuff of my black shirt. "She found it out somehow."

"Dragons sometimes will tell a human lover without meaning to," Drake said. "In the height of passion, especially with a human, the dragon might forget to hide it. Most humans wouldn't understand what they were hearing in any case."

The silence that followed was absolute. Colby looked at the ceiling, but Drake frowned at me, unaware he'd said anything that might upset me.

The voice of the magic mirror floated from the saloon. "I know for a fact that Micky-kins has never let slide one syllable of his name around here, no matter how much passion he's been in with Janet. And darlings, Micky and Janet shag *a lot.*"

"But if he were the witch's lover," Drake went on remorselessly. "He might have told her, as I said, without meaning to. She has gained power over him somehow, and that seems the most likely way."

Colby put his hand on Drake's shoulder. "Drake, my friend, take some advice. Don't ever tell a Stormwalker who's the daughter of a goddess from Beneath that her boyfriend is cheating on her. Not unless you want to end up as a smoking hole in her tile floor."

Drake still looked puzzled, but I didn't blame him. Drake lived with dragons and worked with dragons, with little contact with humans, and so he could only think like a dragon. Mick sometimes did that—he'd ruthlessly pursue the truth without worrying about pesky things like hurt feelings. Mick's own feelings for me had amazed him, and he'd watched them develop in wonder, like a nature-lover watching a butterfly unfold.

"It's all right, Colby," I said. "Drake isn't wrong. How do I know what Mick gets up to, or who he's with when he's not here?"

"Does it even matter?" Pamela broke in. "Whichever way the witch snared him, she did it, and if she decides to send Mick to fry us, we won't be safe from him. We have to consider Mick not as our friend, but as the witch's weapon. Cassandra explained to me how much trouble we could be in for." Pamela, a Changer who could become a wolf, thought like a wolf. Friend. Enemy. Protect one, kill the other.

"You know where Mick's lair is," I said to Colby. "Even if he hasn't left his name lying around as you say, Cassandra believes I might pick up a clue to it in the vibrations of material objects. I can read auras of things and places—I might be able to figure it out from those."

"Maybe," Colby conceded. "But if I take you there, and you figure out the name, then I could figure it out too. You want to trust me with that?"

I didn't, but I didn't have a choice. "It's in the middle of the Pacific, right? If we go at night, can you fly me out there?"

"Love to. But . . ." Colby jerked his thumb at Drake.

"But Colby is on probation and may not fly anywhere as a dragon," Drake said smoothly.

Oh, perfect. "Probation?" I glared at Colby. "What did you do this time?"

Colby looked hurt. "Hey, why do you automatically assume I'm guilty?"

"Because I've met you. What kind of probation?"

"I have to work for them," Colby said before Drake could answer. "If I'm a good dragon, and do whatever they say for a year, they won't make me face a trial."

"In any case, he will not be allowed on any search for Micalerianicum's name," Drake said. "I will undertake the journey with you, once I get Colbinalius back to the compound."

"No," I said at once. While I didn't much want Colby to discover Mick's true name, Colby I could at least browbeat. I wasn't at all certain I could control Drake.

"There really is no other way," Cassandra said in her clear voice.

I hated this. I balled my fists, my body still weak and tired from all the crying I'd done. "Let me think about it," I said.

Before anyone could answer, I turned away and made my way into the kitchen, in time to see my grandmother hanging up the phone. "Who was that?" I asked.

"None of your business. I can have private phone calls if I want to."

I gave up. "Colby and Drake are here."

"I know that. Ineffectual lizards. I have work to do. If you fly off with them, you'd better have some kind of hold over them so they won't drop you."

As much as she exasperated me, I couldn't say she was wrong.

The phone rang again. Grandmother and I lunged for it at the same time, but I was faster and snatched it up. "Hello?"

The voice of my cook, Elena, rang down the wire. "I don't want to talk to you. I want to talk to Ruby."

I'd had no idea that my grandmother and Elena even knew each other. Grandmother looked pointedly at me until I meekly handed her the phone and left through the back door. I was no longer in command here, and I knew it.

With the newly made wards keeping out malevolent magic, Cassandra and I were able to find and remove the deterioration spell on the hotel. Maya and Fremont still had to make another round of repairs, but this time, the repairs should stick. Neither was happy, but they went back to work.

I asked Drake to stay there with Colby while we figured out how to get out to Mick's lair and who would go. I also wanted Drake close to keep him from sending a phalanx of dragons to simply kill Mick and Vonda, end of problem. So far Drake seemed willing to wait for a less destructive solution, but he couldn't hide his impatience with human slowness.

With everyone staying in, the hotel was quickly filling up. Pamela and Cassandra said they'd return home now that the roads were clear, but Maya and Fremont took me up on my offer of rooms so they could keep working without worrying about driving back and forth to town. Everyone was getting free room and board. If they started complaining about lack of maid service, I'd throw them out.

I squeezed in one more person as it turned out, because at sunset, Emilio Salas drew up in his police car and helped Elena out of the backseat. Elena looked me up and down as Emilio followed her, carrying two large suitcases in his strong hands.

"You look terrible," Elena told me. "I'll start my corn soup."

Salas set down the suitcases and blew out his breath. "Janet, will you please explain to her that a police car isn't the same thing as a taxi?"

Elena had excellent hearing. "A police car is better for the icy roads, and now my daughter won't have to drive me in bad weather. I'll give you some black bean chili to take home with you."

"Can't argue with that." Salas cheerfully picked up the bags and carried them upstairs.

When I tried to enter the kitchen and find out what Grandmother and Elena were up to, I discovered that they'd locked the door. I gave up. As long as they were cooking, I'd let them whisper about whatever they wanted.

For now I wanted to find Mick's lair, and I was all out of maps of the South Pacific.

Colby followed me into my office and closed the door. It was the first time we'd had a chance to talk alone, and Colby gave me a grave look as he sat on my sofa and propped his booted feet on my desk. "Janet, you can't let Drake take you," he said. "He's dragon council, and you can't risk giving the council Mick's name."

I had to agree. "What do you suggest we do, sneak away in the night?"

"Yep."

"Drake will come after us."

"Cassandra's a damn powerful Wiccan. She can put a binding spell on him. Or something."

My eyes narrowed. Colby's attitude was a bit too casual.

"What about the binding spell on you?" I had been studying his aura and now saw the spell, lines like faint black cords wrapping his body. "You want Cassandra to remove it, don't you?"

"Wouldn't say no."

"What happens to Cassandra when the dragon council finds out she freed a dragon they're holding? Especially when dragons don't trust witches in the first place?"

Colby evaded my gaze. "She can say I coerced her."

"Right. Nice try."

He shrugged. "It was worth a shot."

"If you think I'll throw everyone I care about to the wolves to get Mick back . . ." I trailed off because I wasn't so sure I wouldn't.

"Janet, sweetheart, I'd love to tell you to forget about Micky and shack up with me, see what things are like with a *real* dragon, but Mick being enslaved is a danger to all dragons. If you can't get him free, you need to figure out what the witch bitch wants and prepare for a fight."

I knew that. Grandmother was right: this wasn't the time for grief; it was the time for planning and for action. Time to pull in every favor owed me from everyone I could think of, and find this witch and stop her. If Vonda Wingate wanted war with me, whatever her reasons . . .

"You've got it, honey," I whispered, fingering a framed photo of Mick and me. We were leaning against Mick's bike, Mick's arms around me, both of us smiling and happy. "You've got it."

Favors. I called Coyote's cell phone again once Colby went back to the saloon for more beer, but again I got no answer. I hadn't seen Coyote in my dreams lately either, naked or clothed, in human form or coyote.

I called my father, who also didn't like to answer the phone. His reluctant tones floated over the line from Many Farms. "Who is it?" he asked instead of saying hello.

"Hi, Dad."

I heard him relax. Pete Begay didn't like to talk on the

phone, saying that he found it uncomfortable to not see a person's face or eyes when they conversed. He wanted to connect with the whole person, he explained, not only the voice. I doubted he'd ever use e-mail, which took away even the voice.

"Janet?" he said in delight. "How are you? Are you well?"

My father considered it the height of rudeness to jump past greetings into what a person had actually called to talk about. He thought it more important to discuss family and friends rather than immediate problems, and I couldn't say I disagreed. I dutifully asked about my niece's last basketball game, and was pleased to hear her team had won. I heard my father's worry about the heavy snow, the worst they'd seen in years.

"Grandmother is still here," I finally was able to mention. "Why did she come down?"

"To look after you." I heard surprise that I'd had to ask.

"I'm a grown woman, Dad. I don't need looking after."

"She worries about the signs. She has seen the *karmii*. Do you understand what they are?"

I grew cold. "Jamison told me." Harbingers, Jamison had said. Pointing to evil. "Where did Grandmother see them?"

"In the hills west of here. She said they showed that evil was brewing and that she knew it was brewing near you."

Of course, when Grandmother saw evil things, she immediately thought of me. "Do you know if the *karmii* hurt people? Or just point out the evil?"

"They find evil and destroy it."

Perfect. Had they been trying to destroy me while I'd clung to the seat in Nash's SUV? Could I reason with them? I remembered my numb terror as I'd watched them close on me with mindless determination. Probably not.

"Do you think you can talk Grandmother into going home?" I asked. "My cook has reappeared, so I don't need Grandmother to make the meals, and I don't like you left there alone."

"I'm not alone. Your aunts have been stopping by to look after me." His voice went wry. "Maybe a little too often."

My father rarely said a bad word about the overprotective,

domineering women in our family, and his admission made
me laugh. Ever since the night my father had brought me
home, confessing that I was his child, my aunts and grandmother had dictated every moment of Pete Begay's life.

Or so they'd thought. My dad and I had managed to escape the house often enough to walk the land, to drive out
under the stars and watch the moon rise. I treasured those
moments of my life, and missed them.

"I like that your grandmother is staying there with you,"
my father said. "Remember, Janet, that when you think you
are the most alone, you are not."

Without further explanation, he hung up, and I was left
with a silent phone. My father might believe in long hellos,
but not long good-byes.

Wondering what he'd meant, I booted up my laptop and
examined the pictures I'd taken out at the sinkhole before
I'd met Gabrielle. I saw nothing new. Petroglyphs, tons of
them drawn so close together they overlapped one another,
but no sign of the *karmii*.

I knew that Jamison Kee was as traditional as my father
about communication, so I didn't bother to e-mail the pictures to him. I e-mailed them to Julie, instructing her to
show them to Jamison for me. I knew that she would.

The next favor I needed wasn't quite so easy. I'd pretty
much used up my favors with Nash Jones, and whatever
help he gave me now would go into my debit column. Ow-
ing favors to Nash wasn't comfortable, but I didn't have
much choice.

When I called the sheriff's department, though, Deputy
Lopez told me that Jones wasn't there. No, he hadn't gone
home; he'd headed down my way a little while ago and even
now should be starting his raid.

Fifteen

The abrupt wail of sirens proved Lopez right. I clicked off my phone and ran out of my office in time to see county and state police flying into my parking lot. Before I could wonder which of my guests Nash was after, I saw that the police weren't targeting my hotel but Barry's bar.

Bikers liked to congregate at the Crossroads Bar. The bar was located on a quiet back highway, tucked away from most attention, and Barry, a biker himself, kept a pretty good handle on things. Violence rarely erupted at the Crossroads Bar. That's not to say Nash didn't like to walk through the place every once in a while to remind everyone there who was in charge.

Nash usually didn't do it with ten DPS cars plus his entire department to back him up. He must have gotten a tip about a drug or arms deal going down, or maybe he'd heard that a wanted criminal had stopped to toss back a few.

The cops, led by Nash, poured into the bar as the sun slid below the horizon, bathing the winter evening in darkness.

My hotel guests, including Grandmother and Elena, came out to watch, and I counted heads.

"Wait a minute. Where's Colby?"

Drake hissed, coming alert. "He's in there."

"How do you know that?" I asked.

"I know."

He didn't explain, but I assumed that Drake could feel Colby's whereabouts through the binding spell.

What the hell was Colby doing? Helping Nash out?

No, I realized a second later. The crafty dragon must have gotten wind that Nash would be coming to the bar, Nash who negated pesky spells wherever he went. I wouldn't put it past Colby to have called in the tip. Nash wouldn't wait for confirmation of a drug deal going down—his policy was arrest first, ask questions later.

These thoughts must have occurred to Drake at the same time, because we both sprinted out of the hotel and ran like crazy across the parking lot. Drake had a longer stride, but I hung in there and made it to the bar's front entrance alongside him.

The state cops tried to keep us out. I could hear Nash in his stentorian tones telling everyone to get on the floor, hands on their heads. Drake turned and ran around the building, looking for the back door. I knew where it was—a door in the wall that led from Barry's kitchen to his trash containers.

What barreled out the back door wasn't Colby but three large human bikers carrying black pistols. The state cops came pounding after them, and in a few seconds, bullets would fly.

"Get down!" one of the cops shouted at us.

A thug decided to take me hostage. Even as I fought him, he got his beefy arm around my neck and shoved the barrel of the pistol against my throat. The cold of the weapon aroused my rage, but it was true that if he pulled the trigger, I would die.

The cops looked furious that civilians had showed up to complicate their bust. Despite me in a chokehold, gun at my throat, they looked in no way disposed to drop their weapons and let the bad guys get away. Maybe they thought that me dying would be worth the price.

One of the thugs shot a state policeman in the chest, and the cop fell, but his bulletproof vest saved him. My thug stepped in front of everyone and used me as a shield.

I didn't have time for this. My Beneath power fluttered close to the surface of my psyche, ready to go. The very thing I'd been trying to avoid for months—using magic to kill for my convenience—raised its head, and for a second I feared I'd simply destroy everyone in sight. But I had to get away from them, to find Colby. I didn't have time to consider the feelings of violent criminals who were happy to use a young woman as a human shield.

When I looked up at my captor, he jerked, and I knew my eyes had turned ice green. The man's finger tightened on the trigger.

My magic twisted the pistol in half. The biker screamed when the pieces exploded from his hand, and I laughed. The Beneath magic surged again, and I barely kept myself from blowing a crater into the desert outside Barry's bar.

A bullet flashed past Drake's face, and he looked annoyed. He'd not hit the dirt when the cops commanded it—not Drake the arrogant dragon. He looked annoyed at me too. He flicked fire from his hand in two precise bursts, combusting the pistols of the other two bikers. The three stared at us for one stunned moment, then ran off into the darkness, each in a different direction.

One of them sprinted for my hotel. Damn it. I grabbed the sleeve of Drake's elegant leather coat.

"Stop him! My grandmother's in there."

Drake gave me another look of irritation, but he turned and loped off toward the hotel. Cops peeled off to go after them, and others followed the other two thugs into the dark desert.

I slipped into the bar through the back door and found the place in chaos. Barry was swearing, his shotgun in his hands, shattered bottles and glasses all over the floor. The state and county police were walking through the patrons, cuffing each one of them. I found Jones in a far corner, his head still sporting a bandage, bending down to slap cuffs around Colby's wrists.

I hurried to them, slipping on the alcohol- and glass-laden floor. "Let him go, Jones."

Nash hauled a smiling Colby to his feet. "Every person in this place resisted arrest, including Colby. I'm taking them in and sorting it out at the sheriff's department."

"Is that legal?"

Nash didn't bother to answer, which meant it was legal according to Vigilante Jones.

Colby winked at me. "It's all right, Janet." He meekly allowed Nash to steer him out the front door with the others, into the open air.

I examined Colby's aura as I followed and found it clean and free of the dark binding threads. Nash must have drawn off the spell when he'd touched Colby to cuff him.

I saw Drake break from the knot of cops and start for us. He'd have sensed the spell fail and was on his way to do something about it.

Colby looked at me. "Ready?"

"Nash," I said. "I'm really, really sorry about this."

"Now what are you talking about?" Nash demanded.

The cuffs burst apart under Colby's strength and clinked to the ground. I grabbed Nash and pulled him down as Colby erupted into several of tons of dragon, right over the litter-strewn parking lot. Nash started swearing.

Drake snarled as he ran for us. Colby swooped out of the darkness, reached down, and plucked me up in his talons. I bit back a scream as I rose with sickening swiftness into the freezing air, and then Colby streamed west with me toward the rapidly darkening horizon.

Drake followed us. As fast as Colby winged his way toward the Pacific, Drake remained hard on his tail. Colby was a smaller dragon—at least small compared to Mick—his hide fiery red streaked with black. Drake was completely black, his eyes shining in the darkness as he came on, and he was half again Colby's size.

Would Drake fire us out of the sky? If Colby ended up a dragon smear on the ground, I would be a smaller smear next to him. I had no way of knowing whether Drake would try to preserve my life or decide I was worth killing to get to Colby.

Colby managed to remain in the lead as we chased the sunset. I'd had no idea dragons could fly so *fast.* The icy wind bit me as I huddled inside Colby's talons, wishing he'd given me time to grab my coat. I hunkered down the best I could, but I'd be frozen solid by the time we reached Mick's lair.

I assumed we were headed to Mick's lair. Colby had freed himself from Drake's binding spell—would he honor my request to help me find Mick's name, or was he taking me someplace of his own? I couldn't communicate with Colby when he was in dragon form, and I wasn't telepathic, so I had to shiver, huddle, and wait.

I saw the enormous bulk of lights that made up Los Angeles and the surrounding metropolitan area, the lights glittering like jewels all the way down the coast to San Diego. Then the cities dropped behind, and an updraft from the ocean sent Colby soaring high.

As we winged out over the Pacific, I noticed that Drake was keeping pace, not catching up. I doubted he planned to let Colby go; he must want to come with us to find Mick's lair.

I grew sleepy, which worried me. If I fell asleep, if Colby relaxed his talons, would I fall? Would Colby bother to catch me, or would he swipe and miss? I didn't think my Beneath magic could keep me from splatting on the surface of the ocean, hundreds of feet below me.

The air warmed. From the faint glow that was the horizon, I could tell we'd turned south, Colby flying far and fast. Drake kept his pace, neither firing nor trying to overtake us. He followed us through the night until night was gone and the eastern horizon began to lighten.

I felt the drafts change, and Colby began circling, spiraling lower and lower like a bird in descent. My exhausted body began to sweat, my clothes now too heavy for the climate.

Colby touched down and released me before he morphed back into a man. Drake landed a little way from us, and by the time I'd unfolded myself and started rubbing my sore limbs, he had become human as well.

I found myself in tropical paradise. The island was volcanic, like the Hawaiian islands, a massive mountain rising from the sea and covered in green splendor. Colby had landed in a large clearing surrounded by trees and thick undergrowth. I heard the rush of a waterfall on one side, with surf pounding out of sight somewhere beyond the dense rain forest.

It was beautiful, in a hot, steamy way. I looked up and around, watching the sky brighten to powder blue. The surrounding trees and bamboo were dotted with flowering plants, and the steep wall of the volcano rose above us, a huge fold of rock cutting into the sea. There was magic in these hills, different from the dry desert magic I was used to, but as powerful. The Polynesian gods had been here, but long ago, and now the island belonged to mortals.

"So where is the lair?" I asked. I imagined a long hike through dense jungle-forest or a climb up that mountain, which must rise at least ten thousand feet. Something I'd enjoy on a nice long vacation with a massage and a mai tai at the end of the trail, not something I wanted to face after an exhausting overnight journey.

"You're standing in it," Colby said.

I looked around in surprise. I saw the cleared-out area covered with lush grass, and I realized the meadow had been cleared on purpose, probably so a dragon could land here. "I thought he'd have a cave."

"He does. Somewhere." Colby waved a hand at the mountain. "Several of them. But I mean that the whole island is his lair."

"Oh."

Mick had never mentioned that he owned an entire island in the middle of the Pacific. I knew there were no people here—human beings leave traces of themselves, and this place was completely unspoiled. How resort builders or researchers had missed it, I had no idea, but very likely, Mick had cloaked it with magic. "How did *you* find it?"

Colby shrugged. "Trial and error the first time. This time I knew what to look for."

"Are you telling me that we have to search this entire island for traces of Mick's true name?"

"Yep."

I heaved a sigh. Drake had said nothing, only viewed the vast greenery in silence.

Both he and Colby were completely naked, but dragons didn't share the sense of shame humans did. They dressed when interacting with humans, but they could take clothes or leave them. Though I'd been raised to be modest, I'd stopped noticing naked dragons and naked gods, which showed how different my life had become from what I'd thought it would be.

Colby was tattooed all over, his skin like living art. Drake's dragon tattoo spread across his back and down his arms, the spikes of wings rising up his neck. He had no tattoos on the front of his buff torso, and I distractedly noticed his nice six-pack and good pecs. With his black hair and dark eyes, Drake was a handsome man, but give me Mick with his bad-boy blue eyes and wicked smiles anytime.

"We'll have to fly it," Colby said. Which meant more motion sickness for me, but I didn't see any other choice.

It took all day. The sun rose, heating the already warm air, the humidity holding in the heat. I found it difficult to believe that hours ago I'd stood in my slushy parking lot, the temperature a toasty thirty-seven degrees. It was about eighty-five here, with about that percentage of humidity, though when Colby lifted me above the trees, the bracing ocean wind cooled me.

We flew across valleys where waterfalls cascaded hundreds of feet into the rain forest below. These valleys cut deep into the island, which, if I remembered correctly from travel brochures I'd longingly perused, must be about as big as Molokai in the Hawaiian chain.

By nightfall, Colby hadn't found whatever it was he looked for. I fretted, hating to leave my hotel unprotected, no matter how well we'd warded it. And of course I'd been without my cell phone when Colby grabbed me, so I couldn't check in. I had a piece of magic mirror with me—I liked to always keep a shard handy—but whenever I looked into it, it was dark, and I couldn't get it to respond. That worried me more than I liked to say.

Drake helped us search but kept Colby in his sight at all times. I grew hungry and very thirsty. Though the waterfalls fell to clear, freshwater creeks, I wasn't certain how safe the water was to drink, and I hadn't had the foresight to stash water purification tablets in my pockets when I got up this morning.

Finally, as the long day began to fade into night, Colby dove sharply into a pocket between mountains, one we'd circled before. This time, he crashed through the canopy of trees and landed in another big clearing. It was too dark to see much of it, but from what I could tell in the dying light, it wasn't much different from the other valleys we'd explored.

Colby had barely set me down before becoming human again, laughing in triumph. "Knew it was here somewhere."

"What is this place?"

I was sore, sick, hungry, and dehydrated. Back here in the dark, away from the bracing ocean air, the humid heat was stifling. My clothes clung to my body, my jeans heavy with the dampness, my hair irritating on the back of my neck.

"It's the heart of his lair," Colby announced. "This is where the dragon hides when he needs to hide, where he stashes his most precious things, where he'll come eventually to die. If Mick's name lingers anywhere on this island, it will most likely be here."

"*Now* you find it," I said sourly. "When it's too dark to see anything." The sun set rapidly in these latitudes, and behind the dense forest, we stood in blackness.

"You don't need light to find the name," Drake said. He hadn't spoken much all day, but his dark voice was as strong as ever, not dry and scratchy like mine. "But if you must have light . . ."

He threw a fireball high. It exploded into a light spell, the same kind Mick liked to use, illuminating the clearing like a million fireflies.

I gasped, and I heard Colby's sharp intake of breath.

Drake's light showed us a charred ruin. The entire clearing had been burned out, every tree, vine, and tangled bit of undergrowth destroyed to its roots. The rocks left behind were blackened like lumps of charcoal, and I saw the glitter of gold, melted, coating the rocks, mud, and debris.

It was an amazing piece of destruction. Only molten lava could have caused this damage, except that no hardened black lava remained. The only other thing that could have obliterated this place was dragon fire.

"He destroyed his own lair." Colby sounded both awe-struck and sickened. "No dragon would do that. The heart of the lair is a sacred place."

Drake lowered his hand, and the light spell died. As the fire faded, stars came out overhead, bathing the stubbled landscape in a kinder light.

"He is lost to us," Drake said, his voice holding a note of sadness I'd never heard from him. "Micalerianicum is lost."

"Or not." Colby was looking at the sky, studying the stream of stars the clearing bared.

Colby grabbed me and jerked me aside at the same time a huge black dragon swooped in, mouth open, fire roaring, coming right for us.

Sixteen

Mick fired what was left of the clearing, belching flame that ate everything in its path. Without Colby taking to wing and grabbing me up with him, I would have been one of the things roasted.

My stomach dropped as Colby did one of his whizzing turns, but I realized after a few panicked seconds that Mick wasn't aiming at us. He'd come to finish burning out the clearing, destroying the last of what he was. Drake rose, his dragon as large as Mick's, ready to stop him, but he dove out of the way when Mick shot a stream of fire at him.

Mick was big, dangerous, and he didn't care. This was the side of Mick other people saw—the dragon lord, the monster, the force of destruction. I understood why people feared him, why they turned green and sidled away when his eyes went black and determined. Any gentleness I'd ever seen in him had gone. The witch had taken it away.

Trees went up in flame, towering pillars of fire ringing

the clearing. Mick burned everything down to the rocks and soil, until the black volcanic gravel gleamed through the mud. Twice Drake tried to stop him, and twice Mick drove him away. Colby, smaller than Mick, had the sense to hover above and outside the clearing, out of range of Mick's flame.

Mick rose from the fiery lair, climbing up and up, his huge body outlined by the stars. He swung among them like another constellation, but just when I thought he'd wing away from us, back to his witch, he turned and rushed at Colby.

Colby did his zinging hop backward, leaving bile in my mouth. Mick swooped by, giving us a foot to spare, his wings folded behind him as he arrowed past. He cocked his head as he went by, and I looked straight into Mick's black and silver eye, which was cold—ice-cold—no fire within.

"Mick," I whispered.

But he was gone, shooting past. He opened his vast wings to pump him up into the night and disappeared.

Colby banked left, carrying me back to the clearing where we'd started. He set me on the ground, morphed back to human, and grabbed at me with human hands as I collapsed, numb and spent, to the grass.

Drake insisted we stay the night before heading back home. I didn't want to. I'd been gone twenty-four hours already, and I longed with all my heart for dry desert cold and my grandmother's scolding. Drake gave me a grave look, shook his head, and said, "The human woman needs to rest or she risks death."

Colby, damn him, agreed with him.

Drake proved himself useful by fashioning a shelter for me against the rain that had started to patter down. Darkness brought sudden cold, and the clouds that had formed against the high mountain now spread their bounty to the lowlands. Drake must have done this before, because the tropical roof he tied between the trees was pretty damned watertight. He ordered Colby to guard me and said he'd forage for food.

Drake took a long time to return, and when he did, he brought me not whatever fruit was in season or some unfortunate tropical bird he'd snared, but a Hawaiian plate lunch in a plastic container. We weren't that far, he explained, from Hawaii's Big Island.

I hadn't thought I could eat a bite, but suddenly the meat and rice and fruit seemed a very good idea. "Don't tell me you went into a restaurant naked," I said around mouthfuls.

"I keep stashes of clothing in various places in the world, in case I need to move among humans."

"Your lair's around here too, is it?"

Drake didn't answer. I gathered from the chill in his silence that my question was the height of rudeness. The gleeful look on Colby's face confirmed it.

Once I'd eaten, my stomach settled a little, and exhaustion hit me. I huddled under the shelter, longing for my coat, and discovered that Drake had thoughtfully brought me a blanket.

I slept fitfully, my dreams filled with Mick and fire, sorrow and worry. After a long time of tossing and turning, I woke abruptly in the pitch-dark, unaware what time it was. Drake was nowhere in sight, but Colby lay next to me, human and naked, snoring loudly. In his sleep, he'd stolen most of the blanket.

I let him have it. I got to my feet as quietly as I could and walked away from the shelter.

I made my way out of the clearing and down to the beach, where I could breathe the fresh air that came over the sea. The rain had abated, the clouds thinning to tatters before a running wind. The moon had set, but the stars shone above me in dense proliferation, reminding me of the petroglyphs the ancient artists had drawn in the sinkhole. Without man-made lights spoiling the sky, the pueblo peoples must have seen and drawn the same swirls of stars I looked at now.

I saw him by that starlight, an upright man walking with strong steps toward me down the sand.

I stopped. I knew in my heart Mick hadn't come out here because he'd been miraculously released or because his love for me had overridden the spell. He'd come for a reason, the witch's reason.

I waited for him to approach. Mick hadn't dressed; his naked skin glistened in the starlight where spray dampened him. The dragon tattoos on his arms looked blurred, out of focus, as though the dragons shivered, as I'd seen them do the night Mick had been taken from me. Mick's eyes were white and cold, but fire flickered in them as he stopped and looked down at me.

I cleared my throat. "Nice lair you have here. Long way to go for takeout, though."

"You need to leave." His voice was so different, no longer the easygoing tones of my beloved Mick. "You won't find what you seek here."

I folded my arms, both to keep myself warm and to hide the fact that I was shaking. My finger found the turquoise-and-onyx ring that still clasped my finger, and I stroked the cool silver. "What I'm seeking is you. I won't let that bitch have you, Mick. If she wants a fight, I'll give her one."

"You are not what she wants. She doesn't care whether you live or die."

"No? What does she want, then? And why all the crap with Ted and my hotel?"

I knew Mick wouldn't tell me, even before he gave me a stony look. "Leave Magellan. Go back to your native land and stay there. For your own good."

"Is it my hotel she wants? Why? The damn thing stood empty for years. Why is she just now trying to move in?"

Again, the unhelpful stare. "I can tell you this, Janet. Take your grandmother and go home, or you will die."

My shaking calmed as I thought things through. "If Vonda Wingate is so big and bad, why does she need a dragon to deliver messages for her? She had to use you to get through the wards to put the damaging spell into my hotel—which means she's not as all-powerful as she'd like to be."

"She is stronger than you understand. This is her warning."

"Gods, Mick, listen to you." I stepped to him, looked into

his hard face, my heart aching because I wanted to touch him and didn't dare. "She's made you destroy the heart of your own lair. Drake told me it was sacred to you. Doesn't that mean anything? Plus you tried to kill me, right after you gave me this." I held up my hand, letting the stars reflect on the ring.

Mick's gaze went to the ring, and for an instant—the barest instant—I saw his eyes become blue.

The flicker fed my hope and made me reckless. He was in there, somewhere, my Mick. I grabbed his arms, but Mick jerked away with a snarl. "Don't touch me!"

"Mick, come back to me. Don't let her have you. Please!" I was crying and begging, and I didn't care. I loved this man, and I knew, somewhere deep inside him, that he still loved me.

Mick pushed me from him so hard that I stumbled, and by the time I regained my balance, he'd lifted both hands and surrounded them with fire.

"I'm ordered to kill you if I have to," he said. He gave me a sickening parody of his usual grin. "It's nothing personal, baby."

I rested my weight on the balls of my feet, ready. "Tell me one thing. Are you sleeping with her?"

He gave me a look of disgust. "I don't have sex with humans."

"Except with me, you mean."

"And for that, you die."

The little aside gave me the time I needed. Mick's fire burst from his hands, but I threw up a shield of Beneath magic, drawing on the barest remains of the passing rainstorm to ground me. My shield deflected Mick's fire into a little circle around me, and sand melted into glass.

My defense pissed him off, and again I saw the monster that was Mick, the dragon who wanted to crush the puny human. The sneer he'd made about sex with humans had been real. I was seeing the Mick from long ago, from before the dragon council had sent him after me, before he'd watched me and decided that maybe humans, especially Navajo biker-chick Stormwalkers, weren't so bad.

He threw fire at me again. But Mick had trained me to fight, to reach for and control my powers. I was no longer the child who burned down buildings by accident until she fled, crying into the storm. I was no longer the young woman running away from what she was, who feared killing a bunch of human bikers in a bar when they tried to mess with her. I wasn't even the Stormwalker determined to, yet afraid of, confronting her goddess-from-hell mother.

I was the Janet in control of her newly awakened goddess powers.

Well, nearly in control of them.

I surrounded myself with Beneath magic, making a bubble of it as Gabrielle had when I'd fought her in the snow. Mick's fire streamed at me, the sand burning and boiling in its wake. I sweated as it struck my barrier, my skin blistering even behind the bubble.

"I taught you," Mick said, as though he knew what I was thinking. "I taught you everything. I know all your tricks, Stormwalker."

"Maybe you taught me some. But we spent time apart, Firewalker, five years apart. I learned plenty of other things then. Without you."

"I watched what you learned. I've always been watching you."

He had me there. Mick had watched and protected me when I thought I was alone and vulnerable, which I hadn't learned until much later.

"Stalking me," I countered.

Mick shrugged. "Whatever."

I wasn't going to win a battle of words. I rarely won arguments with Mick when he was sane. I doubted enslaved Mick would pull his punches.

So I didn't pull mine. I grabbed the fading wind, built it into my own little microburst, mixed it with Beneath magic, and threw that at him. Mick's flame widened, sucking the wind into himself at the same time keeping the Beneath magic out. My power pulled back into my hands with a jerk.

Mick didn't give me time to recover. Another wave of flame came at me, and another, and another, engulfing my little bubble in heat. My hair crackled, my skin blistered. Mick was going to roast me alive.

He circled closer, a smile on his face, ready to kill me and enjoy it.

I gathered wind and blew it at him, following it with a whip of white magic that cracked through the fire and across his skin. His eyes widened in rage, and he came for me.

My bubble burst under the next fireball, the magic evaporating like water. I ran. I pounded down the beach and straight into the waves as streams of fire followed me.

The water slapped me, salty and cold. Mick came after me. He was pissed as hell, and his fire boiled the sea. Bubbles formed around me, the water roiling as Mick decided to steam me like a lobster. He strode into the water, like a very good-looking sea monster, and I could do nothing against him. The rainstorm was now completely gone, and it hadn't been much more than gentle in the first place. I had only my Beneath magic left.

I could kill Mick with that raw power, but Mick knew I wasn't prepared to kill him. The witch must be counting on that too. I didn't want Mick dead. I wanted him free.

"What is your name?" I shouted at him. "Come on, Mick. *Tell* me!"

Mick ignored my plea. He kept coming, me treading water now, my clothes soaked.

"You have to be in there somewhere, Mick. Please, tell the witch to kiss off and come back to me."

Mick had finished with banter. He was the most frightening when he was quiet, focused, deadly. That deadly focus was now trained on me.

His next burst of fire flowed around me, so hot it burned even the water. I realized dimly that he knew my Beneath magic could shield me as it had on the beach, but that I'd corner myself in a trap of my own making. He'd surround me with fire and heat until the shield failed, and Mick was a long way from tired.

Mick didn't bother with another burst of flame once he neared me. He reached, physically, through the fire, immune to his own dragon magic, and grabbed me around the throat.

I couldn't scream, couldn't do much of anything but kick and flail and try to beat him. Mick was a big man, with three times my strength. I'd always loved how he kept that strength gentled for me, even during our wildest sexual escapades, but he wasn't gentling it now.

He lifted me out of the water, one hand around my neck. He didn't squeeze, didn't shake, simply lifted me until I was face-to-face with him, until I knew the hard power of his hands that would take my life.

Except he didn't take it. He held me fast, my clawing not making a damn bit of difference. With the other hand, he ripped open the pocket of my jeans. When Mick's fingers closed around the shard of magic mirror I kept there, I understood.

I kicked him squarely in the balls.

Any man kicked by a hard motorcycle boot between the legs should fold over in exquisite pain, but Mick just looked at me. He pulled up the shard of mirror, his hand bleeding as the glass cut him. I stopped clawing at his death grip and started going for the mirror. I couldn't let him have it.

Mick heaved me away from him, one-handed. I flew backward and landed hard on the water, the flames still licking it. I went under but fought my way upward, coughing and spluttering. The mirror was screaming, its high-pitched keen echoing through the deep valleys of the island.

The mirror would be compelled to obey him, because Mick and I had woken the mirror from dormancy with a spell we'd worked together. It had to obey me too, but right now, Mick held the shard, and it was Mick bouncing fire magic off it, doubled in strength, directed at me.

I dove. Down into coral that waited to scrape the hell out of my face and hands and rip my jeans. Startled fish burst apart as I invaded their space. I kicked and swam, well under the water, and surfaced right next to Mick.

His eyes were pearl white, his hands dancing with red light, the mirror screaming. "Oh, Mommy, help me!"

I dove into Mick and at least made him trip, but I couldn't get him down. I jumped aside as his mirror-enhanced flame came for me, but my clothes caught fire, and I had to roll back into the water. I looked up, weakening, to see Mick with the mirror reflecting red. Behind Mick rose another dragon, huge and black, wings beating the air, poised for the kill.

"No!" I screamed.

But Drake wanted to kill. He pounced on Mick, ready to tear him apart, and Mick, armed with the mirror, turned to incinerate him. Only Drake's dragon hide saved him from the fire that lanced him, and he shot upward, screeching.

Undaunted, Drake attacked again, intent to kill. I tackled Mick's legs, trying to drive him to his knees, but if he hadn't felt me kicking him in the balls, me landing on the backs of his knees was like a gnat landing on a buffalo.

I climbed up him, going for the shard of mirror, and Mick fought me all the way. This allowed Drake to swoop in, talons extended, and I don't think he minded that I might die along with Mick.

But Mick was ready. He lifted the shard, out of my reach, and the fire that he reflected from it ripped Drake across the chest.

Drake's hide opened to the bone, a torrent of blood raining on Mick and me and the mirror. As Drake screamed and took to the air, Mick let fly another blast that struck Drake on the underbelly.

Drake ponderously flapped away, but he didn't make it far. He wheeled and fell into the thick trees, and the *boom* as he struck the ground reverberated through the valley.

I didn't stop to watch or wonder. I went for the shard.

Colby flew in and landed yards away, then ran for us. He closed his arms around my waist, trying to pull me away from Mick, and I fought him off.

"Get the mirror!" I screamed. "Don't let him have the mirror!"

I suddenly adored Colby, because he didn't stop to ask questions. Colby matched Mick in human strength, and facing that coupled with me clawing at him, Mick suddenly had to truly fight.

Mick punched Colby across the chest, but as he did, I sank my teeth into Mick's bloody hand. When he flinched, his grip loosened, and I whipped the shard from his fingers. I cut him deeply, and cut myself as well.

At my touch, and the touch of my blood, the mirror homed in on me.

Mick, eyes wild, clamped his hand around my wrist. I felt my bones give, screamed as they broke. I grabbed the shard with my other hand and threw it as hard as I could. As it arced toward the water, I directed Beneath magic at it, which caught in its reflection and arrowed back to Mick.

Mick had to drop me. The white-hot Beneath magic missed him, shot into the trees, and obliterated them.

Mick looked at me in surprise. That blow had been intended to kill, something Mick had not believed I'd try. I gave him a smile, trying to mask my own surprise that the burst had been so strong.

"Sorry, baby," I said. "Nothing personal."

Colby was digging through the water trying to find the mirror. Mick snarled at me, turned and sprinted down the beach, then morphed, shrouded in darkness, into his dragon. He took wing and flew into the dawn, a beautiful black dragon outlined against gray sky. My heart ached as I watched him lift toward the rising sun.

"Damn it." Colby stood up, hands on hips. "Can't reach it."

I hobbled over to him, torn between wanting to curl into a weeping ball and wanting to puke my guts out. I told myself I had time for neither and made it to Colby's side. Nothing glimmered in the water, but I'd seen the mirror drop into it, free of Mick.

"We have to find it." My voice grated, my useless wrist hurting like hell. "You never know what kind of creatures exist in the ocean." Nasty ones, according to my grandmother.

"I'm here! I'm here! Don't leave me, for the love of the gods!"

The voice echoed to me from our left, and I saw morning sunlight glimmer on something on the coral. I reached for it, closing my eyes in relief as I picked up the piece of glass.

"This is what Mick came for." My panic rose even through my pain, burns, and exhaustion. "I have to get back to the hotel. *Now*. Before Mick figures out a way to enter it and get to the original."

Seventeen

We found Drake collapsed, still dragon, in a stand of crushed trees. His eye was filmy white, his hide covered with blood. He still lived, though his breathing was labored and loud.

"We'll have to leave him," Colby announced. "If you want to get back to your hotel anytime soon, we can't take him with us."

I knew damn well why Colby wanted to leave Drake behind, and it had nothing to do with getting me back to the hotel quickly. Colby was free from the council's binding spell, and he wanted to fly off before Drake was strong enough to renew it.

"What's to keep Mick from returning and killing him?" I asked.

Colby shrugged. "If Micky wants your mirror, why should he?"

I didn't know, but there was more going on here than met the eye. If Mick managed to take the mirror away from the hotel, he could do a lot of damage. The mirror had to obey him, as it had to obey me. Maybe the mirror couldn't directly murder me while I had power over it, but Mick could use it to destroy everyone else in my life.

But if there was the slightest chance Drake could figure out Mick's name while lying here soaking up the earth of Mick's lair, wouldn't Mick return to prevent that?

"Dragons heal quickly, and I can help," I said. "We can't leave him."

"We don't have time—"

Colby broke off as thin, dark tendrils of magic emanated from Drake's mouth. Drake hissed softly, and the threads wound themselves once more around Colby's aura.

"Oh, this is so not fair," Colby muttered.

Drake's binding spell tightened, putting Colby right back into Drake's power, as strongly as he'd been before Nash had negated the spell.

"We heal him," I said firmly. "And then you heal me, and we go. With Drake. I'm going to need all the help I can get."

By the time Colby landed behind my hotel, it was dark again, the day gone. We'd lost hours on the trip east, and Colby claimed he couldn't fly as fast because of the binding spell. That might have been true.

Colby had carried Drake in his human form, because Drake wasn't well enough yet to fly. Drake didn't like that, but I didn't have time to consider his feelings.

I'd tried to have a serious talk with Drake as Colby carried us back, difficult to do when held by a dipping, floating, soaring dragon. Drake had told me he'd hold off advising the dragon council to kill Mick, but only for twenty-four hours. No matter how much I pleaded, that was all he'd give me.

I didn't have time either to consider the feelings of Paco Lopez, who waited in my lobby, looking apologetic. Lopez stared at me when I limped in, my face windburned, my clothes covered in dried blood. I was still favoring my wrist though Colby's and Drake's healing magic had fused the bones. However, Lopez had learned not to question the weirdness that went on around me, and he got down to business.

"Sorry, Janet," he said, lifting his cuffs and making for Colby. "Nash says I have to bring him in."

At least I'd been able to let Colby dress. We'd come in the back door and stopped off in my bedroom, where I'd let Colby and Drake wait while Cassandra brought them clothes from their rooms. Now, without a word to Lopez, Drake dragged himself up the stairs and into his room.

Colby shrugged and held out his wrists. "Fine by me. Take me in."

"No." I stepped between the two men. "I need Colby here. Tell Jones he'll have to deal with it."

"Janet, if I go back without him, Jones will tear my head off," Lopez said. "Give me a break. I'm too young to die."

"Colby wasn't doing anything illegal in that bar. What's the charge?"

Lopez cleared his throat. "Resisting arrest."

"He wasn't resisting. Nash is just touchy. I'll vouch for Colby."

"That won't be good enough, Janet. Jones will be down here in no time, and I'm much nicer than he is. You know that."

Colby grinned. "Don't worry. I'll be happy to talk to the fine sheriff."

"No," I said. "I can't afford for you to run off again, and I don't have time for you and Drake to fight it out. I need you, Colby."

Colby looked affronted. "I can't believe you think I'd desert you, Janet."

Nice sentiment, but I still didn't trust him.

"Please," I said to Lopez. "Tell Nash that I do need to talk to him but that he has to leave Colby alone."

"I'm just a deputy trying to keep his job."

"Tell him I stopped you from taking Colby. He'll believe that." I stepped up to Lopez and looked him in his dark eyes. "Because I will."

Lopez put away his cuffs. He had no magic in him, even

though he believed in it, and he'd seen me do some crazy things. Dangerous things. Deadly ones.

He didn't agree to blame me, and I didn't think he would, but at least he left. Colby gave me a cheerful grin and a thanks and ran upstairs to clean up, and I went to talk to the magic mirror.

The saloon was empty, the hotel still closed. I helped myself to a bottled water from the refrigerator and looked up at the mirror. It hung silently, the bullet hole in its center a testimony to my violent life.

"Everything is warded tight," I told it. "He can't come in."

"Oh, girlfriend." The mirror shuddered, glass tinkling. "What *are* we going to do? I was so scared out there, I almost peed my pants."

"Why were you dark when I first looked into the shard?" I'd have loved to be able to communicate with Cassandra, to have her witch magic help me find a trace of Mick's true name. Not that it would have done any good, I realized in retrospect.

"He came here," the mirror said, dropping to a frightened whisper. "He looked through the window, searching. I didn't want to show him anything—where you were, where I was."

"He knew anyway," I pointed out. "He found us."

"That's because Drake and Colby weren't subtle about changing and flying off. Jonesie had to convince all those gorgeous men in uniform that they were tricks played by the meth dealers to distract the cops while they got away. And I saw Mick talking to Barry, who pointed the way Colby and Drake had flown. Probably wasn't hard to figure out where they were going."

Plus when the dragons had touched down in Mick's lair, they'd likely set off all kinds of magical alarms. But I hadn't been worried about stealth—I'd assumed that once I found Mick's name, everything would be all right.

Instead I had a sore wrist, a dehydrated body, and an injured dragon upstairs.

"When we were searching the island, did you sense anything? Any music, any touch of his name?"

"No, sugarplum. I would have said."

I was back to square one.

"How the hell am I going to find it?" I asked. "How the hell did *she* find it? If dragon names are so elusive, how do witches figure them out?"

"I don't know, honey bun," the mirror said. "But I've seen a dragon enslaved to a witch before. Believe me, it wasn't pretty."

I stared at the mirror, my wan face and wide brown eyes reflecting back at me. "You know a witch who enslaved a dragon? How did she do it? Who is she? Where can I find her?"

The mirror sighed. "She's long dead, hot lips, sorry. It was the witch who first made me, oh, a couple hundred years ago, a long time before someone drove me out here. She already had the dragon when she made me, so I don't know how she got his name. That bitch had power to spare, but it wasn't good enough for her, oh no. She enslaved a dragon, and she made a magic mirror. I knew all of it was too much for her to handle, but would she listen? Noooo. After all that trouble, she died, and I went dark. It was hell."

"How did she die? What happened to the dragon?"

"Now, that's not a nice story. The dragon, he got pretty weak in the end, because the witch magic drained the dragon's magic out of him. One day, he morphed into a dragon and ate her. But there was so much of her magic wound around him that when she died, he did too. He looked relieved, poor thing. Last thing I saw before I went dark was him falling over dead."

I hung on to the edge of the bar, my heart sinking. A bad story on top of fight wounds on top of a Hawaiian plate dinner and an erratic flight back was not what I needed right now.

Yes, I did, I told myself. I had to know what I was facing.

"Is it you she wants?" I asked the mirror. "Not the hotel?"

The mirror shivered again. "If she wants me, she'll have to kill you and Micky first."

"I'm thinking she's fine with that," I said.

"Please don't let her." The mirror's voice was small and subdued. "I like you, Janet. Even if you're the offspring of a crazy Beneath goddess, with runaway magic that could melt me like hot lead, I really want to stay with you."

What a sweetie. I wanted the mirror to stay with me too, because if a witch did get hold of it, there was no telling where she'd stop. Besides, the mirror was right—I'd have to be dead before the mirror obeyed another master.

"Thanks," I said. "You've helped."

"Sure thing, honey pie." The mirror sounded mournful. I gave its frame a pat as I left the saloon and went upstairs to check on Drake.

Drake looked better, if unhappy sitting in my over-stuffed chair drinking tea Cassandra had brewed for him. He didn't like witches, but he would accept all the healing magic he could get. Dragons—at least if Mick was anything to go by—hated to be unwell.

"If you've come to ask for more time, I can't give it to you," he said. A book lay facedown on the table beside him, something by John Locke. He saw me looking at it. "Micalerianicum accused me of knowing little about humans. I thought I'd start with their political philosophy."

"As long as you remember that there's more to human history than dead English philosophers. I need more time."

Drake heaved a sigh. "I am being kind to give you twenty-four hours. I am taking into account the fact that you saved the life of a member of the dragon council last fall, although you did it to save Micalerianicum in a roundabout way. Twenty-four hours is generous. If you can't free him by then, the council will have to take steps. The witch can't live."

"And Mick?"

Unhappiness flickered in Drake's dark eyes. "An unfortunate but acceptable casualty."

I leaned down and gripped the lapels of Drake's fine silk shirt. "It's not acceptable to me. If Mick becomes a casualty, so do you."

He believed me. But though I saw self-worry in Drake's eyes, what frightened me more was that it didn't dim his determination. "If it must be," he said. "We must stop this witch even if it means that I pay with my life."

His words froze my heart. Dragons feared so very little. When they were afraid of something or someone, it was best to take notice.

I released him. "My priority is to get Mick free. If you try to stop me, I'll stop you."

"So be it."

I had to give Drake points for attitude. I knew ours was a temporary truce, and that when his time limit was up, he'd be my greatest enemy.

"Twenty-four hours," he said from behind his book as I left the room. I closed the door firmly and went back down to the kitchen.

At least Grandmother and Elena had unlocked the door. They weren't cooking—they sat at the kitchen table, tea steaming between them, talking intently in low voices. The air in there was cool, a refreshing change from the tropical rain forest of Mick's island, the heat turned down the way Grandmother liked it.

"Everything all right here?" I asked them.

Grandmother took a sip of tea. "You are a mess, Janet. As usual." She spoke English, so that, if Elena didn't know Diné, she'd be able to follow my grandmother's admonishments.

"We had an encounter," I said.

"I know. The mirror told me. Now what will you do?"

I scrubbed my hand through my hair, noting that the dragons' combined healing magic hadn't done anything about my subsequent headache. "I don't know what I'm going to do. I'm out of ideas. If you have any, they would be helpful."

I broke off as I saw a flash of movement outside the back door, someone walking by in the dark parking lot. Not Mick—I would have sensed him. "Who's that?"

"No one," Grandmother said quickly.

Elena and Grandmother looked guilty as thieves. I frowned at them and marched out the back door.

"Hey!" I called to the man who was walking swiftly toward the railroad bed. I ran to catch up with him. "Where the hell have you been?"

Coyote stopped and waited for me. He wore a sheepskin coat against the cold, his black braid shining in the moonlight. I understood why I hadn't realized who was skulking outside; Coyote could hide his aura from me when he wanted to.

He shrugged. "Around."

"Around? That's all you can say? Why haven't you been helping? I've been frantically searching for Mick's name, for some way to get him free, and you haven't been helping!"

I seized his arms, fearing he'd shift and run from me, or simply vanish like smoke. Coyote could do that.

"Janet . . ."

"Shut up! You know you can make it all better. You can wave your hand and everything will be right. Why haven't you fixed it? *Why?*"

I screamed the last word. I found myself beating my fists on his chest before his strong arms came around me.

"Hush now, little Stormwalker."

I didn't want to cry and be comforted. I wanted him to *do* something. But I couldn't help leaning against him, searching for solace in his strength.

Coyote's clothes smelled of warmth and wood smoke and the homey scents of my grandmother's cooking. His hands on my back steadied me, and his heartbeat under my ear sounded human and normal.

I sniffled. "Why do you smell like my grandmother's stew?"

"She fed me. Well, what she really wanted was for me to bow down and worship her masterful cuisine. But hey, it was a free bowl of stew, so why not?"

I lifted my head. Despite the amusement in his voice, Coyote's dark eyes held sympathy and worry.

"Why haven't you helped Mick?" I asked.

"It's tricky, Janet, even for me. It's not a simple matter

of negating a spell." He let go of me, brought up his broad hands, and laced his fingers together. "See, the true name gets all tangled up in the witch's psyche—she's as much bound to him as he to her. The dragon's anger at being trapped only feeds the spell. That's why, if someone like you learns the dragon's name, then you have a chance of getting him free, because Mick has much stronger emotions wrapped up in you. If I tried to free him . . ." He jerked his hands apart. "I might end up killing him, and even I need the true name to do it."

"You're a god. Can't you find out his true name?"

"I'm a Native American god. The dragons have their own gods, their own rules. Dragons are smart enough to hide their names from tricksters like me."

My hope was fading fast. "But you must be able to do *something*."

"Maybe. Can't promise."

I thumped him again and pushed away. "Go out there and look, then. I have twenty-four hours—now twenty-three and change—before Drake rounds up the dragon council to take out Mick. No trials this time, just death. An acceptable casualty, Drake said."

"That's typical." Coyote glanced at the stars. "I wish I could help you out, Janet, but your grandmother, she's sent me on a mission."

I gaped at him. "Wait. *What?*"

"Your grandmother has sent me to do something for her." He glanced back at the hotel, its lights warm against the darkness. "She and your cook can be pretty insistent."

"Since when do you take orders from my grandmother?"

He shrugged. "I like to humor her. Besides, she reminded me how wicked she is with a broom."

I remembered my grandmother long ago chasing a coyote away from our house in Many Farms, her broom coming down solidly on the beast's hindquarters. The coyote had yelped and run off. I'd since figured out that the culprit had been Coyote himself, sneaking around peering into windows as he liked to do. *Watching me?* I wondered. He was always watching me.

"What does she want you to do?"

Coyote dropped a kiss on the top of my head. "Sorry, Janet. Gotta go." He shoved his hands in his pockets as he turned and continued his swift walk toward the empty railroad bed.

"Wait! Don't you dare run away from me!"

Coyote had made it to the top of the railroad bed by the time I started scrambling up it after him. I gained the top in time to watch him trot down the other side as a coyote and then disappear. Completely.

I saw nothing but darkness, snow clinging to juniper and grasses, and moonlight glittering on frost. My breath fogged in the air as I called Coyote's name, but I knew that he was gone.

When I stormed back inside to confront my grandmother, I found that she and Elena had locked the kitchen doors again. I could have magicked my way in and demanded they talk to me, but I had doubts about how much they'd tell me, and I was too exhausted to fence with Grandmother tonight.

I made myself soak in a bathtub but not collapse in despair this time. I tried to focus my attention on the soap suds, on finishing the healing of my wrist, on the soft comfort of clean towels. But I went through the motions with my heart like lead in my chest.

I dressed in clean clothes, feeling physically better but with my mind still spinning. I had no idea what to do next, short of holding Vonda Wingate upside down over a vat of piranhas until she promised to release Mick. I wasn't certain where I'd find piranhas in the desert or whether I could get close enough to Vonda to grab her, but it made for a satisfying vision.

But I knew I couldn't bluster and blast my way out of this one. I needed to be stealthy. I needed to plan. I needed to *think*.

Thinking wasn't aided by the arrival of Nash, still in his sheriff's uniform and coat, looking for Colby. He'd taken off the bandage, showing where a patch on the back of his head had been shaved.

I met Nash alone in the lobby. The hotel was quiet, everyone having either gone home or retreated to their bedrooms. Grandmother and Elena were still locked in the kitchen.

"Let it go, Jones." I leaned back against the reception counter and folded my arms. "Don't you have a mountain of paperwork to do, after all those arrests last night?"

Nash regarded me with an ice-cool gaze. "That's why I have deputies."

"Must be nice to be so powerful. You know Colby had nothing to do with whatever was going down in Barry's bar, I know you do. Colby was trying to help me out, and he needed you to negate a binding spell so he could do it."

Nash shook his head, his gray eyes still flinty. "I mostly wanted to arrest him to shut his smart-ass mouth. Tell him to consider it a warning."

"He does have a mouth," I agreed. "I've been meaning to ask you this, Nash, but I haven't had the chance. Could you arrest someone for me?"

"Who? Why?"

"Ted Wingate and his wife."

Nash looked interested, eager even. He tapped fingertips on the polished wooden counter. "What for?"

"Kidnapping and assault."

"Kidnapping . . . When the hell did this happen?"

"A couple days ago. They have Mick."

Nash's alert expression vanished. "I need something better than that, Janet. I saw Mick earlier today."

"It's a magical kidnapping. You can arrest them for *something*, can't you? You were ready to lock up Colby for mouthing off."

He wanted to. I saw it in his eyes. Nash was a stickler for rules, but I knew that if anyone could find a way to arrest the Wingates without ever breaking a rule, it would be Nash Jones.

I had to wonder about his magic-negating ability and the enslavement spell as well. Would Nash's magic dissolve the spell, as it had the binding spell that held Colby? Or would the enslavement spell kill Mick if Nash's negative magic tried to pull him free? The spell Drake had wound around Colby was a simple tethering spell, like a magical leash. Drake hadn't stopped Colby from thinking. Mick's entire aura had changed, the enslavement spell holding his mind and psyche rather than his body. Another thing to ponder and worry about.

Nash watched me narrowly. "Why don't you tell me exactly what is going on?"

I had to. I sat down with him facing me on a leather sofa under one of my art photos of the mysterious beauty of Chaco Canyon, and told him.

I left nothing out. I started with Ted's hotel inspection, and told Nash about everything in between that and my sudden trip to Mick's Pacific island lair. Nash Jones had been an Unbeliever for a long time, and he shot me skeptical looks when I babbled about Mick's true name and dragon enslavement, but to his credit, he listened without argument.

"Mick has tried to kill you?" he asked in a hard voice when I finished. "Twice?"

"He wouldn't have if he hadn't been ordered to. I know why the witch wants me dead—I'm the biggest threat to her—but I can't figure out why she did the elaborate inspection thing if she just wanted Mick to steal the mirror. Which will do nothing for her until Mick and I are both dead."

Nash waved aside overarching goals and villain motivation. "You're not certain that my antimagic, or whatever it is, will work to destroy the spell?"

"Coyote says its tricky, and I'm inclined to believe him."

"I broke the binding spell on Colby, you tell me," Nash pointed out.

"Yes, but that bound Colby's body only. The one around Mick involves much more, Coyote said. I want you to arrest the Wingates not to try to negate the spell, but so I can corner Vonda Wingate, study the spell, look for her weaknesses. Cassandra can help with that, and Coyote can too, if I can find him again. This will be more like diffusing a bomb than breaking down a door."

"But we might have to break down a door to get to the

bomb," Nash said. "While Mick, a dragon, tries to fry me, eat me, or just squash me. Plus Wingate could shoot me before I get near his wife."

"I think Ted Wingate's a coward," I said. I'd made him afraid of me, anyway.

"Plenty of cowards are dead shots."

"Stop thinking of difficulties."

"Not difficulties; contingencies," Nash said. "We need to know every possibility before we go in, and what we'll do to counteract each."

"We have to do it within twenty-four hours," I told him. "Twenty-two now."

Nash gave me an aggrieved look, but at least he didn't get up and leave me alone. He was going to help.

Before we could start formulating any plans, Grandmother came out of the kitchen, followed by Elena. The two women, one in long skirts, the other in jeans and a too-bright polyester top, made straight for Nash.

"We need your help, Sheriff Jones," my grandmother said. Standing, she was the same height as Nash sitting down. "Come into the kitchen and talk to us. Now."

"Grandmother . . ."

"*Now*." Grandmother turned and marched away, followed by Elena, after giving me one of her dark looks. Nash, damn him, rose quietly and obeyed.

Eighteen

Grandmother told me to serve Nash coffee while she and Elena sat down with him at the metal-topped kitchen table. Grandmother was keen on hospitality but preferred me to do the labor of it. I poured coffee without fuss, curious as to what they wanted from him.

"Gabrielle Massey," Grandmother said. "We need to find her."

I splashed coffee next to Elena's cup, and Elena gave me an annoyed look. I quickly wiped up the spill and returned the coffeepot to its place on the counter.

"I don't want her anywhere near you, Grandmother."

"I am not asking *you*, Janet. I'm asking the sheriff to look up her records and find her. She's important."

I granted that, but I wanted to be the one doing the finding. Gabrielle could kill my frail grandmother in a heartbeat.

"I did look her up," Nash said. "After meeting her, I was curious."

Of course he would have. I sat down. "Might as well tell us what you found."

Nash took a sip of coffee, held the cup as he talked. "She was born in Whiteriver, lived there for fifteen years, and then was reported missing by her parents. A runaway. She surfaced again three years later in Las Vegas, when she was arrested for shoplifting. Charges were dropped, and she went on living there, saying she had no intention of returning to Whiteriver. She was eighteen by then, so her parents apparently didn't try to get her to come home. Two years after that, the Masseys were killed in a car accident, on a road on the Rim, her father apparently driving under the influence. Gabrielle was living in Albuquerque by that time. After her parents' funeral, she dropped out of sight again, until turning up here. She's now twenty-four, has a record of several arrests for shoplifting and vandalism, but no convictions."

Her file sounded much like mine, only I'd finished high school and taken a degree at NAU. But except for that, Gabrielle and I might have been the same person.

"Where is she now?" Grandmother asked.

"No record. She isn't renting, hasn't purchased anything high dollar, like a car, doesn't have credit cards, no longer lives on the reservation, doesn't have a job. She's dropped off the radar."

"Except that she's around here somewhere," I said. "We've seen her."

Elena moved her coffee cup in gentle circles. Elena, who was from Whiteriver. "I remember Gabrielle as a child," she said. "A troublemaker if I ever saw one. Her father was an off-and-on drunk. Perfectly nice when he was sober, but once he hit the bottle, mean as can be."

"So many are," Nash said.

"Alcohol is evil," Grandmother said, giving me a fierce eye. She did not approve of me having a bar for my guests and living next to a biker bar.

"That could explain why Gabrielle ran away," I suggested, ignoring her. I'd had the benefit of a kind, loving father to take care of me, and I felt a twinge of sympathy for Gabrielle.

"Of course it does, but I remember how distraught her mother was." Elena shook her head. "Bad blood, that one.

I've told my daughter and my friends to keep an eye out and tell me if she comes back."

"No," I said in a loud voice. "Gabrielle is dangerous. Your daughter doesn't need to go anywhere near her."

"My daughter is a smart young woman. She can find things out without hurting herself."

"You don't understand *how* dangerous, Elena. She's the daughter of the goddess that made me."

Grandmother's face was pinched. "We all know that. But Gabrielle's very powerful. She either has a hand in Mick's enslavement, or she can be an asset to getting him free."

"We will look," Elena said stubbornly. "Either help us, or stay out of the way."

The amusement in Nash's gray eyes was hard to miss. He liked meeting people who could put me in my place.

It was true that we needed to find Gabrielle. I needed to pin her down and figure out what her purpose was, and Grandmother was right that she could be helpful—but only if we could control her. I had doubts about that. Gabrielle reminded me of myself when I was young and unsure of my place in the world, but Gabrielle had an arrogance that I had lacked. I'd tried not to hurt people; she didn't seem bothered by such things.

"I didn't say I wouldn't help," I said. "Elena, your daughter and friends can keep a watch for her, but tell them that they are by no means to approach Gabrielle or let on that they're looking for her. I don't trust her not to kill an innocent bystander just to prove she can."

Nash broke in. "Much easier if I do the searching. I have official ties, friends in the tribal police I've already contacted."

"Official records don't tell everything," I said. Mine certainly didn't.

"But law enforcement officers are human beings, Janet," he said. "They know everyone, and they gossip among themselves. Not everything we know gets put down in an official file, only the things we can put there legally."

Good to know. I imagined that gossip about my youthful exploits was rife.

I stood up. "Understand something. Gabrielle is unpredictable and dangerous. I want to find her, yes, but I don't want any of you going near her. None of you is strong enough to face her. Leave her for me."

"If she tries magic on *me*, it won't work," Nash said. "Right?"

"Who knows? We haven't tested how much you can take. Give Gabrielle a wide berth if you find her, and call me."

"No, call *me*," my grandmother said.

"Grandmother . . ."

"I'm not a simple old woman who needs to be protected."

"I know that, but . . ."

I was saved from the ensuing, and never-ending, argument by the ring of my cell phone. As usual, it was lying somewhere in my office, the tiny peal sounding through the open kitchen door.

I did my usual scramble out of the room and desperate sprint across the lobby, my boots skidding on the tiles as I lunged into the office to snatch the phone out from under a stack of papers. I'd wisely set it to ring many times before it rolled to voice mail, and I managed to catch it on the very last ring.

"Janet?"

"Naomi?" I panted, surprised. "Hey, how are you?"

"It's Jamison." Naomi's panic came through the phone and roused my own.

"What about Jamison? Is he all right? Did Mick hurt him? Don't trust Mick. If you see him, get away from him."

"Slow down. This has nothing to do with Mick. Jamison went to the sinkhole. He got excited about those photos you sent him, and he's gone to take a closer look. I think he's searching for another entrance to the cavern under it. He was too wound up to explain, he said. I'm so worried he'll go out there and get hurt. Could you—?"

"Go find him and beat some sense into him?" I relaxed a little, but not completely. "Sure. But seriously, Naomi, if you see Mick anywhere in town, don't approach him, don't talk to him, don't even wave at him. He's . . . not himself."

"I'll take your word for it." She sounded doubtful.

"And if you see Coyote, tell him to call me. Not that he'll listen."

"I'll try." Naomi hesitated. "Can I come with you?"

"No. I'm sorry, but no. There are things in that hole— might be things in that hole—that I don't want touching you. I'm not sure what they'll do. You stay put, and Nash and I will get Jamison."

As I spoke to her, I dashed around my office tucking a piece of magic mirror into a chamois bag, pulling on my warmest boots, fetching my jacket. I convinced Naomi to stay home and look after Julie—I knew I'd never talk her into staying safe for her own sake, but she'd do anything to protect Julie. She sounded relieved that I'd take Nash with me.

"I'll get Jamison. Don't worry." I sounded so reassuring as I hung up, but I was anything but reassured.

Outfitted against the cold, I made for the kitchen again and gave Nash a tight smile. "I need you, Nash. Sorry, Grandmother. We gotta go."

Because Nash didn't like people poking around his accident scenes, he was happy to drive me in his SUV over the dark roads to the sinkhole. He was ready to arrest Jamison on the spot, and right now, I'd be happy to let him.

Jamison wasn't at the sinkhole. A Flat Mesa police officer guarding the hole told us no one had been near all afternoon or all night. I shivered, the moon close enough to setting that its light didn't help us much. Why couldn't Jamison have come prowling during daylight?

Answer: because under cover of darkness, he could roam around in his mountain lion form. He'd see better in the dark, his thick fur would keep him warm, and he could scramble nimbly up and down rocks.

Nash and I crouched by the hole, and Nash flashed his powerful lantern around the steep sides and the debris. Nothing. Even the petroglyphs didn't look as densely drawn as before, which was weird. This entire place was weird.

"Naomi said she thought Jamison was trying to find another entrance," I said as we stood up. "You've lived around here all your life. Are there caves somewhere?"

Nash scanned the horizon. It was truly dark here, the lights of Flat Mesa hidden behind a rise of land. The stars were hard and cold against black sky, and the moonlight faded and was gone.

"I know a possible place, but those roads are snowed over. Low priority, won't get plowed."

I glanced at his SUV with its big tires. "The magic of four-wheel drive?"

Nash gave me a sour look. He had great affection for his vehicles, and bumping his new sheriff's SUV over a primitive, hole-filled road in the snow filled him with loathing. But Nash was also a law-enforcement officer at heart. If a citizen of his county might be in trouble, he couldn't leave without recovering said citizen. Nash gave me a brief nod and led the way back to the truck.

How he found the road in the pitch darkness with all landmarks buried in snow, I had no idea, but he did it. Nash drove slowly between two snow-covered fence posts that were barely far apart enough to admit the SUV, and started down a track to nowhere.

The truck listed and bounced, the gears whining as Nash strained to take it slow and steady. I had to admit he was a hell of a driver. We bounced slowly along, the new radio and computer system on his dashboard emitting a crackle or beep every once in a while. Nash had GPS, which explained how he could find the road's location, but not how he could see the strip of it unwinding before us.

This road hadn't been graded or raised, and we followed the contours of the land. Every dip might end in a canyon, every rise might end at a cliff. Nash navigated snowy washes that I'd never have dreamed of attempting, bending the SUV to his will.

After about half an hour of this, Nash halted the truck, without bothering to pull off the road. He set the gear and the brake but didn't turn off the SUV or its lights.

"Over that way." He motioned to a snow-covered mound of rocks illuminated by his headlights. "I used to play out here as a kid. It hasn't changed much."

I slid out of the SUV and he followed, bringing his big flashlight. We were the only ones for miles around, the snow clean and untrodden, the rocks poking in square regularity through snow-covered scrub.

I'd been born and raised in the country, and I knew that the earth beneath us was all connected. The bones of it ran through the bed of the world, and amazing things could be found just below the surface. Magellan and Flat Mesa had an elevation of about six thousand feet, but this part of the land was essentially flat—deceptively so. Canyons cut through the iron-rich sandstone to spill water from the high mountains south of us. The plateau makes all kinds of things possible—dry and wet caves, shallow but sharp-walled canyons, sinkholes—the connections of the earth world. The sinkhole and whatever Nash was leading me to would connect, somehow. It remained to be seen whether that connection was the right one.

"Here." Nash shone his light on a crack between boulders, and I slid to a halt beside him. Darkness yawned beyond the crack.

"Wait. Move the light this way." I pointed at a patch of muddy snow. "There."

We both saw it, a large paw print, the track of a mountain lion. *Jamison*, I thought. Changers' beasts were larger than normal animals, and this mountain lion would be about two hundred pounds. I squinted into the darkness, wondering whether Jamison's lion would be big enough to get stuck down there.

We squeezed cautiously between the boulders. Nash went first, and for once, I was fine with that. If someone tried to attack us magically, Nash could absorb it; if they attacked us physically, he had weapons.

"How would Jamison find this place?" I whispered. The tunnel beyond the opening was narrow, not much room between the sandstone walls.

"Naomi must have told him about it. She used to play out here too."

"And Maya?"

"Maya was younger than we were and had her own friends. Naomi and I were considered kind of nerdy."

Interesting. "You never thought about hooking up with Naomi?"

"No." The word was neutral, uninterested. "I wasn't her type, she wasn't mine. We stayed friends until I joined the army. She got married but I didn't like her husband. Her first husband, I mean. Jamison's fine."

Naomi's first husband was Julie's dad. Naomi never talked about him, but I gathered from Jamison that the scumbag had left Naomi because Julie had been born deaf. The man blamed Naomi for that; Julie's father had dumped them both. After ten years, Naomi had found Jamison and lived happily ever after. Now I needed to find Jamison and make him go the hell home so they could keep living happily ever after.

Nash led me a long way down a narrow, rocky tunnel, both of us grunting around boulders jutting into the passageway. The ground underfoot wasn't nice and level, it was strewn with gravel and obstructed by rockfall, the floor sometimes thrusting so high there was only a few feet between it and the ceiling. We'd at least left behind the bitter cold of the winter night, though the chill in here was substantial.

Nash stopped so abruptly I barely kept myself from running into him. He stood at the top of a long rockslide, boulders tumbling away from us into a high-ceilinged cavern. I'd love to say it was a majestic place of stalagmites and stalactites, but nothing so grandiose. It was a big hole in the ground, nothing more, and it had a mountain lion in it.

The mountain lion sat on its haunches, staring at the wall above it. It moved so little that it might have been carved of stone, like one of Jamison's amazing sculptures.

When Nash's light touched him, the mountain lion turned with a low growl, eyes green and glittering.

"Jamison?" I asked.

The lion growled again, this time in irritation. Lips pulled back from fangs, and Nash eased his pistol from its holster.

I put my hand on the weapon and forced it down. "It's Jamison. Turn off the light. He doesn't like it."

"Well, I don't like the dark," Nash snapped.

"He wants to shift. Turn it off."

"You can read his mind?" His skepticism rang clearly.

"No, but I recognize Jamison annoyed when I see it. Turn off the flashlight. Trust me."

Nash heaved an aggrieved sigh but flicked the switch. The cave became inky black, the growling increased, and I heard what sounded like a crunch of bones. More silence, broken only by the slither of fabric and then Jamison said, "All right."

Nash flicked on the lantern. Jamison stood in front of us, clad in jeans and in the act of pulling on a T-shirt.

I understood why he'd wanted darkness. Unlike dragons, who saw no reason to put on clothes unless absolutely necessary, Jamison was a modest man. He didn't like people watching him shift, and only Naomi got to see him naked.

"These caves are dangerous," Nash said to him.

"Then why are you down here?" Jamison countered. "Especially you, Janet."

"Naomi got worried."

"And you shouldn't be here," Nash finished, still the sheriff.

"I'm not trespassing," Jamison said. "These caves are part of the S.J. Ranch, and Samuel has given me permission to walk this land anytime I want. I come here looking for stones to carve. I was going through the photos Janet sent me and realized where I'd seen drawings like them. Here."

He gestured to the top of the cave, but Nash didn't move his light. "So you came to investigate, alone, in the middle of the night?" Nash asked him.

"It was late afternoon when I started. Took me longer to find what I was looking for than I thought."

"What *did* you find?" I asked. "Nash, please, I need to see this."

Finally Nash raised the lantern and shone it on the wall where Jamison pointed.

I sucked in my breath. The highest point of the walls and the entire ceiling were covered in petroglyphs. Whorls of stars, animals, humans with triangular torsos, plants, and abstract symbols had been chipped out here, there, and everywhere, overlapping one another as they had in the sinkhole.

Among these the spidery, skeletal hands of the *karmii* began to glow, and as we watched they started skimming across the ceiling, coming directly for me.

Nineteen

Jamison sucked in a breath. "Those weren't here a minute ago."

"No," I said. "They're sensing evil."

Three guesses as to who was the evil. Jamison the Changer who took such good care of his family? The diligent sheriff who could absorb and negate all magic? Or the Stormwalker whose mother was a goddess trapped Beneath?

The hands multiplied, glowing with the sickly light I remembered from the sinkhole. Nash snapped off his light, and the glow continued, the *karmii* now flowing down the walls.

"Nash—no!"

Nash had started to walk for the wall, his hand out. He looked at me. "What are they? How are they moving?"

"They point the way to evil," Jamison said.

Nash had been an Unbeliever all his life, and even now that he knew magic was real, he didn't simply accept things without question. "What evil?"

"Me," I said.

"You're not evil. A pain in my ass, yes, but not evil."

"Haven't you been paying attention?" I asked him. "You saw my mother coming out of the vortex; you've watched me kill with my Beneath magic."

"To save other people's lives, yes. Your methods are not the most reassuring, but you're not evil."

I warmed at his praise, but I didn't think the *karmii* would take his word for it. Nash walked straight to the wall, ignoring me and Jamison, and put his hand right over a skeletal one.

He jerked but didn't pull away. Under his palm, the *karmii* squirmed like a bug trying to get out from under a boot. Light shot up Nash's arm, then dispersed as suddenly as it started. When Nash lifted his hand away, that *karmii* had vanished.

Just the one. The other thousand or so lingered, pulsing, watching, waiting.

"Did it burn you?" I asked. "Or give you frostbite?"

Nash showed me his hand, whole and unblemished.

"We need to go," Jamison said.

The *karmii* had stopped for now, but if they continued down the walls and reached the floor, they could flow through that to me. My leg ached with the memory of the *karmii*'s frozen touch, and that had been only one of them. What would happen if the entire horde poured over me, crawled up my legs, dragged me down? I shuddered, pivoted, and headed for the rockfall at the entrance.

Which was suddenly blocked by my sister, Gabrielle. "Hey, Janet," she said, giving me a wide smile. "Sheriff, you left your truck running." She held up her hand, the keys dangling from her fingers.

The *karmii* stopped for a split second, then they went insane. Another thousand or so sprang to life and homed in on my evil little half sister.

"Gabrielle!" I shouted.

She looked up, and for the first time since I'd known her, I saw her eyes fill with fear. The *karmii* whirled, silent in their fury, and dove straight at her.

I scrambled up the wall of fallen rock, grabbed Gabrielle, and started hauling ass up the tunnel. The *karmii* followed, flowing fast through the walls ahead of us. Could they follow us all the way out of the cave? When I'd left the sinkhole they hadn't come after me, but that didn't mean they couldn't.

The *karmii* lit the tunnel so brightly we didn't need a flashlight. Gabrielle ran, me right behind her. We reached one of the places where the floor rose toward the ceiling, and the *karmii* were waiting, filling the space. We'd have to try to squeeze past them, and they'd have us. Would they simply freeze us to death? Or keep us alive while they burned the skin from our bones?

"Let me." Nash shoved past me and Gabrielle and put his back to the wall.

I gasped as the *karmii* flowed behind him, his skin lighting with them until I could see the blood pulsing through his veins. The hands fled from him, bunching together on the opposite wall and the ceiling, waiting.

Nash grabbed Gabrielle and squeezed her between him and the space of the wall he'd cleared. As soon as Gabrielle touched the rock, the *karmii* tried to zoom back, but Nash shoved her hard, and she fell past, free of them. Giving Nash a look from her wide brown eyes, Gabrielle fled on up the tunnel.

"Janet." Nash was body squashing the *karmii* again. As soon as he'd cleared a space, he moved a body width, and I dove between him and the wall.

I scraped my flesh on rock and heard Nash swear as I dug him in the ribs. But Nash was strong, hard with muscle, and my little body flailing past him didn't faze him. As soon as I landed on the rock on the far side, he dove after me, hauled me to my feet and started pushing me ahead of him.

Jamison came behind with the flashlight, and when I glanced back I saw that the *karmii* were nowhere near him. No evil in Jamison, the earth-magic shaman.

I heard Gabrielle screaming. I tried to pick up the pace, but I was too slow for Nash. He squeezed past me and half-crouched, half-ran up the tunnel, sure-footed on the rocks. The *karmii* flowed rapidly past him like a river of light.

Jamison reached me, panting, and together he and I picked our way more cautiously up the tunnel, the *karmii* leaving us alone.

We caught up to Nash and Gabrielle at the entrance between the rocks. Nash was circling Gabrielle, trying to beat back the *karmii*, which filled the outer cave walls, roof, and floor. Nash could clear a foot, but as soon as Gabrielle stepped there, the *karmii* returned full force.

"Hey, *karmii*!" I shouted. "You want evil? Suck on this!"

I manifested a ball of Beneath magic—not difficult because I was scared out of my mind. I raised the light above my head, and the *karmii* froze. I threw the bright ball of magic far back into the cave, and the *karmii* went for it like beetles to a corpse. I conjured another one while Nash hustled Gabrielle out, and Jamison ran after them, still carrying the flashlight.

I threw my second ball of magic, turned, and sprinted out of the cave, praying I was right that the *karmii* couldn't follow us out into the open air. I had to brace myself on the thick rocks at the opening, and the *karmii* came for me. I pulled my hand away the split second before the skeletal fingers could touch me, the air of death brushing my skin.

I more or less fell out of the cave, rolling on rocks and snow and frozen ground until I landed on my back on flat land. Jamison held out his warm, solid, living hand and helped me to my feet.

I stood up, hanging on him while I tried to catch my breath. Gabrielle sobbed with terror. Nash's method of comforting her was to shake her by the shoulder and shout, "You're all right! Stop that."

Gabrielle flung her arms around Nash's neck and planted a kiss on his cheek. "Thank you, Sheriff. You saved my life."

Nash looked embarrassed and annoyed. "Just give me back my keys."

Gabrielle lifted them out of his reach with a little smile, and as she did so, something dove at us from the night, firing flame before it with the precision of a laser beam. The stream of fire hit Nash's SUV, and before we could move, the truck exploded into a blue white fireball.

The dragon that had targeted the truck winged his silent way skyward, no screech of triumph following. It was a huge black dragon with a silver white eye, Mick's fiery aura clinging to it like a second skin. He flapped his wings once and disappeared into the desert night, leaving us stunned, shivering, and Nash swearing in frustrated rage.

Nash called Lopez to come and get us, stating that the deputy had the only other vehicle in the county capable of traversing the road. Nash was furious, and stormed around in the snow, saying many choice words about dragons in general and Mick in particular. Hopi County didn't have a lot of money, and Nash had wrecked two trucks in the space of a week.

At least the oily fire was warm. I hunkered in my leather jacket and waited next to Jamison, who'd morphed back into a mountain lion to better take the cold.

"What dragon was that?" Gabrielle asked me in anger. "Can't your boyfriend keep them under control?"

I looked at her in surprise. "That was Mick."

"Really? What happened? You two have a fight?"

"No." I put my hand on Jamison's furry back, drawing strength from him as well as warmth. "Are you telling me you don't know?"

"Know what?" Gabrielle seemed genuinely confused. Maybe my grandmother was wrong about her involvement.

I swallowed, hating to say the words. "Mick has come under a witch's thrall. She enslaved him—I don't know why. I mean, I know she wants his power, but I don't know why she chose Mick."

Gabrielle stopped. "What witch?"

"Pretty sure it's a woman called Vonda Wingate."

Gabrielle's mouth dropped open. "*What?* That *bitch*! I'll kill her!"

"You do know her, then." So my grandmother and Elena hadn't been wrong after all.

Gabrielle's eyes flared green, and for a moment, I saw

my mother very clearly in her. "I'll kill her," she repeated, her voice low and firm.

The Beneath power was strong in her, and I knew she could kill Vonda without blinking. Which meant Mick would die too, and Gabrielle wouldn't care.

I grabbed for her, but Gabrielle stepped back, her face flooded with rage, and disappeared. My hands closed on empty air.

Damn it. I don't know how Gabrielle did that or where she went when she did. All I could do was stand at the end of a snow-covered road next to Nash's burning truck and fume and worry.

I knew Gabrielle hadn't reached Vonda Wingate, because when Lopez arrived with the fire department, he casually mentioned that Vonda and Ted had left the county that morning, Ted up and quitting his job. Where they'd gone, no one knew, but no one was very sorry they'd left.

Nash remained with the firemen to answer questions, and Lopez drove me and Jamison back home. My cell phone didn't work all the way out here—someone else had reported the fire, probably the owner of the ranch—or I would have called Colby and Drake to fly me out of there so I could hunt for Gabrielle.

As it was, I had to sit moodily in the back of Lopez's SUV with Jamison, dressed again, right next to me. While I wasn't a touchy-feely kind of girl, Changers liked to be tactile, touching for greeting, comfort, friendship, love. Jamison had comforted me, leaning against me in his mountain lion form as we waited; now he comforted me with his warm hand on my shoulder and his stoic silence.

It was dawn by the time Lopez dropped me off at the hotel. Jamison, tired, got back into the car to return to his own house, where I'm sure Naomi would first hug him, then ream him out for going to the caves by himself. Elena, up and dressed, made me a staggeringly wonderful breakfast while she and Grandmother grilled me about what had happened.

"The *karmii*," Grandmother said. "I might have known."

"What can they do?" I munched savory beans and eggs in fresh corn tortillas and washed it all down with rich coffee. "They didn't follow us out of the caves, but there were plenty of boulders for them to slide through just outside it."

"They thrive in darkness," Grandmother said. "They search for evil, and they absorb it. They don't like light or good earth magic, so they avoid it." Which explained why they'd fled from Mick's light spell in the sinkhole and didn't bother with Jamison at all.

"Can they be considered a good thing, then?" I asked. "If they absorb evil? They tried to kill Gabrielle." *And me.*

Elena returned to her stove. "*Karmii* are neutral things. Mindless. Shamans use them to detect the presence of evil, but *karmii* are tricky. If they believe the shaman has evil magic, they'll turn and kill him, even if he invoked the *karmii* to protect him. They have no mercy or compassion."

I'd seen Elena run people out of her kitchen at knifepoint without mercy or compassion. I supposed such things were relative.

"You saved Gabrielle," Grandmother said, giving me a hard look. "Why?"

I remembered my panic when I saw the hands flowing toward Gabrielle, and the real terror on her face.

"I don't know. I didn't want to watch them kill her. She doesn't deserve that."

"Why not?" Elena demanded. She turned from the stove, her spatula dripping. "She killed her own parents, after all."

Twenty

My hand jerked on my coffee cup. "What?" I rapidly reviewed the information Nash had spouted to us last night at this very table. "Nash said her parents had been killed in an accident while Gabrielle was living in Albuquerque."

Elena shrugged and turned back to whatever she was frying. "I had a long talk with my daughter about her last night. She remembers the incident plainly—I was working in New York at the time. Gabrielle was living in Albuquerque, yes, but she'd come home that day to argue with her parents about something. My daughter doesn't know what, but the Masseys' neighbors talked about screaming and shouting coming from their house. Then both Gabrielle's parents ran outside and jumped in the car, terrified, and drove away fast, her father driving, as drunk as he was. Gabrielle never came out, and no one in Whiteriver saw her again. But her parents drove into the mountains north of town and had the accident on one of the hairpin turns. Car flipped down the hill and burned. Gabrielle wasn't reported at the scene of the accident, but you tell me that she can appear and disappear at will."

I sat back, my chest tight. I imagined the Masseys, Gabrielle's human parents, frightened by their monster of a daughter, fleeing her, only to have her manifest in front of them on a mountain road. Her Beneath magic could certainly have wrecked the car, flipped it, burned it. I'd seen how casually she'd blown up Cassandra's car.

To be fair, Elena didn't know this for certain, going on four-year-old hearsay from neighbors and her daughter. The roads along the Rim could be perilous, especially in any kind of bad weather, and accidents happened. But I shivered as I met my grandmother's gaze.

"You see why you shouldn't defend her, Janet?" she asked.

I warmed my freezing hands on my coffee cup. "You thought I'd be like that, didn't you, Grandmother?"

"When your father carried you home, you stinking of Beneath magic? Of course I did."

"You could have killed me," I said. "No matter what Dad wanted."

"I could have." Grandmother acknowledged this with a nod. "But I also knew you had your father's blood, and Peter was always a good boy. My son has a river of kindness in him, as did his father."

I caressed my coffee cup to hide my surprise. Grandmother rarely talked about her late husband, my grandfather, who had died before I was born. There was one photo of Jacob Begay in the house, a stern-faced Navajo, long hair neatly braided, who looked much like my father. There was wisdom in my grandfather's face but not arrogance. He'd been the sort of man, my father had told me, who helped others without demanding anything in return, not even thanks or acknowledgment. The fact that he'd made someone else's life better was reward enough, my father had said.

Dad had always thought of himself as falling short of his father's legacy, no matter how hard he tried to be like him. The fact that my dad hadn't abandoned me, but kept me and raised me, without fuss or demands, in defiance of my grandmother, told me he'd achieved his father's status.

"I wish I'd met Grandfather," I said.

"You have. In your father. Which was another reason I

let Peter keep you. I didn't have the heart to take you away from him."

"Thank you for that."

"You proved yourself," Grandmother said. "Finally. Though you must be diligent at all times about your magic. And about Gabrielle. We need to find her and trap her. Go tell that witch of yours to come up with some kind of binding spell. She's good enough."

The words were a dismissal, my grandmother loving but never sentimental. I chewed the last bite of my meal, carried my dishes to the sink, and left her and Elena whispering together again.

Cassandra couldn't put a binding spell on Gabrielle if we couldn't find her, and I couldn't help Mick if I couldn't find him either. I went to the saloon to have a serious talk with the magic mirror.

"Micky doesn't have a piece of me with him," the mirror said. "I'd know. I bet the witch told him not to bring one, in case you could spy on them."

"Then why did he try to take you from me when we fought at his lair?"

"To use me against you. Micky wanted to kill you, honey, that was for sure."

He had. I'd seen it in his eyes.

"Could you help him get free if I could get you to him?" I asked.

"No, girlfriend. I'd still need his true name, and he never told it to me."

Wise of Mick. I wouldn't trust a magic mirror with something that powerful, especially a magic mirror as mouthy as ours. "He told me he saw the sheriff's department lift pieces of my bike out of the sinkhole. What happened to that mirror?"

The magic mirror hummed to itself for a few minutes. "Got it. It's in a big room. Dust. Not much light. Nowhere near Micky."

"A warehouse, maybe? Can you show me?"

More humming, then the mirror clouded over. When the mist cleared, I was looking at a strange angle down to a floor about six feet below. It was a warehouse, all right. Shelves, daylight filtered through dust, metal walls. Not a big one, because I could see three of the walls and blue sky outside the high windows. Probably storage at the sheriff's impound lot.

"Does Mick know it's there?"

"Don't ask me."

"I wasn't really." I chewed on my lip. "I was thinking out loud."

"Well, honey, how am I supposed to know the difference?"

"If Vonda wanted you, she would have sent Mick or Ted to fetch the piece by now. Which means that she doesn't consider you important."

"Not important? Oh, I am *so* offended."

"I mean you aren't what she's after. So why did she try to drive me out of the hotel?"

The mirror cleared its throat. "Are you asking me, or are you still thinking out loud?"

"I'm asking you. What's in this hotel that she could want?"

"Its location? It's on the Crossroads."

I knew it didn't mean the hotel's convenient placement at the intersection of two highways. The Crossroads was a magical crossroads, Jamison had told me, the defunct railway built along a ley line that traversed the desert. A magical place, where the line between the real and the psychic blurred.

"Could be." I'd have to ask Cassandra's opinion on that. But Vonda's motives were of secondary concern to me while Drake's twenty-four hours ticked by. Once I got to Mick, I could worry about what Vonda truly wanted.

The image of the warehouse shelving dissolved, and I found myself looking again at my thoughtful face, hair still damp from my shower, the saloon lit with morning light behind me.

"I'm going to the sheriff's department," I said. "Keep an

eye on the place, especially on Drake, and help Cassandra
with anything she needs, all right?"

"If I do all that, will you give me a good polish?"

I patted its frame. "Of course."

"Will you be naked?" it asked hopefully.

"No."

The mirror sighed. "I can never catch a break."

I caught a break because Maya arrived to continue
her work on the wiring, and she had no problem driving me
to Flat Mesa and the sheriff's department instead.

"How are things between you and Nash?" I asked her as
we drove up the cleared road.

The heavy snowfall was melting, but the land to either
side of the black strip was still white and unbroken. The sky
was white gray, but the clouds were thin and high, not storm
clouds. No blizzard today.

Maya shrugged. "All right, I guess. He took me to that
fancy restaurant in Winslow a couple weeks ago. We stayed
the night at the hotel."

Winslow had a Harvey Girls railroad hotel that had been
restored to its former glory, with a restaurant with food to
die for. "Romantic," I said.

"Briefly. Then we went home."

"Nash is getting used to having someone to care about,"
I said.

"Bullshit, Janet. Nash has had years to get used to me.
How much time does he need?"

"He's is afraid of powerful feelings, and the feelings he
has for you are powerful. I know about that kind of fear,
Maya. It's frightening to know that another person has such
control over your emotions, your very life. You try to push
away, but you never can do it."

"Is that what you did with Mick?"

"Pretty much. I walked out on him, stayed walked out for
years, because he'd had all the control in the relationship,
and I had none."

Maya looked at me, her beautiful eyes telling me she wanted to hope. "Are you saying that I have all the control with me and Nash? Are you serious?"

"You do, which is why he keeps pushing you away. He's not afraid of you taking care of him; he's afraid he'll like being taken care of, which to him means weakness. I think in that thick skull of his, he's afraid of weakness, because it might make his PTSD flare up again. Nash loves his job, and he doesn't want to lose it."

"Wow," Maya said, gripping the wheel. "I had no idea I was so threatening with my albondigas soup."

I grinned. "I'm not saying he's not an idiot. I'm saying you need to feel sorry for *him*, not yourself. Keep at him. You'll tame him."

"Janet, the relationship counselor."

"Yeah, I'm one to talk."

"I'm really sorry about Mick, but you know that he loves you. I've seen the way he watches you. He'd die for you."

Would I die for Mick? I hid my sudden tears by looking out the window at the bright snow. Yes, I thought I would. But I hoped I wouldn't be called upon to do it.

Lopez went with me to the impound and let me take the mirror from the box on the shelf. I swallowed as I saw the other pieces strewn in the boxes. Six years of my life, a pile of metal parts. I stuffed the mirror into the pocket of my leather jacket and left the warehouse.

"Jones wants to see you," Lopez said before I could re-join Maya.

"What for?" I asked, but Maya had heard and was already leaping down from her truck.

Without waiting for me, Maya strode into the sheriff's department and down the hall. I hurried after her, catching up to her on the threshold to Nash's office.

Maya walked inside, plopped down on one of the visitor's chairs, and yanked off her hat. Nash glanced at her briefly, without surprise, and transferred his gaze to me.

"Close the door."

I complied. "What's up?"

"I think I found Gabrielle. Where she's living now, anyway."

"Gabrielle?" I heard the sharpness in Maya's voice. "The one Janet claims is her half sister?"

"Severely dangerous half sister," I said. "Where?"

"Snowflake. Close enough to her home in Whiteriver, but far enough away that people might not recognize her. She's renting a room under an assumed name—Janet White."

I jumped, and the magic mirror in my pocket said, "Ooh, girlfriend, that's just mean."

"Her idea of a joke, maybe," I said.

Maya tapped her hat on her thigh. "Weird sense of humor."

"If she hadn't used that name, I might not have taken a closer look," Nash said. "My friend at the Snowflake police— I went to high school with him—told me there was a Native American woman of the same age who'd moved there a few months ago, calling herself Janet White. It raised my suspicions, so I followed up. She took a room with people renting out space behind their garage. She hasn't been there in the last couple of nights, though."

Woe to anyone who tries to hide out in a small town, where almost everyone drew pictures together in the first grade. I'd grown up in such a place, made even more fishbowl-like by connections—clan, cousins, grandparents, extended to the nth degree. Gabrielle would have been noticed and talked about, though if she kept to herself there was less risk that people in a town off the reservation would recognize or remember her.

But while Nash had provided a good lead, I doubted we'd find Gabrielle in Snowflake. She had disappeared last night vowing to kill Vonda Wingate, and I didn't doubt that Gabrielle was putting all her energy into hunting her.

"I put out a warrant for her arrest," Nash said, finishing.

"What for?" Maya asked.

"Blowing up my truck out on the S.J. Ranch."

Maya's mouth was a round O. "Your new black truck?"

"The sheriff department's SUV." Nash's mouth was a thin line. "Criminal damage to county property."

"Gabrielle didn't do that," I broke in. "Mick did."

Nash gave me an unblinking look. "I didn't see Mick out there last night. I saw Gabrielle."

"Mick was a dragon."

"There's no such thing as dragons," Nash said. "At least not according to Hopi County's judge. He'd rather I give him a vandal with a record of vandalizing than claim that the SUV was blown up by a fire-breathing dragon."

I opened my mouth to keep arguing, but Nash gave me a steely look and I stopped. Nash would do what he wanted.

"Fine," I said. "If your friend in Snowflake manages to corner Gabrielle, tell him to be damn careful. And call me. Maya, you need to take me home."

Maya was on her feet. "What about this Gabrielle and Nash on S.J. Ranch? Why didn't you bother telling me about that, Nash?"

I opened the door and all but dragged Maya from the office. "Nash was helping me find Jamison. I'll tell you about it on the way."

Maya gave Nash one final glare, which Nash returned with a spirited one of his own, and I pulled Maya out and down the hall. I swore those two would combust one day.

Out in the truck, I asked Maya, "What are you doing for the rest of the day?"

"Working for you. And listening to you explain about your half sister and Nash."

"And I promise to explain, if you drive me to Snowflake. I doubt Gabrielle will be there, but I'd like to have a look at where she's living."

Maya agreed with a little too much enthusiasm. As we left Flat Mesa and took a route around the sinkhole to the highway south, I told her about what had happened at the cave where Nash and I had found Jamison. Maya had been an Unbeliever, like Nash, for a long time, but she drank in my story. She couldn't hide her flash of pride when I explained how only Nash could make the *karmii* back off enough for us to get out safely.

Maya still wasn't thrilled that Nash hadn't told her

about the adventure, but she agreed with my need to find Gabrielle.

Snowflake sits on the highway from Holbrook to the mountains, on a fairly flat area of the plateau, the highway cutting through the heart of the old town. The town was so named, not because it gets much snow, but because its founders' last names were Snow and Flake. We passed tall statues that honored the men, and Maya turned off into a residential street.

"I don't remember Nash giving us an address," she said.

I shrugged. Nash hadn't given me the address because I knew he didn't want me trying to find Gabrielle myself. He had very firm ideas about what was police business and what was civilian business. "We'll ask around," I said.

I'd gotten very good at asking, in a casual way, for information. Before I'd moved to Magellan, I'd helped out people who were desperate to solve puzzles that the police couldn't or wouldn't—missing persons, strange hauntings, inexplicable events. Some problems turned out to be supernatural, some decidedly human. In any case, I often had to begin in a town I didn't know, with people I didn't know, and I'd learned to ingratiate myself. I wondered whether Gabrielle had learned the same skill.

It didn't hurt that Maya had a few friends here, and within half an hour, Maya and I had learned that Gabrielle was renting from people called Thompson. Maya, who knew the streets of the town better than I did, drove me back to a small house in a late-twentieth-century development.

The Thompsons looked normal enough, a late-middle-aged couple whose children had grown and gone. Photos of said son and daughter and grandchildren dotted every available surface, along with photos of the Thompsons vacationing and several group photos in front of a church.

They didn't know much about Gabrielle, however.

"She keeps to herself," Mrs. Thompson told me. "We don't see her often. Her room has a separate entrance, and she has her own key."

"Has she been here lately—in the last few days?"

Both Thompsons looked at me blankly. "Haven't talked to her," Mr. Thompson said. "You say you're friends of hers?"

"I never met her," Maya volunteered. "I'm just the driver."

"I'm a friend." I debated whether to float the "half sister" relationship, but decided not to. "I'm getting worried about her."

"Why?" the woman asked sharply. "Is she in trouble? She seems nice. What's she into?"

"Nothing." Well, besides Beneath magic, blowing up vehicles, and threatening to kill a witch I needed to keep alive for a while longer.

"She said she was Apache," Mrs. Thompson said. "Are you Apache?"

"Navajo," I answered, holding on to my patience.

"I thought you two tribes hated each other."

What kind of stuff did she read? "I really need to find Gabrielle," I said. "Can you let me into her room? She might have left some sign of where she was going."

"Sign?"

I nodded. I'd noticed the well-thumbed paperbacks beside an armchair, on ghosts and haunted places. "I'm a bit psychic."

The woman looked suddenly interested, and Mr. Thompson, who'd gone back to watching television, said, "Don't see why not. She doesn't have anything to steal."

I wondered how he knew that. Maya and I followed Mrs. Thompson out and down a flagstone path to a door behind the garage. She knocked on the door then opened it to reveal a small room, about ten feet square, that held a bed, a cabinet, a small chair, and not much else. Another door led to a tiny bathroom.

I felt a stab of pity for Gabrielle as I walked inside. The room was clean, the bed stocked with pillows and blankets, but the space was stark, without personality. No television, no books, no pictures. The bathroom held essentials only: toothbrush and toothpaste, soap, shampoo, hairbrush. No makeup, jewelry, perfume. It was as though Gabrielle went through the motions of being human but nothing beyond that.

Mrs. Thompson watched us curiously, then I told her I

could sense the vibrations better if we were alone. She left, still looking interested, and Maya rolled her eyes.

I noted that Gabrielle had put no warding over the doors, or anything that felt magical and would alert Gabrielle that someone had entered. I had to wonder why—either Mr. Thompson was right that she had nothing to steal, or else Gabrielle felt safe from all comers. Or she simply didn't care.

Maya sat on the bed, while I went into the bathroom again to open the medicine cabinet. Nothing in that either, not even aspirin. I wondered whether Gabrielle got magic hangovers as I did or if she managed to avoid them. She certainly hadn't stocked up on painkillers.

"Janet."

Maya's voice held a strange note. I left the bathroom to find her standing in front of the cabinet that she'd opened. I stopped.

Gabrielle kept no clothes in her closet, not even empty hangers. Instead, the walls and doors were coated with newspaper clippings, blown-up photos, printouts from Internet sites, and glossy sheets from magazines. The subject of these photos wasn't me, but the stern face and cool gray eyes of Hopi County's handsome sheriff, Nash Jones.

Twenty-one

It was a bizarre shrine. Gabrielle had taken some of the photos herself: of Nash's house, of him walking out to go to work, of him washing his truck in his driveway, clad in shorts and shoes and nothing else. One had been snapped through Nash's half-open blinds while he pumped iron on his exercise machine. The others came from articles on Jones as the youngest sheriff ever elected to Hopi County, on Jones the war vet, on Jones who'd made drug busts, uncovered a human traffic smuggling ring from Mexico, stopped small-arms dealers, and generally kept the populations of Flat Mesa and Magellan safe. Handsome Nash in his uniform, shooting at the range, Nash driving his SUV over desert roads, Nash talking into his radio.

"She's stalking him," Maya said, her face stark with shock. "She's stalking *my* boyfriend."

I sat down on the bed, my legs suddenly weak. "Yeah, she is. We need to tell him."

"How can you be so calm? Why is she doing this? What does she want?"

I remembered the woman in the hospital in Flagstaff who'd claimed to be Nash's mother. She'd gone for Nash before Mick had killed her, but I don't think she'd been human. I still wasn't certain what she'd been, but she'd fed on my Beneath magic and became stronger. I'd assumed the woman had been trying to kill Nash, but now I wondered whether Gabrielle had sent her to kidnap him.

"I'm pretty sure Gabrielle wants to have his baby," I said.

"His *baby*?" Maya's eyes were wide in outrage and fear. "What the fuck?"

"Nash negates the most powerful magic out there," I said. "A child from a woman with pure Beneath magic, coupled with the DNA of someone who can absorb all magic, would be damn powerful. My mother—my real mother— wanted that too. She wanted me to couple with Nash and bring her the resulting child."

Maya's already wild eyes went rounder. *"What?"*

"I stopped her. Mick and I stopped her."

"When the *hell* did this happen?"

"Last May. Mick and I made sure she failed, but if my mother has sent Gabrielle in my place . . ." I got to my feet. "We need to find her."

Maya slammed herself between me and the door. "Nash never told me this. *You* never told me this. How could you not tell me?"

"I'm sorry." I was truly sorry, because Maya didn't deserve any of this, but I needed to worry more about Gabrielle right now. "Of course Nash wasn't going to confess that he was almost raped by a crazed goddess, if he even understood half of what was going on."

"What about you?" Her dark eyes flashed pain, betrayal, fury. "What, did you *forget* that your mother wanted you to get pregnant by my boyfriend?"

"I didn't want you to know about it once he was safe. You and Nash have enough problems."

"Problems that are none of your business." She stabbed a

slender finger at me. "Don't you think I deserved to know? What else has gone on with Nash that you haven't told me? Is he secretly married to someone else? Has he had a sex change? Come on, Janet, you seem to know everything there is to know about Nash Jones, while I—the woman he's *dating*, for crap's sake—know next to nothing."

"I know that he's in love with you and always has been," I said.

"Oh, right, Janet. You claimed not an hour ago that I had all the control in my relationship with Nash. Explain to me how I'm supposed to believe that, when crazy magical women are after his sperm? Because of his ability to *not* do magic? It's the stupidest thing I've ever heard."

I pressed my palms together, forefingers to my lips. "I'm sorry, Maya. I really am sorry. You can hate me later, but right now, I need to find Gabrielle, and I need to warn Nash. He's thinking that she's nothing but a petty vandal, but if he arrests her, and she's in his custody . . ."

Maya screamed in fury. She shoved her way past me and attacked the papers taped to the cabinet walls. She ripped and clawed, shredding the images of Nash into so much confetti. I should have stopped her, but I didn't have the heart. Let her get back at Gabrielle as best she could. When I next faced Gabrielle, I didn't want Maya anywhere near her.

"Will this help?" I handed Cassandra a folded piece of paper with strands of Gabrielle's hair I'd taken from the hairbrush in her bathroom.

Cassandra studied the black threads of hair and nodded. "It will. For both location and binding."

Hence why leaving behind traces—hair, nail parings, anything—was a bad idea. Witches can use them to find a person's essence, or to bind or manipulate the person. I was surprised at Gabrielle's lack of caution—no wards on the doors, her hairbrush in plain sight. But maybe she simply didn't know. Beneath magic, which was pure energy, was very different from witch magic, which used the connectedness of all things to work effective spells. I'd known nothing of witch magic before I met Mick, and Gabrielle hadn't had the training I had.

Cassandra started her spells in my private third-floor office, and Maya planted herself in the lobby, so she'd be on hand the moment Cassandra located Gabrielle. Maya had never had much faith in Wiccan magic before, but now she resolutely waited for the results.

I called Nash and told him that by no means was he to approach Gabrielle, and if any of his connections found her, they were to call me first. I told him what I'd found in her room, and I told him why I thought she was stalking him. I'm not sure he believed me, but he sounded a bit unnerved.

"I know how to do my job, Janet," he snapped over the phone.

"Jones, she's not a perp with a pocketful of meth. *You* might be able to withstand her magic, but your deputies can't, and the police in Snowflake can't. You should call off the warrant before someone tries to arrest her and gets killed."

Letting a criminal get away was not in the Nash Jones codebook, but he growled, "For once, I think you're right. But if I see her, I'll do my best to make her answer for what she's done."

"If you see her, you *call me*."

"Fine."

Jones hung up on me. I wasn't sure if he meant he'd call me first, or if he'd try take Gabrielle down and call me afterward.

Drake and Colby were still upstairs, Drake honoring his twenty-four-hour window with dragon stubbornness. Dragons never went back on their word, but if I didn't find Mick and free him in the next eight hours, the same dragon honor would send Drake back to the council to round up a posse to hunt down the witch and kill her, no matter what that did to Mick.

I had to find Mick before they did. My mind was a jumbled mess, worries clogging my thoughts. Gabrielle and Drake both wanted the witch dead, and neither was bothered much by the fact that her death would kill Mick. I knew

I needed to be calm and think, but when I closed my eyes, trying to find the meditation exercises Jamison had taught me once upon a time, they eluded me. I could only feel the weight of the silver onyx-and-turquoise ring Mick had slid on my finger as his pledge to me and wonder if I'd ever see Mick's bad-boy smile again.

I studied the ring. Turquoise for protection, healing. Onyx for more protection, and silver for love. The stones flowed around the ring in a pattern for strength, courage, and again, protection.

I kissed the ring softly, then let my gaze focus on it, reaching again for my meditative state. It cut my heart to study Mick's beautiful gift to me, but at the same time it made me realize that he was still part of me.

As I concentrated on the ring, the power of the stones became visible, like heat waves in a desert summer. Linked, intertwining: protection, healing, love, all laced with the tiniest bite of Mick's fire magic.

I brought the ring to my cheek, closing my eyes again. Mick's magic, the merest touch, kissed my skin, and I opened my eyes and looked at the ring.

Mick had given me this right after both Maya and Pamela had reported seeing him with Vonda, just before he'd had to go to her. Some part of him had known, even if his conscious mind hadn't remembered his encounters with her, that he was being taken. He'd given me a ring filled with protective magic, and laced it with a tiny bit of dragon magic.

I took off the ring and examined it closely, pouring my concentration into the stones. Had Mick left clues for me in it? Maybe a piece of his name or an idea where to find it?

If he had, I wasn't able to unlock the secret, no matter how much I probed and concentrated, no matter how deeply I tried to meditate. I found no music that might be a dragon name, no part of Mick to tell me where he was, or even if he were still alive.

Damn it. I balled my fist, brought it down on my desk, and left the office.

I went back to the bedroom and started going through the

drawers that held Mick's belongings, looking for clues, anything. Like Gabrielle, Mick traveled light, having nothing more than spare jeans and shirts, socks and underwear, hairbrush, toothbrush. Nothing that he'd poured his true name into to sing to me as soon as I touched it.

I made the mistake of lifting one of his T-shirts to my nose. It smelled first of the laundry but then of Mick, his scent, his fire. I sank to my bed, hugging that shirt and burying my face in it.

I would get him back. I would lie in this bed with him again and wrap my arms around him while he smiled down into my face and made my body sing. I didn't care what I had to do or what kind of magic I had to use. I would bring him home.

"Janet."

Pamela stood in my doorway, and I didn't even question that she was back in the hotel. Where Cassandra went these days, so did Pamela. "Cass said to tell you she made a breakthrough."

I folded Mick's shirt carefully and put it back into the drawer before following Pamela out into the lobby. Maya tossed aside the magazine she'd been pretending to read and went upstairs with us.

Cassandra sat cross-legged in the middle of my third-floor office, a map of Arizona and New Mexico spread before her and strewn with black sand. Cassandra looked out of place on the floor in her business suit and no shoes, slim legs folded, smudges of black on her silk blouse. Her eyes were tired.

"You're not going to like this," she said as I entered.

"Why not?"

"I found her, and she's still there." Cassandra pointed at a red dot on the map.

I leaned closer and saw that the dot lay next to the words "Flat Mesa." The dot pulsed. Cassandra moved her hand, and that bit of the map enlarged outward, as though she used the zoom function on a computer. The streets of Flat Mesa separated and became distinct, even showing houses and trees and cars. Cassandra stopped the map on a long, low ranch house set back from the road with a black F-250 parked in front of it.

Maya made a noise of anguish and ran out of the room. I lunged after her, but my cell phone rang. For once I had it with me, and the caller ID readout said "Jones."

I slammed it to my ear, but I heard a woman's voice, not Nash's.

"Hey, big sis. You need to get over here right now and bring your wicked Wicca. Better hurry, or Jones and I will go one on one." A click, and she was gone.

Twenty-two

We had a hell of a time convincing Maya and Pamela to stay behind. I didn't want volatile Maya anywhere near Gabrielle, because Gabrielle might simply kill her without blinking. Pamela wouldn't have a much better chance.

I finally convinced Pamela that she needed to keep Maya safe, and Colby, also chafing because he couldn't leave the house without Drake, agreed to keep an eye on both of them. All three of them watched us go, not happy, Pamela growling and swearing under her breath. But muscle wouldn't help us against Gabrielle, only magic, and I wasn't certain even Cassandra and I together would be strong enough.

We took the rental car Cassandra was using to Flat Mesa. Cassandra drove, and good thing too, because she drove calmly and kept the car on the road. I'd never have been able to.

Darker clouds were gathering to the north and east, dimming the light. A storm would give me some advantage, though it might not be enough.

Nash's house looked quiet enough when we reached it. He'd cleared his driveway and front walk, the yard looking neat even draped in snow. We walked to the front door without bothering with stealth, found the door unlocked, and entered the house.

Nash was sitting on the bench of his exercise machine when we walked in. A handcuff enclosed one wrist; the second of the pair was locked around an upright support bar of the machine. Gabrielle sat on a bar stool at the breakfast bar, eating a sandwich and looking at one of Nash's gun magazines.

"This looks nice," she said, holding up a picture of an automatic rifle. "What does it do?"

"Guns drive me crazy," I said, moving to her. I rested my arm on the breakfast bar and squarely met her gaze. "If you don't fire them right, they kick, and the chemicals and metal interfere with magic."

"Really?" Gabrielle turned a page, studied another weapon, and closed the magazine. "That's interesting. You brought the witch. Good. I need you to do something for me."

"Let Nash go, and we'll discuss it."

Gabrielle smiled. The silly look she'd affected around Nash during our previous encounters had vanished. She was hard and dangerous and no longer played. "Nash is mine. He's my reward for all the trouble I've gone to."

"Your reward will be me letting you live," I said. "Maybe."

I purposely didn't let my magic build—actually, I beat it down as it rose with my panic. If Gabrielle thought me ready to fight, to kill, she might hurt Cassandra and Nash. Gabrielle couldn't harm Nash magically, but she could blow up his house or shoot him with one of his many guns.

Cassandra whispered rapidly under her breath. She'd caught me off guard with a powerful binding spell last year, and she let fly one just as powerful at Gabrielle.

Gabrielle casually held up her hand. The binding spell hit whatever force Gabrielle shoved in front of it, and the spell rushed back toward Cassandra with blinding speed. Cassandra gasped and snapped off the spell the instant before its returning web could touch her.

Damn. Why couldn't I do things like that?

"I didn't ask you to bring the witch so she could bind me," Gabrielle said in a hard voice. "I need her to do a locator spell, to find Vonda Wingate."

Cassandra tucked back a wisp of hair that had escaped during her spell attempt. "Don't you think I've been trying? I've been doing locator spells on her for two days. She's shielding herself, and doing it very well."

"Plus she has Mick's magic to help her," I said. "Mick knows amazing defensive spells." Spells he'd showed to me. I wanted to die with grief.

"I know that Vonda has Mick," Gabrielle snapped. "And she will pay—oh, she will pay for going behind my back like this."

"I'm starting to not much care what you do to her." I sounded so calm I amazed myself. "But I won't let what you do hurt Mick."

"Whatever. She enslaved him so she could use him to kill me. Well, guess what? Vonda's not taking *me* out, I'm taking her out. She's not getting her hands on my prize."

We both looked at Nash, who scowled back. "Janet, get me out of these cuffs. Now."

"Do it and I kill Cassandra," Gabrielle said.

I folded my arms. "If you kill Cassandra, she won't be able to do your locator spell."

"Then I'll find another witch," Gabrielle said impatiently. "Cassandra's here because she's handy."

My blood heated. "Is that how you see people? Handy for when you need something?"

"Don't you?"

I didn't answer, not liking the nasty feeling that she might be right.

No. I shoved the thoughts aside. Gabrielle was trying to get under my skin.

"Let Nash go, and we'll help you find Vonda," I said. "I want to find her myself."

Gabrielle grinned again, the smile wrinkling her nose. "We'll get her, sis. Don't you worry. If Cassandra does well, I'll let her go. But Nash stays with me."

"I won't bargain with my friends' lives. They go free, no matter what."

Gabrielle's eyes hardened. "I came to this county for one reason, and one reason only. That reason is Nash. Vonda is busy fucking things up, and I need to stop her, but sorry, Nash belongs to me."

"You can't bind Nash, Gabrielle. You can't fight him. He can resist anything magical you do to him. You can't win this one."

Gabrielle gave me a patronizing look. "I can threaten his lover, can't I? Nash will do anything to keep that Hispanic bitch safe. Anyway, it isn't him I need but his seed. So I can give Mother the child she truly wants."

Nash stopped rattling the handcuffs and stared, his gray eyes like chips of ice. "What the hell?"

"Gabrielle," I said. "Listen to me. You don't need to worry about pleasing our mother. She's locked behind the vortex anyway. You can't get to her—she's no longer a part of us."

"Don't be an idiot, Janet. She's not dead, and we certainly can get to her. You and I are powerful enough to open the vortex together, whenever we want. I'll take Nash and our child to Mother, and this time, she won't turn me away."

In the heavy pause that followed, I heard the wind pick up outside, not with the might of a storm, but in a nice, steady, chill breeze.

"She turned you away?" I asked, forcing myself to sound unruffled. "I hadn't realized you'd met her."

Gabrielle nodded. "It was four years ago, in your little town of Magellan, at that stupid Ghost Train festival the wannabe Wiccans have at Christmas. I was thrilled to finally meet her, but you know what?" She stopped, the hurt in her eyes vast and troubling. "Mother didn't want me. I hadn't turned out right, she said, because what she needed was a daughter with a combination of Beneath and earth magics. That's what it takes to open the vortexes. My father, she said, had only pretended he'd had shaman powers. He'd tricked her. And so I was useless to her."

Four years ago. And four years ago, Gabrielle Massey's

parents died in an accident on a lonely highway. "Is that why you killed them?" I asked softly.

Gabrielle couldn't meet my gaze. "I was so angry. I finally knew why I was different, why I had all this incredible power inside me, but Mother didn't want me because the man whose seed I came from lied to her about being a shaman. Massey *lied* to her so he could have sex with her—while he was already married, by the way, to Anna, a very kind woman. I went home and told him what I knew. The stupid drunk. They were on that road because he was running away from me. He was terrified of me. I didn't flip the car. When I stepped out in front them, he couldn't stop, and they went off the side. I never touched them."

The pain in Gabrielle's eyes was worn, yet still fresh, as she relived a memory that had never lost its sharpness.

"I'd always hated him," she said in a broken voice, "but I'm sorry about my mom. His wife, I mean. Anna couldn't have children, and she raised me, even though she didn't understand what I was."

Cassandra and Nash watched us, their stillness filling the room. I couldn't help picturing Gabrielle standing on the dark road, watching in horror while the car rolled down the mountainside, seeing the people who'd taken care of her since babyhood suddenly wiped from her life.

"Gabrielle," I said, my voice firm. "You don't want to be with our mother. She's evil, and I mean evil in the purest sense of the word. She has no concept of anything but coldness. She won't accept you, and she won't love you, no matter what you do, no matter who you bring her."

"You don't get it, Janet." Gabrielle sneered at me. "I don't want to be *loved*. I want what she offered you. Mother was ready to give you all the power in the world, to let you have anything you wanted, to have you live by her side as a goddess. And you said no." Gabrielle got up off the stool. "You said no, you stupid bitch, and you sealed her in. You took what I wanted, what should have been *mine*, and you threw it away."

White power crackled in Gabrielle's hands. Gods, I wanted to knock her over the head. She needed a good talking-to about evil and the ways of hell-goddesses. *After* I got my friends free of her.

"What she offered me was a sham," I said. "Mother didn't want me ruling by her side; she wanted to use me to give her Nash."

Gabrielle rolled her eyes. "So? Haven't you learned, Janet, that in this life, you have to take what you can get? No one gives you anything. Nothing is free. If the price of the power that should be yours is capturing a handsome sheriff, good enough for me."

I knew one thing—though I felt somewhat sorry for Gabrielle, that didn't mean I'd hand her Nash or help her open the damn vortexes. Gabrielle might want to confront our mother to get over her abandonment issues, but I couldn't risk the fate of the entire planet so Gabrielle could play Mom-likes-me-best.

"Tell you what," I said. "We'll help you find Vonda. You help me get Mick free. Then you can do what you want to Vonda. That's the only bargain I'm making right now."

"Who cares about Mick? I need to stop Vonda. She's snared herself a dragon so she can kill me. I have to find her and kill her first."

"Why should she want to kill you? What did you do to her?"

Gabrielle heaved an aggrieved sigh. "I didn't do anything to her. My mistake picking a witch with delusions of grandeur. She'll use Mick to eliminate me and go after what she wants."

"Which is what?"

"Hell if I know. When we find her, we can ask her."

"Only if you let Nash go," I said doggedly.

Gabrielle hopped back onto the stool. "Sorry, sis. I'll spare you and your precious friends, but Nash is mine."

"No, bitch," Maya's voice came from the front door. "Nash is *mine*."

Nash rose as far as he could from the bench, yanking at the handcuffs. "Maya, get the hell out of here!"

Maya had a gun in her hands, which I recognized as the semiautomatic with which she'd once tried to shoot me.

I didn't pause to puzzle over how Maya had gotten away from Pamela, because Pamela herself was coming up the driveway.

"Maya, I've got this," I said. "Turn around and get out of here, and take Pamela with you."

Maya fired. She had a damn good aim. The bullet went straight for Gabrielle, and would have slammed through her chest if Gabrielle hadn't thrown up a shield of magic to deflect it.

The bullet stopped, stuck in the bubble of Beneath magic as though suspended in resin. Gabrielle studied the bullet curiously, then moved her gaze to Maya.

"Good shot, *chica*." Gabrielle's hand came up, and her Beneath magic sailed, clear and true, toward Maya.

I leapt the short distance to Maya and tackled her. We both went down, and Gabrielle's magic blasted out the front-door frame, making Pamela dive aside. A tail of the Beneath magic caught me on the arm, and I grunted in pain. My own Beneath magic rose in me like fury, ready to strike back.

I reached for the wind instead. The approaching storm was still weak, but I found wind and falling snow and streamed them through my hands. I knew, based on what we'd done out on the highway, that if I started a Beneath magic fight with my little sister, we'd destroy Nash's house and half the neighborhood.

Gabrielle's defenses wavered under my Stormwalker magic, and I saw her realize that I wasn't as weak as she'd thought. Furious at my attack, she wound up into a Beneath magic rage.

"No!" I shouted. "We can't do this here."

Cassandra made it to Nash's side. I smelled a bite of witch magic as she opened the handcuffs. Nash was up, making for Gabrielle. Pamela, eyes wolf white, was right behind him.

"Nash, no!" I yelled. "Stop! We all have to stop."

"I want her out of my house." Nash kept moving fearlessly toward Gabrielle, ready to pick her up and bodily throw her out.

I grabbed him. "You can bounce her all the way out of Hopi County later, but as much as I hate to admit it, I need her to help me with Mick."

"Why?" Maya asked. She pushed hair out of her face and climbed to her feet, still holding the gun. "She said she didn't care if Mick died. I heard her."

"I'm going to make damn sure Mick doesn't die. But Vonda is a powerful witch with a dragon, and Gabrielle can keep her busy while I do what I need to do."

"I told you, Janet, I'm going to kill Vonda," Gabrielle said. "You can't stop me."

"Fine, as long as you wait until Mick is free. Maya, go home. Pamela, take her. Neither of you can help. Cassandra, start that locator spell." I shoved Nash's magazines to the floor, clearing a space on the counter.

Maya's dark eyes snapped in rage. "I'm not going anywhere. Not while this bitch can't keep her hands off my boyfriend."

Gabrielle smiled at her. "I'll make him happier than you ever can, sweetie. When Nash gives me his baby, I'll make him a god."

Maya sighted down the pistol at Gabrielle. "The only one having Nash's baby is me."

I saw Nash have an uh-oh-did-I-forget-the-condom moment, before he realized Maya was speaking metaphorically. "Maya, for God's sake, do what Janet says," he growled.

"I refuse to step meekly aside while this person tries to rape you. She can't do it if I have a gun pointed at her brain."

I had to admire Maya's courage. She was the only non-magical person in this room, and she'd already seen what Gabrielle could do. I cursed Maya's stubborn stupidity at the same time, but admitted she had guts.

"Maya, if you're staying, sit down over there and keep out of the way," I said. "Pamela, make sure she doesn't shoot anyone. Gabrielle, you stand here next to me, and I swear to the gods, if you touch anyone in this room, I'll fry you so fast you won't know what happened. Cassandra, start the spell."

Cassandra, the calmest of all of us, spread out her map

and opened a vial of black powder. "Fine," she said. "I'll need to borrow some salt."

Cassandra couldn't find Vonda. She tried many different variations of her spell, but at each attempt, her black sand and white salt lay in neat piles on the map and didn't move. We postulated that Nash's non-magic might be interfering, but taking the map out far behind the house and performing the spell again did nothing.

"She's shielding, and the shields are strong," Cassandra said. "Plus, I don't have anything personal of hers."

"Try to find the dragon then," Gabrielle said. "We can follow him to her."

"You can't find Mick with a locator spell," I answered. I knew this from experience. Once, during the five years Mick and I had been apart, I'd gone to a witch and asked her to locate Mick—I told myself that I simply wanted to see that he was all right. But I'd been missing him, heartsore, and I wanted to know where he was. The witch, a good one, had never been able to find him. It turned out that Mick had been very close, as usual, watching me, but he'd instinctively shielded the locator spell. All dragons did that, he told me later.

"We'll go to the witch's house then," Gabrielle said, brow furrowed. "See whether she left something behind that will help us."

"Not if she's a good witch, which she obviously is," Cassandra answered. "I keep my own apartment meticulously clean, knowing that one stray hair could betray me."

That explained part of Cassandra's fastidiousness. I suspected, though, that she'd be as neat as she was regardless.

"What about Ted?" I asked. "He's human. She'd shield him when he was near her, but the minute he's out of her range, would he show up? And then lead us back to her? Can you—I don't know—cast a timed spell that will show Ted as soon as he's out from under her shield?"

I knew as soon as Cassandra looked at me that she was a powerful witch indeed. She didn't even flinch at my crazy suggestion but nodded thoughtfully. "I've never done that, but I could try it. I warn you that she might be able to cast a spell that shields him always, no matter how far he gets from her; plus I'd need something of Ted's. A shirt, nail parings, a sample of his handwriting."

Maya reached into her back pocket and pulled out a folded piece of paper. "How about this?"

It was the list Ted had made of the faults of my hotel. The paper showed boxes ticked with neat checkmarks, and Ted's comments written with sharp up-and-down letters. Maya had the original.

"Perfect." Cassandra smoothed out the paper, writing side down, on the map. "This might take a while, so I urge you, don't interrupt me."

"Sure thing." Gabrielle straightened from where she'd been leaning on the counter and walked purposefully down the hall to Nash's bedroom.

Nash strode immediately after her, and Maya, with a snarl of anger, charged after him. Pamela folded her arms and leaned against the counter, two feet from Cassandra's side.

Nash had guns back there, and Maya still had hers. Gods, I wanted to put a binding spell on the lot of them.

Cassandra found Ted Wingate after a few hours—whether Vonda hadn't shielded him, or Ted wasn't with her at all, or Cassandra was just that good, I never knew. She put her finger on a line on the map of New Mexico and said, "He's there."

There, I saw when we zoomed in, was a casino and hotel run by one of the small New Mexico tribes, located on a back highway, a little off the beaten path. I'd stayed there before, when my peripatetic life took me along New Mexico's byways. The turnoff to the hotel was about ten miles east of Gallup, which meant nearly two hours from Flat Mesa.

"Will they still be there when we get there?" I asked. "Or are they making a pit stop?"

Cassandra rubbed her forehead, streaking it with her

black powder. "I'm not good enough to know that. But they must be there for a reason, because Mick could fly them anywhere they'd want to go. Either that or Ted's on his own, nowhere near his wife or Mick."

"I'd like to talk to Ted, regardless," I said with determination. "If he's alone, he can't move any faster than we can."

"We have dragons," Cassandra pointed out. "Colby and Drake."

Letting Drake fly us there—he would never let Colby do it without him—would be risky. Drake might take the opportunity to kill Vonda while he had the chance, screw his deadline, which was four hours from now. Or Vonda might be able to discover Drake's and Colby's names and trap them as well. I still had no idea how she'd known Mick's. Then we'd have three dragons to face instead of one.

I explained this to Cassandra. She nodded as she lifted the edges of the map and poured the powder and salt into a bowl. "Then we drive."

Twenty-three

Again convincing Maya to stay behind was difficult. I needed Cassandra with me, and I didn't want to let Gabrielle out of my sight. I also needed Nash, who would be my most formidable weapon.

"I want you and Pamela here," I argued with Maya. "You have to make sure Drake doesn't come after us, but tell Colby to watch in the magic mirror without Drake knowing. If everything goes to hell, we might need to call the dragons in, regardless."

Maya was furious. "You can tell Colby that on the phone. You don't need me to deliver messages."

"I also want to know what Grandmother and Elena are up to. They've been entirely too secret in that kitchen of theirs. And I need someone to try to find Coyote."

"Anything else?" Maya asked sourly.

"I think that about covers it. Ask Fremont to help you, and tell Colby to stay alert."

I made a move toward Nash's truck, but Maya stepped in

front of me. "Janet, Nash thinks he's invincible for some reason, and I don't mean against magic. He has this idea in his head that he can't be hurt. Either that or he doesn't care that he can be." She shot a vicious glance at Gabrielle, who was climbing into the backseat of Nash's pickup. "Nash isn't stupid enough to fall for Gabrielle, but he is stupid enough to think she's harmless."

"I know." I gave her shoulders a squeeze. "Believe me, Maya, I'll keep her far away from him. I don't trust Gabrielle an inch, which is why I want her right next to me. And a long way from you."

I stopped before I said anything sentimental, like "You're my only girlfriend, and I don't want to lose you."

"You bring him back safe to me," Maya said, scowling. "Or we'll have words."

"I will. I promise. Don't linger here; go back to my hotel with Pamela. The witch can't touch you there, but she might figure out what we did and backtrack Cassandra's spell to Nash's house. You'll be safer at the hotel."

She gave me a look full of fire. "And when you come back, we'll talk about what else you haven't told me about Nash and these women who want to make babies with him."

I raised my hands. "Fine. I'll bring the tequila."

She flashed a sudden smile at me, remembering our first girls' night at her house. We'd started out enemies and ended up . . . lesser enemies and very drunk.

I looked at Maya for a few seconds, then on impulse I grabbed her in a hug. Neither she nor I liked girly-girl hugs, but her arms came around me, and she held me tightly for a moment.

"Go," I said, and ran for the truck.

Because Nash drove, we cruised the speed limit all the way, neither above nor below. Cassandra and I sat in the front seat with Nash, while Gabrielle lounged behind us on the half seat. When I'd ridden in this truck last fall, Nash had stashed in it a first aid kit that could have supplied an emergency room, plus enough gear for a seven-day hike in the

remotest part of the earth. A glance in the back showed me
the large first aid kit was still locked in place. Good thing,
because we might need it.

The road into New Mexico from Holbrook ran straight
across fairly flat land, the road bisected at times by shallow
canyons. As we approached Gallup, canyon walls rose to
line the freeway, and with them, the storm clouds. Snow began to fall gently as we approached Gallup and then passed
it, the freeway looping away from the town.

I pressed my hand to the window, smiling to see the flakes
of snow home in on my fingers. I let them go, not wanting
to endanger us as we sped on into growing darkness.

The winter light faded, by the time we pulled into the
parking lot of the hotel and casino, ten miles south and east.
The high-rise hotel with its huge lighted sign was incongru-
ous on this lonely stretch of road through a river canyon, with
mountains rising to the south. But these days, tribes needed
the money casinos brought in, especially the smaller tribes
that had no other resources, and so there existed a swank
hotel in the middle of nowhere.

We walked in to lights and noise and a swirl of people.
We were a disparate bunch, Nash in his workout clothes,
Gabrielle and I in jeans and leather jackets, Cassandra in her
skirt suit with tasteful black pumps and turquoise jewelry.
The clerk behind the desk blinked once, but her training took
over, and she asked in a friendly voice whether she could
help us.

As a hotel owner, I'd learned that, for both security and
to protect your own liability, you never volunteer information about your guests. If someone asks to see a guest, you
call the guest's room yourself and don't give out the room
number. If no one answers in the room, you offer to leave
a message from the inquirer. The last thing you want is for
some crazed stalker to go charging upstairs, endangering
your patrons.

I wasn't sure how to ask whether Ted was here without
alerting him, but I saw Gabrielle open her mouth to simply
demand they hand over Ted, Vonda, and Mick. I pulled her

out of the way and let Cassandra smile and Nash take out his badge and show it to the woman behind the desk.

"You're no fun, Janet," Gabrielle said as we walked away. "We're all-powerful, half-goddess women. We should be able to take what we want whenever we want it."

"You watch too many movies."

"What else is there to do in Snowflake? Oh, look, video poker."

I felt like a mother with an unruly teenager. I let Gabrielle plop onto a padded stool in front of a poker machine. She slid a credit card into a slot, which I couldn't grab before she'd fed it in. The lights blinked and the computer dealt a hand.

"Is that your credit card?" I demanded. "Do you even have any money?"

"Relax, big sis. I have plenty of money stashed away, and I lifted the credit card from Nash."

I dove for the button that would cancel the game, but she batted my hand away. "Just one. He won't even miss it." She picked the cards she wanted to keep, chose her bet, and pushed the button for the next deal. Three different cards came up, none matching what she already had.

"You bet twenty dollars on a pair of twos?" I asked. "Someone needs to teach you how to play cards."

"I know how to play cards. It's called gambling. The bigger the risk, the greater the thrill."

I canceled the next hand and pulled her off the stool. "Risk your own money. Besides, I see Ted."

Ted was playing blackjack. My annoying hotel inspector with his tan and his golden brown hair flashed his charming smile at the dealer, a young woman who kept her smile neutral while she dealt him another card. Ted was winning, chips stacked in neat piles next to his hand.

The young woman turned over her own cards, a nine and a three, followed by a king. "House busts," she announced. She passed chips to Ted and two others at the table.

Ted chuckled and raked his win toward his pile. "That's all right, little lady. Maybe you'll get me next time."

Gabrielle scooted onto a chair next to Ted, boldly took one of his chips, and pushed it at the young woman. "Deal me in."

"Hey." Ted's glare softened into a smile as he looked Gabrielle up and down, obviously not knowing who she was. "Well, now, I guess I don't mind if you want to sit next to me, little gal."

Ick. I leaned on the table on Ted's other side. "Hi, Ted."

Ted swung around, and all the color drained from his face.

I smiled. "Be careful how you talk to my sister."

"Your sis—" Ted broke off.

I drew on the storm outside, which had started swirling in earnest, and showed Ted, under the table, the white ice whirling in my fingers.

"Sit tight," I told him. "Let Gabrielle finish, and then we'll go upstairs."

Ted gave me a tense look, clearly remembering my ice-queen magic at his office. On his other side, Gabrielle glanced at her cards, a jack and a six, and asked for a hit. I resisted rolling my eyes, and the dealer turned over an eight.

Gabrielle shrugged as the dealer raked away the chip. "Sorry, Ted," she said. "Maybe I should bet more on the next one."

"No, we're done." I put my hand on Ted's shoulder, letting the cold of the snow burn through his shirt. "Pick up your chips, Ted."

"I've got them." Gabrielle swept them into her hands and walked away. Ted had no choice but to follow.

Gabrielle went to the cashier's cage and handed over the chips, eagerly snatching up the stack of hundreds and twenties the cashier pushed back at her. She pocketed the money with a wink at Ted, who choked but said nothing.

Cassandra and Nash were no longer at the front desk as Gabrielle and I walked Ted out of the casino, but I didn't want to look for them. If they'd found Vonda, Cassandra would have alerted me, and I didn't want to risk losing hold of Ted.

We waited for an elevator to empty; then I pushed Ted

into it, my hand firmly on his elbow. His entire arm was cold now, and he shivered. I waited for Ted to let me know what floor. He said seven. I hoped for his sake he wasn't lying.

"Gabrielle, you *stick* on a sixteen," I said in an admonishing tone as the doors slid closed. The elevator swiftly rose. "You really need to learn about odds."

Gabrielle fingered the wad of cash in her pocket. "You don't stick if you're trying to lose other people's money. Thanks, Ted. Consider it payback for the trouble you've caused me."

"I don't even know who you are," Ted said.

"You don't, but your wife does. Who do you think paid your way into that job in Flat Mesa? Or rented your house? That was me, Gabrielle, your fairy godmother. All you had to do—*all* you had to do—was get Nash Jones over to your house and have Vonda hold on to him for me. But, no, you two had to play your own little game, and now you're going to answer for it. You don't take money for a job and then don't do the job."

"I think Ted became a little too fond of his work," I said. "As the inspector, I mean, making sure I couldn't possibly pass his little tests. I bet you enjoyed making out that check sheet and waving it in my face."

Ted's own face was pale, his lips blue, as the cold from my hands seeped into his blood. "I didn't have a choice. Vonda said I had to."

"Vonda needs to answer a lot of questions. I sure hope she's here."

"She is." Ted's lips compressed from more than cold. "She sent me off to play so she could be alone with your boyfriend."

My heart constricted, but I refused to let him worry me. One thing at a time.

The elevator doors opened. Gabrielle danced out before us. "Which one?"

"Seven twenty-six," Ted said in a dull voice.

Gabrielle ran down the hall, not bothering to be quiet. She stopped in front of room 726, and blasted the lock with a beam of Beneath magic. Ted made a strangled noise.

I shook my head. "I can't do anything about her. Gabrielle's kind of out of control. But you know what little sisters are like."

Gabrielle was smart enough to step aside as she slammed open the door. I felt the witch in there, powerful, her aura a strange smoky color, and mixed with hers, the fiery red of a dragon.

I closed my eyes a brief moment and prayed with all I had that we wouldn't find them in bed. If that happened, I didn't know what I'd do. I'd try to kill Vonda, and there would go my hope of getting Mick safely free.

The core of me twisted into a ball of pain as I shoved Ted inside in front of me. Vonda lounged on the bed of the large half suite, but she was dressed. Mick stood across the room from her, looking out the window, his back to me. He wore a sleeveless T-shirt, baring the dragons on his arms, which vibrated with the same shivering movement I'd seen before.

Something warm flooded through me when I saw him. He was Mick, the man I loved, strong, safe, alive. Everything in me wanted to go to him and slide my arms around him from behind, resting my head on his broad back. I wanted to touch him, smell him, feel his hard body, reassure myself that he was all right.

I missed his warmth in my bed, his sleepy eyes regarding me from his pillow, his slow smile as he suggested we make love again. I missed riding with him on the highway, my arms wrapped tightly around him, feeling wild and free and, at the same time, safe. He was my Mick, and I wanted him back.

"What are you doing, Ted?" Vonda asked, not in the least alarmed at our dramatic entrance.

She sat up, and I faced Vonda Wingate for the first time.

Vonda wasn't pretty, at least not to me, but like Ted, her looks were striking. She wore her blond hair cut close in an angular style, and her eyes were very blue in a face too pale for my taste. She had slimness without being bony, more like a person who worked out a lot and ate very little. Her white sleeveless shell, gray silk skirt, and the black pumps she'd dropped next to the bed were as tasteful as anything Cassandra would wear. Vonda had paired the ensemble with pretty silver jewelry.

I understood at once why my grandmother and Elena called her "Shadow Walker." Shadows danced through Vonda's aura: gray, smoky, dark. She was human, and yet her magic had built upon itself until it had consumed her. It clung to her like scum on the bottom of a dirty bathtub. She might look like a well-off woman in her forties, but I knew this was the picture she chose to project. I couldn't guess what she actually looked like, but likely something old, because I sensed great age in her.

The most unusual thing about Vonda was the sheer amount of magic swimming in her. If Nash was a magic void, Vonda Wingate was a magic well. She'd been filled to the brim with all kinds of magic: witch magic, shaman magic, *chindi* magic, and now, dragon magic. The magic swirled around her in the shadows, part of her and separate from her at the same time.

She looked at me, and I suddenly understood my danger. A woman who sucked up magic from others would be more than thrilled that a Stormwalker with Beneath powers had just walked into her lair. She'd simply add me to her collection.

It wasn't my magic mirror that Vonda wanted, I realized with clarity. She would have to kill me and Mick to use the mirror, and Vonda wanted me alive. Magic mirrors, though rare, weren't unique. I was.

When Vonda had first come to town, she hadn't simply grabbed me and sucked me dry. I would have fought her, possibly killed her. She hadn't been strong enough then.

She was strong enough now, because she had a dragon, a dragon whose magic she'd imbibed, a dragon who did her bidding. Mick still didn't turn around.

"So you are the Stormwalker." Vonda's tone was neutral, not betraying the eagerness I read in her. She looked me up and down, from my messy black hair to my mud-splotched motorcycle boots, unimpressed.

I gave Ted's arm a squeeze, and he shuddered with cold. "I have your husband," I said. "You have my boyfriend. How about a trade?"

My words were cut off by Gabrielle, who decided to launch herself at Vonda. Vonda coolly watched her come, and I saw wards on the walls around her spring to life. The magic in Gabrielle's hands twisted around her own wrists, and Gabrielle screamed.

"Mick," Vonda said.

Mick turned. His eyes were gray white, his face hard and expressionless. He lifted his hand and streamed fire at Gabrielle.

Gabrielle managed to block it with Beneath magic, but she panted with the effort, her eyes wide with fear and rage.

"Mick," I said.

Mick's gaze landed on me, his fire died, and my heart broke.

I looked into the eyes of a stranger. Whatever part of Mick had loved me was gone. This man wouldn't smile at me over dinner in a fancy restaurant, wouldn't growl as he licked the inside of my wrist, wouldn't whisper naughty things to me as we stood together in a crowded room. Gone was the man who'd taught me how to control my magic and fix up my bike, who kept me warm when we curled up to sleep, who'd kissed syrup off my lips in the morning.

When Mick had startled me with his proposal of marriage, I'd put him off because I thought I'd have plenty of time to think about my answer. I'd ponder the question awhile until I got used to it, and then I'd tell him what I wanted.

Facing Mick now, I realized that there was no such thing as enough time. Time is snatched away swiftly, while we in our arrogance think it will always be there for us. I'd spent five years traveling alone, trying to figuring out who I was and coming to terms with it, before I'd returned to the vortexes and my mother and faced my fears. I'd been very lucky in that time that I hadn't lost my father or grandmother, that I'd had a home to return to whenever I liked. That Mick had secretly watched over me and kept me safe.

I could have lost everything in those five years, and the thought had never once occurred to me.

Now I realized that I had to hang on to what I had and savor all of it for as long as I could. So that when whatever I had was taken away—and it would be—I'd have no regret that I hadn't savored enough.

"Mick," I said softly. "You can be free of her. Tell me your name, and we can break the spell."

Behind me, Vonda laughed. "If it were that simple, don't you think he'd have done it by now? He's finished with you, Stormwalker. The dragon fights for me now. He'll do anything for me."

Her arch tone made me know she wanted me to picture them in bed together. I remembered the scorn in Mick's voice, when he'd said *I don't have sex with humans.* He'd meant it, but I couldn't know what Vonda had compelled Mick to do since I'd last seen him. I swallowed, trying very hard not to imagine them together. I wondered how Ted felt about it.

I glanced back at Ted in time to see him try to sidle out of the room. I started to shout to Gabrielle to stop him, but Nash walked in at the moment and pointed his nine-millimeter at Ted's head.

"Stay where you are."

"Are you all right, Janet?" Cassandra asked as the heavy door swung shut behind her. I sensed the crackle of magic in her, the makings of her binding spell.

"Your pet witch," Vonda said. She rose from the bed, went to the wet bar, and started clinking ice from a bucket into a glass. One glass. She wasn't offering. "And the very interesting Nash Jones." Her gaze lingered on Nash, the muddy gray of her aura brightening as she studied him. "A magic void. I've heard of a spell that can make a void, but not inside a person. No wonder Gabrielle wants you."

I saw Nash's interest in her comment about a spell, but he was too professional to be distracted.

I pretended to ignore Vonda, as though I'd sized her up and dismissed her. She was a threat, and a big one, but I had to solve the problem of Mick before facing her. After that, the gloves would be off.

"I'm fine," I answered Cassandra. "Keep Gabrielle away from Vonda."

"Screw that," Gabrielle snarled. "This bitch messed with me. She *used* me."

She had. Vonda must have been delighted when Gabrielle asked for her help in snaring Nash. Gabrielle, in her arrogant naïveté, had handed Vonda, the magic well, a dragon and a Stormwalker, and now Nash as well.

I didn't have time right now to sort out Gabrielle's problems. I shut out the rest of the room, quietly reached for the storm outside and the Beneath magic within me, and walked toward Mick.

He hadn't moved, not to stop Nash or Cassandra, or even to glance at Vonda pouring a drink for herself. Mick watched me as I closed the space between us, and I watched Mick.

His eyes were mostly white, his pupils black pinpricks, the beautiful blue of his human eyes gone. I hated that, but I forced myself to focus. Nothing in this room mattered but getting Mick free. Nothing.

"Mick," I said. "Your name."

He still wouldn't answer, didn't speak a word. I took another step, now within arm's length of him, my magic ready.

Mick was ready too. He reached out, not with his fire, but with his bare hands. As soon as I was close enough, he grabbed me around the waist, whirled with me, and threw me at the window.

The windows didn't open in this fairly new hotel. Buildings with sealed windows creeped me out—why would you want to entomb yourself in glass and concrete?

But as Mick tossed me at the window, it suddenly wasn't there. A rectangle of flame melted it, and I flew right through the hot glass and out into the swirling snow, seven stories from the ground.

Twenty-four

First came screaming. Second came me catching the storm and whirling it around my body so fast that the air currents cushioned my fall.

"Cushioned" is a relative term. I bounced off the roof of a car in the dark parking lot, setting off its alarm, rolled down the hood, and landed, hard, on my feet. I staggered, trying to get my balance. The wind had picked up, and the snowstorm raged around me, snow clinging to my clothes. I must have looked like a drunken abominable snowman.

I made it to the edge of the parking lot and stumbled into the desert. Dizzy and scared, I heaved my guts out.

When I straightened up again, trying not to sob, it was to see Mick standing five feet away from me. He was alone, no Vonda or Gabrielle behind him. Snow swirled around him, whitening his dark hair, but he didn't seem to notice the cold.

"We can't do this here," I said. "Too many people. Why can't you just tell me your name?"

No answer. Mick walked toward me, and I backed away,

straight back into the parking lot. I didn't want to fight him here, not near all these people, with more zooming by on the highway. I could lead him out into the desert, but this wasn't my terrain. But if I could lead him to a place of my choosing . . .

I turned and sprinted across the lot. Five motorcycles had been parked close together, a group inside either gambling or staying the night. It was easy to freeze off the lock of the first one I came to, and start it up, not with magic, but with know-how. I drove it out of the lot without looking back.

I saw the flaw in my plan as I moved onto the highway. Mick could simply return to Vonda and obliterate my friends.

But he didn't. Maybe he saw the wisdom of the two of us facing off for once and for all, or maybe Vonda had ordered him to drag me back to her.

Either way, Mick started up his own bike and chased me up the highway, toward the interstate.

When I reached the 40, I headed west, to home and the territory I knew. I leaned forward, not worrying about speeding, and opened up the bike. It was a good Harley, and someone had tuned it into a fine machine. The CCs throbbed under me, and we went like a dream, no hard shaking as sometimes had happened with my own bike.

The headlight cut through the snow, which turned to sleet, then back to snow again as we went. This was a big storm, I could feel it, swallowing the sky for miles.

Mick pulled alongside me, and we rode neck and neck. He wasn't chasing me but making sure I didn't get out of his sight. Side by side we rode at ninety miles an hour down into the canyons, the lights of Gallup flying by on our left, and then across the state line.

I would take him up to Canyon de Chelly. It was in the middle of the Dinetah, the Navajo Nation, my land, my home. The canyon was a mystical place, an ancient place, and my Stormwalker powers would be strongest there.

But when the exit to the north 171 came up, Mick ran his bike up on my right side, nearly swerving into me, so I had to dive into the left lane. I missed the exit, and the two of us sped around a slow-moving semi, ending up side by side again down the middle of the road.

Mick stuck to my right. He didn't want me pulling off, doubling back. He stayed there for about fifty more miles, until he zoomed to my left again, forcing me down the ramp to Holbrook.

This highway led south, right through town. Again, I couldn't stop and risk people, so I rode through until we made the other side. The best place to go from there was my hotel, but Mick again had a different idea. I was trying to lead him; he was herding me.

Mick forced me onto the road I'd been riding when the sinkhole happened, and he stuck right by me as we flew down the highway. Our speed reached one that would make Nash write us fourteen tickets, but Nash was back in New Mexico, and his deputies obviously had better things to do than man the speed trap on a snowy night.

Therefore, Lopez and the other deputies weren't there to see Mick and me zoom by, swing around the black barrier now heaped with snow, and race toward the gaping hole at breakneck speed.

Mick was going to run me into the sinkhole. Well, screw that. I and a bike had already fallen down there once. I wasn't about to do it again.

Right before we reached the hole, I yanked my handlebars sideways and ditched the bike in, well, the ditch. The bike slid out from under me, and I rolled through soft snow and muddy grass to come to a halt in icy water.

Mick didn't ditch his motorcycle. He ran it right at me.

I scrambled to my feet and ran like hell on feet numb with snow and water. Mick came on. I noticed distractedly that the sinkhole had gotten bigger. Lopez's geology professor had warned us that the hole might widen, as the ceilings of the caverns below weakened further. Mick was chasing me right toward the edge.

Between falling from a window and the first incident of the sinkhole, I was developing a healthy fear of heights—or rather, of falling from heights. But I couldn't afford to let

Mick be in too much control. If he chased me until I fell into the hole, I'd be flailing around trying to save myself and possibly die. I needed to gain some advantage here, much as it terrified me.

When Mick turned his motorcycle to take another run at me, I took a deep breath, whirled wind and snow around me like heavy blanket, and jumped straight into the sinkhole.

I didn't scream this time but curled my arms around my body and tucked my face to my chest. The storm cushioned my descent a little, but still I landed hard on the rocks that had snagged me and Nash the first time.

The storm swirled away from me, shooting upward to join the winds above. Everything went quiet.

And dark. I struggled for breath, noting how the air, though cold, was more bearable down here than on the surface. I had my leather jacket against the elements and the rocks, but I groaned as I sat up and brushed dust from my hair.

I didn't want to risk a light spell. I couldn't do light spells with storm magic, and using Beneath magic would alert the *karmii*. I stilled my labored breathing, hoping that, if I used no magic at all, the *karmii* would leave me alone.

But I was too agitated, and Beneath magic swam through my body, filling it like the magic that filled Vonda. Both of my magics were whirling inside me as much as the snow and ice whirled in the blizzard above.

Mick hadn't followed me down, and I no longer heard the throb of his motorcycle. He hadn't even glanced in to see whether his prey lived or died. Maybe he figured that I couldn't get out, that the *karmii* would finish me. Or that I'd be trapped here while he went to get Vonda.

The sinkhole began to glow. Dread clogged my throat as drawings of wiry hands appeared on the rocks in front of me, then behind me, then above, then below. The breath went out of me at the same time I felt a hot draft over my shoulder from the beating of massive wings.

Mick floated by, above me in the night. I forced myself to my feet and hunkered as close to the rock wall as I could, nearly whimpering when the *karmii* reached out to me. Mick turned and dove at the hole, his fire burning a streak through the dark.

Here it was then. Mick and me. Facing each other, alone.

Me in a hole with the *karmii* dancing around me, Mick above, trying to burn me alive. The hole was plenty big enough now for Mick to dive into it, but he kept flying, sending his flame roaring down to roast me.

There was nothing to save me from him. Mick, a dragon, was able to take my Stormwalker magic and resist it. I pressed my hands together, drew them to my chest, and closed my eyes.

I saw inside me what I'd seen when I'd saved Mick last fall, my Stormwalker magic and my Beneath magic twining around each other like black and white, yin and yang. Whirling together into one solid foundation.

When I opened my eyes again, my entire body sparkled. Earth magic and Beneath magic, a powerful combination. As far as I knew, I was the only being in the world who had it. I thought Vonda wanted it, thought that her desire for my magic would keep me alive. But Mick didn't seem to care about keeping me alive. He was going for the kill.

"Ice," I whispered, and the ice in the storm bent to my will.

It flowed through my fingers, freezing my body. Ice crackled through my hair and my skin and shot upward from my hands to meet Mick's arrow of flame.

Fire and ice met with an explosion that rocked the sinkhole. The impact tried to lift me off my feet, but I held on to the tight braid of both my magics and stayed put, my hands together. Mick screamed and beat the air before he swooped down for another pass.

I laughed up at him. "Come on! Let's see what we can do!"

We were going to kill each other. Him by burying me in fire, me by burying him in snow. Legends would be sung about this battle between the dragon and the Stormwalker, the flame and the ice.

Mick laid down fire to incinerate the hole. Rocks crackled and broke, tree roots burst into flame, and the fire sucked oxygen from the air. I would have burned alive but for the bubble of ice I formed around me to deflect the fire. Mick blasted me again and again, trying to wear me down, but I held on, my sweat forming into instant ice on my skin.

My next stream of ice hit Mick's flame, and he had to fight his way skyward, roaring with rage. Mick wheeled back, sucked in a breath, and blasted me with fire.

The heat of the volcano that had created him flowed down at me like molten lava. My defensive shield of ice was enough to deflect it, but the rocks around me couldn't hold. They crumbled and melted, sandstone not strong enough to withstand the heat.

Rocks jerked out from under me, and I fell. And fell and fell. This rockslide, if anything, was bigger than the first that had opened the sinkhole. Tons of rocks cascaded around me, battering me, smothering me. My magic snapped and broke, and so did one of my ribs. The pain made me sick, but I didn't have time for that as I rolled and tumbled down the shaft.

I hit hard at the bottom, and I had enough presence of mind to scramble out of the way of the rocks coming down on top of me. I crawled through sharp gravel toward a light, moving mindlessly, and wriggled through a small hole as rocks filled the shaft behind me.

The impact of the last rocks propelled me forward, and I landed on my stomach, my broken ribs aching. There was light in here, and I saw why when I managed to roll over.

I was in the cave in which we'd found Jamison. Petroglyphs had been chipped into the reddish walls in thick clusters, stars and comets and constellations. I could see them because of the *karmii*, thousands of them, skeletal hands flowing down the walls and across the rock floor in a race toward me.

"No," I whispered. I reached for the storm, managing to let my body vibrate with it. The *karmii* sensed my earth magic and paused, as though debating.

I rolled over, groaning, and got to my knees. Cradling my arm across my stomach, I climbed painfully to my feet. The *karmii* gave me a clear circle about two feet in diameter, but they waited, watching. When the storm died, I would too.

The circle of *karmii* followed me as I hobbled through the cave, searching for the rockslide that led up to the tunnel Nash had brought me through. Outside, a dragon waited to roast me alive. Down here, petroglyphs waited to freeze me to death.

Janet.

"Coyote!" I screamed.

Where was he? I scanned the cave but saw nothing, no tall naked man, no large coyote. Damn him. I swore I was taking a rolled-up newspaper to his nose when I faced him again.

Janet.

"What? I'm right here! Where are you?"

Here.

I raised my head to look in the direction of the voice and found him. Sort of. Among the dense whorls of petroglyphs on the ceiling, someone had drawn the face of a coyote.

"What are you doing?" I shouted. "Get down here. Blast these things away from me. Help me get out of here. Help me fight Mick."

I'm not really with you, Janet. I'm projecting. I'm thousands of miles and an age away.

"An age? What's that supposed to mean?"

It means I can guide you, but you must do this yourself.

"Oh, of course." I started crying as I spoke, tears smearing on my cheeks, and my rib cage *hurt*. "Do you see anyone else in this cave to help me? No. It's just me, with broken ribs, surrounded by drawings who think I'm some kind of walking evil lodestone. Mick is trying to kill me, and my friends are trying to keep my sister from killing the witch who enslaved him—so Mick can stay alive to kill me. Now my strongest ally is saying he's nothing more than a chipped-out drawing on a wall?"

Only you can save Mick, Janet. You must use his true name.

"I know that! What is it?"

As I told you, dragons can hide such things even from the gods, especially from gods that are not theirs.

I kicked the floor, spattering gravel over the *karmii* who didn't move or even notice. "Then what good are you?"

You know Mick's true name.

"No, I *don't*! That's why I wanted you to find it, that's why Colby took me to Mick's lair. The name is not at his lair, it's not in the ring, it wasn't in the wards at the hotel. It's not even in his toothbrush. Trust me, I checked!"

He tells it to you when he makes love to you.

"That's not what Mick says when we make love." Various dirty suggestions and graphic descriptions of how I made him feel, yes; names that sounded like strings of music, no.

I know what he says. That is different from what he tells you.

"Oh, very clear, thank you. And why haven't you bothered to tell me this before? I might have had time to figure it out."

I didn't know. It is one thing I learned on my travels through the earth and time.

"Where the hell are you? What did my grandmother send you to do? Why aren't you helping me instead?"

That is between me and the lady crow. I'm helping her because she doesn't like the word 'no.'

Tell me about it. "Wait—you said you traveled in *time*? You can do that?"

Gods can. Time isn't linear to us as it is to you. Remember when I said Mick and I had tangled, that he claims I violated his territory? It was on this search. It happened just now. Or back then, whatever is your perspective.

I'd have to think about that later, if I lived long enough. "That's all you can tell me? That I already know Mick's name, except I don't know what it sounds like, how I know it, or how to use it?"

Yes.

"I'm developing a serious dislike for you."

Aw, Janet, don't be like that.

"If I get out of this alive, you and I are going to have

words. And when we're done, you're going to wish I'd been my grandmother with a broom."

I'm sorry you have to be alone for this, but it's the only way. You have to face Mick, and you have to face him naked— without magic and without tricks. Just you.

"Literally naked?"

Well . . .

"Go away if you aren't going to tell me anything useful."

Alone. I'm sorry. You have to go out there and face him.

Or face him in here. The dust at one end of the cave stirred, the *karmii* lighting it like sun inside a cloud. Through that cloud stepped Mick.

Twenty-five

When you have sex with someone, it changes your relationship with them forever. You might think you're keeping something casual, but after sex, you know things about that person that no one else does, and they know many things about you. If you break up, even if you say you want to keep things friendly, knowing that you shared a private part of yourself with the other person can lead to resentment or out-and-out rage. The rage is especially strong if the other person betrayed you—you gave them all you had, trusted them with your secret self, and they turned that knowledge against you.

I faced Mick knowing that I'd shared things with him I'd shared with no one else in the world. He'd taken a naïve young woman, alone and vulnerable, and shaped her into a confident magic wielder and experienced lover. I'd surrendered myself into his capable hands; and Mick had taught me more about myself than I would have ever discovered on my own.

Now Mick stood before me, tall and naked and beautiful,

and he'd use the knowledge he'd acquired to hurt me. The thought was already breaking my heart.

"Does Vonda want me dead?" I asked him. "I thought she wanted my magic."

Mick said nothing as he came toward me. He held no fire in his hands, but I sensed it lurking below the surface, his dragon tattoos writhing with it. The tattooed eyes glittered, not in a friendly way.

The *karmii* backed off from Mick—to them, he was the good guy, an earth-magic being—and kept their circle around me. If the storm outside died, or if Mick beat me back so that I lost my grip on it, the *karmii* would leap upon me and smother me with their burning cold.

"You must know," I continued. "Why go to all this trouble? Gabrielle thinks Vonda enslaved you to kill her, but you've never gone after Gabrielle. Only me."

"You need to be eliminated."

Gods, he sounded like the Terminator. But that movie villain had nothing on a tall dragon-man who could incinerate me in the space of a thought.

"Why?" I asked him. "What am I standing in the way of?"

"The universe."

I'm sure that meant something. "The universe. Right. I have a lot of power, yes, and I can open vortexes, true, but if Vonda kills me, I won't be opening any vortexes for her."

"It has nothing to do with the vortexes."

I hated that he answered in Mick's familiar voice, the one that tickled inside of my ear when he whispered my name in the night. But the voice was without inflection now, as Mick stated simple facts.

"With what, then?"

Mick closed his mouth. The witch had probably put a silence spell on him as part of the enslavement, allowing Mick to answer only questions that didn't come under the spell's umbrella.

"The hotel deterioration was all a diversion then?"

Mick didn't answer, but the answer told me something. If he wasn't allowed to say, then it might not have been a diversion after all.

Did Vonda Wingate want my *hotel*? Not my dragon, my powers, my sister, or my magic mirror. The hotel itself.

"If I'm going to die here, I'd like to at least know why," I said.

"I don't want to kill you, Janet."

"Well, that's a relief. Although I'd believe it more if you didn't say it in that robotlike voice."

"But I have to kill you. You're in the way."

"Which means that if I'm alive, I can stop Vonda and her evil plans—whatever they are."

"I'm a fighter, a warrior. I don't give a damn about her plans. I just want the kill."

He did. I saw it in his eyes, which were black but swimming with white sparks. He wasn't my beloved Mick anymore. He was a dragon at the height of his powers, and I was a Stormwalker with a broken rib surrounded by entities that would kill me the minute I used my Beneath magic.

"She believes that I love you enough to not kill you," I said. Tears formed in my eyes as my emotions slipped. "But she's wrong. I do love you, but if I have to kill you to survive, to keep the witch from what she wants, I will."

Mick didn't wait. No last-minute taunts, no "Let's do this." He simply let fly with the fire.

I grabbed the wind whipping around on the surface, sucked it down the tunnel behind him, and buried the fire in whirling white snow. The flame easily burst free and flew around the room, encircling the *karmii* that encircled me.

"Oh, this is so not fair," I said.

I yanked the piece of magic mirror out of my pocket, called a handful of the Beneath magic and Stormwalker magic mixed together, and directed it at the mirror. The mirror screamed, and I didn't blame it, because I had no idea what this would do to it.

The mirror absorbed my magic, screeching and moaning, and then it fed it back tenfold. The flames receded a little, the circle of them drawing back, and the *karmii* did too. Mick watched me, his head tilted to one side, studying me with that dragon curiosity.

Curiosity. While we were fighting to the death.

I slammed more magic into the mirror. The piece started to shudder and then it broke apart in my hands.

I followed the pieces down, grabbing the shards even as they cut my hands. Breaking a magic mirror doesn't diminish its power—it simply means that you have more pieces to work with.

I swept the shards into my hands, all but one. That piece had landed in the middle of the *karmii*, and I couldn't reach it. The *karmii* pulled back from it, because the mirror had been created by solid earth magic, silicon and silver. The mirror was a good guy in the *karmii*'s opinion.

A snake of flame reached the shard, and the mirror slid to Mick. Mick calmly picked up the piece and directed a thin spire of flame into it.

The mirror kept screaming as Mick turned the mirror to me and released the magic. The flame, doubled in strength, came straight for me.

I yelled and hit the dirt, frantically pulling wind and ice over me to deflect the fire. They did, barely. The heat of the flames singed my hair, made my clothes so hot the fabric melted to my skin.

I got to my feet, eyes stinging with heat and smoke. Mick had figured out the perfect way to kill me. He'd driven me down here where the *karmii* would keep my Beneath magic penned, and he'd absorb any storm magic I threw at him. He could use the magic mirror we'd both awakened against me, and I'd die.

The dragons for years had been afraid of me, but Mick, who knew me and loved me, was the only dragon who'd figured out how to destroy me. He'd stripped me of everything, and I had nothing left.

You have to face him naked, Coyote had said. *Without magic and without tricks. Just you.*

Mick had effectively rendered my magic useless, except for a thin layer of defense. And Coyote wanted me to drop that too?

I drew a long breath. Coyote drove me crazy, but he was a god. He'd been right before, and there was a good chance that he was right now.

There's always a first time for him to be wrong, the practical voice inside me said. *He'd admit that.*

I pushed my hair out of my face, dismayed when part of it came away in a burned mess. I flung away the hank and, in a fluid move, stripped off my jacket and half-disintegrated shirt. The clips that held my black lace bra closed were burning my back, and I ripped off that too.

Naked and alone. Without magic.

I knew that Coyote had meant *naked* metaphorically, but I couldn't help think he'd appreciate me stripping off half my clothes to face Mick. I could picture Coyote's grin, the shine to his dark eyes.

I drew another breath. I deliberately dropped the pieces of the magic mirror, tossing them to land smack among the *karmii*. The skeletal hands drew away from them like bugs skittering back from a growing pool of water.

"What are you doing, girlfriend?" the mirror called. "Don't leave me here!"

Without lifting my hand I called off the storm magic. The wind swirled around me once, the ice stinging my bare flesh, and then it died. I loosened the entwined magic inside me and let it flow to its disparate parts.

I had to close my eyes for the last part, which I didn't like, because I imagined Mick's fire cutting me in half like a laser the second I took my gaze from him. But maybe he was curious enough to wonder what insane thing I was doing now.

I let my mind drift, thinking of calm things—the moon rising over the mountains I'd walked with my father, a stream tricking between rocky banks, the endless sky over my home. I'd found my greatest peace alone there with my father, in the silence between us that was serene and happy.

I remembered that peace and the love I'd always felt from him, which kept me going in times of loneliness, uncertainty, and downright fear.

I pictured my father, Pete Begay, with his wise eyes, the kindness that radiated from him like warmth from a hearth fire. Wrapping my senses around that peace, I let my Stormwalker magic and my Beneath magic recede until they were the tiniest of sparks buried inside my psyche.

I opened my eyes and at first worried when I couldn't see anything. Then I realized that the *karmii* had faded. One or two lingered around the edges of the cave, but with my Beneath magic at low ebb, they'd stopped sensing it and had retreated, their job done.

The only light came from the fire in Mick's hands, which lit him with a red glow. It showed me his hard and handsome face, the nose that had been broken, his hair hanging loose, his eyes dark in the shadows. He was still a beautiful man.

"Mirror," I said, my voice so steady it surprised me. "Some light please?"

I didn't need to use magic to make the mirror obey, because the mirror had magic of its own. That is why magic mirrors are such sought-after talismans—they can work when the mage's defenses are down. And they always protect their masters.

Clean, white light sprang from each of the shards and lit the cave like a bank of LEDs. The light wasn't bright enough to flood the cave but enough that I could see what I was doing.

I spread my arms. "Here I am. No magic. Nothing. Just me. Just Janet."

"Good," Mick said. "You make my job easier." He didn't say, *Stupid human*, but his body language radiated the thought.

Mick squished the fire in his hands into a ball. I stood and watched him, forcing fear from me. *Peace*, I told myself. *Trust Coyote.*

"Mick," I said as he worked. "I love you."

No answer.

I lifted my hand, letting the light dance on the band of silver, turquoise, and onyx. "I kept the ring you gave me. I didn't give you an answer that day you scared me to death talking about marriage, but I've decided now."

Mick looked at me, then at the ring. I swore I saw a brief blue spark in his eyes, but I couldn't be sure.

He went back to making his fireball. "Throw the ring away. It's no longer important."

"It's important to me. You gave it to me."

"Trust me, Janet. Take that ring off and throw it from you as far as you can."

His voice ended in a harsh note. I studied the band, silver for love, turquoise for healing, onyx for protection. Healing, love, protection. Around and around the ring they went. Entwined, unbroken.

"No," I said.

"You should have gotten rid of it after I left you. I thought you would."

"Well, I didn't." I turned the ring to catch the light. "Since I'm going to die here, tell me your name. Your true name. I want to hear it once, even if it's the last thing."

"Nice try."

I shrugged. "I had to." I lowered my hand and started walking toward him, pretending I didn't fear him. My inner peace was no match for the terror of moving closer to the man who was coldly preparing to kill me. He didn't give a damn about my inner peace, or about my love for him, or about the ring.

Except that me still having the ring bothered him. That intrigued me enough to keep walking to him though my fear begged me to run the other way.

Mick looked down at me with hard, cold eyes when I reached him. "I'm going to kill you, Janet."

"I know." I knew it, and I accepted it, and suddenly, I was no longer afraid.

Whether I lived or died, I was not going to kill Mick. I would get him free, if it was the last thing I did, and now it looked as though it *would* be the last thing I did. I loved him, as I loved my father and my grandmother, and my last act on this earth would not be to slaughter someone who had taught me how much selfless love could accomplish.

"Why don't you fight me?" Mick asked.

He genuinely wanted to know. I'd seen his dragon curiosity at work, and now he brought it to bear on this question.

Why would the puny Stormwalker shut off her power and wait to die? Foolish, foolish Stormwalker.

"I don't want to," I said.

"I'm being controlled by another, and her wish is for me to kill you. I have no choice but to obey."

"I know. But it doesn't matter. I love you, Mick, the real you that's behind the puppet Vonda controls. Because what you and I had means something to me, and she can never take that from me. It might be over between us now, but it meant something, and I'll never forget that. I'll never forget *you*."

"You'll remember me only for the seconds it takes you to die."

"Maybe." I stepped closer to him, looked right up into his eyes. "I love you, Mick. Tell me your name."

"I can't. Even if I wanted to, the spell is too strong."

The ring tingled on my hand, so cool in the heat of the cave. It didn't contain his name, no. He'd have been compelled to destroy it if it had. But Mick had put a tiny bite of his essence in there, the spark of dragon fire I'd sensed. He'd made the confusing proposal to me and slipped the ring on my finger.

"Yes," I whispered. I lifted my hand to Mick's arm, pressing my fingers and the ring against the dragon on his biceps. "My answer is yes. I'll marry you."

A spark stung him, and he jerked. Mick looked swiftly down at me, and for an instant, the horrible gray in his eyes cleared, and the clear blue of Mick shone through.

"Your name," I said. "Hurry."

Mick pushed me off with a growl, and my hope died. I'd thought that maybe the name would burst from him when he felt a touch of his own, untainted magic, but perhaps the spark wasn't big enough. I couldn't reawaken my own magic to amplify what was in the ring, because the *karmii* would strike.

Amplify.

I held up my hand, thrusting the ring into a beam from one of the mirror shards. "Hey, magic mirror. What do you make of this?"

"Ooh, honey," the mirror said in delight. "*Love* the bling. Think he'd give me one?"

Mick began to growl. His curiosity about what I was trying to do kept his fire at bay for two more seconds, but two seconds was enough.

The mirror grabbed the glint from the silver ring, bounced it across the five or so pieces of itself scattered on the floor, then slammed the five beams together. I grabbed Mick and dragged him straight into that light.

The dragon fire in Mick's hands burned me to the bone. I grunted with pain but didn't let go until the beams from the mirror shot into his eyes. Then my senseless fingers lost hold of him, and I folded, groaning, to the floor.

The skin of my hands was gone, blackened and burned, the blood and muscle oozing around the ring, which still clasped my finger. I saw the splinter of bone that had broken sticking through the disgusting mass. I curled up onto myself and whimpered in pain.

Mick roared. I don't mean he shouted like a human; I mean he roared like a dragon. An earth-shaking, earsplitting, oh-gods-I'm-going-to-die-if-he-doesn't-stop roar. It went on and on, and rocks began to fall on us, and the mirror shrieked. I couldn't move my hands to clap them over my ears. I could only squeeze my eyes shut, clench my jaw, and pray.

The roar built and shook, tumbled and spun, rocking the cave and the earth above and beneath it. The shaft that led to the sinkhole exploded in dust as more of the surface fell down.

The sound wound up until I couldn't take it anymore. My eardrums were about to burst—no, maybe my entire head—when the roaring turned into a string of music so sharp and pure that my heart began to break.

I looked up and saw Mick standing in the light. His fists were clenched, the dragon tattoos writhing up and down his bunched arms. His head was thrown back, his wild hair straggling across his face, but his now-black eyes were wide-open. So was his mouth, and from it issued that sound, the music that sounded of the most beautiful string of chimes, and wind, and ringing crystals.

The music filled the cave and wrapped me like a cocoon. The mirror caught the vibrations and reflected them back, amplifying the music as it had amplified the spark of dragon magic in the ring.

Mick's name. His true name, the entire beauty of it. My mind drank it in, the music finding the empty spaces in my body and filling them.

Mick looked at me. The black receded from his eyes and blue filled them, the brilliant blue I'd looked up into in that hotel in Las Vegas, when he'd laid me down and made love to me for the first time.

"Janet." The light played over Mick's bronzed body, his wide shoulders, the dragons on his arms, his thick phallus, his blue black hair, and the eyes that held the blue of twilit skies. "I give it to you," he said.

His name. His gift to me. The music flared and flooded me, then it faded, the last notes dying like a breeze whispering through wind chimes.

That was my last thought before the magic mirror's light winked out. My eyes rolled back into my head, and the cave's gravel cut what was left of my skin as I fell face-first onto it.

Twenty-six

I swam awake to the sound of Mick's voice. I felt a warm hand in my hair, and I smelled Mick, the good scent of his human body and the fiery spark of dragon magic.

I opened my eyes and was rewarded by the sight of his face hanging over mine, and his blue eyes. I lay on his lap, which was bare, nothing between me and the warm goodness of Mick.

I couldn't imagine where we were, and I didn't care. The place was dark and dusty, and pebbles cut into my legs, but I was with Mick, on his lap, his big hands cradling me, his whispers healing me.

"Hey, baby," I murmured.

Mick closed his eyes, and when he opened them again, they were filled with tears. "Janet." He gently touched my arms, and I hissed in pain. Something had burned me and burned me bad.

"Janet, love."

This was more like it. Mick whispering endearments instead of trying to kill me with his fire. I liked this dream.

"Move your arm," he said.

No. Too comfortable. Moving meant pain.

"Come on, sweetheart. I need to know that you're all right."

"Want to sleep," I whispered.

Mick lifted me. I groaned, every part of me protesting. I stopped protesting when I found myself resting against his chest, the warmth of him against my cheek. Mick cupped his hand around my wrist, which had skin on it again, but the skin was red and sensitive to the touch.

"Ow!" The pain cut through my fogged senses and my mind began to clear.

We were still in the cave, which was lit only by a single shard of magic mirror. That shard was tiny and threw light like that of a pencil-thin flashlight. We all-powerful magic people couldn't have thought to bring a real flashlight, could we?

Mick was gazing at me not with the cold malevolence of an enslaved dragon but with the fiery concern of the man who'd rescued me six years ago. His healing spells were winding through my body, restoring my hands and arms he'd burned, the ribs that had cracked. Skin covered my hands again, solid, whole, unbroken. But, gods, it *hurt*.

Mick kissed the top of my head. "I want to tell you . . ."

I waited, but he didn't finish. He kept kissing me, stroking my hair, his body shuddering. I realized, after a stunned moment, that Mick was weeping.

Mick, my bad-ass biker boyfriend who could stand against a horde of demons without flinching, who'd faced my hell-goddess mother Beneath and laughed at his impending death. I raised my hand, touched his face, and marveled to feel tears on my fingertips.

"Not your fault," I whispered.

"I fought her with everything I had. Everything. And it wasn't enough. She still made me hurt you. Gods, Janet, I watched myself hurt you, heard the things I said to you."

"Hey, I didn't go down so easy." I brushed a tear from his rough face. "I think I did pretty good, in fact."

"I forced you down here to kill you. I knew the *karmii* would keep you pinned and stop you using your Beneath magic, the only way you can fight me."

"I know. It was a good idea." I lifted my hand, where the ring, miraculously, still clasped my finger. "What did you do to the ring?"

"Put a piece of my aura into it." Mick touched the silver, which vibrated a little, and I smelled the good smell of dragon fire. "I felt the compulsion spell start on me, so I went to a friend, a Zuni who's a shaman. I knew I couldn't fight the spell, and he couldn't either, but I asked him to help me put a tiny bit of aura into the ring, enough that it might touch you when I was gone. So that you wouldn't forget me, the real me, no matter what happened."

"You didn't give it part of your name, then?"

"There's no way to do that, and at the time, I still didn't know what was happening to me. I never remembered meeting Vonda, but then all of a sudden, she was singing my name, calling me. I'm an arrogant dragon, Janet. I never thought such a thing could happen to me, so I never took precautions."

Mick was so strong I would never have thought it possible either, and I knew he'd beat himself up about it for a while. "So how did the ring bring you back?"

"It held a piece of me that wasn't wholly enslaved. It allowed me, when the magic mirror multiplied that piece, to release enough of me from the spell so that I could give you my name. Giving it to you, the most powerful magical being around, took it away from her."

I didn't feel like the most powerful being around. I felt weak, sick, and magicless. I shifted, rock digging into my backside and thighs. "We couldn't be talking about this in some nice cushy hotel room?"

"I didn't want to move you. It's freezing outside, and I doubt I have the strength to go dragon right now. I don't even have enough to make a light spell."

And between the two of us, we had nothing but one pair

of jeans, and I was wearing those. "I don't suppose my cell phone survived."

"You're amazing, Janet."

"Why? Because I've broken another cell phone?"

"Because you didn't give up on me. You could have found a way to kill me, or you could have killed Vonda. Why didn't you?"

"Why do you think?" I wriggled, trying to get comfortable. "I didn't want you to die."

Mick stared at me in surprise. "I made sure you were alone and defenseless. I tried to kill you for her. Why didn't you protect yourself?"

I squirmed again; the damn cave floor was too hard. "Because I love you, you idiot. Vonda's the enemy, not you."

Mick kept looking at me, his eyes so blue, even in the darkness. I'd seen tenderness on his face before, but what I saw now was more than that—a deep joy, sudden understanding coupled with astonishment.

"Janet." His voice was clogged with emotion.

I wanted to see where that emotion led, but we couldn't relax yet. "By now, Vonda will have realized she's lost her dragon. I hope she packs up Ted and runs off, but I'm thinking she won't."

Mick nodded, still watching me with that awe. "She'll try to take another dragon. Drake or Colby, maybe."

I sat up suddenly, wincing when my head pounded. "Drake. Crap. His deadline."

"What deadline?"

Fighting, nearly dying, and excruciating pain had distracted me from the fact that Drake was about to call the dragon council and have them round up an army of dragons to hunt and fry Mick. "Drake gave me twenty-four hours to free you. He'll be coming to kill you."

"No, he won't."

"Why not? How do you know?"

"The magic mirror," Mick said. "It broadcasted into the dragon compound. They'll have seen our fight, seen me break from the spell."

"But now the council will know your name too—not to

mention Drake and Colby. And so will the magic mirror. This is so not good."

Mick shook his head. "It doesn't work that way. I didn't tell you my name; I *gave* it to you."

"While they listened."

"You didn't hear it with your ears; you heard it inside your head. They just heard me screaming."

"Oh," I said, relaxing. A little. I remembered Mick's long, drawn-out roar of pain, and I felt his body shaking even now. Vonda had reduced him to this, and for that, she'd pay.

"We have to deal with the witch," I said, my voice strengthening.

I started up, made it an inch, and fell back against Mick. I couldn't deal with a hangnail right now.

Mick held me in arms that felt so good. "Not yet. You need to get better before we leave. We're safe enough down here."

"With no light, and petroglyphs that can freeze me to death."

"Hey, darling, I'm here." The magic mirror's voice from the inch-wide shard sounded tiny and shrill, as though it had breathed helium. "At your service."

"The *karmii* will alert us to any danger," Mick said. "That's what they were made for, to protect the shamans who came down here to capture the magic of the stars."

I looked up at the walls. Comets and star clusters danced in the light from the mirror. Under these stars I lifted up, wound my arms around Mick's neck, and kissed him.

Mick made a raw noise in his throat. I pulled him closer, deepened the kiss, sliding my tongue into his mouth. It had been too long since I'd touched him, too long since I'd held him and taken comfort in his body.

He kneaded my back, pulled me up into him. Our lips brushed and bruised, the kiss awakening our hunger instead of slaking it.

I knew Mick wouldn't push me, because he worried about hurting me. He always worried about hurting me. I opened my jeans myself and wriggled out of them, and Mick's hands landed, warm, on my thighs. I wrapped my legs around him, touching him with hands that were whole and healed, thanks to him.

"Wait," he said.

Mick's eyes were black again, but the sparks in them bore the red of fire, not the white of shadow magic. Mick got to his feet and pulled me up with him. Both of us were coated with dirt and sweat and spattered with blood, and half my hair was singed. I didn't care. Mick lifted me in his arms, and our mouths sought each other, the warm kissing turning to craving.

"Ground's too rocky," Mick said between breaths.

I nodded, not really hearing him. Mick was hard and ready, and I was open, and all my pain went away as soon as he slid into me. I threw my head back and shouted for the pure joy of it.

Mick leaned me against the smooth cavern wall, the stone cool on my back. He cushioned me with his arms so I wouldn't get scraped, considerate of me even in the madness of passion.

We'd never been quiet lovers, and we saw no need to hold back now. I knew the magic mirror was listening, but it was tiny and pointed at the ceiling, so anyone watching would see only the ancient glyphs. They'd hear us, yes, but let them eat their hearts out.

I wrapped my legs around Mick's hips, held on to his shoulders, kissed his throat. My mouth fastened on his neck, me suckling him while he loved me hard. I could tell Mick was entirely free of Vonda because he took joy in every moment.

I gasped in sudden release, too quickly, Mick groaning right along with me. I had no memory of finishing, only me falling, landing on Mick in sudden and blissful exhaustion, and the shard of magic mirror crooning, "Oh, lovers, that was *good*."

Colby was still at the hotel. His frown filled the small shard of mirror, his light blue eyes angry under dark brows.

"No one's here but me and Drake."

"No one?" I asked in alarm. "Where's Maya? I told her to stay with you."

"Probably in New Mexico. She and that wolf-girl took off out of here not long after they got back. With Maya driving. Your grandmother and your cook went with them. It was their idea."

"*What?* And you let them?"

"'Let' isn't the word for it. Your grandmother snuck out the back while I was trying to keep Maya from going out the front. The Changer woman started fighting me, and Maya made a run for it. I couldn't run after them because I'm under the effing binding spell. I can't leave the hotel without Drake, and I can't shape-shift. I tried to contact you, but you were . . . busy. Take a bigger piece of mirror next time. I couldn't see a damn thing."

"What about Drake? Why did he let them go?"

"They're not dragons, so he couldn't be paid to care. Drake called off the vendetta on Mick, but not on Vonda. Drake's on his cell right now, conference calling with the dragon council. They're debating what to do. That should take about five years."

Or five minutes. When dragons decided to act, they acted swiftly. I didn't mind the dragons taking down Vonda, but my grandmother and Maya and everyone I cared about were with her. And as Colby said, Drake couldn't be paid to care about anyone but dragons.

Mick took the mirror from me, and I paced the cavern, trying to keep my Beneath magic from flaring out in my rage and panic.

"Hey, Micky," Colby said. "You look like your old self."

"I am my old self. Get Drake off the phone and tell him I'm using my dragon lord status to call dragons to converge on the site in New Mexico, but they are not to engage until my command. Understand? Do *not* engage. We have civilians involved, plus a witch who is an expert at dragon enslavement. And we'll need someone to pick us up at the rock cave on the S.J. Ranch. Got all that?"

"Fine. Only, don't keep me in the dark—let me see what's going on." He growled. "I *hate* being out of the action."

"I'll buy you a beer," I promised.

"Yeah, yeah. Good hunting."

The mirror went dark, Colby gone.

"You trust the dragon council?" I asked. "How do you know they won't use whatever dragon army you call to burn down the casino?"

Mick looked up at me from where he'd stretched out on the cavern floor, calm and quiet even though the rocks must be cutting his backside. "Using my status means the council is honor-bound not to override my orders. I'll hold them to that."

Damned dragon honor. Mick fully believed the council would do as he wished, and I knew enough now to believe it too. Even Colby, who bent rules to suit himself when he could, wouldn't violate dragon honor.

"Why did you tell Colby to have someone pick us up? We can't wait. My grandmother, my cook, and my best friend are rushing into the arms of an all-powerful witch."

Mick got to his feet, easily, casually, as though we had all the time in the world. Dragon arrogance. "I can't become dragon yet. Notice that I still can't conjure a light spell."

"You healed me."

"I did, and it took the last bit of magic I had. But I'd have been compelled to heal you, even if I hadn't wanted to. Now that you have my name, I'm honor-bound to help you. And you me."

He turned and made his way to the rockslide we had to climb, his tattoos looking normal again. No more shivering.

My mouth went dry as I watched him go, his last words ringing in my ears. I had the feeling this was going to get complicated fast.

Deputy Paco Lopez picked us up in a sheriff's SUV. He averted his eyes when he saw Mick stark naked and me topless under the jacket I'd retrieved, and I knew he was adding this incident to his list of weird things he knew about Janet Begay.

Lopez gave Mick a blanket, pretended to buy his explanation that he'd lost his clothes trying to save me from the caves, and politely didn't arrest either of us. He drove us from the ranch to the Holbrook road and the sinkhole, so Mick could fetch his clothes and his motorcycle.

The sides of the sinkhole had caved in during our fight, filling the hole with debris and ruining the straight-sided effect. I wondered whether the caverns below would buckle some more, possibly across the whole valley, and bury the rock caves. That would be too bad, because all those petroglyphs would be lost, and I had a feeling they were important as well as being beautiful.

Mick had left his bike well back from the lip of the sinkhole, his clothes folded neatly next to it. He'd taken time to do that before he turned dragon and came to kill me.

The bike I'd stolen was wrecked and unusable. We left Lopez frowning over it, mounted Mick's bike, me zipping my jacket to my chin, and prepared to race back to New Mexico.

As soon as we were out of Lopez's sight, Mick opened it up, and we flew down the road at an astonishing speed. The snow had stopped falling, but the road was covered with it and icing over. Mick somehow kept his Harley under us as we sailed down the highway toward Holbrook, me clinging to him like a spider.

An accident west of Gallup clogged lanes on the 40 with halted eighteen-wheelers, snowplows, and DPS. Mick charged around all of these at about a hundred miles per hour, catching the attention of every cop in sight. They were too busy to chase us, but I knew they'd radio ahead. Sure enough, several cars full of New Mexico's finest sprang out at us on the other side of Gallup, lights blazing. As soon as we hit the reservation, the tribal police joined in.

Mick never slowed. He ate up the few miles to the casino and swung into the parking lot, skidding out the bike as he stopped. I was off and running toward the hotel as three state police cars and two tribal dove into the lot with us.

"They've got my grandmother!" I screamed as men with weapons leapt out of patrol cars and tried to surround me and Mick. "They've kidnapped my grandmother and are holding her hostage upstairs!"

My panic wasn't faked—Grandmother's earth magic was well-grounded, but I had no idea whether she could hold her own against a witch like Vonda. The fact that Cassandra hadn't contacted me in any way meant that things were bad on their end. And not only was Vonda in there, but also Gabrielle, my not-so-stable half sister with powerful magic and violent tendencies.

The cops tried to stop me, of course, but I was strong and wiry and slipped by them. I was in the elevator in short order, leaving Mick to deal with them, doors closing on their warnings to me to stop.

All was quiet on the seventh floor as I hurried down the hall. The door to suite 726 was closed, and I heard only silence behind it.

But I could sense the auras in there—the bright white one of Gabrielle, the strange shadowy one of Vonda, Cassandra's pale cream. I didn't sense Nash, but that was normal. I also sensed the auras that shouldn't be there—Maya's tinged with angry red, Pamela with the white spark of her wolf, the dark green of Elena, and the crackling black and red of my grandmother.

The door wasn't locked. I opened it and walked right in.

There was a vortex in the middle of the floor. How it got there, I had no clue, but there it was, swirling away in the center of the beige carpet, my friends and family and all the furniture pressed against the walls. The white-hot evil I sensed from the vortex made my scalp prickle. Though I'd heard no sound in the hall, the room, now that I stood in it, was filled with sound—a roaring, screaming, maddening sound that poured up from the vortex.

I realized that the room was missing one person. "Where's Ted?" I shouted over the noise.

For answer, Gabrielle pointed at the vortex. The rest of my friends turned to me, either furious or terrified. All except Vonda, who stood quietly, unperturbed.

"Gabrielle," I yelled. "What did you do?"

Gabrielle looked up at me with a mixture of horror and anger. "*I* didn't do anything! It was her." Gabrielle pointed to Vonda, who stood casually, her gray silk outfit as pristine as ever. "She opened the vortex and fed her own husband into it."

Twenty-seven

This was all kinds of bad. That the vortex had opened here meant that the hotel had been built on one.

What had the hotel builders been thinking? Hadn't the shamans warned them? Or had someone had the great idea that building a hotel on a vortex would attract more business, maybe make the odds in the casino favor the house more?

Though I didn't sense my mother's unique brand of evil in this vortex, who the hell knew what was down there?

Vortexes are evil, no matter where they open. They're gateways to Beneath, but Beneath isn't all one place. It's a series of places, like different pieces of hell, each with its own gateway. You can jump into a vortex a few yards away from another and find yourself in a completely different world below. It will still be Beneath, still evil, still full of gods pissed off because they were left behind when the rest of humanity made it out to this world eons ago.

I didn't ever want to visit the world of Beneath again. It had been terrifying and, let's face it, just plain weird. My storm magic didn't work there, and the chances of me getting out once I was in weren't good.

"Gabrielle, what's down there?"

Gabrielle shrugged, her face so wan it was tinged with green. "Demons, I think. Probably a demon master. I don't know. I haven't seen this one before."

"Janet," Grandmother said from Elena's side. "You can't leave Mr. Wingate down there."

I glared around the room. "Please, someone tell me *why* you all let her open a vortex?"

"Like we had a choice," Maya said. She stood with Nash, who looked furious, not at Vonda, but at *me*. Of course.

I pointed at Gabrielle and at my grandmother. "You two had a choice. Why didn't you stop her?"

"I couldn't." Gabrielle's voice was small.

I focused again on Vonda, who coolly lounged against the bed, which had been upended.

"I took away your dragon," I told her. "Mick is free of you. If he tells me that you hurt him in any way, I'll kill you slowly and enjoy it."

Vonda looked bored. "Ted will be fine. I needed his sacrifice to open the vortex. Once I imbibe its magic, I'll be finished, and you all can go home. Safe and sound."

Sure, I believed her. "You can't imbibe the magic of a vortex. It will kill you."

"Not if you take precautions and know what you're doing. I'm experienced at this, Janet Begay. I find it interesting that you have so much magic inside you, and yet you never try to enhance it, never try to build it to its fullest potential. You've gotten misguided advice."

No, I'd gotten good advice from wise people who had compassion. I could barely handle the powers I already had. Why go looking for trouble?

"If you suck down the power of the vortex, you'll destroy this hotel and everyone inside it," I said. "Sorry, I don't like to throw away lives like that."

"But you don't have to. I could teach you much."

"Janet, don't listen to her," Grandmother said. "She has a silver tongue, that one."

"No kidding," I said.

Vonda smiled. "These people all claim to care about you. It's sweet."

"Let them leave."

"I will. Really, I will. They don't have much power that interests me—well, none that I haven't already taken from others." She glanced dismissively at Pamela, Cassandra, and Elena, not even seeming to see Maya. "Except Nash. And you."

Maya broke in angrily. "Why the hell does everyone want to get their hands on Nash?"

"Because he's unique," Vonda said without heat. "What I couldn't do with power like his. The bargain is this, Janet. You and Nash stay, and all the rest of these people can go home."

"I'll stay," Nash said at once. "If everyone, including Janet, leaves."

My friends, being my friends, all started arguing at once. Gabrielle's voice rose above the others. "You don't want *me*?" She sounded hurt.

Vonda answered. "Gabrielle, sweetie, you have powerful Beneath magic, but Janet's is as powerful, and she's wrapped it around earth magic, something no one else has ever done. I want that."

Gabrielle started for Vonda, but I grabbed Gabrielle and pulled her aside, speaking rapidly in a low voice. "Stop it. I need you. I don't trust her not to kill everyone as soon as you all walk out, so I need you to protect them. Especially Grandmother and Maya. Got it? Find Mick, tell him what's going on. But protect them. All right? You're stronger than anyone here, the only one who can keep them safe."

Gabrielle just looked at me. No eager happiness that I was trusting her, no anger that I wanted to use her. Only a thoughtful light in her eyes as she studied me.

Finally she nodded. "All right."

I didn't smile in relief or throw my arms around her. Gabrielle played her own game, and if she'd agreed, it was for her own reasons.

"Please," I said.

"Let it go, Janet. I said I would." Gabrielle turned to the others. "You heard her. Out. When Janet takes down the mean old witch, we can come back and dance on her entrails."

I needed to have a serious talk with Gabrielle.

I thought I'd have to fight Maya again, but Nash laid his hands on Maya's shoulders and spoke to her in a quiet voice. I saw Maya nod and Nash bend to kiss her. When Nash let Maya go, she walked away with tears in her eyes, but she went.

Grandmother gave me a long and defiant look as Elena followed Maya out. "I hope you know what you're doing," Grandmother said to me in Navajo.

"I don't, but this is the best chance I have to keep you safe. Watch Gabrielle."

"Oh, I intend to."

"And then we're going to talk about why you came out here in the first place," I said.

"I had my reasons. I'm not a stupid old woman, you know."

"I never said you were. Now let me and Nash deal with Vonda." I didn't want to mention the dragons Mick had put on standby, not knowing how much Navajo Vonda might know.

Pamela almost dragged Cassandra out of there, the only one who didn't protest about leaving me and Nash alone. Pamela's world was Cassandra, and when Cassandra was safe, Pamela was happy.

Nash gave me an inquiring glance, and I knew he wondered about Mick. Mick hadn't come charging up here, which meant he was planning something. Those cops wouldn't have distracted him for long. I hoped that Mick was quickly and quietly evacuating the hotel.

I shrugged at Nash, and he closed the door, leaving us with Vonda and a vortex.

"Now," Vonda said. "Would one of you please fetch Ted for me? I like him and want to keep him around."

I questioned her taste, but Ted was human, a civilian, as Mick termed it, and he didn't deserve to die a horrible death in a vortex. Really, he didn't, I told myself.

"It should be me that goes down there," Nash said. "Magic can't hurt me."

"*Maybe* it can't hurt you," I said. "The rules Beneath are different."

"Then what do you suggest?" he snapped.

Vonda didn't help; she watched us with cool indifference.

I sighed. "You have a rope?" I asked Nash.

"In my truck. With a grappling hook."

Of course he did. "Something in your truck doesn't help us much."

"Yes, it does," Vonda said. She didn't move, but suddenly, a rope and grappling hook rested at her feet.

My heart beat rapidly in surprise. Teleportation magic didn't exist, or shouldn't. Witches pushed and bent reality to make things happen—they cast spells that defended or healed or attacked or simply revealed something—but they weren't like television witches who popped in and out or snapped their fingers to produce what they wanted. The laws of physics still applied to mages. Moving something through space took vast amounts of energy, and it was easier to simply pick up something and carry it.

Somehow Vonda had learned these tricks, the most difficult magics in existence, and she didn't even look strained. The bitch.

"And a harness," Nash said calmly.

A harness appeared in the pile. Nash, who'd been a fierce Unbeliever until he'd met me, said nothing as he skirted the vortex, which looked like a tornado that had sucked away half the floor, and picked up the gear.

"Before I do this," he said to Vonda as he strapped on the harness. "Tell me what I am."

Vonda lifted her plucked brows. "Bring me my husband and then we'll talk."

"No," Nash said. "Now."

"Why do you think I know?"

"You seemed to know so much about everyone here. What about me? How did I become this way?"

Vonda's lip curled. "It's very complicated. I doubt you'd understand."

Before Nash could growl at her again, I made a wild stab. "Does it have anything to do with my hotel? And why you want it?"

Vonda looked at me with a flicker of anger, and did I detect worry? "We're wasting time. My husband might be being eaten by demons even as we speak."

"I don't notice you leaping to his rescue." I moved to the wet bar, which was happily in an alcove away from the vortex, opened the refrigerator, and took out a water bottle. The cardboard collar on the bottle said that the hotel would add four dollars to Vonda's bill if it was opened. I ripped off the collar, unscrewed the lid, and took a long drink.

"Answer Nash and answer me," I said. "You wanted me out of my hotel because you wanted the hotel. Not because it's close to a vortex, because there's one right under this hotel, which obviously you know how to open, and I don't notice you trying to take over this place. It's not the magic mirror. I thought maybe it was because of the Crossroads, but you could more quickly take over Barry's bar, which lies even closer to the ley line. Barry's human and easily disposed of, even with all his biker friends ready to shoot you. So what is it?"

"Really, Janet, you'd let my husband die?" Vonda asked me. "A helpless human?"

I took another sip of water. "I never liked Ted."

Vonda didn't want to tell me. I saw in her face that once she explained her desires to me, she knew I'd try to stop her obtaining those desires. Which meant that she wanted something dark and horribly dangerous that would make her darker and still more dangerous. I planned to stop her no matter what, but the more specifics I knew, the easier my task would be.

I watched her weigh her need for more power against Ted's life. Despite her neutral expression, the indecision in her eyes was interesting. She must really love Ted. Why, I had no idea. I wondered if I'd experience the same turmoil if someone had told me that to rescue Mick, I'd have to let go of something vastly important to me, maybe my magic itself.

I knew with sudden clarity that for me, such a choice would be simple. No turmoil about it. I loved Mick, and I'd give up all the secrets of the universe, the answer to magic itself, to keep him safe.

I took another quick sip of water to hide my bewilderment. This stage of my love was new and fragile, and I viewed it in wonder.

Vonda pressed her hands together, her silver bracelets clinking. "There was once a great mage," she said. "An Apache shaman who grew to such power that he was asked to leave his home and not come back. This was a hundred and more years ago, when the railroads were new, bringing more and more settlers out into Indian lands. The Apache followed the Crossroads from his home in the mountains down to Magellan, to a hotel that had just been built next to the railway line."

"The man who owned the hotel didn't want to let him in," Vonda continued. "The hotel was for whites only, but the Apache shaman refused to leave. Because the shaman was old and pathetic, and it was snowing, the owner let him sleep in the basement for a night. The next morning, the old man was gone."

"And this Apache shaman put a spell on my hotel?" I asked.

Vonda ran slender fingers up and down her bare arms. "No one knows. No one actually saw the man leave. He simply vanished. The owner didn't care. He was happy that the old Indian had moved on. But a mage who stopped at the hotel a few years later felt a vast magic there and sought its source. He found it in your basement, a sink of magic, vibrating with potential but impossible to tap." She drew a sharp breath. "There is a spell, you see, known only to the most powerful mages, that can be put on a specific thing to attract magic to it—a talisman, a place, a building in this case. It absorbs magic, sucking in more and more as time goes on, until the power it's built is incredible."

"And that's what you say happened to my hotel?" I said doubtfully. "The shaman put a spell on it to absorb magic? I've lived there almost a year, have worked wards all over it and deep into the walls. Why wouldn't I have known it was a magic sponge?"

"The spell is very subtle. Only a powerful witch or shaman who understands these things would find it, and without the right knowledge, the magic can't be tapped. But you were attracted to the hotel, weren't you?" Vonda smiled at me, her eyes still cool. "Why else would a young Navajo photographer, who thought herself a free spirit, decide it a good idea to open a *hotel*. A run-down place that hadn't been successful for any other owner before her?"

Good point. I remembered when I'd ridden past the Crossroads the first time and seen the hotel standing abandoned next to the biker bar. A square, brick, rather ugly thing, windows gone, stones crumbling, unwanted and alone. I'd felt an affinity for it, a need to pat its walls and reassure it that I'd take care of it. I'd been able to get the building cheap because no one wanted it—no one wanted even the land it was on. I'd stubbornly put the hotel back together and had fought time and again to hang on to it.

"You see?" Vonda said. "You sensed its power, even if you didn't know why. I have a feeling that's why your witch Cassandra came to you. She was attracted by the magic sink, but she must not know how to unlock its power, because she would have by now if she could." Vonda took on a dreamy look. "All that potential, and it's just sitting there. Protected by you and your dragon boyfriend and your magic mirror, while it quietly imbibes all your magics at the same time."

"It's draining us?" I asked in alarm. But my magic and my ability had *grown* since I'd moved in. She made no sense.

"No. That's the beauty of it. The magic uses your power to enhance its own. It builds but doesn't destroy." Her dreamy look turned wistful. "And now you won't let me have it."

"Damn right I won't." Vonda was a magic stealer. Letting her get hold of a well of sparkly magic that had been building for a hundred years would not be a good idea. She'd unmake the world just for the fun of it and then take Ted out for pizza.

"What has all this got to do with me?" Nash asked in a hard voice. "Am I linked to the hotel somehow? I'm negative magic while it's positive?"

"Nice theory, but no," Vonda said. "But you're similar to the hotel. Just as a mage can create a power sink, a mage can create a power *hole*. A place from which all magics are driven out, or maybe the magic is absorbed and negated, canceled. The spell I'm thinking of is very, very difficult, almost impossible for all but the strongest mages. It was first created to be a defensive spell, usually put into a talisman and to be used only for the short term—if the mage knows he has to go up against a very strong magical being, say. The talisman would cancel out the magic of the attacker—in theory. I've never actually seen such a spell in action."

"I never remember anyone giving me a talisman or casting a defensive spell on me," Nash said. "Or a spell of any kind, not that I'd have believed it anyway."

"I'm not sure exactly what happened to you," Vonda said, looking at him thoughtfully. "But if a group of very powerful mages combine efforts, they can sink the magic negativity into a larger thing, such as a building. Or sometimes a person if that person is strong enough to hold it, but that's very rare. Mick told me your history. I'm willing to bet that in Baghdad, you led your men into a building that had been turned into a talisman for magic negation, probably by a group of mages working together. They must have been very powerful. Spells like that have a great sense of self-preservation. When the bomb went off with you in the building, the spell likely dove into the strongest thing it could find. You."

Nash's face drained of color until his unshaved whiskers stood out stark against his skin. "Are you saying that my men died, but I stayed alive so that a *spell* could survive?"

"It chose you, Nash Jones," Vonda said. "Knowing that you were the strongest person in that building. You grew up around vortexes in that little town of yours. It's possible that a spark of magic lingered in you, and the spell was drawn to it. Or maybe it just sensed your strength. You are a very strong man." Her gaze roved up and down him in appreciation. "But no matter how it happened, you now possess some of the greatest negative magic that I have ever witnessed."

"Can the spell be reversed? Or taken out? Or wear off?"

Vonda shrugged, silver clinking again. "Who knows? I do know that I want what's in you. So does Gabrielle, and so does Janet's mother. How deliciously powerful I could be if I could siphon off that negative energy but keep it from taking away my own magic. I tried to do it while you were unconscious in the hospital, but it didn't work."

I remembered the woman who'd pretended to be Nash's mother while he lay in the ICU. I'd thought Gabrielle had sent her to kidnap Nash, but I realized now that not even Gabrielle was powerful enough to create a slave from nothing. "What was that thing?" I asked. "How did you do that?"

"A simple spell," Vonda said offhandedly. "An animated talisman, infused with my magic, and fashioned to look like Nash's mother. It was supposed to steal his magic and bring it back to me, but I had no idea at that time how strong Mick was. Or Nash." She ran her tongue over her pale lips.

"How the hell did you know what my mother looked like?" Nash snarled.

"Photos. You have one of her in your office. Ted snapped a picture of it for me when he went to talk to you."

The ever-handy Ted. I remembered Nash telling me, irritated, that Ted had barged into his office to accuse Nash of doing his job badly.

"Asshole," Nash said.

"It didn't work, so the effort was wasted. Your Stormwalker friend and the dragon protect you well. But of course they do—they want your magic to serve *their* needs, not anyone else's."

I noticed I was crushing the water bottle in my hand, and I set it down. "If you want to keep Nash alive to take his magic, why are you making him go into a vortex?"

Vonda looked surprised. "If his negative magic isn't powerful enough to survive a vortex, then it's of no use to me. This is a good way to find out."

"You are one sick woman," I said. "But you're right

about one thing. I won't let you get your hands on my hotel, and I won't let you get them on Nash. We should go, Nash. Let her fish up Ted on her own."

"I can't." Nash's face was nearly green, but he shook his head. "I can't deliberately let a man die when I can save him. Even a man as irritating as Ted." He looked up at Vonda. "But when I bring him back, you and he are leaving my county. My state. No, the entire Southwest. I'm putting you two in every police database in the country and sending the info around the world. You do anything to anyone ever again, I'll be alerted, and when I find you again, I won't hold back."

His voice was cold, Nash at the end of his tether. He would never deliberately hunt and kill another person—unless they broke the law. Then they wouldn't have a prayer of escaping the wrath of Nash Jones.

"All right, hurry up," I muttered. I couldn't walk away from Ted either. Demons from Beneath could be nasty, and even Ted didn't deserve death at their hands.

Nash gave me a nod, dug the grappling hook through the carpet into the cement floor, and dove straight into the vortex.

Twenty-eight

I started for the rope, but Vonda reached me before I could and shoved a cold pistol into my ribs. "Not you."

I brought up my Beneath magic to squish her pistol in half, but she slapped me with a touch of it herself, canceling mine out. The vortex, responding to our little play, yawned wider.

This could get ugly fast. "Let me help him. Nash is my friend."

"I want to see what happens to him. Or what he does to the vortex."

The rope stretched tight, the grappling hook creaking as it swayed. I prayed that Nash had fixed it right, though he seemed to know what he was doing. There was no sound from below us, only the rushing, roaring noise of the vortex.

"If Nash dies, you're going in there headfirst," I said.

"And you with me."

Fine. I could kill her down there as well as I could up

here. "How did you acquire Beneath magic? Witches are earth magic."

"Correction, witches are *supposed* to have only earth magic. I learned to be open-minded."

"But how did you get it? The more important question: who from?" Or did I mean *from whom*? I'd never done well with English grammar.

"From Gabrielle." Vonda smiled. "The day I met her."

Shit. "Does she know?"

"No. Gabrielle thinks she is powerful, but I am more powerful."

"You're a leech," I said. "You suck power from others the same way a leech draws blood. What happens if you get too bloated with magic? You explode?"

Interesting thought. Taking inventory of myself, I knew she hadn't taken power yet from me. Why hadn't she? And could I overload her if she tried?

"I learned a long time ago how to make sure I don't hurt myself," Vonda said.

"How long ago? Are you even human?"

"I am. A hundred years and more I've been imbibing magic." She looked me up and down and smiled. "You'll taste good."

"A hundred years. Like the Apache in your story. Are you him? Is that why he disappeared? You changed form?"

"No. He died. I killed him and buried his body under the railroad bed. *After* I took his magic. Well, what was left of it, damn him."

I leaned against the wall, still wary of her pistol. "Why don't you tell me about it? While Nash and Ted are busy fighting for their lives?"

Vonda shrugged as though we chatted at a cocktail party, a boring one. "I lived in Magellan back then, very young, about sixteen. My mother was a night bird, a lady of the evening, if you will, and naturally, I became one too. I'd lived in Magellan long enough to understand that the vortexes held magic, and that I held magic. And that I was strong. The hotel owner hired me to go down to the Apache and keep him quiet. The Indian smelled and was filthy, and I didn't want to touch him. But the hotel owner promised to pay me a large sum—large for those days—and down I went. I figured out pretty quickly that he was a powerful shaman, too powerful for his own people's comfort. I stole that old man's magic tricks, but he'd already dumped most of what he had into the walls of the hotel, locking it in with spells I couldn't break. That made me very, very angry. So I drained him of everything he had left. Once he was too weak to fight me, I stuck a knife into his chest."

Heartless bitch. "And carried him upstairs and buried him in the desert with no one knowing?"

"Oh, the hotel owner knew. He helped me bury the man. Who cared? He was only an old Apache, outcast from his tribe. We didn't have to be PC in those days."

I doubted Vonda had ever caught on to treating anyone with dignity, no matter who they were or what their culture. "So that makes it all right?"

Vonda laughed, and she really shouldn't have. "Janet, I was young and broke. I wanted his magic, and I wanted the money. The Apache was like an animal to me, one ready to die. I did him a favor."

When Nash came out that vortex, I was pushing her in. End of story.

I imagined the terror of the old man in the dark of my basement, fear shining in his eyes, as the beguiling woman stole the last of what he was. Vonda hadn't even had the decency to return him to his home, his lands, his people. She'd dumped his body, and he'd disappeared as though he'd never existed. Had he been able to find his ancestors? Or was he still out there wandering, searching? I'd never seen any ghosts on the railroad bed, but others, including Fremont, claimed to.

"And now you're back to see if you can take the magic out of my basement," I said. "Why did you wait so long to return to Magellan?"

Vonda looked annoyed. "Because I knew I wouldn't be strong enough to tap into the magic. It took me decades to build up my powers and educate myself. No one wanted that old hotel, and I thought I could simply come back when I was ready and take it. And then you moved in. A Stormwalker with Beneath magic, drawing wards all over the place. Then your dragon turned up and added *his* magic. Irritating. I had to watch and plan, but once I'd learned how to suck away a dragon name, I struck. I don't care that you've taken Mick away from me. I'll fight you, and I'll win. I'll get your magic and the rest of the shaman's magic from your hotel. And then I'll be invincible."

"You know . . ." A familiar male voice came from the door, one I'd last heard talking to me from a wall in the cave. "I always wondered what happened to that old shaman."

Coyote walked in, his hands in the pockets of his denim jacket, his dark eyes watchful. I let out a quiet breath in some relief. About damn time.

"I looked for him for a long time before I decided he must have died," Coyote said. "You buried him under the railroad bed, eh? Not good."

Vonda drew herself up, uncertainty flickering in her eyes. "I'm not afraid of you, Trickster. I can take your magic too."

"I'd be afraid of me." Coyote grinned. "You don't know everything."

"I've learned. I've studied. God magic is a little different, but it can be done."

I saw the shadow detach from her, the strange, smoky piece of her aura that floated across the room and made for Coyote. The blue nimbus of Coyote's own aura encircled him, but when the shadow touched it, the blue dimmed.

"No!" I yelled.

"Don't worry, Janet," Coyote said, but his face had lost color. "I always have a trick or two up my sleeve."

I swung to face Vonda, bringing my own magic to bear. I had to stop her.

"Can we come in now?"

My grandmother chose that moment to push her way into the room, Elena with her. Behind them came Mick.

"Mick—crap—get them out of here!"

Mick, his eyes firmly blue, closed the door and locked it. "It's all right, Janet."

"No, it isn't! Vonda's stealing Coyote's magic. Nash is down there." I pointed at the vortex. *And you're still too weak to use any dragon magic.* I kept that to myself.

"And I have a god," Vonda said, another shadow snaking out to surround Coyote. "Much better than a dragon."

Damn it, we had to stop her.

"Don't kill her," Elena said.

In her polyester yellow pants and bright top, her hair in a black bun, Elena could have been any of the RVers playing the slots in the casino downstairs. My grandmother still wore her more traditional skirts, but as she took a stance next to Elena, I saw the crow in her aura, the hint of black feathers, the dark eye, the anger.

"I have to," I babbled at them. "If she takes Coyote's power, we're done for. Everyone is done for."

"She won't have it." Elena unfolded her arms, hands at her sides. I'd watched those plump hands chop vegetables for stew with graceful competence, and now her fingers hung loose, relaxed.

"You stole something from me, Shadow Walker," Elena said to Vonda. "From my family."

I stared at her. "The Apache?"

"He was my great-great-grandfather. My ancestor. His power should have passed down through the generations to me."

Vonda didn't look concerned. "That's the way it goes. He was gone long before you were born."

"We are always connected to the ancestors, ignorant witch. Family—past and present—all connected. That's what you don't understand. There is no break. You took from me. Now I will take from you."

"You can't," Vonda said. "You have no magic, old woman."

"I have a little," Elena said. "I have the latent magic of my family, still there in spite of what my great-great-grandfather did."

"Liar." Vonda sneered. "If you had even a spark of that old man's magic, you would have already retrieved what he left at the hotel. I don't see that you have, so you must not know how."

"I know how." Elena's voice was matter-of-fact. "But I know the magic is safe where it is. When I saw Janet and her dragon move in to the hotel, I knew my great-great-grandfather's legacy would be protected. And now I look after it too."

"You can't take it," Vonda said with conviction. "You're not powerful enough. You can't work the spells."

"No power comes without a price," my grandmother broke in. "You pay a price for anything you take in life. Even if you avoid the price as long as you can, it will someday find you."

Did her words make Vonda uneasy? If so, the woman hid it well. "*You* can't take it either."

Grandmother shrugged, not looking worried.

"For me, the price would be too great," Elena said. "I have all I need. I have a family, and I have my friends. And my friends in this room are very, very strong."

Fear flickered across Vonda's face, and she looked at Mick. Mick was grinning that wicked grin that turned me inside out, and I felt his aura flare. No more weakness; he was a full-strength, full-powered dragon.

Mick ripped sudden fire through the shadows around Coyote, severing them from Vonda. Vonda gasped, and quickly, before the shadows faded, Elena stepped into them and grabbed them with both hands.

Coyote's blue nimbus burst out as strong as ever. It surrounded Elena and the shadows, and the shadows started swirling through Elena's hands and into her body. Elena looked at Vonda, a smile on her face.

I knew that smile. Elena used it when someone was foolish enough to bother her or, worse, tried to steal a morsel of food while she sliced up something with her wickedly long knife. The smile would be followed by choice words in the Apache language and her knife rising until the intruder whirled and ran.

Vonda had stolen much more than mushrooms for the stew. She'd told me that she'd viewed the old Apache as little better than an animal, as though he didn't matter. But every life mattered, because every life was connected to every other life in the world. A part of that old and powerful Apache man lived on in Elena, and he wanted his revenge.

Elena started chanting words I didn't understand. More shadows unwrapped from Vonda and streamed toward my cook, and Vonda started to scream. My grandmother, next to Elena, simply watched.

As Vonda's shadows left her, one by one, the vortex started to shrink. In alarm I grabbed Nash's rope. "Nash!"

I felt warmth at my side as Mick joined me. In spite of the craziness going on in this room, I felt the surging joy of working side by side with the man I loved, the two of us understanding each other so well that we didn't have to speak or even signal. Mick started pulling up the rope, grunting with the effort of it, and I whirled in time to defend him from Vonda's attack.

She was losing the magic that kept her looking like a cool, successful forty-year-old woman. Vonda's silk skirt and blouse began to hang on her body as she shrank, her limbs growing thin and wasted. Her face became pinched, skin receding to the skull, and still she fought with strength. The power she'd acquired was vast.

I didn't pity her. Vonda had stolen for years from the magical, siphoning what she wanted from them. She'd tried to steal Mick from me, taking the one person in my life who'd always believed in me. I wouldn't forgive her for that.

Elena kept chanting, her eyes closed, a look of vast concentration on her face.

The next part happened so swiftly that for a long time afterward I puzzled over the exact sequence of events. Nash's hand, blackened with soot, met Mick's, and his face, just as blackened, appeared within the whirling madness of the vortex. Nash had his arm looped under Ted's, dragging the man up and out. Ted was alive, but barely, his face as black with soot as Nash's, and cut and bleeding.

At the same time, the door burst off its hinges, sailed across the room, smacked into the again-whole window, shattered the glass, and tumbled out into the night.

Gabrielle stormed in on a wave of Beneath magic, her

hands full of white fire. I tried to get in her way, but she flew across the room, and her boot heels connected with Vonda's chest.

Gabrielle landed on her feet as Vonda went down, and smiled a wide, mad smile. "Die, bitch. That's the last time you suck magic out of me."

"Gabrielle, no!"

My shouting went unheeded. Gabrielle fired up her magic and flung it at Vonda, and the vortex went crazy.

The whirlpool of it expanded, sending the rest of us slamming into the walls of the big room. Vonda screamed and screamed as Elena stole from her and the Beneath magic burned her, Vonda's body dying as it should have done a hundred years past. Nash and Ted gained the floor, what was left of it. Mick smacked his fire at Gabrielle as she wound up to throw more Beneath magic at Vonda.

All the while, Elena was chanting, chanting, Vonda's shadows sliding into her hands. When Elena opened her eyes, they were white with power. She'd become the Shadow Walker, while Vonda slowly crumpled into ash.

With the last of her strength, Vonda shoved Gabrielle toward the vortex. Gabrielle flailed on the edge, and I screamed and grabbed for her.

Ted, lifting his head, seeing what was left of his wife, wailed in sudden grief. I saw his hand go to the pistol Vonda had dropped, and before I could draw breath to shout, he'd aimed it at Gabrielle and pulled the trigger.

The gun exploded from the energy in the room, but the bullet sailed straight and true. Gabrielle didn't notice, trying to keep herself—and me—out of the abyss, and the bullet shoved itself right into her side.

Gabrielle fell to her knees as blood gushed from the wound. I clamped my hands around her wrist as she slid backward into the vortex, my feet braced on the floor where reality met Beneath. I felt Gabrielle go slack, and her weight started dragging me into the vortex with her.

She looked at me in pathetic confusion, pain clouding her eyes. "I'm sorry, Janet."

"No!" I yelled at her. "I've got you. I'm not letting go. You're not giving up."

But she was slipping, falling, and I either had to release her or be pulled down with her.

And then Mick was there. Without a word, he laced his strong arm around my waist and wound a string of bright magic around Gabrielle. The two of us hauled her, inch by inch, bleeding and coughing, back to the carpet.

Vonda was dead, and Elena had all the magic. Gabrielle was down, bleeding. And still the vortex was there.

"Damn it," I said, gritting my teeth. "Mick, help me. We have to close it."

He and I had closed a vortex before. But that had been in the middle of a raging storm, when I'd been supremely powerful. The storm outside had died, now when it would have been so helpful, and I couldn't risk using my Beneath magic. The vortex rose like a vast drain, and in a few moments, we'd all be cascading down its pipes.

"Janet," Mick said, his voice so calm that it reached me even through the roar. "Give me a little of your magic."

I wasn't sure what he meant, but I drew forth a spark of Beneath magic and fed it into his hand. Mick smiled, and I felt him wrap that spark of magic within a fireball of his own and fling it at the vortex.

The vortex crackled with fire all along its edges, but other than that, nothing happened. Mick frowned, as though puzzled, that dragon curiosity again. I wanted to scream at him.

Cassandra appeared in the doorway, Pamela behind her. Maya was with them, and neither stopped her running to Nash.

Coyote joined me on my other side, watching the vortex, not bothering to help, damn him. Cassandra pressed her hands together and began to chant, magic flowing from her like a river of smoke. Still the vortex yawned, the power in it massive. It was hungry, and it wanted us.

Gabrielle lay still on the carpet, with Nash pressing his hand to her side, trying to stop the bleeding. He'd taken the gun from Ted, who was now on his hands and knees, weeping over the pathetic remains of Vonda.

Gabrielle opened her eyes and struggled away from Nash. He tried to stop her, but Gabrielle kicked away and lunged for Vonda's body. She scraped it up, silk fabric and all, and hurled Vonda into the vortex.

The vortex flared, the magic hitting the ceiling and tearing plaster from it. The automatic sprinklers engaged, pouring a sudden cascade of water over us.

Mick and I smacked the vortex with magic, and Coyote, next to me, finally decided to help. My grandmother calmly walked to Coyote's side, closed her eyes, and started to whisper in Navajo.

It wasn't going to close. I silently swore at whoever had decided to build the hotel on top of a damn vortex. Their fault we were all going to be sucked into hell. Would it stop with us? Or swallow the entire hotel?

Wind whipped through the room, burning my still-healing skin. The water from the sprinklers became a deluge. We'd land in Beneath exhausted and soaked, and then have to face whatever demon master was down there.

I thought I heard a rustle of wings, so many wings. The kachinas? I wondered. The Hopi gods, come to help us? Or to shove me and Gabrielle in for using too much Beneath magic?

Through the middle of this tumult, Elena quietly approached the edge. She stood at Grandmother's side, stretched out her hand and, without any noticeable effort, let one of the shadows drop from it.

The vortex trembled. Whatever the hell kind of magic had been in that shadow, the vortex didn't like it. Elena watched, unperturbed, as the vortex boiled and whirled, trying to belch out what she'd thrown into it.

"Now!" Coyote shouted.

He grabbed my hand and Grandmother's on his other side. I caught on and seized Mick's hand, who in turn caught Cassandra's, who took Pamela's, then Maya, who held on to Nash, and all around the circle. Elena stood next to my grandmother, both hands over the vortex.

I felt us connect—Stormwalker, dragon, witch, god, crow, Changer, shaman, and the void that was Nash. It was heady, it was powerful, too powerful to contain. We fought the Beneath magic of the vortex, battling it back as it tried to reach for and obliterate Elena.

The backlash was incredible. I gritted my teeth, trying to stay on my feet. Mick's strong hand on mine kept me grounded, but I barely remained upright. His love for me and the music of his name flowed through the connection between us—it was wonderful but also seriously distracting right now. I kept wanting to stop to absorb more of the music. His name was part of me now, filling me with Mick and his magic. Earth magic, dragon magic, more than enough to ground me.

The vortex yawned wider, and Gabrielle screamed. But Nash was there, standing in front of her, guarding her from the deadly pull. The vortex touched Nash and shank back.

It was lessening. Under the combined power of our magic, the vortex started to give up. Elena held out her hand and dropped another shadow. She shouted in a high-pitched, wailing voice, blowing out every light in the room.

The vortex swirled once, then with a rush and a roar, winked out of existence.

The room went black but for the fingers of dawn that touched the broken window, and the pattering of water on the carpet was loud in the sudden silence.

Twenty-nine

The morning sun burnished the emergency vehicles filling the parking lot. Medics surrounded a frightened Gabrielle, and I stuck next to her in case she panicked and tried to kill the nice humans trying to help her. Grandmother and Elena planted themselves by the stretcher, once again looking like nothing more than two harmless older ladies who'd come to the casino for an exciting night out.

The hotel manager, of course, wanted to know why we'd wrecked the room. The window was broken out, the lights were destroyed, the furniture was shattered against the walls, and everything had been soaked by the sprinklers. Plus the door to the room was now in the parking lot. Coyote walked off with the manager, talking rapidly. I wondered if Coyote would use his magic to make the man forget all about us, or whether one of us would be writing a large check.

Nash turned over the handcuffed Ted to the New Mexico police, and I noticed Mick fading into the shadows while the police loaded up Ted and drove away with him. Nash did not look good—pale smudges of skin showed through the black on his face, and his clothes were soot-marked and torn, as though he'd fought his way through a fire. When I looked at him, wanting to ask what had happened to him, Nash put his arm around Maya and walked away from me.

No sign of dragons in the powder blue sky. They'd obeyed Mick's command not to attack, and Mick must have sent them away again. I loved a man who could keep everything straight.

"Grandmother," I said in a low voice as the paramedics loaded Gabrielle into the ambulance. "You and Elena knew all about Vonda and the Apache shaman in my basement, didn't you? Any reason you didn't bother telling me?"

"We didn't know all about it," Grandmother said. "We suspected, once we discovered she was a Shadow Walker, but we didn't know for certain until we heard Vonda tell the story."

I ground my teeth. "*This* is what you and Elena were conspiring about in the kitchen? And Coyote right along with you?"

"I don't have to share everything I do with you, Janet. I have my own friends, my own puzzles to solve."

"Coyote's important errand was to discover all he could about Vonda?"

"Yes."

"When I could have used his help figuring out Mick's name," I finished. "You still should have told me."

"I didn't want you to try to stop us going after the Shadow Walker," Grandmother said. "You were too worried about what would happen to Mick if she died, and rightly so. Besides, Coyote wasn't able to find Mick's name."

"Because Mick had to tell me the name himself." My anger softened. "I get that now. Vonda's shadows sucked Mick's name from him, but when Mick gave it to me as a gift, it was stronger than Vonda's pull."

"Because your emotional tie to Mick is powerful," Grandmother said. "Very powerful."

Mick's arms came around me from behind, his wonderful heat surrounding me. "Exactly."

Grandmother sniffed. "Firewalkers are always sentimental." She gathered her skirts and started to climb into the ambulance, Elena after her.

"Where are you going?" I asked them in surprise.

"To the hospital. We've decided to look after Gabrielle. She needs us."

"She's my sister and not your responsibility."

"I know she's your sister," Grandmother said. "Which means she's trouble. I trained you; now Elena and I will train her. Go home, Janet, and leave us to it."

The ambulance doors slammed behind her before I could say good-bye, the med techs wanting to get Gabrielle to the hospital as quickly as possible. The lights went on, the siren wailed, and the ambulance hurried out of the parking lot and onto the highway.

I leaned back against Mick and sighed happily. "Let's go home."

He kissed my hair. "You don't want to rest here awhile? Plenty of beds. Room service. Anything you want."

Tempting. We were a long way from home, and I didn't relish the cold ride back. But no. "I don't think I should stay in a hotel right on top of a vortex. Too dangerous. Let's go to my nice, safe hotel with the magic sink in the basement, the nosy magic mirror, and Colby and Drake the irritated dragons."

"We'll send them all away and lock the doors, then I'll cook you a kick-ass breakfast."

"Now, that I can go for."

I snuggled under his chin and basked in the beauty of standing with my lover, mine once more, with the rising sun illuminating the New Mexico landscape. This was happiness.

"Hey!"

I jumped at the harsh voice. A large human male in a T-shirt and biker vest had approached us. He had shaggy hair, a salt-and-pepper beard, huge arms covered with tatts, and he carried a gun in a shoulder holster under his vest. Several similar-looking men backed him up.

"I think you took something of mine," he said.

The motorcycle. Well, shit.

I did not want to tell this tall, angry, armed man that I'd wrecked his Harley on a lonely road seventy miles from here. "Hopi County Sheriff's Department," I said, trying on a smile. "You'll find it there."

"Hopi . . . Where the hell is that?"

"Flat Mesa," Mick said, voice rumbling. "Arizona."

"It was an emergency," I put in.

The biker drew out his pistol. "Listen, bitch, you'd better take me to this Podunk town, and you'd better hope that nothing happened to my ride, or you'll owe me for the rest of your life. Your boyfriend too. Got it?"

Damn it. I'd tried to help him; really I'd tried. I didn't want to use Beneath magic so near a vortex, but I couldn't risk the man shooting Mick.

Before I could raise even a spark of magic, another pistol pressed into the man's temple, and I heard the click of a handcuff.

"I'd be happy to escort you to Hopi County to locate your bike," Nash Jones said. "At *my* sheriff's department. And you'd better hope that the weapon I just witnessed you threaten my friends with is registered and that when I search you, you're clean. Your colleagues can come with us, if they want. Or they can go. Now."

The other bikers backed away and left their fellow to his fate. Nash plucked the pistol out of the biker's hand and clicked the second cuff around the man's other wrist.

"Take her home," Nash said to Mick, and then gave me a severe look. "We'll talk about the stolen motorcycle later."

Without further word, Nash started pulling the biker toward his truck, his voice droning the man's Miranda rights.

Maya, who'd been waiting for Nash, threw up her hands in exasperation. "Really, Nash? I thought we were going to spend the night here. Don't you *ever* take vacation?"

Nash didn't answer but shoved the perp into his black

pickup. He turned around, crushed a kiss to Maya's mouth, then left her with a stunned but glowing look on her face.

One month later

Early March brought rain but an end to the frigid weather. I'd reopened the hotel a week after our New Mexico adventure, and business was booming, with a backlog of reservations that would last me all the way through the summer.

Elena was back in the kitchen, as prickly as ever, behaving as though nothing unusual had happened. She still glared at anyone who interrupted her prepping, and now that I knew she had amazing magic at her disposal as well as sharp knives, I gave her all the space she wanted.

Colby hung around as well. Still bound to the dragon council, but at least allowed to come and go between the hotel and the dragon compound near Santa Fe, he decided it was fun to drink in my saloon and irritate me. But strangely, Elena started to like him, and even let him into the kitchen. I wondered if Elena was gearing up to enslave a dragon now that she had all the magic Vonda had accumulated. So far, though, it looked as though she only enslaved Colby with sweet tamales and cornbread fritters.

Grandmother had taken the recovering Gabrielle back to Many Farms, and I wasn't certain how I felt about that. On the one hand, I knew that if anyone could keep Gabrielle under control, it was my grandmother. On the other, I worried about the rest of my family with Gabrielle's destructive magic. But then I thought about my nosy, gossiping aunts visiting the house every day, and I had to smile.

Mick and I . . .

Mick took me to the Winslow hotel for a much-needed vacation, and we rarely left the bedroom. I showed him how much I'd missed him, and he showed me how grateful he was to me for rescuing him. We had to put sound-smothering spells on the room so we wouldn't be asked to leave.

Sometimes we simply held each other in the moonlight and listened to the trains rumble by. Mick would touch the ring on my finger, and I'd sing notes of his true name. We were bound in the dragon way, he said, and the way he whispered that made me shiver in delight.

My promise to marry him still held, but we hadn't told anyone about our engagement. It was fun, having a lover's secret.

I didn't see much of Nash Jones, except for when he sternly summoned me to the sheriff's office to lecture me about stealing the motorcycle. He'd found meth on the biker he'd arrested, plus learned that the biker had stolen the gun he'd waved in my face. Said biker was languishing in Nash's jail, unable to make bail, on charges of assault, possession, dealing, theft, and other things. I'd have to be a witness, Nash told me, but he let me off with a warning about the motorcycle.

He said nothing about Vonda, or the vortex, or his rescue of Ted, who was in jail in New Mexico for shooting Gabrielle. Nash brushed me off coldly when I tried to ask him what had happened inside the vortex.

So I asked Maya. She breezed into the hotel on a morning in early March, ready to check the maintenance work she'd done in the basement. Once she and Fremont had restored everything from Vonda's last deterioration spell, my electricity and plumbing had worked like a dream.

The basement fascinated me now that I knew magic had been sunk there, though I couldn't discern anything different about it. I found no spots where magic dragged at me or jumped up and down and screamed at me, and even the piece of magic mirror I flashed around couldn't distinguish the long-dead shaman's magic from any other. Elena never said that she'd tapped into it, or even mentioned it at all. Maybe the Apache's magic had so long permeated the bones of the hotel that the magic simply had become part of the structure.

"Did Nash tell you?" I asked Maya as she checked her wiring. "About what happened to him in the vortex?"

"Yes," Maya said. "And he told me not to tell you."

"It might be important. I'm worried about him."

"So am I."

"Maya . . ."

Maya took off her work hat, ran her hand through her hair, and leaned one foot back against the wall. "You're right. It was awful. Nash has been spending nights at my house, and one time, I woke up and found him crying. He was pretty pissed off that I'd caught him, but I made him tell me what was wrong." She gave me a heartbroken look. "Janet, when Nash went down into the vortex, he found himself back in that building in Iraq, the one that blew up when he and his men were in it. It happened all over again—the explosion, the fire, the walls collapsing, his men screaming. Only this time, Nash knew he'd be able to save one man: the asshole Ted Wingate. Nash said he knew none of it was real, but at the same time, he didn't have a choice about who he could save. He had to bring Ted back, and all the others had to die. Again."

I listened in horror. "Oh, gods." Whether some demon Beneath or Vonda herself had made Nash relive the worst day of his life, it had been an act of pure cruelty. "Poor Nash."

"He's getting better. Slowly. Don't you dare tell him I told you."

"No." Some secrets needed to be kept.

"Nash doesn't blame you," Maya said. "But he doesn't want to see you. Or Mick, or anyone really, because . . . well, Nash isn't good with letting people see him vulnerable."

"At least he's talking to you."

"Yeah." Maya put her hat back on, her eyes soft. "He's talking to me. I'm going to move in with him."

That caught me by surprise. "Yeah?"

"We talked about it and decided we'd live in his house in Flat Mesa. It's closer to his office. Besides, I need to do *something* about his décor. The whole weapons and weight machine look has got to go."

Wow. Maya's house was beautiful, and I imagined she'd work her magic on Nash's plain one.

Nash Jones shopping for furniture and curtains. It boggled the mind.

I left her, my thoughts whirling, and went back upstairs.

Mick met me in my bedroom and gave me a long, bone-melting kiss. I loved this man, this dragon-shifter with the hard body, who stood in front of me in jeans and nothing else. I knew there was nothing else, because Mick's jeans rode low on his hips, no underwear in sight.

"Can we tell now?" I asked him. "Our friends will drive us crazy, but I think they should know. Happy secrets should be shared."

Mick kissed me again and shrugged. "Whenever you're ready."

Now I was excited. I knew the first person I wanted to tell, so I took out my cell phone and called the number of my home in Many Farms.

Gabrielle answered. "Hey, Janet. Your grandmother is one amazing bitch."

I agreed. "How's it going?"

Gabrielle made a sound of disgust. "She wants me to do all these rituals, morning, noon, and night. Tedious, time-consuming rituals. Gods, tell her to at least let me go to the movies once in a while."

I couldn't help but smile. "Do the rituals. I hated them too, but they helped me. A lot."

"Snotty big sister," Gabrielle said. "Come on up to Many Farms and take me out of here. I want to have some fun."

"Only if you can control yourself. No killing people."

"Oh, all right. If you insist." I knew by her tone that Grandmother had already had an effect on her.

"Is my dad there? I need to talk to him."

"He's here. He's the only nice person around here. Your aunts are just scary."

This from the crazy daughter of a crazed hell-goddess. I smiled. "I know they are. Put him on."

"Janet?" Pete Begay's gentle voice came to me through the line, and my eyes got misty. "How are you?"

We had to go through a discussion of about how Mick was and what he was doing, and Elena, and my friends, and all my aunts and cousins. Mick had his arms around me the whole time, distracting me by pressing little kisses to my ear, my neck.

My father said, "Gabrielle is doing better. Your sister is . . . interesting."

I wanted to laugh. *Interesting* was one way to describe her, and I'd never, ever have let her anywhere near my father without my grandmother around. "Yeah, she is."

I closed my eyes, picturing my father staring at the wall as he always did when he talked on the phone, clutching the receiver in a death grip. "I need to tell you something, Dad," I said before he could speak again. "Mick asked me to marry him. I said yes."

"Janet." I heard his happiness as well as a tug of tears. "I am so very happy."

My stoic father would never jump for joy, but I could tell he was pleased. I heard my grandmother in the background yelling, "What? What are you so very happy about?"

"I have something to tell you myself," my dad said, ignoring her. "I too have met a woman and have asked her to be my wife."

I stopped, words dying in my mouth. Mick had heard too, and he looked at me in surprise.

"Are you still there, Janet?" my dad asked.

"Dad." I coughed. "What did you say?"

"I said, I have asked a woman to marry me. She consented. We will marry this year. You have never met her, Janet, but I know you will like her."

"Who?"

My grandmother snatched away the phone. "Her name is Gina Tsotsie, and she's from Farmington. She'll do well enough. Now, what is this about you?"

The rest of the conversation was surreal. I'd been chuckling to myself about the bombshell I'd dropped, and Dad had dropped a bigger one on me.

My father, getting married. I told myself that it was about time. He'd never had a wife, not really—my goddess mother seducing him hardly counted. I had to meet the woman who'd worked through Pete Begay's shyness enough to get him to agree to marry her. It must have taken her some time. So why hadn't he—or my grandmother, who I now wanted to strangle—*told* me?

"Are you all right, Janet?" Mick asked after I hung up. He lounged against the dresser, his body distracting. We'd done some deep, satisfying lovemaking well into this morning, and the loose feeling of it lingered in my bones.

"Fine. A little anti-climaxed, but fine."

"Then maybe it's a good time to give you your engagement present."

I touched the ring, which I treasured, not only because it contained a piece of Mick's aura, but because he'd given it to me. "Wasn't this it?"

Mick grinned, sliding heat up and down my spine. "Not quite."

His jeans's dipping waistband showed me the sharp-lined fire tattoo across his lower back as he turned and led me down the short hall outside my bedroom to the back door. Mick took my hand in his, opened the door, and took me outside.

I stopped.

Parked behind the hotel was a gleaming, beautiful, heart-tugging little Harley, all shining in the morning sunlight. It was a Softail, customized by Mick, obviously, beautiful black with red flame highlights.

"Mick . . ."

He touched the handlebars. "A little over 1500 CCs, modified to make the ride smooth as silk. I figured you were about ready."

I'd never forget my little Sportster that had died a violent death in the sinkhole. We'd been through a lot, that girl and me. Losing it had been like losing my closest friend, and you don't replace your closest friend without grieving for a while.

Mick had known that it was time. And he'd brought me exactly what I needed.

I squealed like an eight-year-old and launched myself at Mick. I threw my arms around his neck and my legs around his hips, and he laughed as he held me. I wiped the smile from his mouth by covering it in kisses.

Mick's strong hands cupped my hips, his laughter going low as he caught my lips with his. The kisses turned promising, but he lowered me to my feet. "You can thank me later," he said.

And I would. Later would be the best he ever had.

Before I could grab the helmet and gloves that Mick had included, a Native American woman I didn't know walked around the hotel, saw us, and came over.

She was tall and broad-shouldered, a Changer, I saw in her aura. Bear, I guessed, from her large build, her dark eyes, her careful but powerful way of moving. She set down the overstuffed suitcase she carried and fixed a steely gaze on me.

"Are you Janet Begay? The Diné who owns this hotel?"

"That would be me," I said.

Mick watched her, hands on his hips, saying nothing, but subtly readying his fire magic.

"You can stand down, Firewalker," the woman said, sounding amused. Her voice was contralto, her words slow and deliberate. "I mean no harm to you, or your Stormwalker. I am seeking my ex-husband."

"Ex-husband?" I ran through a mental list of my guests, wondering which of them had a Changer for a wife. There was always Ansel, my Nightwalker—I didn't know much about him, apart from his fondness for stamps and old movies.

Coyote walked through my back door, a beer bottle in his hand. Why he'd been coming to my room with a beer I didn't know, but that was Coyote.

He saw the woman, and stopped dead. The bottle slid from his fingers to shatter on the hard dirt.

"Son of a bitch," he whispered.

"Coyote?" I exclaimed. Even Mick looked stunned. "Wait—you mean *Coyote* is your ex-husband?"

The woman smiled, showing sharply pointed teeth. "I knew I'd find him here."

"Shit," Coyote said.

"Coyote," I said, keeping my voice calm. "You were married?"

"A long time ago," he growled.

I grinned and leaned back against Mick. "Now, this I gotta hear."

"In due time," the woman said. "First you, Janet Begay, will give me a room." She shot Coyote a look that made him turn brick red. "And then you will tell me *all* about what he's been up to."

Dear Reader,

Please turn the page for a sneak peek of Primal Bonds, *from the Shifters Unbound series I write as my alter ego, Jennifer Ashley.*

Twenty years ago, shape-shifters of all kinds were rounded up and made to live in Shiftertowns. They are forced to wear Collars—half-magic, half-tech—designed to keep their violent tendencies at bay.

The Shifters are tamed now, Collared, safe . . . but are they?

Primal Bonds *is the story of Sean Morrissey, Feline Shifter and Guardian of his Shiftertown—the man who sends Shifter souls to the afterlife. When Andrea Gray, a half-wolf Shifter, seeks refuge in the Morrisseys' Shiftertown, Sean agrees to claim her, sight unseen, so the humans will allow the transfer. He never dreams that the challenging Andrea, with her gray eyes and fearless attitude, will be the woman that stirs the wild mating frenzy within him.*

Primal Bonds, *available now, will be followed by* Wild Cat *in January 2012. Also look for* Pride Mates, *re-released by Berkley Sensation in July 2011.*

See the Shifters Unbound website for excerpts, book blurbs, "The Human's Guide to Shifters," and more: http://www.jennifersromances.com. (Choose "Shifters Unbound" from the right-hand menu.)

Allyson James, aka Jennifer Ashley

One

Andrea Gray had just set the beer bottle in front of her customer when the first of the shots rocketed through the open front door. The bar just outside of the Austin Shifter-town had no windows, but the front door always stood wide-open, and now a cascade of gunfire poured through the welcoming entrance.

The next thing Andrea knew, she was on the floor with two hundred and fifty pounds of solid Shifter muscle on top of her. She knew exactly who pinned her, knew the shape and feel of the long body pressing her back and thighs, trapping her with male strength. She struggled but couldn't budge him. Damned Feline.

"Get *off* me, Sean Morrissey."

His voice with its Irish lilt trickled into her ear, swirling heat into her belly. "You stay down when the bullets fly, love."

A ferocious roar sounded as Ronan, the bouncer, ran past, heading outside in his Kodiak bear form. Andrea heard more shots and then the bear's bellow of pain. Bullets splintered the bottles above the bar with a musical sound, and colorful glass and fragrant alcohol rained to the floor. Another roar, this one of a lion, vibrated the air, and the hail of bullets suddenly ceased. Tires squealed as an engine revved before the sound died off into the distance.

Stunned silence followed, then whimpers, moans, and the angry voice of Andrea's aunt Glory. "Bastards. Human lickbrain assholes."

Shifters started rising, talking, cursing.

"You can get off me now, Sean," Andrea said.

Sean lingered, his warm weight pouring sensations into Andrea's brain—strength, virility, protectiveness—*you're safe with me, love, and you always will be*. Finally he rose to his feet and pulled her up with him; six-feet-five of enigmatic Shifter male, the black-haired, blue-eyed, Collared Feline to whom Andrea owed her freedom.

Sean didn't step away from her, staying right inside her personal space so that the heat of his body surrounded her. "Anyone hurt?" he called. "Everyone all right?"

His voice was strong, but Andrea sensed his worry that he'd have to act as Guardian tonight, which meant driving his sword through the heart of his dying friends to send their bodies to dust and their souls to the afterlife. The Sword of the Guardian leaned against the wall in the back office, where Sean stashed it any night he spent in the bar. Since Andrea had come to work there, he'd spent most nights in the bar, watching her.

She'd also seen in the two weeks she'd lived next door to Sean Morrissey that he hated the thought of using the sword. His primary job was to be called in when there was no longer any hope, and that fact put a dark edge to his entire life. Not many people saw this, but Andrea had noticed.

Andrea was close enough now to Sean to sense his muscles relax as people assured him they were all right. Shifters climbed slowly to their feet, shaken, but there was no one dead or wounded. They'd been lucky.

The floor was littered with glass and splintered wood, the smell of spilled alcohol sharp, and bullet holes riddled the dark walls. Half the bottles and glasses behind the bar had been destroyed, and the human bartender crawled shakily out from under a table.

A wildcat zoomed in through the front door and stopped by a clump of humans not yet brave enough to get up. Feline Shifters were a cross between breeds: lion, leopard, tiger, jaguar, cheetah—bred centuries ago from the best of each. The Morrissey family had a lot of lion in it, and this wildcat had heavily muscled shoulders, a tawny body, and a black mane. It rose on its hind legs, its head nearly touching the ceiling, before it shifted into the tall form of Liam Morrissey, Sean's older brother.

The human males at his feet looked up in terror. But what did the idiots expect if they hung out in a Shifter bar? Shifter groupies baffled Andrea. They wore imitation Collars and pretended to adore all things Shifter, but whenever Shifters behaved like Shifters, they cringed in fear. *Go home, children.*

"Sean," Liam said over the crowd, eyes holding questions.

"No one in here got hit. How's Ronan?"

"He'll live." The anger on Liam's face mirrored Sean's own. "Humans, a carload of them." *Again*, he didn't say.

"Cowards," Glory spat. Eyes white with rage, the platinum blonde helped another Shifter woman to her feet. The Collar around Glory's neck, which she wore like a fashion accessory to her body-hugging gold lamé, emitted half a dozen sparks. "Let me go after them."

"Easy." Liam's voice held such calm authority that Glory backed off in spite of herself, and her Collar went silent. Liam's Collar didn't spark at all, although Andrea felt the waves of anger from him.

One of the Shifter groupies raised his hands. "Hey, man, it had nothing to do with us."

Liam forced a smile, stuffing himself back into his ostensible role as bar manager. "I know that, lad," he said. "I'm sorry for your trouble. You come back in tomorrow, why don't you? The first round's on me."

His Irish lilt was pronounced, Liam the Shiftertown leader at his most charming, but the humans didn't look comforted.

Liam was stark naked, except for his Collar—a large, muscular male, gleaming with sweat, who could kill the men at his feet in one blow if he wanted to. As much as they pretended to want the thrill of that danger, Shifter groupies didn't like it when the danger was real.

Ronan staggered back in, no longer in his bear form. Ronan was even bigger than Liam and Sean, nearly seven feet tall, broad of shoulder and chest and tight with muscle. His face was sheet white, his shoulder torn and covered with blood.

Andrea shook off Sean's protective hold and went to him. "Damn it, Ronan, what were you doing?"

"My job." The amount of blood flowing down his torso would have had a human on the floor in shock. Ronan merely looked embarrassed.

Sean got to the man's other side. "In the back, lad. Now."

"I'm fine. It's just a bullet. My own fault."

"Shut it." Sean and Andrea towed the bigger man to a door marked "Private," and Sean more or less shoved him into the office beyond.

The office was ordinary—cluttered desk, a couple of chairs, a storage cabinet, shabby sofa, and a small safe in the wall that only the bar's human owner was supposed to know the combination to. Andrea knew good and well that Liam and Sean knew it too.

The Sword of the Guardian leaned against the wall like an upright cross, and threads of its Fae magic floated to Andrea from across the room. Andrea had no idea whether pure Shifters could sense the sword's magic as she, a half-Fae, half-Lupine Shifter could, but she did know that the Shifters in this Shiftertown regarded the sword, and Sean, with uncomfortable awe.

Sean pushed Ronan at a chair. "Sit."

Ronan dropped obediently, and the flimsy chair creaked under his weight. Ronan was an Ursine—a bear Shifter—large and hard-muscled, his short but shaggy black hair always looking uncombed. He didn't have an ounce of fat on him. Andrea wasn't used to Ursines, having never met one before moving to Austin. Only Lupines had lived in her Shiftertown near Colorado Springs. But Ronan had proved to be such a sweetheart he'd quickly overcome her uneasiness.

"I can't stay in here," Ronan protested. "What if they come back?"

"You're not going anywhere, my friend, until we get that bullet out of you." Sean snatched a blanket from the sagging sofa and dropped it over Ronan's lap. Shifters weren't modest as a rule, but maybe Sean thought he needed to protect Andrea from a bear in his naked glory. Ronan, admittedly was . . . super-sized.

"I thought I'd be away from the door maybe a minute." Ronan's deep black eyes filled. "What if someone had gotten hurt? Or killed? It would have been because of me."

"No one got hurt but you, you big softie." Sean's voice took on that gentle note that made Andrea shiver deep inside herself. "You frightened away the bad guys before anything worse could happen."

"If I'd been at my post, I would have blocked the door, and none of the bullets would have gotten inside."

"And then you'd look like a cheese grater," Sean said. "And be dust at the end of my sword. I like you, Ronan. I don't want that."

"Yeah?"

Andrea set down the first-aid kit she'd fetched from the cabinet and perched on the edge of the desk, her hand on Ronan's unhurt shoulder. "I don't want that either."

Ronan relaxed a little under her touch—he needed touch, reassurance, all Shifters did, especially when injured or frightened. Andrea wanted to give Ronan a full hug, but she feared hurting him. She kneaded his back instead, trying to put as much comfort as she could into the caress.

Ronan grinned weakly at her. "Hey, you're not so bad yourself, for a Fae."

"Half Fae."

Anyone else mentioning her Fae blood made Andrea's anger rise, but with Ronan it had turned into friendly teasing. Ronan squeezed her fingers in his pawlike hand.

"This is going to hurt like hell, big guy," Sean said. "So

just remind yourself who you'll have to answer to if you turn bear on me and take my head off."

"Aw, I'd never hurt you, Sean. Even if I didn't know Liam would rip my guts out if I did."

"Good lad. Remember now. Andrea, hold the gauze just like that."

Andrea positioned the wad of sterile gauze under the ragged hole in Ronan's shoulder as Sean directed. Sean sprayed some antibacterial around the wound, reached in with the big tweezers he'd dipped in alcohol, and yanked the bullet from Ronan's flesh.

Ronan threw his head back and roared. His face distorted, his mouth and nose lengthening to a muzzle filled with sharp teeth. Blood burst from the wound and coated first the gauze, then the clean towel Sean jammed over it. Ronan's hands extended to razorlike claws, which closed on Sean's wrist.

Sean pressed the towel in place, unworried. "Easy now."

Ronan withdrew his hand, but not before a blue snake of electricity arced around his Collar, biting into his neck. He howled in pain.

Damn it. Andrea leapt to her feet, unable to stand it any longer. She batted the surprised Sean's hands aside and pressed her palm directly to the wound. Folding herself against Ronan, she held her hand flat to his chest.

The threads of healing spiraled in her mind, diving through her fingers into Ronan's skin, swirling until she closed her eyes to fight dizziness. She sensed the threads of Fae magic from the sword across the room drifting toward her, as though drawn by her healing touch.

Ronan's skin knit beneath her fingers, tightening and drying, slowly becoming whole again. After a few minutes, Andrea opened her eyes. Ronan's breath came fast, but it was healthy breathing, and the blood around the wound had dried.

Andrea drew her hand away. Ronan probed his injury, staring at it in amazement. "What the hell did you do to me, Andy-girl?"

"Nothing," Andrea said in a light voice as she stood up.

"We stopped the blood, and you heal fast, you big strong Ursine, you."

Ronan looked from Sean to Andrea. Sean shrugged and gave him a small smile, as though he knew what was going on, but Andrea saw the hard flicker in Sean's eyes. Oh, goody, she'd pissed him off.

Ronan gave up. He stretched and worked his shoulder. "Slap a bandage on me, Sean," he said in his usual strong voice. "I need to find my clothes."

Sean silently pressed a fresh wad of gauze to the wound, secured it with sterile tape, and let him go. Ronan kissed the top of Andrea's head, clapped Sean on the shoulders, and banged out of the office, his energy restored.

Andrea busied herself putting things back into the first-aid kit. Sean said absolutely nothing, but when she turned from tucking the kit back into the cabinet, she found him right behind her, again invading her personal space.

It was difficult to breathe while he stood over her, smelling of the night and Guinness and male musk. She had no idea what to make of Sean Morrissey, the Shifter who had mate-claimed her, sight unseen, when she'd needed to relocate to this Shiftertown.

A mate-claim simply meant that a male had marked a female as a potential mate—the couple wouldn't be officially mated until they were blessed under sun and moon by the male's clan leader. All other males had to back off unless the female chose to reject the male's mate-claim.

When Andrea had wanted to move to Austin to live with Glory, her mother's sister, Glory's pack leader had refused to let Andrea in unless she was mate-claimed. The pack leader had the right to disallow any unmated female to enter his pack if he thought that the female would cause dissention or other trouble.

Andrea, a half-Fae, illegitimate Lupine, was considered trouble. When Andrea's mother, Dina, had become pregnant by her Fae lover, Dina been forced from the pack. That same pack now didn't want her half-Fae daughter back. But Andrea had needed to flee the Shiftertown in which she'd been living in Colorado, because a harassing asshole, the

Shiftertown leader's son, had tried to mate-claim Andrea for his own. He hadn't taken her answer—*no way in hell*—very well.

Glory had turned to Liam, the Austin Shiftertown leader, as was her right, to appeal her pack leader's decision to keep Andrea out. Apparently the arguments between Glory's pack leader and Liam had been loud and heated. And then Sean had cut the arguments short by claiming Andrea for himself.

Why he'd done it, Andrea couldn't figure out, even though Sean had explained that it had been to keep the peace between species in this Shiftertown. But if that was all it was— a formality to satisfy a stubborn pack leader—why did Sean watch Andrea like he did? He'd not been happy with Liam for hiring her as a waitress, and Sean made sure he was at the bar from open to close every night Andrea worked. Didn't the big Feline have better things to do?

Sean was tall and blue-eyed, and he radiated warmth like a furnace. Andrea loved standing close to him—*How crazy is that? I'm hot for an effing Feline.* She'd thought that after what Jared, the harassing asshole, had done to her, she'd never have interest in males again, but Sean Morrissey made her breath catch. To her surprise, Sean's mate-claim had awakened her instincts and made her come alive. She'd never thought she'd feel alive again.

"What?" she asked, when Sean made no sign of moving.

"Don't play innocent with me, love. What did you just do to Ronan? I watched with my own eyes while that wound closed."

Andrea had learned to be evasive about her gift for her own safety, but she somehow knew Sean wouldn't let her. If she didn't answer, he might try to pry it out of her, maybe by seizing her wrists and backing her against a wall, looking down at her with those blue, blue eyes. Well, a girl could hope.

She made herself turn her back on his intense gaze—not easy—and start straightening the shelves in the cabinet. "It's something I inherited through my Fae side. Of course it's through my Fae side. Where else would I have gotten it?"

"I didn't notice you mentioning that you had healing magic when you arrived. I didn't notice Glory mentioning it either."

"Glory doesn't know," Andrea said without turning around. "I had a hard enough time convincing Glory's pack to let me move in with her, not to mention the pair of Felines who run this Shiftertown. I figured, the less of my Fae part I revealed, the better."

Sean turned her to face him. His eyes had gone white blue, an alpha not happy that a lesser Shifter hadn't bared every inch of her soul to him. As much as Andrea's gaze wanted to slide off to the left, she refused to look away. Sean might be an alpha, but she'd not be a pathetic submissive to his big, bad Feline dominance.

"Why keep such a thing to yourself?" Sean asked. "You could do a hell of a lot of good with a gift like that."

Andrea slid out of Sean's grip and walked away. First, because it proved she could; second, it got her away from his white-hot gaze.

"The gift isn't that strong. It's not like I can cure terminal diseases or anything. I can boost the immune system, heal wounds and abrasions, speed up the healing of broken bones. I couldn't have magicked the bullet out of Ronan, for instance, but I could relieve his pain and jump-start his recovery."

"And you don't think this is something we should know about?"

When she looked at Sean again, his eyes had returned to that sinful, summer-lake blue, but his stance still said he could turn on her anytime he wanted. If Andrea hadn't been intrigued by Sean the moment she'd laid eyes on him in the Austin bus station, the man would terrify her. Sean Morrissey was different from Liam, who was a charmer, in your face, laughing at the same time he made damn sure you did whatever it was he wanted. Sean was quieter, watching the world, waiting for something, she wasn't certain what.

It had been one hell of a long ride from Colorado to central Texas, but Andrea had had to take the bus, because Shifters weren't allowed on airplanes, nor were they allowed to drive cross-country. Glory had brought Sean with her when she'd picked up Andrea from the station. Tall, hard-bodied, and black-haired, Sean had been dressed in jeans and a button-down shirt, motorcycle boots, and a leather jacket against the February cold. Andrea had assumed him to be Glory's latest conquest until Glory introduced him. Sean had looked down at Andrea, his hard-ass, blue-eyed stare peeling away the layers she'd built between herself and the world.

She remembered thinking, *I wonder if he's black-haired all the way down?*

Sean, being the alpha he was, had sensed her distress and exhaustion and pulled her into his arms, knowing she needed his touch. He'd smelled of leather, maleness, sweat, and cold February air, and Andrea had wanted to curl up in a little ball against him like a wounded cub. "You're all right now," Sean had murmured against her hair. "I'm here to look after you."

Now Sean stood patiently, waiting for her explanation. The damn stubborn Feline would stand there all night until she gave him one.

"I wasn't allowed to talk about it in Colorado," Andrea said. "The Shiftertown leader gave my stepfather permission to let me use it, but they didn't want me telling people how I healed them. I understand why. Everyone would have freaked if they thought I was using Fae magic on them."

"That's a point," Sean conceded. "But we're not as easily, as you say, *freaked*, around here. You should have told me, or Glory at least."

Andrea put one hand on her hip. "My life as a half-breed illegitimate orphan hasn't exactly been pleasant, you know. I've learned to keep things to myself."

"And you thought we'd treat you the same, did you, love?"

Damn it, why did he insist on calling her *love*? And why did it sizzle fire all the way through her? This was crazy. He was a *Feline*. If Sean Morrissey knew little about her, Andrea knew still less about him.

"Well, you're part of us now." Sean came to her, again stepping into her space, a dominant male wanting to make her aware just what her place was. "You're right that not all Shifters are comfortable with Fae magic, but my brother has to know about your healing gift, and my father. And Glory has a right too."

"Fine," Andrea said, as though it made no difference. "Tell them." She moved to the door, again deliberately turning her back on him. Alphas didn't like that. "We should go help clean up out there. Does the bar get shot up often? I should get hazardous duty pay."

"Andrea."

He was right behind her, his warmth like sunshine on her back. Andrea stopped with her hand on the doorknob. Sean rested his palm on the doorframe above her, his tall body hemming her in. She remembered the feel of him on top of her on the floor, the tactile memory strong.

"Glory says something's been troubling you," Sean said. "Troubling you bad. I want you to tell me about it."

Andrea shivered. Damn Glory, damn Sean, and no, she didn't want to talk about it.

"Not now. Can we go?"

"It's my job to listen to troubles," he said, breath hot in her ear. "Whether I'm your mate yet or not. And you will tell me yours."

Andrea's tongue felt loose, her pent-up emotions suddenly wanting to spill out to this man and his warm voice. She clamped her mouth shut, but Sean stunned her by saying, "Is it about the nightmares?"

She hadn't told anyone about the nightmares, not Glory, not Sean, not anyone, though Glory might have heard her crying out in her sleep. The nightmares had started a week after she'd moved in with Glory, when they'd risen in her head like a many-tentacled monster. She didn't know what they meant or why she was having them; she only knew they scared the hell out of her. "How do you know about my nightmares?"

"Because my bedroom window faces yours, love, and I have good hearing."

The thought of Sean sitting in his bedroom, watching over her while she slept, made her shiver with warmth. "There's nothing to tell. When I wake up, I can't remember anything." Except fear. She had no idea what the images that flashed through her head meant, but they terrified her. "I really don't want to talk about it right now," she said. "All right?"

Sean ran a soothing hand down her arm, stirring more fires. "That's all right, love. You let me know when you're good and ready."

From the feel of the very firm thing lodged against her backside, Sean was good and ready now. One part of him had definitely shifted.

Andrea deliberately leaned on the door and pressed back into him. A jolt of heat shot through her, the fear of the nightmares dissolving. After Jared, Andrea thought she'd be afraid of Sean, turned off, ready to run. Instead, Sean made her feel, for the first time in years . . . playful.

"So, tell me, Guardian," she said, lowering her voice to a purr. "Is that where you carry your sword, or are you just happy to see me?"